WHAT READERS ARE SAYING ABOUT KAREN KINGSBURY'S BOOKS

Karen's book *Oceans Apart* changed my life. She has an amazing gift of bringing a reader into her stories. I can only pray she never stops writing.

> Susan L.

Everyone should have the opportunity to read or listen to a book by Karen Kingsbury. It should be in the *Bill of Rights*.

> Rachel S.

I want to thank Karen Kingsbury for what she is doing with the power of her storytelling—touching hearts like mine and letting God use her to change the world for Him.

> Brittney N.

Karen Kingsbury's books are filled with the unshakable, remarkable, miraculous fact that God's grace is greater than our suffering. There are no words for Ms. Kingsbury's writing.

> Wendie K.

Because I loaned these books to my mother, she BECAME a Christian! Thank you for a richer life here and in heaven!

> Jennifer E.

When I read my first Karen Kingsbury book, I couldn't stop.... I read thirteen more in one summer!

> Jamie B.

I have never read anything so uplifting and entertaining. I'm shocked as I read each new release because it's always better than the last one.

Bonnie S.

I am unable to put your books down, and I plan to read many more of them. What a wonderful spiritual message I find in each one!

Rhonda T.

I love the way Karen Kingsbury writes, and the topics she chooses to write about! Thank you so much for sharing your talent with us, your readers!

Barbara S.

My husband is equally hooked on your books. It is a family affair for us now! Can't wait for the next one.

Angie

I can't even begin to tell you what your books mean to me…. Thank you for your wonderful books and the way they touch my life again and again.

Martje L.

Every time our school buys your next new book, everybody goes crazy trying to read it first!

Roxanne

Recently I made an effort to find GOOD Christian writers, and I've hit the jackpot with Karen Kingsbury!

Linda

When Karen Kingsbury calls her books "Life-Changing Fiction™," she's merely telling the unvarnished truth. I'm still sorting through the changes in my life that have come from reading just a few of her books!

Robert M.

I must admit that I wish I were a much slower reader ... or you were a much faster writer. Either way, I can't seem to get enough of Karen Kingsbury's books!

Jillian B.

I was offered fifty dollars one time in the airport for the fourth book in the Redemption Series. The lady's husband just couldn't understand why I wasn't interested in selling it. Through sharing Karen's books with my friends, many have decided that contemporary Christian fiction is the next best thing to the Bible. Thank you so much, Karen. It is truly a God-thing that you write the way you do.

Sue Ellen H.

Karen Kingsbury's books have made me see things in ways that I had never thought about before. I have to force myself to put them down and come up for air!

Tabitha H.

Other Life-Changing Fiction™ by Karen Kingsbury

9/11 Series
One Tuesday Morning
Beyond Tuesday Morning
Every Now and Then

Lost Love Series
Even Now
Ever After

Above the Line Series
Above the Line: Take One
Above the Line: Take Two
Above the Line: Take Three
    (spring 2010)
Above the Line: Final Cut
    (summer 2010)

Stand-Alone Titles
Shades of Blue
Oceans Apart
Between Sundays
This Side of Heaven
When Joy Came to Stay
On Every Side
Divine
Like Dandelion Dust
Where Yesterday Lives

Redemption Series
Redemption
Remember
Return
Rejoice
Reunion

Firstborn Series
Fame
Forgiven
Found
Family
Forever

Sunrise Series
Sunrise
Summer
Someday
Sunset

Red Glove Series
Gideon's Gift
Maggie's Miracle
Sarah's Song
Hannah's Hope

Forever Faithful Series
Waiting for Morning
Moment of Weakness
Halfway to Forever

Women of Faith Fiction Series
A Time to Dance
A Time to Embrace

Cody Gunner Series
A Thousand Tomorrows
Just Beyond the Clouds

Children's Titles
Let Me Hold You Longer
Let's Go on a Mommy Date
We Believe in Christmas
The Princess and the
    Three Knights
Let's Go Have a Daddy Day
    (spring 2010)

Miracle Collections
A Treasury of Christmas Miracles
A Treasury of Miracles for
    Women
A Treasury of Miracles for Teens
A Treasury of Miracles for
    Friends
A Treasury of Adoption Miracles

Gift Books
Stay Close Little Girl
Be Safe Little Boy
Forever Young: Ten Gifts of Faith
    for the Graduate

KAREN KINGSBURY

Shades of Blue

ZONDERVAN®

ZONDERVAN.com/
AUTHORTRACKER
follow your favorite authors

We want to hear from you. Please send your comments about this book to us in care of zreview@zondervan.com. Thank you.

ZONDERVAN

Shades of Blue
Copyright © 2009 by Karen Kingsbury

This title is also available as a Zondervan ebook.
Visit www.zondervan.com/ebooks.

This title is also available in a Zondervan audio edition.
Visit www.zondervan.fm.

Requests for information should be addressed to:

Zondervan, Grand Rapids, Michigan 49530

Library of Congress Cataloging-in-Publication Data

Kingsbury, Karen.
    Shades of blue / Karen Kingsbury.
       p. cm.
    ISBN 978-0-310-26694-5
    I. Title.
PS3561.I4873S53 2009
813'.54—dc22   2009028795

Published in association with the literary agency of Alive Communications, Inc., 7680 Goddard Street, Suite 200, Colorado Springs, CO 80920. www.alivecommunications.com

Interior design by Michelle Espinoza

Printed in the United States of America

---

09 10 11 12 13 14 15 • 22 21 20 19 18 17 16 15 14 13 12 11 10 9 8 7 6 5 4 3 2 1

To Donald, my Prince Charming...

This is the fall we've been waiting for, my love. All our boys at our wonderful Christian school, and you there teaching and coaching in the midst of it all. For two decades I've watched other people's kids be blessed by your talents as a teacher and coach, and now ... finally ... those kids will be our very own. I rejoice every day as I watch you and the boys drive off to school together. In this very short season, I can't wait to see how God uses your time with our precious young men, in helping them learn, in mentoring them, in giving them the great privilege of being the coach's sons. The list is long. I only know that after so many years of praying and dreaming about this time, I don't want to miss a minute of it. Thank you for your faithfulness, my love. For consistently loving me and our kids, for always leading us back to the Lord again and again and again. Thank you for praying about this wild and amazing ministry of Life-Changing Fiction™ and for supporting me through every step. I love you more now than ever, if that's possible. The music plays on, in this great scene in the story of our lives. Let's keep dancing, keep singing, and keep falling deeper in love with every glorious day. I love you always and forever.

To Kelsey, my precious daughter...

I remember six months ago putting your birthday in my countdown clock on my phone and looking at the seconds as they fell away. Because even if I stared at those numbers for a long time, I couldn't quite grasp that my baby girl would be twenty this year. And now … here you are. No longer a teenager. Along the way of your wonderful childhood we ushered in so many beautiful chapters. Watching you grow to a toddler we lost the baby you once were. But we were dizzy with love over what we had gained. Then we watched you grow into a preschooler, chattering and tossing your long blonde hair and making best friends with our cat, Orky. Along the way we lost the toddler, but we were in awe of what we had gained. And it's been that way with every stage of your life. We no longer have that sweet baby or the curious toddler. The precocious preschooler and the kind kindergartner are also gone. We've said good-bye to Kelsey the grade school girl, and we let go of the tomboy middle schooler with mud stains on her soccer uniform. The high school girl with braces on her teeth and a song on her lips has grown and gone away too. And yet there you stand, a part of all of those girls, but at the same time all grown up. A beautiful, faithful young woman. Kelsey, from the time you were very little we said you were one-in-a-million. Now that you've come this far, you've proven us right. You love God, you treasure your relationship with me and your dad and your brothers, and you are choosing to live for the Lord with every decision you make. We are so proud of you, honey. God's great plans for your life are right here on the brink. Keep on, sweetheart. Because one day we'll look back and remember the short time when you were a college girl, twenty years old, with all of life ahead of you. I love you so much, honey. You'll always be my little Norm.

To Tyler, my lasting song …

I love that you are branching out, Ty, that you've taken time to write music and work on your piano playing. One of the highlights of this past year was the moment when you told me you absolutely knew God was leading you into a future of Christian music. Then watching you start to pen songs from the overflow of your heart, songs that talked about God's greatness and purpose, His mercy and grace. How great is our God, that He would lead you in this direction. I've also seen your heart grow attached to the special friends in your life who love God as much as you do. Another gift from our Lord. I am so grateful for your place at our local Christian school! I've seen your faith become strong and personal, and I've watched you hold your shoulders back, head high as you lead with compassion and set an example for your peers. Keep pushing the limits, Ty. And as you take the stage for whatever's next this year, know that I'll be cheering you on. Let's enjoy this coming season, and the ones that follow it. With your Dad there teaching you in so many ways, I see you becoming more like him with every passing season. Your music fills our home, and I can't imagine the deafening silence that lies in the not-too-distant future when you go off to college. In the meantime, keep singing for Him. I am so proud of you, Son. I love you always.

To Sean, my happy sunshine ...

I love your heart, Sean. I love that you are always looking for a chance to sidle up to me and talk about every topic that breezes through your heart. You and I can sit for hours talking about different job descriptions, or the state of our nation's faith or political climate. We talk about God and heaven and why it is that some people won't turn their hearts to Him. One of the things you've often said lately is that you don't know how you'll learn to be a grown-up. "What if I don't know how to pay bills?" you'll ask. Or, "I won't have any idea how to run a house, Mom." And sometimes, "I hope I make it as a pro athlete, because I'm not sure I can do anything else very well." It touches my heart that you care so much about the future and what's ahead. But our job—your dad's and mine—is to help you relax a little. God will make the next step clear when it's time for you to take it. Kids don't become grown-ups all at once or overnight—even though it sometimes feels that way to us. God will walk you through it, and we will too. I guess the great thing is that you care so much. You're a conscientious young man with a great heart for God. Not long ago I told you that as you got older, if you went to the public high school, you'd either end up very lonely—the way Kelsey was through high school—or you'd get dragged into the incessant partying and immoral choices of most athletes at our local school. I love how you've watched for whether I was right. Just the other day you said, "I'm so glad we're going to the Christian high school. Remember what you said about being lonely? Well, last weekend the kids we know had a big party, and me and Josh didn't get invited." You had a knowing look in your eyes. "It's because they know we won't drink, Mom. So you were right about being lonely around that crowd." I wanted to stand up and shout, "Yay for God!!" We are so blessed to have you boys starting high school with your dad at such a wonderful school. I can't wait to see all the ways you grow in the coming years, and how you start to understand the details of life that today seem so elusive. And don't worry about being a pro athlete, Sean. You're great at lots and lots of things. I love you so much. Hold tight to Jesus. In life, He'll help you suit up exactly where He wants you to play.

To Josh, my tenderhearted perfectionist...

Starting a new school and leaving friends you've known all your life is never easy. Yet you, my dear son, have made this transition with optimism and faith—and for that I will always be grateful. It was the same way when Dad homeschooled you boys for those years. You didn't complain, but rather looked for the positive in each situation. That's the case now, and I know that God will bless you for it. You have embraced the new kids at your Christian high school, knowing that it is a different situation than the one you would've found at our major public school.

There won't be crowds of kids, but there will be a class you'll be close to, and pep assemblies that are more fun than what's happening down the street. And there won't be the constant pressure to drink and party, nor the assumption that as a star athlete you'll have physical relationships with girls. For the most part, you will be surrounded by kids like yourself. In making this decision, your dad and I prayerfully asked God where you and your brothers belonged. God made it very clear. We know you would've been a standout athlete at the big public school, but that is not what this time in your life is about. We did not adopt you so that you could be popular or have your name in the headlines. Rather, we brought you here asking God that we might raise you as a godly young man, one who will honor Him and one who will lead your future family and generations to come with the faith and knowledge you learned here with us. Here's the cool thing. You'll be even more of a standout at your smaller Christian school. And you'll be a leader too. I can't wait to watch it all play out, Josh. I'll be in the front row, cheering you on always. I love you so much! Hold on to Jesus!

To EJ, my chosen one …

What I love about you, EJ, is the way you're always surprising us. You have the driest sense of humor in the family, often making us burst out loud with laughter at the things you say. Though you're easily the quietest of the kids, you are very perceptive, knowing just when to say the right thing and finding perfect timing to put a smile on our faces. But the words you said the other day made me smile in a different way. One of your siblings was commenting that getting A's wasn't that important. As long as a class was passed, that was what mattered. You gave a puzzled look. "Not me. I say get the highest grade of all. That way you can do anything you want when you grow up." Now, for some kids that might be the natural response or something they might've repeated based on a parent's teaching. Not you. For years you would grow bored of school and we would struggle to keep you interested. Then, after being homeschooled by your dad, you had a change of heart. You try harder than anyone, and you look with anticipation for your report card. You've been on the honor roll at school for the past few years, and now I know why. You want the chance to grow up to be whatever you want to be. I couldn't be happier about that, EJ. Whether God has in mind for you to be a pastor or a doctor, a politician or a civic leader, a businessman or a teacher and coach like your dad, you'll go after the dream and you'll get it. Because God will honor your determination to try. I'm so glad you're finding your strength in Him. He is all that matters in the end. We are thrilled with all you're becoming, all you desire to be. Keep your eyes on Jesus. I love you so much.

To Austin, my miracle boy ...

What an adventure you're just beginning, Austin. You and your brothers starting at a new Christian school, a place where you'll make amazing memories and forever friends. I'm so glad you'll be a part of this wonderful community, and I expect that this year is the beginning of a time when God uses you as a brilliant light for Him. You will be a leader at this school, as you have already been a leader for your friends at your elementary school. But even as I am thrilled with all that lies ahead, I still can hardly believe you are at the beginning of middle school. For the last year I've been calculating lasts. Your last back-to-school ice cream social—something that's only done at the grade school. Your last open house, and your last chance to participate in the science fair. Your last time to have recess built into your daily routine. How can it be that my youngest child is no longer in grade school? As difficult as it is to see you grow, it is even more exciting to see all you are becoming. I think of the time at the beginning of last baseball season when the umpire pulled aside our coaches and said, "I love your catcher. I've never seen a boy in this league with as much character and good manners as that young man. Please … tell the rest of your team to take a lesson from him." Wow, Austin. As happy as your dad and I are when you make an out at home plate or when you hit a home run, those things pale in comparison to the way you're being a light for Christ. You grow to be a little more like your daddy every day. Something that must make your Papa smile up in heaven. Keep on, my youngest son. Keep Jesus first and know that I love you always and always.

And to God Almighty, the Author of Life, who has—for now—blessed me with these.

ACKNOWLEDGMENTS

NO BOOK COMES TOGETHER WITHOUT A great and talented team of people making it happen. For that reason, a special thanks to my friends at Zondervan who combined efforts to make *Shades of Blue* all it could be. A special thanks to my dedicated editor, Sue Brower, and to my brilliant publicist Karen Campbell, and to Karwyn Bursma, whose creative marketing is unrivaled in the publishing business.

Also, thanks to my amazing agent, Rick Christian, president of Alive Communications. Rick, you've always believed only the best for me. When we talk about the highest possible goals, you see them as doable, reachable. You are a brilliant manager of my career, and I thank God for you. But even with all you do for my ministry of writing, I am doubly grateful for your encouragement and prayers. Every time I finish a book, you send me a letter that deserves to be framed, and when something big happens, yours is the first call I receive. Thank you for that. But even more, the fact that you and Debbie are praying for me and my family keeps me confident every morning that God will continue to breathe life into the stories in my heart. Thank you for being so much more than a brilliant agent.

A special thank-you to my husband, Don, who puts up with me on deadline and doesn't mind driving through Taco Bell after a basketball game if I've been editing all day. This wild ride wouldn't be possible without you. Your love keeps me writing; your prayers keep me believing that God has a plan in this ministry of fiction. And thanks for the hours you put in working with the guestbook entries on my website. It's a full-time job, and I am grateful for your concern for my reader friends. I look forward to that time every day when you read through them, sharing them with me and releasing them to the public, lifting up the prayer requests. Thank you, honey, and thanks to all my kids, who pull together, bringing me iced green tea, and understand my sometimes-crazy schedule. I love that you know you're still first, before any deadline.

Thank you also to my mom, Anne Kingsbury, and to my sisters, Tricia, Sue, and Lynne. Mom, you are amazing as my assistant—working day and night sorting through the mail from my readers. I appreciate you more than you'll ever know.

Tricia, you are the best executive assistant I could ever hope to have. I treasure your loyalty and honesty, the way you include me in every decision and the daily exciting website changes. My site has been a different place since you stepped in, and the hits have grown a hundredfold. Along the way, the readers have so much more to help them in their faith, so much more than a story with this Life-Changing Fiction™. Please know that I pray for God's blessings on you always, for your dedication to helping me in this season of writing, and for your wonderful son, Andrew. And aren't we having such a good time too? God works all things to the good!

Sue, I believe you should've been a counselor! From your home far from mine, you get batches of reader letters every day, and you diligently answer them using God's wisdom and His Word. When readers get a response from "Karen's sister Susan," I hope they know how carefully you've prayed for them and for the responses you give. Thank you for truly loving what you do, Sue. You're gifted with people, and I'm blessed to have you aboard.

A special thanks also to Will Montgomery, my manager. I was terrified to venture into the business of selling my books at events for a couple of reasons. First, I never wanted to profit from book sales at speaking events; and second, because I would never have the time to handle such details. Monty, you came in and made it all come together. With a mission statement that reads, "To love and serve the readers," you have helped me supply books and free gifts to tens of thousands of readers at events across the country. You understand my desire to give away our proceeds for ministry purposes. More than that, you've become my friend, a very valuable part of the ministry of Life-Changing Fiction™. You are loyal and kind and fiercely protective of me, my family, and the work God has me doing. Thank you for everything you're doing and will continue to do.

Thanks too to Olga Kalachik, my office assistant, who helps organize my supplies and storage area and who prepares our home for the marketing events and research gatherings that take place here on a regular basis. I appreciate all you're doing to make sure I have time to write. You're wonderful, Olga, and I pray God continues to bless you and your precious family.

I also want to thank my friends with Extraordinary Women —Roy Morgan, Tim and Julie Clinton, Beth Cleveland, Charles Billingsley, and so many others. How wonderful to be a part of what God is doing through all of you. Thank you for making me part of your family.

Thanks also to my forever friends and family, the ones who have been there and continue to be there. Your love has been a tangible source of comfort, pulling us through the tough times and making us know how very blessed we are to have you in our lives.

And the greatest thanks to God. The gift is Yours. I pray I might use it for years to come in a way that will bring You honor and glory.

FOREVER IN FICTION

Whenever I receive the completed paperwork for a Forever in Fiction winner, I read through the details of the life being honored in fiction — whether the person is alive or has passed — and I am touched by the real-life stories that come my way.

In *Shades of Blue* you will see three characters named through my donation of Forever in Fiction to various auctions. The first is Francesca (Frankie) Gianakopoulos, a six-year-old girl from Plainfield, Illinois. Frankie was chosen to be Forever in Fiction by her mother, Melissa Gianakopoulos, who won the item at the Trinity Christian School auction. Frankie is a petite girl with dark hair, dark eyes, and a short, sassy haircut. According to the people who know her, one word describes Frankie — angelic. People say they can see an angelic aura about her that is demonstrated in the way she looks at others, the way she speaks, and even the way she moves. She touches the hearts of everyone she meets.

At age three, Frankie was diagnosed with Idiopathic thrombocytopenic purpura — a blood disease that causes her to be severely bruised most of the time. Her blood count is constantly being checked. Although she is forced to deal with an illness she doesn't understand, she has a very strong faith and loves life with a passion. She is especially fond of Lincoln Logs, Legos, and Hot Wheels cars, and she is best friends with all the boys in her class. She is a tomboy who loves seeing her grandparents in Las Vegas, and she is thrilled with visits to Disneyland. She needs to be careful she doesn't get hurt, but that doesn't stop her from playing with her older siblings — Lexa and Christopher. Frankie also loves reading and math. Despite her weekly visits to an oncology clinic, those who love her have committed Frankie to God, and they believe she is in His hands.

In *Shades of Blue*, Frankie appears as one of the kids in Emma Landon's classroom. Because of her illness, Frankie helps Emma understand the value of life—no matter what. Frankie and Emma are very close, and Frankie's faith is one of the factors that ends up helping Emma understand that she must find redemption if she's to move on in life.

Melissa, I pray that your family will be blessed by the placement of Frankie in the pages of *Shades of Blue*, and that when you read this book you will always see some of your precious little girl here, where she will be Forever in Fiction.

Also honored in *Shades of Blue* is seventeen-year-old Kristin Palazzo. Kristin was born in October of 1989 and quickly became a loving little Daddy's girl. Growing up, she loved her black lab, Mollie, her Grammy, and her cousins. She enjoyed taking trips to the American Girl doll store and staying at the family's cabin in the mountains of West Virginia. She loved photography, cooking, reading, swimming, and creating artwork. She enjoyed taking close-up photos of flowers and God's beauty in nature. She had long, straight, dark brown hair and brown eyes. She was tall and slender with a wonderful laugh and a lovely smile. Kristin was quiet, kind, adaptable, unpresuming, caring, creative, easygoing, perceptive, lighthearted, and intelligent. She was humble and never wanted to be the center of attention, and she loved the Lord with everything she had. She was close to her younger sister, Stephanie, sixteen.

When Kristin was ten years old, she got a virus, a simple case of pneumonia. Her condition worsened that night and she was air-transported to the pediatric intensive care unit at Hershey Medical Center. There, she was diagnosed with myocarditis, and she spent seven weeks on life support fighting for survival. Several times she went into cardiac arrest. Though doctors at first gave her a grim prognosis, her family and community rallied in prayer around her, and Kristin finally recovered enough to go home. But she did so with a very damaged heart.

Eventually Kristin was able to return to school, but with every year her heart grew larger and weaker. When she was in sixth grade, she accepted Jesus as her Savior and went on to be the sort of friend who prayed constantly for others — despite her medical issues. At one of her last doctor appointments, the staff told her that she had perhaps one of the largest hearts in the country, a truth that held more than one meaning for her family. Even so, her heart was functioning well enough that she wasn't put on a heart transplant list. She was, though, limited in her daily activities. Just after her seventeenth birthday, Kristin was scheduled to have a pacemaker and a defibrillator implanted into her chest. In anticipation of the surgery, her friends at school threw her a pre-pacemaker party. Even though she didn't like the attention, she loved the support and concern from her friends and classmates that evening.

Throughout the experience, Kristin learned not to get too upset about the small things in life. She was very brave and rarely complained as she tried to live as normally as possible. In fact, many people had no idea what she was going through medically.

The day after Kristin's seventeenth birthday, she was taking a walk across the street when she went into cardiac arrest. By the time the ambulance got there, her dad had been performing CPR for thirty minutes. They got her heart started again and took her to Hershey Medical Center for six more weeks. They tried their best, but on November 26, 2006, she went home to be with Jesus. She was a junior at Lancaster Mennonite School, where her parents dedicated the Kristin L. Palazzo Gallery at the school. The gallery presently displays Kristin's art, but also the work of other students. The people who loved her and knew her best like to say that Kristin will be a much bigger part of their future than their past.

At Kristin's life celebration service with Mount Joy Mennonite Church in Mount Joy, Pennsylvania, more than six hundred people attended. Her favorite Bible verse, Psalm 46:1–2, was recited for all to hear. People left the service that day forever touched by Kristin's life.

Kristin's life was honored Forever in Fiction by her parents—Rick and Lynne Palazzo, who won the item at the Lancaster Mennonite School Auction. I chose to make Kristin a student volunteer for Emma Landon's grade school children, a role that gives Kristin's character the chance to make an impact on Emma. Kristin's love for friends and God, her faith and courage, make her another great example for the struggling Emma. I pray that Kristin's life will touch many of you reading this book as well, and that her parents, family, and friends are honored by her placement in the pages of *Shades of Blue*, where her memory will live on Forever in Fiction.

Finally, in this book, Cassandra Rae Armijo will be honored as well. Cassandra's life was very brief, but it was also brilliant. She was stillborn at just less than six months' gestation. She had beautiful eyelashes, a cute nose, and she was a very active baby until the time of her death. Cassandra would've been the first-born for her mother, the first niece and the first grandchild for her mother's side of the family. She since has two brothers who will not meet her until heaven—Nathaniel and Micah.

Cassandra was placed Forever in Fiction by her aunt, Joanna Williams, the sister of Cassandra's mother—Elisabeth Armijo. I chose to have Cassandra be the baby of one of Emma's teaching colleagues. In doing so, Emma has the chance to see the reality of life that grows within a woman during a pregnancy. This helps to create an awareness for Emma about life and its sanctity. Joanna, I pray that you and your sister and your family are honored by the placement of Cassandra in *Shades of Blue*, and that you will always be touched when you see her in the pages of this book, where her memory will continue to touch hearts and change lives as she lives on Forever in Fiction.

For those of you who are not familiar with Forever in Fiction, it is my way of involving you, the readers, in my stories while raising money for charities. To date, Forever in Fiction has raised more than $100,000 at charity auctions across the country. Obviously, I am only able to donate a limited number of these each year. For that reason, I have set a fairly high minimum bid on this package so that the maximum funds are raised for charities.

If you are interested in having a Forever in Fiction package donated to your auction, contact my assistant, Tricia Kingsbury, at Office@KarenKingsbury.com. Please write *Forever in Fiction* in the subject line. Also, look for occasional offerings of Forever in Fiction on eBay—an attempt to give all my readers the chance to purchase this item while benefiting a charity of my choice.

Shades of Blue

One

CREATING THE RIGHT SPIN USUALLY CAME easily for Brad Cutler, but this time he was struggling. Kotton Kids Clothing was the account of the moment, a lucrative campaign with a high-end product that should've been easy to work with.

He stared out the window and tried to focus. The stunning view from his downtown New York City office on the twenty-first floor of the Westmont Building was hardly conducive to figuring out family moments as they related to soft cotton clothing. Even so, the chaos of Manhattan wasn't the problem. Brad could work anywhere, and on this day, creating a campaign should've been even easier. His office had been transformed, surrounded by soft pastel fabrics, instrumental lullabies, and poster-size images of children — all intended to take him from the frantic pace of the city into another world.

A world of babies and beginnings.

Brad turned away from the window and braced himself against the solid walnut table that spanned the center of the spacious room. Never mind that he didn't have personal experience with babies. This account shouldn't stump him. He believed in the product — Kotton Kids, a luxury high-end organic cotton clothing and bedding line for pampered babies and toddlers. Brad understood the assignment.

But between his understanding of the task and his ability to create unforgettable ad copy stood a virtual wall of stone. Brad couldn't scale the jagged sides no matter how he tried, and worse, there was no logical reason for the barrier. Except maybe one. A sick feeling came over him and he closed his eyes. Earlier today he glimpsed the dance of shadows from long-ago days, the whisper of a memory from an old, almost-forgotten place in his soul.

He stared out the window and the feeling came around him again. The faint smell of summer sand on a North Carolina shore, the shades of blue where sky and sea blur, the feel of her beside him. A memory he hadn't dared think about in years.

You're losing your mind, Cutler, he told himself. *What could any of that have to do with an ad campaign? Help me focus, God.* He raked his fingers through his blond hair and glanced at the clock on the wall. Almost noon. In a few minutes his boss, Randy James, would stop in to see how he was doing, and Brad had no idea what to tell him. Randy James had trusted him with a project that could take the company to the next level this year ... and for years to come.

Randy James. His boss, and in six weeks, his father-in-law.

He paced to the far end of the room where a display of the cotton product covered two chairs and the end of the table. The colors were soft, muted pinks and blues and tans. He picked up a plush blanket and ran his thumb along the satin edge. He'd come up with only a few slogan lines so far, and nothing he was crazy about. *Babies deserve better ...* The words ran in his mind again and he edited them. *Your baby deserves better.* That was closer, but still not the slam dunk he was looking for. *Because your baby deserves the best ...* He let the words hang in the hallway of his heart for a few seconds.

Whatever he chose, the president of Kotton Kids would be in the office Wednesday for the presentation. If the pitch wasn't strong, Brad could lose the campaign. He lifted the blanket and brushed it against his cheek. Softest stuff ever, like a warm breeze across his skin. The product was brilliant. If he failed this assignment, the blame would be his alone.

But still the wall remained.

His eyes moved along the surface of the table, to the photos of the babies. Eight of them under a year old in various baby positions — crawling, stretched out with feet in the air, cradled in a mother's arms. Brad imagined his fiancée, Laura, holding a baby in a blanket like the one in his hands. *Because love is soft … the soft side of love …* He tried to picture the words sprawled across a magazine ad, but he locked onto the eyes of one of the babies instead. A blonde little girl barely standing, braced against a coffee table. She was looking over her shoulder, and with the music and the blanket and his mind-set over the past few hours, there was almost something familiar about her innocent eyes. He shifted his attention to a little boy crawling across a plush carpet, head tilted up, eyes full of mischief. What would it feel like to have a baby look at him like that?

There was the sound of a sharp knock. Brad looked away from the little boy and dropped the blanket to the table. "Yes?"

Randy James opened the door and stuck his head inside, a grin stretched across his face. "You up for lunch? Two Times Square?"

"Uh …" Brad wanted to say no. It was Monday and he needed every hour surrounded by the cotton clothes and baby photos and lullabies, every possible opportunity to get a brilliant slogan on paper. But Randy didn't ask every day, and Two Times Square was one of the nicest restaurants in the Theater District, meaning his boss had a reason for the invitation. There was only one answer. Brad smiled big. "Sure." He hit a button on a remote control and the music stopped. "Of course." He walked around the table, grabbed his suit coat, and followed his boss. The two of them could talk about the campaign over fish and salads. The change of scenery would clear his mind so he could think better when he returned.

Or maybe a good conversation would tear down the wall.

Two Times Square was situated above the lobby of the Renaissance Hotel. Quiet and elegant, the restaurant exterior was made entirely of glass with a view of Times Square that was as stunning as it was surreal. Like the place was hung in a quiet bubble above the craziness below. The maître d' knew Randy. He sat them without a wait, and Randy ordered his usual—a bottle of Pellegrino and a shrimp cocktail to start. Brad agreed to the water, but not the appetizer.

Randy waited until they both had full goblets before taking a long sip and giving the table a light slap. "Six weeks." He sat back, his face beaming. "All this planning and you and Laura will be married in six weeks."

"Six weeks." Brad's heart lifted some.

"I can barely think, I'm so excited." Randy chuckled. "Can you believe it's already here?"

"Feels like we just announced the engagement." Brad gazed through the sheet of glass at the traffic below. That could be it, right? The wedding? The planning and excitement, the countdown and communication with his family back in North Carolina. That might be interfering with his creative process. The wedding was on his mind constantly. He was marrying the girl of his dreams in a carefully planned outdoor ceremony. Then there was the elaborate celebration that would take place at the Liberty House Grand Ballroom across the river from lower Manhattan. All that and they were honeymooning on Grand Cayman Island, after which she would move into his New York flat. All his dreams were coming true over the next few months. Life couldn't be more beautiful.

No, the wedding wasn't the problem. Loving Laura James had never been a distraction, not even now with their big day drawing near. He lifted his eyes beyond the high-rise buildings, up past the enormous animated billboards with their lights and flashing messages that stood out even in daylight. If he squinted at the space between the concrete and steel, he could make out the New York sky. Never as blue as the one over Holden Beach.

He blinked and a once-familiar laughter flirted with his senses in a distant sort of way. Without warning he missed home. Missed it more than he had in four springs at least.

"Brad?" Randy craned his neck a little closer. Concern flashed in his eyes. "You didn't answer me."

"Sorry." A quick laugh, and Brad straightened himself. He took a long drink of water. "You got me dreaming about the wedding. The end of June." Another laugh. "It can't get here fast enough."

Randy's smile slowly returned. "Yes." He relaxed into his seat. "Things are good, right? You and Laura? The wedding plans?"

"They're great." This time his answer came easily and honestly. "Laura's amazing. I'm the luckiest guy ever."

"You both are." Randy picked up the menu, stared at it for a minute, and frowned. "Pumpkin soup. Strange choice for the middle of May."

Randy had his usual — a half order of grilled halibut with sautéed spinach. Brad took the small chicken Caesar. Dinner was at the James' house tonight, after Laura and her mother returned from making final preparations for the wedding. Brad couldn't afford to be overly full.

Not until halfway through lunch did Randy set his fork down. "Tell me about Kotton Kids."

Brad gave a slow nod, his mind racing. "Great product."

"Definitely. Brilliant. With everyone going green, and the quality of the material. They'll capture the market if we handle the ad right."

"I agree."

"We need to knock this one out of the park." Randy dabbed the linen napkin at the corners of his mouth. "I was going through the product line earlier today. Makes me anxious to hold that first grandchild. In a Kotton Kids blanket, of course." He laughed at his wit.

The mention of a grandchild made Brad's stomach drop. He stared at his plate for a few seconds.

"So," Randy tapped his fingertips on the table. He waited until he had Brad's full attention again. "What're you coming up with?"

"A few ideas." Brad's heart rate quickened. He took another drink of water. "I'm building the campaign around the softness of the cloth. Soft justifies the cost, in this case."

"I like it." Randy seemed satisfied with the direction. "Let's meet tomorrow and look over what you have. The meeting Wednesday is only preliminary. Obviously at this point, you don't need more than a basic slogan and a general campaign direction to keep the Kotton Kids brass happy."

"Exactly."

They finished lunch and a Towne Car picked them up outside the Renaissance for the return ride to the Financial District. Back in his office Brad took off his jacket, sorted through his four phone messages, and returned all of them. He saved the call to Laura for last.

"Hey," he heard his tone soften at the sound of her voice on the other end. "How was your morning?"

"Perfect." Her joy filled the space between them. "We confirmed the linens at the Liberty House. It'll be stunning, Brad. Really. Lots of room to dance." She barely paused for a breath. "And this afternoon ... we're taking a final look at my dress. I wish you could go."

"With you?" He grinned, teasing her.

"No, silly. Not really." She laughed. "It's just ... it's so pretty."

"Of course it is." He couldn't wait to see her later. Maybe picturing her in a wedding dress could pull his mind from the faraway place it seemed bent on visiting. He would be with her in just a few hours, but that wasn't soon enough. He ached to hold her in his arms, feel her hand in his. "I can't wait to see you."

"Me too. We talked to the chef at the country club. He gave us a list of food choices. Seafood or a prime rib carving station."

"Sounds great." He closed his eyes and willed the hours to pass so they could be together. "I already know what I want."

"What's that?"

"You." The meaning in his tone grew deeper. "You and always you. Only you."

He could almost hear her smile. "Have I told you how much I love you, Mr. Cutler?"

"Tell me again." He swiveled his chair and stared down at the busy street below.

"I've loved you since the day we met, and I've thanked my dad a thousand times for hosting that office barbecue." A smile sounded in her voice. "You were talking about your faith, and how you wanted to live for God." She took a quick breath. "I don't know. We walked up that path and the sun was setting behind the dogwoods at the back of our yard. And somehow I knew I'd love you till the day I died. Because we believe in the same things, you and I."

The nervous feeling was back. Brad swallowed hard and struggled to keep her from noticing. "I think I knew even before that."

"Really?"

"Since the beginning of time." He focused on the picture of her in his head. "Tell me about today."

They talked another few minutes about the wedding. Laura promised to share more later about the details she and her mom had worked out that day. "Go back to work. By the way, have I told you my dad thinks you're brilliant?"

"Well," he chuckled. "Then I guess I *really* better get back to work."

"And I better go see that dress."

The call ended and Brad found the remote control. Gentle music filled the room again. He could do this. He could come up with a Kotton Kids slogan in the next two hours and prove to himself he was back on his game. The music led him out of his chair and over to the pictures, back to the product. He ran his hand over a snuggly looking one-piece outfit. Infant pajamas in pale blue. Softer than air.

Hmmm. Softer than air? He mulled the words over. *Because love should be softer than air.* No, something shorter. *Love is softer than air.* He focused on the photo of the little girl standing near the coffee table. The one with the familiar eyes. *Because baby love is softer than air.*

Those eyes. He looked away and the words fell apart. What was it about that face? He couldn't possibly know her. He walked a few steps closer, and in a single beat of his heart he knew. He knew with everything inside him. It wasn't wedding plans, or the pressure of a big ad campaign. It was the babies. And he thought of something else. It was the middle of May, so maybe … maybe there was another reason he was being drawn back to Holden Beach.

He pulled his phone from his pocket and checked the date, and there it was. May 15. He should've thought of this before. He stared at the phone and then leaned back against the wall of his office, his eyes closed. In a rush of emotion and heartache, every image on the table fled from his mind. It was May 15, and suddenly there was no ad campaign, no dinner later that night, nothing except the one, undeniable truth shouting at him from every side. The truth was this:

She would be nine today.

Two

THE HAPPY CHATTER OF TWENTY-THREE FIRST graders filled the North Carolina afternoon air and mixed with the breeze through the open windows, reminding everyone that summer was close. Very close.

Emma Landon surveyed her students and held up her hand. "Shh, class, let's remember. We work quietly, okay?"

A chorus of, "Yes, Teacher," came from the kids. They were working on a printing sheet, filling in the missing letters for simple rhyming words like *cat* and *bat*. Everyone but Frankie Gianakopoulos. Frankie was finished long before the others, and now she was sweetly coloring a picture of a horse.

Emma wandered to Frankie's desk. Jefferson Elementary School let out in a few weeks, and Emma always struggled with saying good-bye to her students. But Frankie would be one of the hardest to let go. The dark-haired little angel with the pixie cut and big brown eyes was a picture of life, a ball of energy who never quit on the playground or in the classroom.

"Your picture's pretty," Emma crouched next to the sweet girl. "I like how you used a lot of colors."

"Know why?" Frankie flashed a toothless grin, her eyes sparkling.

"Why?"

"'Cause God gives us so many colors to use, Teacher. That's why."

God. Emma tried not to let the mention of Him dampen her mood. Instead she covered Frankie's hand with her own, careful not to press too hard. "I think you're a wonderful artist, Frankie."

Again the girl smiled, her eyes dancing. "When I have time. 'Cause I like climbing trees and chasing boys too."

"Right." Emma did her best to look serious. "You might have trouble squeezing in enough time for artwork."

"'Cause it's a lot of sitting."

"True." Emma stood and gently patted Frankie's shoulder. Bruises covered the girl's arms and even the tops of her hands. Any pressure was too much for her. Which was why Emma couldn't understand Frankie's insistent belief that God was behind every good thing. God had allowed this beautiful girl to be born with an incurable blood disease, an illness that created a situation of constant danger for Frankie. Once a week she had to visit the oncologist for treatments that left her drained and sick. Even so, no amount of bruising could dim the girl's bright spirit or her limitless hope.

Frankie lifted her eyes once more. "Teacher?"

"What, sweetie?" Emma stooped down again so she would catch every word.

"You're a little sad."

Emma felt her stomach drop to her knees. She forced a quick smile and tried not to react. Nothing was unusual about today. The order of events and assignments, her tone and the way she looked—all of it had been painfully normal. Emma had made sure of it. The day was almost over, and no one had said anything about Emma acting out of the ordinary until now. She swallowed hard. "No, sweetie." She touched her fingers lightly to Frankie's shoulder again. "I'm teaching today. I'm always happy when I'm here with all of you."

Frankie squinted a little. "Yeah, but your heart still seems a little sad." She gave a lighthearted shrug. "It's okay, though, 'cause I prayed for you already. So God will make you happy again."

The girl was as genuine as the Appalachian Mountains, and regardless of the words Emma was saying, the fact remained. Frankie was right. Emma had been sad since the moment she woke up, sad and certain that she could live a hundred years and still be sad on this mid-May day. And God? If there was a God, He wouldn't let her off the hook by taking away the sadness. Not now or ever. Emma stuffed the thoughts deep inside her aching heart. She could hardly tell any of that to this precious child. She felt her smile become more genuine, felt the shock of the girl's pronouncement wear off. "You really prayed for me?"

Frankie giggled. "Course, Teacher. I pray for you all the time."

Emma was always learning something in Frankie's presence. This afternoon was no different. "Well, honey, thank you for that. I'm very glad you pray for me."

"You're welcome." She looked satisfied with herself, and with that she turned her attention once more to the horse picture and a green crayon that sat near the edge of her paper. She picked it up and began adding grass to the field.

Emma studied the girl a few moments longer. She moved on, checking in with a few of the other kids nearby before she noticed a flash of movement near her classroom door. She walked toward it and saw the face of Gavin Greeley, basketball coach for Wilson Middle School, two miles closer to the ocean. *Why doesn't he give up*, she asked herself. *He doesn't know me. If he did, he wouldn't even try.*

As she reached the door, she looked back at her class. "You're working very nicely, boys and girls, so let's keep focused on our own work. Five more minutes and we'll be done." She steadied herself. When her guard was firmly in place, she opened the door and stepped outside.

Gavin had his hands in the pockets of his jeans. "Hey."

"Hi." The tone of her response was almost a question. Against her will, she felt her eyes dance a little. "Aren't you at the wrong school?"

"Early release. Teachers' meetings until three." He grinned and did a slight shrug. "Our group's already finished."

"So you came here?" She leaned against the doorframe.

"I needed to drop off a few camp registration forms. Figured it was a sunny Friday afternoon. Maybe you'd be up for dinner at the beach."

For a single moment, Emma imagined dinner with Gavin, sitting across from him, allowing herself to make small talk about their students and laughing at the funny way Gavin always had about him. The thought faded almost before it was entirely formed.

"I can't." She peered over her shoulder at her students. They were holding their own. Her mind raced for an excuse, so he wouldn't take her rejection personally. "I have to stay late. Then I need to run on the beach. I've got that half marathon in November."

"We can work around that." If he was hurt by her answer, he didn't show it. "I could, you know, sort of run along beside you feeding you grapes and sliced chicken. A little mustard so you don't have to choke it down or anything."

Emma studied him, the tall boyish man with the hopeful look. Years ago Gavin played baseball at Georgia Tech before coming back to North Carolina to teach history and coach middle school. He was thirty-two with the toned, muscled body of a college beach kid, sandy brown hair, tan skin, and green eyes she could easily get lost in.

But she wouldn't let herself. Not now. Not ever.

A sigh hung on her lips and her smile felt as tired as her façade. "Really, Gavin. I can't. Not tonight."

"Did I mention," he took on a mock quizzical look, "I'm running in that same race?"

"Really." She gave a mildly sarcastic nod.

"I am. Exact same one. Outer Banks Marathon."

"Which means …"

He cocked his head, and his charm doubled. "Which means I could run with you, since, you know, I need to train too. We could push each other. Maybe hit the beach a few times a week so we're ready."

She pictured running alongside Gavin Greeley, making their way down the beach and passing the small white wooden cross, the one mostly covered by the tall grass that fanned out from the sandy knolls at the top of the shoreline. The cross she'd placed there. A shudder passed over her, but she didn't show it. Instead she laughed and shook her head. "You're good."

"I could be better."

"Not at running." She shook her head and couldn't keep from laughing. His persistence sometimes had that effect on her. "You're just plain good."

He feigned innocence about what other sort of good she might be talking about. "No, really. I'm not a runner like you." He shifted, and a ray of sunlight splashed across his eyes, making them more brilliant than before. "Here's the thing. If you push me, I might be *really* good." He raised his brow and waited for her reaction.

"Gavin." Her voice was the same one she used for her students.

"Right." He drew the word out, nodding slowly. "Some other time, I mean. You could push me then."

A pang of regret tugged at Emma's heart but quickly passed. She narrowed her eyes. "Okay, seriously … you aren't really doing the marathon, are you?"

"Actually?" His chuckle told her the ruse was over, that this was for real. "I've been training since March. I'm not much of a distance runner, so yeah, I'm doing the half marathon." He flashed another grin. "Maybe we'll see each other at the beach."

Not today ... please not today. She glanced again at her students and then took a step in their direction. "Maybe." For a brief moment she hesitated and allowed a sincerity to her smile. "I appreciate the offer. Really."

"Okay." He gave another lighthearted shrug and took a step back. "See you around."

Emma retreated to the safety of her classroom and raised one hand in his direction. She mouthed the words, "See ya."

And with that, he was gone. Emma shut the door behind him. She turned to her students, and her eyes met Frankie's. The little girl gave her a sad smile, almost as if she understood the battle raging inside Emma's heart. As if whatever prayers the child had lifted to heaven on her behalf were only the beginning of her concern and knowing.

Again Emma walked slowly toward Frankie's desk. "Okay, everyone, if you're finished, take your paper to the red folder on my desk and sit back down."

Most of the students pushed back from their desks and skipped or walked their papers to the front of the room. Frankie stayed seated, her eyes still on Emma. *What is it about her? And how come she looks at me like she can see straight through to my soul?* Emma tried to seem composed and together, the way a teacher was supposed to. She stopped when she reached Frankie's desk. "Everything okay, sweetie?"

"Yes, Teacher." Her expression lightened some. "I was watching you, that's all."

Emma touched the girl's pretty dark hair. "I'm okay."

Frankie tilted her face, analyzing her the way only a child can. "Good." She reached out and took hold of Emma's fingers. "You're the bestest teacher in the whole world." Her eyes shone. "Know why?"

"Why?"

"Because you're nice, and you look like a princess." She gave Emma's fingers a light squeeze and then she released them and struggled to her feet. Her arms were more bruised than usual. "I'll take my paper up now."

Emma watched the way Frankie's first few steps were a struggle, marked by her constant, chronic pain. But three steps along she picked up her pace and looked like any other child. Pain never slowed Frankie, not as long as Emma had known her. She was proof that perfection wasn't needed for life to be beautiful.

Her students were buzzing again, talking out loud and teasing each other, chatting about the weekend and who won the games at recess. Emma let them be. She went to her desk and straightened the stack of papers in the red folder. While the final minutes of the school day ticked away, she stared out the window.

It had been a day like this. Colder, of course. Less humid, maybe, but just as blue. The day that could've changed everything. Memories rushed at her, but she held them at bay. There would be time to think about it later. Down at the beach.

The bell rang and the children obediently lined up at the classroom door. Emma bid each of them good-bye and then settled back at her desk. Two hours later, when every paper had been corrected and filed, and when her classroom was as neat as it would get before school let out for summer, she headed home.

Emma kept the ragtop down on her old red Volkswagen Cabriolet. The salty summer air took the edge off her heartache as she headed southeast for the Holden Beach Bridge. But her solitude was short-lived. No matter how serene the surroundings, questions cut at her, toying with her, taunting her. *What if she'd never . . . What if they hadn't . . . How would it be today if . . .*

She stopped at a light and something caught her eye. She turned and for a few seconds her breath caught in her throat. The stranger beside her was in a Dodge Ram pickup, and in that moment he looked like . . . well, he looked like *him*. Like a face from the past that she could never quite bring herself to forget. The way he might look now at twenty-eight. The same blond hair and rugged face, the same profile.

Crazy, she told herself. *You're seeing things. Ghosts from a time long past.* She blinked away his memory and focused her eyes straight ahead. She'd never get through the evening if she didn't find a way to stay here in the moment. Her soul hurt from so much thinking, so she leaned back against her headrest. Of all the days to see someone who looked so much like him. A sigh rattled around in the basement of her heart before slipping through her teeth.

She reached the crest of the bridge and gazed out at the deep blue Atlantic. At certain times of the year and from certain stretches of beach, a person could watch both the sunrise and the sunset from the island that made up Holden Beach. She turned right on Ocean Boulevard and savored the sun on her face, her dark hair whipping against her oversized sunglasses.

A few hundred homes made up the beach area, most of them double-wides set in a few blocks from the shore, condominiums with ocean views, and the handful of million-dollar houses set right on the water. Emma never drove home without reminding herself how good she had it, how fortunate she was to have a beach house on Dolphin Street, a block from the sand.

She could still hear her grandmother's voice, calling her a week before her death. "I haven't been there for you the way I should've," her words were scratchy and stuck together. "It's time I made up for it."

The beach house was her way of making up.

Emma pulled into her driveway and surveyed the place. It was on stilts, faded white and gray with wood siding weathered by the sea air — the bleached-out look of most homes along the island. On either side of the front porch was a set of stairs that shot out like another pair of angled stilts. Emma put the car's top up and shut the door. At a quick glance, her house looked sort of like an oversized sand crab, its legs jutting down at differing angles, sitting on a grassy section of sand that doubled as her front yard. The house was built in the late sixties, with a charm she wouldn't have traded.

It wasn't beautiful the way some beach houses were, but Emma didn't care. She was a minute from the shore and the eight miles of sand where she could run until her heart no longer hurt. She knew every neighbor up and down Dolphin Street—including a couple of retired teachers who spent most days reading on their front porches. One of them was always up for an evening conversation and a cup of coffee. But tonight Emma was glad they were already inside.

Besides, she wouldn't be alone. She had Riley, her red-brown lab mix, and two cats—Oreo and Tiger. And she had a plan. She was a year away from earning her master's degree in education. After that she'd see about getting her administrative credential. Maybe one day she'd move to Wilmington or Raleigh and be principal of an elementary school. She loved her beach house, but if she got out of Holden Beach, she wouldn't see her past around every corner.

She slid the long strap of her purse across her body and headed through the front door and into the living room.

"Riley! Here boy." Through the window over the kitchen sink she could see a sliver of the Atlantic, and at this hour the sun sparkled against the distant water, beckoning her.

From down the hall came the sound of dog feet scratching against the worn hardwood, and Riley's wagging tail smacking against the wall. He rounded the corner followed by Oreo, a black-and-white, feisty one-year-old kitty, and Tiger, a striking long-haired mix with exotic green eyes and a haughty personality. The three of them napped together on the couch in her room most afternoons, basking in the sun shining through the window and waiting for her to come home.

"Hi, guys. I missed you!" She gave them each a minute of her attention. Then she downed a glass of water and slipped into her running shoes.

She needed to get out, get to the stretch of white sand that made up her backyard. With the memories surrounding her today, there was only one place she wanted to be, one place that would give her any solace whatsoever. With Riley running alongside her, she headed for the water, to the familiar shore of Holden Beach. Where a lifetime ago it all began.

Where it all ended.

Three

THE WHITE WEDDING DRESS HUNG AGAINST the far satin-lined wall at Clea Colet's on New York City's Upper East Side as Laura James and her mother entered the fitting area. Laura's breath caught in her throat and her fingers instinctively flew to her mouth. She couldn't help herself. Now that the dress had been fitted, it was somehow even more beautiful than before.

"It is a dress for a princess." The seamstress had a heavy Italian accent. She stood a few feet away, gazing at the gown, clearly satisfied. She turned her smile to Laura. "I don't know if we ever have a more beautiful bride for that dress."

"The lace … it's exquisite, honey." Her mother leaned in and kissed her cheek. "Like everything about you."

Laura wasn't sure whether to laugh or cry or ask for a moment alone. But staring at the dress, at the elegant lace train that flowed from the silk and taffeta skirt, and at the shirred sleeveless bodice, she was suddenly taken back. Back to the day when she was thirteen and she talked her mom into buying a *Bride* magazine.

With the wedding plans taking up so much of her time, Laura sometimes caught herself saying she'd been dreaming about her wedding since Brad's proposal. But that wasn't true. She'd been planning for this, dreaming about it since she was in middle school, since her thirteenth birthday when her parents presented her with a promise ring and a prayer journal.

"Ask God for the right man," her mother had told her. "And don't ever settle for anything less than that special guy."

Laura had taken her words to heart. A few weeks later the two of them brought home a copy of *Bride* magazine, and Laura had asked a simple question. "How come all the dresses are white?"

Her mom smiled. "White—for many brides—represents purity. Your promise ring means you've made a commitment, honey. To stay pure for your husband, so that one day when you wear a white wedding dress, it'll mean something very beautiful."

The memory faded as quickly as it had come. Laura linked arms with her mother. Then she cast a hopeful look to the seamstress. "Can I try it on?"

"Of course." The slight wisp of a woman hurried to the dress and began removing it from the silk hanger. "You wore the proper underclothing?"

"I did." Laura swapped a quiet giggle with her mom. They had been up and down Madison Avenue earlier that day looking for the right strapless bra and the perfect wedding attire for beneath the dress. What they'd found was beautiful, a mix of satin and lace, much like the dress.

Laura had put the undergarments on in the dressing room at Rose's in the Fashion District, the shop where she'd found the bridesmaids' dresses. Now, with the door to the fitting area closed, she moved to the small stage at the far end of the room, the one surrounded by tall mirrors on three sides, and she slipped off her T-shirt and jeans. At the same time, her mom helped the seamstress, as together they eased the dress carefully over Laura's head.

"Oh, honey ..." her mother stepped back, her eyes soft and wide. Tears welled up despite the smile that stretched across her face.

"You like, Ms. Rita?" The seamstress nodded at Laura's mother. "A perfect fit, yes?" She tilted her head. "You look like someone famous, Miss Laura. Reese Witherspoon, maybe."

Laura and her mother both smiled. The seamstress wasn't the first person to compare her to the blonde actress. "Thank you." Laura smoothed out the skirt and adjusted it so it settled evenly around her feet.

"I guess I never dreamed …" Her mom stared at her. "It's perfect, darling. Definitely."

The dress fit like it was made for her, which after the tailoring, it pretty much was. Laura stared at herself and at the reflection of her mother looking at her from a few feet back, and she knew she would remember this moment as long as she lived. This dress would in some ways represent her entire past and future as they came together in a single day.

Her wedding day.

"You've lost weight, a little, yes?" The seamstress furrowed her brow and pinched the satin fabric near Laura's waist. "We take in another quarter inch?"

Laura laughed. "It's fine. If I lost anything, I'll probably gain it back with the craziness in the next six weeks."

Her mom nodded thoughtfully. "Laura's right. Let's leave it. We can always adjust it the week before if we need to." She pulled a camera from her purse and took photos of Laura, two from the front and a few from each side. "Your father will want to see you. He would've been here if he could have."

"He'll be home for dinner, right? He and Brad?"

"Right." Her mother took a final photo. "Six o'clock on the back terrace. Marta's making her skewered shrimp, steak, and grilled potatoes."

"That'll put the weight back on." She smoothed out her skirt, loving how she felt in the dress, not wanting the fitting to end. "Daddy will love it. Marta too." The full-time housekeeper and chef had been with them since Laura was eleven years old. The family loved her dearly.

The seamstress helped lift the dress over Laura's head, and in a few minutes she was dressed again and back outside with her mother. She hadn't talked to Brad since earlier in the afternoon, but she was looking forward to seeing him. She had no idea how she'd keep the details about her dress quiet.

Again she and her mom linked arms, and with the sun at their backs they walked more slowly down Madison Avenue. "You were a vision in that dress." They both wore their sunglasses, but her mom's dreamy expression was still easy to see.

"Remember when I was thirteen?" Laura looked up, her steps slow and thoughtful. "We bought that *Bride* magazine. You and I talked about my promise ring and white wedding dresses, and we looked at every gown in every ad. Remember?"

"I told you one day you'd have a fairy-tale wedding."

"And I believed you."

Her mother pulled her a little closer. "I've loved being your mom. You've given me nothing but joy since the day you were born, Laura. A part of me can't believe you're really getting married."

Laura grinned, and she felt the thrill of love to the center of her soul. "I found my Prince Charming."

"Yes." They slowed to a stop and her mom pulled her into a tender embrace, one that didn't notice the foot traffic and craziness of Madison Avenue. "You definitely found him."

DINNER WAS ON THE BACK PATIO of the house where Laura had grown up, a six-thousand-square-foot estate situated on five acres in West Orange, New Jersey. The place wasn't far from Essex County Country Club, and only an hour's commute into Manhattan even at the peak of rush hour.

Laura helped Marta set the table. "I have pictures." She couldn't contain the thrill in her voice. "Mom took them at the fitting today."

"Of the dress?" Marta squealed and then lowered her voice to a whisper. She was in her early fifties, a Polish immigrant with white-gray hair, bright blue eyes, and a vibrant faith. "When can I see them?"

"After dinner." Laura looked back at the living room where Brad and her father were discussing one of their ad accounts. "Brad can't know about them."

Laura's mother walked up with two platters of skewered shrimp. "The food's ready. Smells delicious."

"Thank you." Marta walked around the table, adjusting linen napkins, making the table look just right. "How much longer for the men?"

"I'll check." Laura ran lightly back into the house. "Hey guys … dinner's ready."

"Be right there." Her dad sounded upbeat. Whatever the conversation with Brad, it must've gone well. "We're on our way."

Outside, the velvet green lawn flowed from the custom wood deck off the back of the estate to the frame of trees surrounding the James' property. The setting was like something from a movie, and Laura never took it for granted. That God would let them live here, with this life … that He would let her meet Brad — one of her father's favorite ad executives — and that the two of them were six weeks away from a storybook wedding and a happily-ever-after life together. All of it was more than Laura could believe.

I don't deserve this, Lord … Thank You. With all my heart, thank You.

The guys joined them and her father hugged her gently around her neck. "So you and your mother did some shopping in the city today?"

"We made final adjustments on the bridesmaids' dresses," Laura's eyes danced as she looked at her mother. "And, well … let's just say we got a lot done for one day."

Brad locked eyes with her as he made his way around the table. The chemistry between them was tangible as he touched her cheek. "I missed you," his whispered voice was meant for her alone. "I can't wait to be married to you."

His breath against her face, the way his skin felt against hers, Laura was instantly intoxicated by his nearness. Her parents were distracted by Marta, who was bringing the food out. Laura leaned in closer to Brad. "Six weeks feels like forever."

Their eyes met again, but whereas Brad would usually make the moment last or maybe reach for her hand, this time he turned his attention back to her parents. "The steak smells amazing."

Laura studied him for a few seconds, but then joined in the conversation around her. Nothing was wrong. How could it be, when they were in the final stretch of a year of planning for their wedding? She turned her attention to her father and the way he and Brad were chatting. Work could sometimes cause Brad to be quieter than usual, but tonight he was laughing and talking with her dad about the wedding. Everything was fine. They served their plates, and then her father motioned for them to hold hands around the table.

"Lord, these are the times of our lives, and we are grateful with every breath. Thank You for Laura and Brad, for the beautiful love they share and for the way they've lived their lives for You. No two young people deserve each other more, Father. For that and for this food, we thank You."

The evening was warm and the breeze carried with it the smell of freshly mowed grass and the faint sweetness of distant blooming magnolias. Laura waited until the meal was over before she motioned to her mom to distract Brad.

Rita James was as much her best friend as her mother, a vibrant woman with dark blonde hair and an athletic physique from years of tennis and power walking through the neighborhood. She raised her eyebrows and winked at Rita. Then she took hold of Brad's arm. "I have a catalogue in the car. Tuxedo styles." She flashed Laura a quick smile as she led Brad away. "Laura had a few ideas about what you'd like, but come take a look."

As soon as her mom and Brad were out of earshot, Laura took the small camera from her mother's purse and gathered her father and Marta in a corner of the kitchen.

"What's this about?" Her dad's smile hadn't faded since dinner.

"It's her dress!" Marta was the first to Laura's side. "Come on! Hurry!"

"Oh … right. The fitting." He ambled over, but halfway across the kitchen he stopped. "Actually, I think I'll wait till the wedding day. Something else to look forward to."

Laura pictured her dad seeing her dressed as a bride for the first time here, in the house she grew up in. He was right. The surprise could wait. "Good idea." She showed the photos to Marta.

The housekeeper drew a long, exaggerated breath. "Laura! It's perfect." She looked at each picture and then impulsively hugged Laura. "Sweet girl … no bride has ever looked prettier."

They heard voices on the other side of the garage door, and quickly Laura slipped the camera back into her mother's purse. Brad entered the kitchen first, a tux catalogue in his arms. He gave Laura a bewildered smile. "They all look the same."

Her mom was a few feet behind Brad, and her eyes danced at the way they'd tricked him out of the kitchen. She cleared her voice. "I told him you'd help."

Laura smothered a giggle and then turned a semi-serious expression toward Brad. "How about after our walk?"

"Definitely." The confusion in his eyes eased. They worked with Marta to clear the table and load the dishwasher, and then they walked down the long winding driveway and onto the path toward the west end of the golf course. It was a walk they'd taken more times than Laura could remember, and with the sun setting she could hardly wait for some alone time with Brad.

They were halfway down the drive when he smiled at her. "The fitting went well?"

"It's amazing." She smiled. "I wish you could see it."

"You'd make any dress beautiful."

"You showed Marta pictures, right?" His eyes danced as they walked, their pace easy. "The whole get-Brad-in-the-garage ploy."

"Brad!" She uttered a single shocked laugh. "What ... were you standing at the door listening?"

He stopped and moved closer to her, brushing his lips against hers, a kiss defined by the restraint Brad had shown since they started dating. But one that took her breath all the same. "You aren't good at keeping secrets." He pressed his cheek against hers. "Not from me, anyway."

"You can't see it." She hugged him close. "But it's perfect."

"Like you."

She smiled and stopped herself from saying more. After a long pause she linked her hand with his. "What about your day? Dad mentioned a new ad campaign."

"Yes." A sudden tiredness sounded in Brad's voice. "Kotton Kids. I'm sort of stuck on this one. Surrounded by baby pictures all day, and still nothing."

They turned right and headed up a slight hill. "Baby clothes? Is that the campaign?"

"Not any old baby clothes. High-end, organic, produced in an entirely green facility, softest cotton ever. That kind of baby clothes." Brad slid his free hand through his blond hair and sighed. "But nothing came to me." He gave her a weary smile. "Just one of those days."

"It's weird ... how we'll be talking about baby clothes in a few years."

She expected Brad to jump in with a statement about how he couldn't wait, or how wonderful being a father was going to be. Instead he stayed quiet. After a minute or so, he gave her hand a soft squeeze. "Know what kept coming to me today? When I was supposed to be writing a campaign slogan?"

"What?" They kept walking. The path headed downhill here and leveled off a few blocks ahead.

"How we met." He ran his thumb along the top of her hand, something he did when he was feeling sentimental. "How I knew in the first hour that there'd never be anyone as right for me."

"Mmmm." She pictured them drifting off by themselves at her father's employee barbecue four years ago. "You told me you were earning your MBA at night. Remember?" She giggled. "You'd been working for my dad for a year and somehow I'd missed you." His arm felt warm against hers. The sensation was wonderful. "You're amazing at it, by the way. You could sell baby clothes to a bunch of frat guys."

"Maybe." He laughed, but the sound died sooner than usual. "Today was strange." His pace slowed. "I couldn't focus."

She stopped and faced him, her actions more casual than concerned. She took hold of his other hand and let her eyes get lost in his. "Because of the wedding?"

"No." His answer was quick, his face relaxed. "You and your mom make the details seem easy."

"She's been great." Laura thought about the breadth and scope of pulling together a wedding reception for more than three hundred people. A wedding at the Liberty House in Liberty State Park, no less. The celebration would be covered by the local papers and topped off with a fireworks display at the edge of the Hudson River. Her father had spared no expense, and though they had a wedding planner, her mother had coordinated the photographer and videographer, the catering, and the invitations — which went out a week ago. "I love that she didn't make a single decision without our input."

"I'm not surprised." He eased one hand free and framed the side of her face. "Your mom's having a good time with this wedding." The corners of his lips lifted some. "No question about that."

"So it's not the wedding?" If Brad was bothered, she wanted to know why.

He pulled her into his arms and ran his hand along the small of her back. "No. I promise." When he eased back he kissed her forehead, and then rather than linger on her eyes, he took hold of her hand again and resumed their walk. He talked about Kotton Kids and a conversation he had with his dad, Carl, in North Carolina, and how he was looking forward to the honeymoon.

But he didn't bring up the strange way he'd felt that day again.

Not until Laura was getting ready for bed did she realize he had never actually explained himself, never told her what was at the root of his feelings that day and why he'd felt strange. She remembered what he'd said during their walk, how she couldn't keep a secret from him. She smiled at the truth of that statement. With Brad she was an open book, transparent in her feelings, the way she'd been from the beginning. But what about him?

An uncomfortable question bumped against her heart as she climbed into bed. Not that she had any reason to worry, but here was something she hadn't thought about before. She couldn't keep a secret from Brad, true. But for all their closeness and time together, for all their shared faith and dreams and the way she felt she knew everything about him, she wasn't sure about this:

Could he keep a secret from her?

Four

BRAD TOOK THE DRIVE BACK TO Manhattan more slowly than usual, getting through the Holland Tunnel without ever realizing he'd entered it in the first place. The night with Laura and her parents had been perfect. The weather, the dinner in her family's backyard, the walk after. All of it. Their lives and the impending wedding belonged in a Disney fairy tale. How any guy managed to win over a girl like Laura James and wind up so integrally a part of her family was something only God could explain.

But there was a problem.

Brad turned off the radio and focused on the road ahead. He'd stuffed the truth every day since he met Laura, and always he'd told himself the same thing. She didn't need to know. His past was long behind him, and like he reminded himself the last time he was back in Wilmington, he wasn't the same person anymore. Every time his thoughts found their way back a decade, he came out of the process convinced that his past was locked in a dark closet at the backside of his heart, where it would stay. No reason to drag it out into daylight, kicking it and poking it to see if there was still enough life in it to impact his future.

Or his great love for Laura.

He needed to run. Living and working in the city didn't allow him enough time to run outdoors the way he used to do when he lived near the Outer Banks, back when he was a Carolina beach boy with calloused feet and tanned arms. He would have to get on his treadmill and stare at the city lights. Run until the effort it took to draw a breath killed his ability to remember that far back.

It was the Kotton Kids campaign, that's what was doing this. That and the date, of course. He gripped the steering wheel more tightly than before. *God ... why is this happening? Why now? I made peace with You, didn't I? Wasn't that enough? Every mistake and misstep from the past doesn't have to be public knowledge, right? Especially something so awful as ... so awful as that.*

There was no audible answer, nothing that rang across his soul.

Laura's face filled his mind. She was perfect. He remembered seeing her for the first time. He'd been working for her dad nearly a year, and he'd missed the company Christmas party. When he showed up at the employee summer barbecue, Brad was saying his hellos to Randy and Rita James when he saw her across the lawn, a vision in a sleeveless white linen dress. Blonde hair and tan shoulders, but most of all, a smile that filled her face. He wandered over to Phyllis, the secretary who had been with the company almost since the beginning.

He made small talk for a few minutes, then he hesitated and nodded toward the place across the yard where Laura was talking with a group of people. "Who is she?"

"Her?" Phyllis smiled fondly. "Randy James' daughter."

Brad couldn't take his eyes off the young woman. "What do you know about her?"

"She doesn't date. She plays tennis and writes poetry and she visits sick kids at the children's hospital. She's more about God than guys." Phyllis smiled in Laura's direction. "She's just what her daddy says. One-in-a-million."

Somehow he could tell that about her. He thanked the secretary, and half an hour later he'd worked up the courage to position himself near her. Finally he stepped into her path and held up his hand, his heart slamming about in his chest. "I've been meaning to tell you this ..."

Laura looked surprised. She stopped, the wind playing in her blonde hair. "You've been meaning to tell *me* something?"

"Yes." Brad's days as a cutup back at Wilmington High School helped him fight his fear. He kept a mock-serious look on his face, his tone confident. "Here's the deal." He cocked his head to one side and gave an innocent shrug of his shoulders. "I think we're gonna be better off as friends."

She took a moment to register what he said. Then she scrunched up her brow and managed a confused laugh. "Do I know you?"

"Not yet." He did a few thoughtful nods of his head. "But you will. And when you do, I think we'll be better off as friends."

Her eyes were still narrowed, curious. "Why's that?"

"Because, see," he took a step closer and lowered his voice — as if he didn't want anyone to hear the next part. "You're not my type. I like brunettes." Another shrug. "But that doesn't mean we can't be friends." He grinned. "You know?"

She nodded slowly. "And when are we supposed to start this great friendship?"

"Today?" his expression lit up with possibility. "I work for your dad ... this is the employee picnic." He shrugged. "No better time."

Laughter filled the space between them as they both gave way to the craziness of his request. "What's your name?"

"Brad Cutler."

"Hmmm." Laura surveyed him, teasing. "I can't believe it."

"What?"

Humor shone in her eyes. "I've heard about you, but my dad never mentioned this."

"Mentioned what?" His heart was beating more normally by then.

"That you were a struggling comedian."

He laughed a little awkwardly at that. "Meaning you'll be my friend?"

For a few seconds it looked like she might still say no, even after he'd done his best to charm her. But then she laughed again and agreed. "Who can't use another friend?"

He found her a chilled bottle of water and challenged her to a game of horseshoes. She beat him, but only because he'd never been more distracted. They talked about their shared faith and their passion for charity work, their love for MercyMe's music, and their dream of traveling the world. Time flew, and far too soon the party was wrapping up, the employees heading home.

Brad hadn't wanted to leave, but it would've been awkward to stay. He shoved his hands in his pockets, searching for the right words. "You don't ... have a glass slipper, do you?"

"What?" She giggled. Clearly she was enjoying herself the same way he was. "Are you always this funny?"

"I'm serious." He felt his smile let up. "I want to see you again."

"My schedule's pretty full." Her eyes sparkled. "I'm not sure ... I have volunteer work three days next week. The children's hospital is moving its library."

"I can help." Suddenly the idea sounded better than dinner on the Hudson.

Laura laughed, but in the end she welcomed Brad's help. He was at her side each of the three days she worked that week, showing up as soon as he got off work, and by the following weekend they'd found a connection neither of them was willing to walk away from. The whole time he thought about what Phyllis had said about Laura. That she loved God more than guys. He figured that was the way things should be. Loving God more.

He'd been raised that way—to love God above all else. The way he should've loved God all his life. After all, college had been about finding his way back to God, and by the time he met Laura he was ready for a relationship founded on faith. Brad felt challenged and convicted by Laura's innocent beauty, determined that whether he could win her attention or not, he would be the guy his parents had raised him to be. His father, Carl Cutler, was that sort of godly man. Now it was Brad's turn to follow him.

One night that first month, they met for coffee a few blocks from her father's office. They found a table near the window where they laughed over lattes and life. She came from a wealthy socialite family, and her parents were as invested in charity work as they were in their faith.

"The two are inseparable," Laura had told him that night. "Serving and loving God? One and the same."

The more they talked, the more Brad knew for certain. He could never settle for being Laura's friend. She was beautiful and bright, and an easy conversationalist. She told him about burning a pan of broccoli the past weekend and nearly catching her parents' house on fire.

"I can't imagine the guy who gets stuck with me." She tilted her head back and laughed with a full heart. "I mean, seriously. I can't cook at all."

But Brad was thinking the opposite. How lucky any guy would be to win her over. They started slowly, and for the rest of the summer Brad reminded her often that he wasn't interested. They attended church together, and by the time the holidays came that fall, Brad took her for a walk through Central Park. They stopped at the bridge and sat on one of the stone benches.

"I have a confession." He looked into her eyes without wavering, without blinking. From the sound of his voice she would've thought he was admitting something deep and dark, for sure.

Her smile faded. "Whatever it is ... you can tell me."

"I know." He swallowed hard and took her hands in his. "I lied to you, Laura. I can't go on—not another day—without telling you the truth."

By then they were spending nearly every day together, and twice he'd had dinner with she and her parents on their regular visits in from New Jersey. As friends went, they were inseparable. In that moment, though, Laura's eyes clouded with concern, and her hands felt cooler than before. Her voice dropped a level. "Tell me."

He kept his face serious, his tone dire. "I told you ... I love brunettes ... but I don't."

Like other times when he teased her, her reaction took a moment. But gradually her eyes took on a knowing look, and then the shine of laughter familiar between them. "Really? So, let me guess. Redheads, Brad? That what you're looking for?"

"If that's God's will for my life, then yes. Hair color doesn't matter." He mustered up a pious look. "But the truth is ... I'm crazy about blondes, Laura. Just crazy about 'em."

"So you're not looking for a friend, is that it?" She was teasing him, playing along.

"At this point," Brad looked at her with as much sincerity as he felt in his heart, "I'd be honored to be your friend. But you should know one thing."

"What's that?"

"I'm in love with you, Laura James. Completely and totally in love."

She blushed and laughed in response, changing the subject and spending the rest of the next few hours walking with him through the park. But the day was a turning point for both of them. A month later after dinner and another long walk, he took her back to her parents' house and a few feet away from the front steps he put his hands tenderly on either side of her face. "Can I kiss you good night?" He didn't want to push things, but he wanted her to know his intentions.

"I've only kissed one time," she told him. "My high school boyfriend. But he wasn't okay with just kissing. We broke up over it." She looked intently at him. "What about you?"

Brad was genuinely nervous. He'd been this route before and he wasn't proud of it. But he wasn't the person he'd been in high school. "We don't have to kiss." He brushed his thumb against her soft cheek. "I don't ever want you to feel forced. Staying away from all that means as much to me as it does to you. God won't bless what we've started unless we put Him first."

She paused, staring at him. "Really?"

"Yes." He assumed she wasn't ready for him to kiss her, and he was at peace with that. But as he reached for her fingers and started to lead her up the stairs, the look in her eyes changed. She gave a slight pull of his hand and he returned easily to his spot closer to her. "Then maybe you should kiss me good night," she whispered.

Slowly and with the greatest restraint, Brad searched her eyes, making sure she was okay with what was about to happen. Then he moved gradually closer and for the sweetest few seconds he kissed her. When they pulled away, she said something that stayed with him still. "Who would've known you were just like me? About the whole physical thing?"

Pictures from the past lifted, fragmenting into so many red taillights ahead of him. Brad gritted his teeth and wished for a way back. He should've told her then, right then while the time was right. He hadn't meant to, but clearly he'd given her the impression he was a virgin. From that night on, she talked to him as if his virtue was intact, as if he, too, had only ever kissed his high school girlfriend.

Over time he tried on occasion to broach the subject, come clean about choices he'd made his senior year of high school. But he was an entirely different person from the guy he was back then, changed and reformed. Besides, the subject never came up. He and Laura rarely talked about their physical relationship, or the lack of it. He kissed her once in a while, after a particularly great night out or at the end of a meaningful talk. Then, after he proposed to her, they both teased about looking forward to the honeymoon and how wonderful marriage would be. But his past remained buried in the very deepest basement of his soul and he never figured out a way to talk about it.

By now he had convinced himself that the mistakes he'd made nearly a decade ago couldn't possibly have an impact on his life today. He didn't remember who he was back then. Also, it wasn't like he'd told Laura he'd been pure all his life. She must suspect that maybe his past wasn't as pristine as hers, right? Either way, his senior year of high school was forever ago. Another lifetime. Like what happened that year happened to someone altogether different. The person he no longer knew or understood. The guy he used to be.

Brad finished the drive home, parked in his garage, and took the elevator to the sixteenth floor. His flat wasn't large or brand new, but the views were stunning. The place belonged to the ad agency, and Laura's father let him lease it at a discount. He and Laura would begin their lives here.

He changed out of his dress clothes into a pair of sweats and a T-shirt. The treadmill was calling his name. But rather than clear his mind, four miles later he was still wrestling with his past, wrestling with everything he had tried so hard to forget. So that when he finally stepped off he no longer felt like he was in a suite overlooking New York City, but rather walking a North Carolina shoreline he couldn't forget no matter how hard he tried.

The shoreline of Holden Beach.

Five

MONDAY WAS HIGH SCHOOL VOLUNTEER DAY at Jefferson Elementary, and Emma looked forward to it every week. Not so much because she had help with the kids. Her students were never a problem. If anything, she liked when she had them to herself because the class was more focused. Emma looked forward to Mondays for one reason alone.

Kristin Palazzo.

Kristin, a junior at the nearby high school, drove to Jefferson every Monday despite the fact that she was very sick. Much like little Frankie in Emma's class, Kristin lived with a disease, but hers was worse because it affected her heart. Her mother had told Emma early in the school year that Kristin's doctors doubted she'd live to see the end of her senior year.

God hadn't given Kristin any more fair a life than He had Frankie. When Kristin was ten years old, she came down with a simple pneumonia. But instead of getting better, her condition grew worse and Kristin had to be airlifted to the intensive care unit of the children's hospital in Raleigh. Over the next few days she nearly died, and when she finally pulled through, it was with a debilitating case of myocarditis. Her damaged heart meant one thing for certain: Kristin needed a transplant, and she needed it soon.

At exactly 1:30, Kristin appeared at the door of her classroom, her big Nikon camera looped over her neck. She grinned at the kids and then at Emma. "One more day of pictures, and I should be ready!"

The kids giggled, and a few of them covered their mouths. This had been their ongoing delight with their teenage friend, Kristin. Together they were working on a year-long project that would finally be completed in the next week. It was their secret, and Emma didn't dare ask questions or try to find out more about it than was already obvious. Because clearly the project involved photos.

Kristin seemed a little slower than usual as she set her camera down and flipped her long brown hair over her shoulder. A flock of kids surrounded her. "How's everyone?"

"Can you read about Junie B. Jones and the pet day!" Frankie cried out. "Please, Kristin. Please!"

The other kids joined in, begging Kristin for a story. She touched their heads and put a finger to her lips. Emma watched, amazed. She would make a wonderful teacher someday ... if she were given the chance to live long enough. One more time Emma wondered how she could raise awareness about heart transplants. Kristin needed one yesterday.

"Okay, okay," the teenager laughed, and the sound rang through the classroom. She led the kids to the far corner, the one made up of bean bags and soft carpet squares. Over the next half hour she read them the story they asked for, laughing with them at the funny parts along the way.

When it was over, Frankie reached out and took hold of Kristin's hand. "I like stories that make us laugh," she grinned up at her. "Don't you? Don't you like those funny stories bestest of all?"

"I do!" She turned and looked to Emma. "Can I take them out for recess?"

Kristin was only with them an hour each Monday. Emma was quick to give her permission. "Absolutely. I'll be right here."

It was another sunny day, another afternoon that made kids crazy for summer. They had just eight more days of school, so only one more Monday with Kristin. Emma smiled as the kids followed the pretty teenager out onto the play yard. She was like Kristin once a lifetime ago, innocent and glowing with faith. If only she'd stayed that way. She stood and moved to the window for a quick look. The glare of sunlight on the yard made it impossible for the kids to see her, so she sat on the sill and watched.

With the patience and leadership of a mature college student, Kristin helped each of the boys and girls onto a swing, and then as they began pumping their way higher and higher, she snapped what looked like a dozen photos. Again Emma thought Kristin was moving more slowly than usual. Still, she managed to repeat the routine with each child, getting the boys and girls onto the swing, taking their pictures, and then helping them slow down and climb off the swing.

Finally, when she'd taken photos of every student in a swinging position, she rounded them up to return them to the classroom. If God was listening, why wasn't Kristin getting better? With her parents, her church, and Frankie praying, Kristin had more support than anyone Emma knew.

Kristin brought the boys and girls inside and asked them to return to their desks. Then she looked at Emma, and her expression changed. "Can I talk to you?" she mouthed the words. Whatever was bothering her, it was considerable. Kristin never pulled Emma away from the kids during the school day.

Emma raised her hand and smiled at the children. "Let's say good-bye to Kristin."

"Bye Kristin ... bye." Their voices sang through the schoolroom.

"Okay, class. I'll be in the hall for a minute. I'd like you to pull out your reading folder and go over your questions and answers one more time."

The students did as she asked while Emma followed Kristin into the hall. Emma's heart pounded, and suddenly she felt beyond nervous. Kristin never looked as serious as she did right now, so did that mean her condition was worse than before? Was her heart failure at another, more dangerous level? She folded her arms and stared at the girl. "Is … is everything okay?"

"No." Kristin shifted her weight, struggling to make eye contact. She pulled a packet from her purse and held it up. "I need your help." She handed the packet to Emma. "I'm applying to Liberty University, and … well, I need a letter of recommendation."

Emma felt relief flood through her veins. If Kristin was looking at colleges, then she had to be doing better. Maybe they'd even located a heart for her. Emma took the packet and stared for a moment at the university logo on the front cover. "I'm happy to write you a letter." She narrowed her eyes some. "That's exciting … applying to college."

Kristin allowed a half-smile. "My parents don't think so. They … they want me to wait until I have a transplant." She shrugged. "Or at least the prospect of one."

"Oh." Emma's heart fell a little. "Where's Liberty University?"

"It's a Christian school in Virginia." Light shone from Kristin's eyes. "It's only six hours away. Not a bad drive." She sighed and her enthusiasm waned. "I guess I want to be ready to live. You know, if things work out with the transplant."

"Well …" Emma felt tears pushing their way into the corners of her eyes. She blinked twice, resisting them. "I guess I can see both sides. Your parents just want you close by."

"I know." Kristin nodded at the packet. "There's a form inside. You can fill it out." Her smile returned. "I want to be a teacher. Like you."

Emma fought her emotions. She put her hand on Kristin's shoulder. "I have a feeling," her eyes found a deeper place in Kristin's soul, "you'll be a very … very good teacher one day."

Kristin beamed from the glow of the compliment. Impulsively she rushed forward and hugged Emma for a long time. "Thank you. I won't forget that."

Emma drew back and clutched the folder to her chest. "I'll have this filled out for you next time you come."

Kristin glanced back in the classroom and then at Emma. "You know what I wish?"

"What?" Emma could feel the tears again. She willed them away.

"I wish I could be you for just one day. Already grown up, my heart transplant behind me, and teaching a group of great kids like this."

She waited until she could speak. Then she coughed a little. "Hold on … to that dream."

Kristin hesitated, as if there was something else she wanted to say. But whatever it was, she seemed to change her mind. "I will." She had her camera in one hand as she hugged Emma once more and waved good-bye. "See you next week." She held up the camera and grinned. "We'll have your gift by then. The class and I."

The idea put a brighter smile on Kristin's face than anything in the last few minutes. Emma watched her walk down the hall and out the double doors. Very few teenagers on the brink of summer would be more concerned with college applications and creating gifts for others than hanging out at the beach. Even with her weak heart, Kristin could've spent her time like most kids her age. But she wasn't like most kids.

It was time for the students' painting project, so Emma returned to her class. She handed out sets of paint, smocks, and colorful construction paper. All the while she couldn't stop thinking about Kristin, her compassion and conviction, her desire to live life regardless of the odds. To make the tough choices in faith.

Emma certainly hadn't been that type of teenager. She'd been faced with tough choices the summer after her junior year, but she'd … well, she'd taken the easy way out. At least it had felt that way at the time.

There was a tug on her arm and Emma blinked back the past. Frankie was standing there grinning, as if she were completely unaware of the trail of bruises on either of her arms. "Teacher, know what?"

"What, sweetie?" Emma turned so she was facing the child.

"See this?" Frankie held up her painting. The picture showed two girls, one tall with long brown hair, the other small, with short hair the same color. The older girl had something black around her neck and a big heart painted on her shirt. "It's me and Kristin." Frankie pointed to the black object. "That's her camera, and next to it is her big heart."

An ache grabbed at Emma. "Kristin definitely has a big heart."

"My mommy says kind people always have a big heart. So that's Kristin. It's a 'prise for her when she comes next Monday." Frankie handed the drawing over. "You keep it for her, okay?"

"I will." Emma opened her top desk drawer and slid the painting inside. "It'll be safe here."

Emma carried the image of Frankie's picture with her as she left school and long after she was home and changed into her running gear. That and the conversation she'd had with Kristin. It was always like this midway through May. The end of the school year had a way of making her dread the emptiness of summer. The loss of all that might've been was never more painful than during May's good-byes. She headed to the beach with Riley keeping pace beside her. Three miles down the sandy stretch she veered up and away from the water. She'd placed the cross at the top of the beach in a patch of wild sea grass.

The white wooden marker was visible if someone was look- ing for it, but otherwise she doubted many people noticed it. She stopped, breathing hard and fast from her run. Riley found a freshwater stream and helped himself to a long drink, but Emma barely noticed. She stooped down and touched her fingers to the rough-hewn wood. Etched into the cross was a single date.

November 20, 1999. The sun and seasons had worn away the edges, making the letters less prominent. But they remained all the same.

Along with every memory of that day.

Emma stood and crossed her arms. For a long moment she turned her face toward the late afternoon sun and closed her eyes. The breeze was cooler today, and the warmth from the direct sunlight felt good. But it wasn't strong enough to touch the cold inside her soul. If she'd known then what she knew now, there would be no white wooden cross, no unresolved sorrow shading every other color in her life.

No lonely looming summer.

She opened her eyes and stared at the water, at the place where the blues of sea and sky came together. What about Brad? Had he really been gone from her life for nine years? Were there never days when he woke with her in his heart, the way she still woke with him in hers? She could try to find him; the possibility presented itself some days when his memory was so real she could almost feel him beside her.

But in the end common sense always won out. She wouldn't call him when he had gone so long without calling her, without caring how she was doing and whether she'd ever gotten past the choices they made their last year together. If Brad didn't care to contact her, she wouldn't call him either. But that didn't mean she could stop thinking about him.

Especially in November and May.

Riley was finished with his drink. He came to her side, breathing hard, ready for the run back. Emma reached down and patted the top of his head, scratching the softer fur near his ears. "Ready, boy?"

The dog let out a quiet whine in response. He ran a few steps and then stopped and looked back at her. *Come on, Emma. Get over it,* he seemed to say. *Just keep running ... you'll be okay.*

Emma looked back at the cross and bent down one final time, touching her fingers to the wood. She tried to imagine what Kristin would think of her if she knew about the cross and all it stood for. Kristin was the sort of girl Emma had wanted to be, the kind of girl she might've been if they didn't ... if she hadn't ...

Riley whined again, and Emma took a long breath. "Okay ... let's go." She set out down the sandy knoll back to the damp shoreline. She loved running, but lately she used her time pounding the shore of Holden Beach as a way of clearing her heart and soul, a way of searching desperately for the next thing. As if somehow by running she might reach a place where she could finally, fully move on.

The training was good for her. Physically, she felt better than ever, and at this rate she'd be more than ready for the half marathon. The one Gavin Greeley was going to run. For the first mile of the run back home, she thought about Gavin. She liked him, would have liked knowing him better. But he wouldn't want anything to do with her if he knew the truth. He was a good guy, a worship leader at his church of all things. He was holding out for an older version of Kristin Palazzo. Not someone with Emma's wretched past. Not someone capable of Emma's actions a decade ago.

She tried to keep her mind on school and the final week before summer and the gift Kristin was putting together for her. But no matter what she tried, her mind found its way back to the same place. The stretch of sand right here on Holden Beach where she and Brad fell in love. Where they said good-bye. And like every other time she thought about him, she settled on the same sad reality. She missed him deeply, even though she hated him for leaving her, for never looking back. She still missed him. No matter how far she ran, that much would never change.

Six

BRAD WAS GLAD HE'D WORN HIS suit jacket to the Wednesday Kotton Kids meeting. Anything to give him an edge at a time when he couldn't have felt less prepared. His presentation was coming up and he had a feeling he'd barely breathe through the whole thing. *No problem*, he told himself. He could be nervous as long as he hid it from the others.

The meeting opened with Kotton Kids President, Al Cryder, making small talk with Brad's boss, Randy James. They talked about the two grandbabies due in the Cryder family this summer and about Brad and Laura's impending wedding. Randy pulled an engagement photo from his wallet and slid it across the table. "There they are. The happy couple."

Al was a big guy, who looked even bigger in his western suit, ostrich boots, and dark suede ten-gallon cowboy hat. His company might've have been about going green, but that didn't mean Al was about to lose his Texas image. He sized up the picture appreciatively. "Stunning." He grinned at Brad. "There must be hearts breaking all over the city."

Brad smiled, not quite sure what the older gentleman meant. "Yes, sir."

"You know why, right?" The man had a big voice and an even bigger ego.

"I know." Randy laughed out loud and grinned big at Brad. "Look at the two of you. Together you must've broken a hundred hearts, right, Al?"

"Exactly." He nodded at Brad. "You sure your last name's not Pitt? Those movie-star looks probably make people wonder if they should ask for an ad campaign or an autograph."

Brad appreciated the diversion. Anything to keep a positive feel to the meeting, especially since his presentation had so little in the way of substance. "Laura's the one who looks like a movie star. People say so all the time." He looked at Randy. "Isn't that right?"

"You're both striking." Randy leaned back in his seat. "The wedding's at the Liberty House in the state park."

"I know the place." Al slipped a cigar case from his suit pocket, pulled out a single cigar, and stuck it between his teeth. He didn't light it. "One of my kids looked into it. Spectacular views."

Brad made a mental note that Al Cryder liked cigars—lit or unlit.

"We've got fireworks planned. The whole deal." Randy grinned. "I can't wait."

The conversation fell into a natural lull, and Brad felt the unspoken cue. It was his turn. He drew a silent breath and stood, walking to the near end of the room where an easel was set up with a series of oversized posters. The top one read simply, Kotton Kids Presentation.

"Let's get to the matter at hand." Brad flipped the first poster to the back of the easel. *Okay, God ... help me. Please. I'm not ready for this.* He exhaled, steadying himself. "I'd like to go over the various facets of our plan, the scope and breadth we're prepared to bring to this campaign." The words came easily. This was the part of wooing a client Brad never struggled with. "We'll create three tiers of implementation. The first, of course, is our campaign slogan."

Brad felt a fine layer of perspiration build across his forehead. He ignored it, ignored the way Randy watched him intently, waiting for him to unveil the brilliance he was known for. Another deep breath. "In this case, I'm still honing the exact slogan." He moved to the next poster. Across it were written the only words he'd come up with so far. "At this point we'll use our working slogan, 'Kotton Kids—Because Your Baby Deserves the Best.'"

Al Cryder nodded, his brow furrowed. "I like it. We need more, though." He looked at Randy. "Don't you think, James? Something a little different to set us apart?"

"Definitely." Randy laughed, that confident sort of chuckle meant to assure a client that he and his company were fully in control. "Brad's a genius. He's just getting started on this."

"That's right. Just the beginning." Brad wondered if they could see his knees trembling. He kept his tone controlled, confident as he flipped the slogan poster to the back of the easel. "The next tier, of course, is branding. Colors, textures, an advertisement feel that will keep the consumer connected to Kotton Kids."

He winged his way through that section of the presentation. Muted colors, real babies in sepia tones, gentle music. Despite his lack of direction, he gained ground with Tier Two. "We're talking about creating an experience, a feel with this campaign," he told Al. "Parents will see the parents and babies—whether on TV or in print—and they'll want to have that experience with their own kids. They'll believe that only with Kotton Kids' organic clothing and blankets will their personal moments measure up to what they see in the ads."

"Nice. Very nice." Al bit down on his cigar a few times. He tugged on the brim of his cowboy hat. "You're sharp, Brad. I'm sure your future father-in-law is glad about that."

The meeting continued another twenty minutes through Tier Three—geographical areas where they should best focus their attention, and eventually Brad felt himself relax. He'd survived—this round at least. They set up another meeting for two weeks out, on Wednesday, June 2. Brad was grateful for the respite, but the time would pass quickly. Especially with the wedding plans and everything else interrupting his thoughts. He would have to come to the next meeting ready to wow Al Cryder, or they could lose the account. No matter how well today went. Al was a professional, a cunning businessman who had seized a niche in the market with his Kotton Kids line. He would only be pacified with promises and planned tiers for so long.

Al shook his hand before he left. "Brad ... I'm expecting great things when we see each other again."

"Definitely." Brad kept his cool, his composure. "I think you'll be very pleased."

"You will." Randy chuckled again. He patted Al on the back as if they were best friends, merely catching up for an afternoon. "Brad's the best in the business."

"I hear that." Al narrowed his eyes, the unlit cigar still clenched between his teeth. "What are some other campaigns you've worked on?"

Randy answered. "Finley Grilling System ... Wesley Bedding ... Orion Steel Cookware ... Way Cool Lunch Snacks." Randy gave a dramatic shake of his head. "Everything he touches turns to gold."

Al nodded appreciatively. "Very successful campaigns."

"Yes." Randy directed Al out of the room and down the hall. As they walked toward the building exit, Randy was still raving about Brad, about the magic he could work with an ad campaign.

Brad waited until they were out of sight before he felt his shoulders slump forward. He slipped into his office, walked to the wall of glass across the room, and leaned against it. *God ... what's wrong? May 15th is behind me. So why does my heart still hurt?*

Again he heard no answer, but a song came to mind. An old hymn he used to sing as a boy when he and his parents went to church each Sunday. *Create in me a clean heart, O God ... And renew a right spirit within me.* He thought back, thought about the words of the hymn. They were from a Scripture, right? Somewhere in the Bible.

He left the window, sat down at his desk, and opened one of the drawers on the right side. The place where he kept his Bible. But as he reached for it, his eyes fell on something else instead. An envelope tucked in along the inside of the drawer. It held the contents from his old briefcase, the one he'd used right out of college. Old photos and business cards. He hadn't looked through it in years, but now … now it was calling to him more loudly than Scripture.

With tentative fingers, he tugged at the envelope, pulling it free from the other contents in the drawer. Gently he sifted out the contents on the surface of his desk, and then, without warning, he saw it. The photo he thought might still be there.

The picture of Emma Landon.

He didn't want to touch it, as if by letting his fingers come in contact with the photo paper he might rekindle a feeling he could never escape. Leaning over the image, he stared at her, studied her. His first love, his Emma. Eventually he lost the battle and he picked up the picture, drawing it near so he could see her more clearly.

Was this the problem, the reason he couldn't think clearly? Emma Landon? He held tight to the photo and returned once more to the full-size window. He gripped the heavy wooden frames and stared out onto the street below. Laura had asked him if the wedding was troubling him, and he'd answered her honestly. The wedding wasn't the problem.

He was. He understood that clearly now.

A small plaque caught his eye, a framed Scripture verse he'd bought for himself when he started working at the ad agency. It read, "Anyone, then, who knows the good he ought to do and doesn't do it, sins. — James 4:17."

He'd bought it because in the fast-paced life of a Manhattan advertisement firm, wrong decisions were easy. But if he stayed close to God's Word, Brad would always know the good he ought to do. The framed verse was a reminder that doing the right thing wasn't optional. It was his calling. In advertising and in life. But then why hadn't he done the right thing with Emma? No apology or phone call, no going back to make things right. Not once over the last ten years. As if he could push her and the guilt of what happened aside and somehow get over it.

What did that say about him? And how could he move forward when he'd left so much of his past unresolved? Suddenly he knew what he had to do. He would call Jack Reynolds. Jack was a friend of his from church, a Christian counselor. Brad could at least take the questions to him. Brad looked up Jack's number on his BlackBerry and hit the Send button.

His friend answered on the second ring. "Jack, here."

"Hey … Brad Cutler. Sorry to call you during business hours."

"No worries. I was coming back from lunch." There was the sound of city traffic in the background. "What's up?"

Brad decided to come at it from a different angle. "Okay, so I have this situation."

"Okay."

Brad didn't want to get into details. "You know how I'm getting married this summer?"

"Of course." Jack sounded serious.

"Laura's great. Everything's okay with us." He could hardly believe he was voicing this. "It's actually … I mean, this is crazy but … I had this girlfriend a decade ago. We dated through high school, that sort of thing." His stomach hurt. He rubbed his temples and tried to condense the story as best he could. "Anyway, I'm thinking about her a lot, about how things ended."

"Okay." Jack's voice was calm, but still concerned. "Do you have feelings for her?"

"No, no." Brad's heartbeat sped up. "Nothing like that. It's just ... it didn't ... things didn't end well. I owe her an apology, but I never ... it never happened."

"That's unfortunate."

"Yeah, more than that." Brad exhaled. "I keep thinking maybe I can't move forward with Laura until I go back ... I don't know, maybe find her. Make things right so I can put it behind me."

"I see." He had Jack's full attention, no doubt. "Does Laura know?"

Brad felt sick to his stomach. "Not yet. I guess ... I don't want to make things worse. Dig up the past with my old girlfriend. You know, like maybe an apology would only make things worse for everyone."

"Hmmm." He must've moved in off the street, because the sound of traffic was gone. "Every situation is different, and since I don't know the background or what you're apologizing for, I can only talk in generalities."

"Right. That's what I'm looking for." Brad's heart thudded against his chest.

"Generally, people seeking forgiveness must first seek God's forgiveness, and then they must forgive themselves. And yes, sometimes — if the situation allows — part of the healing is finding the person you offended even after a very long time. Making an apology face-to-face."

"So I should talk to her?" Brad's mind was racing. "I mean, if I can find her?"

"If it's possible — and a lot of times it isn't — then yes. Forgiveness between two people can be very healing. Sometimes it's the first step to moving on. Especially when you're about to start this next chapter of your life." Jack hesitated. "But it's a risk. Laura would have to be on board, or she could misunderstand your motives."

Brad felt his world slipping off its axis. "Exactly."

"Of course there's always the other risk."

"Which is?"

"You could fall in love with this old girlfriend again."

"That won't ... that's not what this is about."

"Like I said, I can only talk in generalities. If Laura understands and you feel this strongly about making an apology, I'd definitely consider it. It's never good to start a marriage with unresolved former relationship issues. Even if seeking forgiveness in this case might not be the safest decision."

Brad wanted to explain there was nothing dangerous about saying he was sorry. The idea of him having feelings for Emma again was crazy, impossible. Nothing could pull him away from Laura. But Jack was the counselor, and he'd probably seen this sort of thing before. Going back to Emma Landon wouldn't be without risk.

He appreciated Jack not pushing to find out the specifics. They saw each other at church, so Brad didn't want Jack knowing more than he'd already said. "Hey, thanks, buddy. That helps."

"Anytime." Again Jack seemed content to let the conversation be. "See you Sunday."

"Yeah. See ya."

The realization of Jack's advice settled in around him, and he felt the hurt in his heart double. The problem plaguing him, the heaviness keeping him from his creative best had nothing to do with Laura or their plans to marry. He lifted the photo and stared at it again. It was him. He knew the right he was supposed to do, but he'd buried it all these years. He'd pushed the truth aside through his college days while he immersed himself in his studies and found his way back to God, and again as he made a name for himself in the business world. He knew what he should've done ten years ago and he knew it now. Especially after talking to Jack. The fact was he hadn't done the good and right thing. He'd avoided doing it all these years. The eyes in the picture stared back at him. His precious Emma. How come he couldn't imagine even a single moment of closure for the two of them? Had he really just walked away, just packed up his Honda and his heartache and never looked back?

Ever since then he had believed with his whole being that he could move into his future without digging up his past. Time would take care of yesterday's wounds for both of them. But if that was true, then how come he could hear the waves on Holden Beach, smell the salty summer air even here in his New York City high-rise office? He hadn't wanted to admit that his troubled soul, his scattered thoughts, were linked to Emma or the choices they made the last year they were together. But they were. They must be.

He looked at the picture, deep into her eyes, and the truth was as vivid as the shape of her face. *Whatever happened to you, Emma Landon? Did you move away and start life over the way I did? Do you ever think about us, about what we walked away from?* The questions came unbidden, flooding his mind and consuming his senses. But one fact stood out from the rest, shouting at him, strangling him, stopping him from putting the photo away and getting on with his day. When it came to Emma, there was good he hadn't done—both that summer and every day since. The weight of that was making it hard for Brad to get through the day, let alone consider getting married. All of which could only mean one thing. Whatever the risk, he needed to do the right thing.

It was time to tell Emma Landon he was sorry.

Seven

LAURA'S WEDNESDAY NIGHT BIBLE STUDY WAS made up of the same six girls who had been her friends since they graduated from Orange Christian High School eight years ago. Over time the group had seen its share of changes — heartache and happiness, tragedies and triumphs. One summer after graduation, none of them were surprised when Megan was the first to get married. Since her freshman year, she'd been dating Joey Johnson, point guard on the Orange Christian basketball team, and now they had four kids under the age of five. She told the rest of the group often that though she loved Joey and the kids deeply, the Bible study kept her sane.

Amy had taken a trip to Aruba two years into her college career at New York University and come home pregnant with twins. She still struggled to talk about what happened against her will at a rented hotel room when the rest of her group was out at a night club. She had seriously considered an abortion, but Megan talked her out of it. Raising two little girls left her no time for dating, so Amy remained single and happy. She and the girls lived back at home with her parents.

The dancer in the group, Bella Joy, graduated from New York City's Juilliard, and for the last several years, she spent spring and summer touring Europe with a ballet company. Now, though, she was tired of the travel, tired of coming home to an empty Brooklyn apartment. No matter how great the thrill of dancing professionally, she was praying to meet the right guy, get married, and raise a family.

Anna was a teacher in Jersey City, married to a youth pastor from an inner-city church in the SoHo District. They lived with his parents, and they were expecting their first baby. Anna had no idea how they'd ever find their own place, since there was no way they could afford anything within an hour of Manhattan. Not that Anna minded too much. She loved her husband's parents and the situation worked for all of them. Two years ago, Anna had a scare with a melanoma on her left leg. But doctors removed the tumor, and she'd been cancer free ever since.

Just back from Nashville was Nelly, who sang in the Orange Christian school choir with all the other girls except Megan. Nelly left New Jersey to get her music degree at Belmont University in Nashville, where she fell in love with a rising country music star. Their relationship made the tabloids and culminated in a wedding that graced the covers of *People* magazine. That was three years ago, but after only ten months, the pictures on the cover of the tabloids changed to include a number of girls who were not Nelly. Her husband moved out a year ago and the divorce was quick and painful, without so much as a proper good-bye from the guy. Nelly came home convinced she'd never love again, but this past spring she'd started dating another graduate of Orange Christian, a guy from the class two years ahead of them.

Megan, Amy, Bella Joy, Anna, and Nelly. The best friends Laura could have had, the bridesmaids for her upcoming wedding. By now — after being in so many weddings together — the friends knew the routine. But still they were thrilled for Laura, for the beautiful ceremony and reception that would take place in six weeks, and because she was marrying a guy as wonderful as Brad Cutler. These friends were the ones who knew how hard Brad had worked these past three years — maintaining his full-time job for Laura's father all while earning his MBA. And these girls had been the first to rejoice with Laura a year ago when Brad proposed.

Tonight's meeting was at Laura's house. The girls were gathered in her spacious living room, each nestled into one of the various overstuffed chairs or sofas. Laura surveyed the room and remembered what it had been like sitting with these very girls around the lunch table at Orange Christian. The best friends had seen each other through those uncertain, dramatic high school days and through every stage of life since. Laura believed they would stay friends forever, and what always drew them back together was this—their weekly Bible study. They took turns hosting the meeting, and though there were seasons when one or more of them couldn't be counted on every week, the gatherings were consistent.

The afternoon had been heavy with humidity, but now a light wind had picked up. Laura opened the windows and placed a pitcher of lemon water on the coffee table at the center of the room. Then she joined the others, all of whom had their Bibles open to Luke, chapter 6.

"You know," Nelly set her water down on the floor near her feet. "I just need to say before we get started … I struggle with this section." She absently gathered her long auburn hair in one hand and stared at her open Bible. Back in high school, Nelly was maybe the most carefree of them all, easily laughing and delighting in life's simplest pleasures. But since her divorce, she sometimes allowed an understandable edge to her voice, a cynicism about her faith.

Laura wished there was something she could do to help her friend, because she had a feeling this was one of those times.

Megan generally kept the discussion moving in the right direction, reminding them that they could talk about their personal lives at the end of the study during the time for prayer requests. Now Megan gave Nelly a sympathetic look. "I agree. There's nothing easy about chapter 6."

A quiet came over the room and each of them looked at the section of Scripture. The small heading for today's reading read simply, "Love for Enemies."

Nelly looked around the room. "Why don't we get started. I think there'll be lots to talk about once we get through the verses." She nodded at Amy. "You wanna read the first four verses out loud?"

"Sure." Amy positioned her Bible higher on her lap. "Luke 6:27 through 31. 'But I tell you who hear me: Love your enemies, do good to those who hate you, bless those who curse you, pray for those who mistreat you. If someone strikes you on one cheek, turn to him the other also. If someone takes your cloak, do not stop him from taking your tunic. Give to everyone who asks you, and if anyone takes what belongs to you, do not demand it back. Do to others as you would have them do to you.'"

A pained look filled Anna's eyes. "Did I tell you what happened at the mission downtown?"

The rest of them mumbled quiet no's or shook their heads.

"You know about our work there. We're set up in SoHo to help kids who don't have a chance." She looked at the others. "Well … last week a couple guys from a cross-town gang broke in and smashed our game tables and wrote threatening graffiti across the walls and windows. They did ten thousand dollars' worth of damage." Anna had short curly hair, and she tucked a stray curl behind her ear, doubt casting a layer of helplessness across her sad eyes. "So yeah, I struggle with this too. I mean, what … are we supposed to find the guys who did this and welcome them back, tell them to take another swing at us?"

Laura had to agree. "She has a point. I mean, does God really want us to roll over and die every time someone hurts us?"

Megan leaned over her knees and folded her hands, her eyes on Anna. "I think this is more about our attitude when someone hurts us."

"Our attitude?" Nelly angled her head. She wasn't being argumentative, but she was clearly confused.

A low-flying plane rumbled across the sky outside. Megan tried again. "In other words, we need to love people no matter what. If they harm us, then we need to believe God will restore whatever was lost in the process. The main thing is to love even when it isn't easy."

"Like loving your enemies." Nelly's voice was softer than before. "That's what I mean. This part's hard for me."

Bella Joy read the rest of that night's section. "Luke 6:32 to 36. 'If you love those who love you, what credit is that to you? Even "sinners" love those who love them. And if you do good to those who are good to you, what credit is that to you? Even "sinners" do that. And if you lend to those from whom you expect repayment, what credit is that to you? Even "sinners" lend to "sinners," expecting to be repaid in full. But love your enemies, do good to them, and lend to them without expecting to get anything back. Then your reward will be great, and you will be sons of the Most High, because he is kind to the ungrateful and wicked. Be merciful, just as your Father is merciful.'"

A silence hung over the room for several seconds. Finally Amy raised her brow and pursed her lips. Her cheeks filled and she exhaled like someone who'd just had her eyes opened. "Wow. I never really focused on these verses. That's a powerful kind of love."

"Or maybe it's just craziness." Nelly shared a look with Amy. "Don't get me wrong, I want to please God like all of us. But there's a line when it comes to people who've hurt us. I mean really, truly ripped out our hearts."

Laura watched her two friends and tried to imagine the kind of pain they both must be feeling. Amy had been date-raped, which was practically all she'd told them about her time in Aruba. For Amy to love this man who had harmed her and taken advantage of her? It seemed an unreasonable request, a particularly painful one. Especially when Amy's greatest enemy of all was the father of her two girls. And Nelly? Knowing that the love of your life betrayed you in a way that made you a public spectacle? Again, loving him still seemed more than God could ask of a person.

"The reality is, we can't love like that on our own," Megan took a drink of her water. "Remember Jesus on the cross? Some of his last words were a cry to His Father, that the people killing Him might be forgiven. That's the only way we can love our enemies. Because He did it first."

Amy sighed. "It's a goal, that's for sure."

"Exactly." Nelly crossed her arms. "In my heart of hearts I want to be that close to God, that I could love however and whomever He asks me to love."

Anna pulled her knees to her chest and rocked a bit. "I guess that's why we need the Scriptures as a whole, not just the parts." She closed her Bible. "I mean, Philippians 4 tells us that we can do all things through Christ who gives us strength."

Laura sat back, still struggling with the concept. "Hmmm. Strength to do whatever He asks. Even loving our enemies." If she had been harmed like Amy and Nelly, Laura was pretty sure she'd have excused herself and gone home early tonight. The way Amy and Nelly were handling the topic, she had a deeper respect for them than ever before.

The study went longer than usual. After they finished with the verses, the conversation shifted to the wedding. Laura shared the last-minute details she and her mom were working on, and she showed them the photos from her fitting.

"You know what I think?" Amy put her arm around Laura's shoulders. She and the others had formed a tight cluster around Laura on the sofa. "I think some of us have lives right out of a storybook. You, especially."

"Let's pray it stays that way." Amy's smile was genuine, without any of the self-pity she could've been feeling.

They closed the night by praying right where they sat, a circle of friends that neither time nor tests had torn apart. They prayed for Megan to have patience with her young children and for Amy to find strength as she raised her twin daughters. They pleaded with God to help Bella Joy find the love of a godly man, and for Anna and her husband not to be discouraged by the recent vandalism at the youth center in SoHo. They prayed for Nelly's current relationship, that the two of them would be wise in the time they spent together, and that God would make it clear if this was a guy who would stay and not run. Finally they asked that Laura and Brad would continue to draw close to the Lord and to each other in the final weeks leading up to their wedding. And that the storybook start would, indeed, lead to the sort of happy ending only Christ could provide.

When the study was over and the girls were gone, Laura sat alone in her living room, staring out the window at the outline of trees against the moonlit sky. Her parents were out to dinner and wouldn't be home for another hour, so for now she relished the quiet. The girls were right. Her life really was something from a storybook.

In some ways, the truth brought an uneasiness, a fear Laura couldn't quite define. Somewhere along the path of her life, she would of course run into a bump in the road, or a broken road, for that matter. But whatever lay ahead, she had this certainty above all: Brad loved her and he loved God. He would stand beside her through the seasons of life, and when it rained ... well, when it rained, he would be her shelter.

She was sure of it. And that would make it easier to love her enemies when the time came.

Laura checked her watch. Brad would call in twenty minutes, because that's what he always did. Mondays were his day at the gym, the evening when he pushed himself the hardest. Sure enough, like clockwork, her cell phone rang just before nine o'clock. "Hey, baby," she smiled as she answered. "Just a minute." She ran lightly to the swing out back and settled in. From here, she had a full view of the waxing moon. "There. I took you outside. It's too nice out to sit indoors."

"It is." His voice was more serious than usual. "I walked a mile on the rooftop track after my workout. I love Manhattan in May."

"You walked on the roof?" Laura knew that wasn't part of his routine. "Don't you usually finish up with a swim?"

"Not tonight." He sighed and the sound rattled with uncertainty. "I needed to think. Figured I could do that better outside."

He needed to think? There it was again, the slight hint of concern, the suggestion that somehow six weeks before their wedding everything wasn't as wonderful as it should be. She worked to keep her tone light. "What'd you think about?"

The silence on the other end lasted only a few seconds, but it felt like so many long minutes. "I don't know … home, maybe. North Carolina." He sounded confused, like he couldn't accurately define his feelings if he tried. "The Kotton Kids campaign is still stumping me." Another sigh. "I think I'll take Friday off and fly to Raleigh. Spend time with my dad. Maybe I'll find the slogan on the beach."

Laura fought the panic welling inside her. "Do you want … me to go with you? Maybe the wedding's getting to you."

"It's not that." His tone was tired, strained. "I think I need to do this alone, Laura. I miss my dad a lot. Maybe it's just starting this new chapter in life and losing a sense of what I left behind." He hesitated. "Does that make sense?"

"Um … sure." The panic grew, but she refused to acknowledge it. She wanted to know everything, every last detail of his thought process. But she didn't want to be pushy or overbearing. The details would come. She kept her tone light. "If you need to go home … you should go."

For the first time in the conversation, Brad seemed to understand how he must've sounded. "Baby," a weak groan came from him. "Don't think for a minute this is about you. It isn't."

"I don't think that." She tried to utter an awkward laugh, but the sound died on her lips. "I mean," she allowed the sweetness in her voice to fall away. "What am I supposed to think? It's six weeks before our wedding and you're lost in thought at work and at the gym, looking for a chance to go back to North Carolina. Then you say something about not wanting to lose the past." A sound more cry than laugh came from her. "Come on, Brad. How do you expect me to feel?"

This time his tone was marked with frustration. "You have to trust me. I love you, baby. I can't wait to marry you." He brought his voice back down a notch. "This … whatever this is … isn't about you. I promise. I'll be gone for the weekend, and I'll work things out."

She squeezed her eyes shut. *God … give me the words. Why do I feel like everything's falling apart?*

In response, sure as God's love, one of the verses from earlier that night came to her. The last line from what they'd read together. *Be merciful, just as your Father is merciful.* Laura breathed in the truth and waited while it worked its way through her heart and soul. She tightened her hold on her cell phone and shifted her gaze to the dark side of the night sky. *Be merciful,* she told herself. "Listen. I'm not sure I understand, but … you have my blessing on this, Brad. Go to North Carolina." She felt the beginning of peace spread through her. "I'll be here when you get back."

"Thank you." The relief in Brad's voice was immediate. "I'll figure things out, and when I get back, we'll talk. It's just something I have to work through."

"Okay. I trust you." The panic still wanted to consume her, but she denied it. Mercy would win out tonight, because that's what God was asking of her. If Brad needed time away, time with his parents back in North Carolina, then she would understand and support his decision.

"You're alright?" His tone was tentative.

"I'm fine." The words were easy. Her feelings could follow. "Let's get some sleep."

The call ended with promises to talk the next day. Brad would buy a plane ticket and fly into Raleigh Friday morning. As Laura hung up, she could barely believe what had just happened. Brad was having doubts. Not about her, maybe. But doubts all the same. Nothing else could explain his deep thoughts and pensive mood. Nothing else would have sent him packing for North Carolina. She wondered how she might've responded if the girls hadn't met for their Bible study that night. But they had met, and now Laura had chosen to love, to show him mercy by trusting Brad and refusing to stand in his way. The Bible was right. It didn't feel great, but this was true mercy, true love.

A love that was possible in God's strength alone.

Eight

BRAD HADN'T LIED TO LAURA, NOT at all. He reminded himself of this fact often over the next couple days, and again as he caught a ride to LaGuardia for the 7:55 nonstop to Raleigh. He wasn't going to call Emma or look her up. Never mind the photo he'd found in his desk, this trip wasn't about her. He'd told Laura the truth. The trip was about himself, about going home and looking for closure. It was about having an honest conversation with his father, and hopefully gaining from that talk a sense of how to walk away from the past for good.

His dad was picking him up, and Brad suspected the two-hour drive to Wilmington would give them a good start on the conversation. At least they would have time to catch up before Brad got to the heart of the matter. No one knew the terrible details about Brad and Emma's final summer together. Brad was very close to his parents, but he had never found the time or courage to tell them the truth about what happened. Now that was about to change. He was close to his mom, but he needed the sort of advice only his father could give.

The American Eagle commuter plane rumbled through a patch of turbulence. Brad looked out the window. Small planes didn't bother him, even though at six-foot-one he couldn't quite find a comfortable position for his legs. He didn't have a seat-mate. If he kept his eyes on the window, he could pretend he was asleep and avoid all conversation with anyone—even the flight attendant.

Already he could feel the strain of the city melting away. How long had it been since he'd seen his parents? Since he'd walked along the beach with Wilmington's own Carl Cutler? He closed his eyes and pictured his dad, his eccentricities and endless love. Even with everything that weighed on Brad's mind, a smile tugged at his mouth. In all the world there was no one just like old Carl. No one in Wilmington more prepared for whatever life might bring.

The man was a decorated retired sergeant in the army, a strong leader who had served in Germany at the beginning of Vietnam. He still ran his life with the discipline of a military mastermind. For one thing, he was crazy about lists. When Brad was growing up, he and his older sister and their parents would often take one of their infamous road trips. Old Carl had a list for road trips, a list that detailed every item that absolutely must be taken when they left, even for a few nights.

Brad felt his smile fill his face. There were the usual things, of course. A flashlight, first-aid kit, extra water, and jumper cables. But the list was nearly two pages long and also included must-have items like bolt cutters, safety goggles, WD–40, 3x5 cards, a hard hat, an ironing board, and a hammer. Not only that, but the entire list was alphabetized.

"That's my trip list," his dad would say, each word slow and deliberate. His southern drawl made him sound like the Looney Tunes' Foghorn Leghorn. "I like to be prepared."

No one was more prepared than Carl Cutler.

In addition, his dad kept lists in a file cabinet, and smaller lists in his wallet. Some were erroneous notes to himself about which grocery stores were having sales on which food items — most of them having expired years earlier. Also in his wallet were small pieces of paper with lists of what his kids did and didn't like to eat. Last time they were together, Brad had gone through the contents, teasing his dad that no guy had a wallet so thick. Tucked amidst receipts and outdated coupons was a single piece of paper that said, "Brad: Doesn't like onions, mayonnaise. Likes Mountain Dew, Sunkist, G. Ale." There was a similar list for his older sister and his mother.

"Really, Dad?" Brad had asked when he found the strange, small list. "How often do you look at this?"

His father didn't mind his family teasing him. He smiled as he took the list and tucked it safely back in his wallet. "Often enough."

Over the years, it was Brad's mother who stayed up late talking to him, easily expressing her love and pride, her concern and interest in his life. If Brad analyzed his parents, he was more like his mom. But from the place where he sat now, this far removed from his life in North Carolina, he had learned more about love from his father.

For one thing, love was harder for his dad. Carl was a man's man, tough to the core. He didn't easily pick up the phone to tell Brad he loved him. But he did pick up the phone. "Any travel on the horizon?" he'd ask in his unhurried way.

Brad would tell his father about his brief upcoming business trips to Chicago or Detroit or Denver, wherever his ad campaigns took him. A few days later in the mail would be a package from his father—a map from the automobile club, complete with sections his dad had highlighted. Certain restaurants and points of interest. The better hotels. Often he highlighted a specific line in a tourist attraction entry, something like "half off Navy Pier's Ferris wheel on the first Friday of the month."

As if Brad would have time to take in an amusement park in Chicago.

Either way, the maps were one way his father could demonstrate the love he didn't often speak of. Another way was his propensity to purchase whatever item Brad was currently promoting. If Brad worked on the ad campaign of a product, his dad bought the item. Every single time. On one of his last visits a year ago, Brad walked into the house and saw a case of Way Cool Lunch Snacks on the kitchen counter.

"Dad?" Brad looked from the box to his father. "When did you start eating packaged lunch snacks?"

His dad would chuckle and brush off the comment. "Don't eat 'em. Just want to support your advertising."

Brad tried to explain the reality to his father. "One purchase isn't going to make a difference, Dad. Really. Don't buy the stuff I'm working on unless you'll use it." He lifted a package of jellied fruit snacks from the box. "You don't care about this stuff."

His father's smile was content and unwavering. As if to say he might not care about Way Cool Lunch Snacks, but he did care about his son.

Lately his dad was into metal detecting along the beach. That and entering sweepstakes. Sometimes, if the contest allowed, he'd enter the same sweepstakes a dozen times, driving to different post offices to drop off his entry in an attempt to somehow increase his odds. The night before last year's *American Idol* finale, his dad called to inform Brad that he'd won an *Idol* Party Package. "Don't know much about the *Idol* show." His dad sounded nonplussed. "But it's another win."

For all his eccentricities, his father was kind and warm to everyone who passed through the Cutler home. That was especially true for Emma. His dad even had a silly nickname for her—Emma Jelly Bean. "Because that girl has all the sweetness and color of a bucket of jelly beans." He would wink at Emma. "Emma Jelly Bean. Better than a string bean."

So it had stuck. Emma Jelly Bean.

The flight smoothed out and remained uneventful. Brad stared out the window and let himself go back—even just a little. He and Emma had been playmates in grade school. She didn't have a dad and her mom worked two jobs, so she was home by herself often. By the time they were in sixth grade, Emma phoned him nearly every afternoon.

"Why does that girl keep calling?" his mother finally asked. She wasn't upset, just curious. "Doesn't she know boys are supposed to call first?"

"There's no one at her house after school." Brad wasn't interested in girls at that point. He was a seventh-grade boy, looking out for a friend. He shrugged as he grabbed an apple. "She calls me because she wants to hear the sound of another person."

His answer must've touched his mother. He could tell because tears formed in her eyes and she softened her tone. "That's sad."

"I know. I mean she's safe and everything," Brad took a bite of the apple, "but I figure I can talk for a few minutes."

His mother was on the phone to Emma's mom later that night. "She can come home with Brad and stay here until you get off work," she offered. "That way they can do their studies together."

Emma's mother was thrilled with the arrangement. She delivered papers before sun-up and worked at the local pharmacy, sometimes until seven o'clock during the week. The deal was good for Brad and Emma too. They studied together and did Brad's chores together, and on warm spring days when they were finished, they would ride their bikes to Wrightsville Beach and watch the sailboats come and go from the marina.

Brad could easily picture her as she looked back then—long dark hair and exotic eyes, the full lips and skinny legs that she didn't grow into until they were in high school. Of course they fell in love. There'd never been any question about whether they'd wind up together, right? By the time they realized how they really felt about each other, the decision was already made. They'd been in love as long as they could remember.

The hurt spread through his chest, a physical pain over all they'd lost that awful summer. The two of them didn't stand a chance after what happened, but that didn't excuse him from how he handled the ending. There had been no explanation, really. No long good-bye, and most of all, no apology. Just a sudden and certain realization that they could no longer stay together.

The pain between them was that great.

Brad stopped the memories cold. He closed his eyes and thought about the wedding. He pictured Laura walking down the aisle, the innocent, trusting love in her eyes. Was he really willing to jeopardize even a little of the adoration she felt for him? And what about her parents? He appreciated the expense and trouble Rita and Randy James were going to so that the big day would be an event no one would forget. But he didn't need an elegant ballroom overlooking Ellis Island and lower Manhattan, or acres of perfectly manicured grass or the flowers that would line the pathways to and from the ceremony site to the Liberty House.

All he needed was Laura. She — not Emma — was the love of his life. Brad was sure about that much. But why had he so willingly let go of Emma and all they'd shared, the way they'd grown up together? And how come he couldn't remember ever finding closure for himself or that part of his life? That was the problem. He wasn't sure he could move into a life with Laura when his heart was still hurting over something that happened a decade ago. Hurting as much as if it had only happened last week.

The plane landed on time in Raleigh at 9:35, and sure enough, his father was waiting for him on the other side of security, a smile stretched across his face as he spotted Brad. He raised his hand and mouthed the words, "Hi, Son." His father wore black dress pants, a crisp white button-down shirt, a black vest, and a striped bowtie.

As if to reflect that Brad's homecoming even for a weekend was a special occasion indeed.

Brad walked up to him, set down his bag, and stepped into his father's arms. His dad could say more with a hug than some men might tell their sons in a lifetime. He took hold of Brad's bag and pulled it behind him as they started walking to the parking lot. The seven-year-old truck was bound to be in the back lot, where it wouldn't get any unnecessary dings or scratches. And Brad knew better than to try to pull his own bag. His father wanted to help, and this was simply one way.

His dad winked at him. "Good to have you home, Son. Very good."

"Thanks, Dad." Brad could almost feel himself relaxing. "I think the city was getting to me."

"You know … there are lots of day trips you can take from the city. Upstate New York's full of attractions. I'll send you some maps, so next time you don't have to get on a plane to get away."

Brad smiled and let the comment go. He was here for a reason. His dad would find out soon enough. "Hey, Dad … you have a little time this afternoon?"

His father thought for a moment. "In fact, I do. Wanted to do a little metal work down at Carolina Beach, but that can wait."

"How about you keep the plan. Wrightsville Beach instead. I'll go with you and we can talk there."

"Good idea." They reached his father's truck, and with the ease of someone who hadn't lost any strength, his dad swung the suitcase into the bed of the truck.

The ride home was mostly small talk — the latest sweepstakes and his dad's belief that maybe this year he'd found a way to crack the Publisher's Clearing House contest. "That's the big one."

"Biggest of all." Brad savored the way it felt simply being with his dad. They were quiet for a few exits, and his father turned to him. "The wedding's coming up."

"Yes." Brad breathed in sharp through clenched teeth. "That's some of what I want to talk about."

His dad glanced at him, then nodded thoughtfully. "That can wait for the beach."

"Yes."

Two hours later they pulled into his parents' driveway, and Brad marveled over how the place never really aged, never changed from what it had been when he was growing up. They went inside, and on the counter was a Finley grill, the kind Brad had designed a campaign for late last year. Brad started to say something about how his father didn't even like the taste of grilled food, but he stopped himself.

It was one more thing that wasn't going to change, and besides, Brad was touched by his dad's gesture. "Doing a lot of grilling, Dad?" He tapped the top of the machine and grinned at his father.

"Trying to get healthy, Brad. You know how it is."

His mother entered the room from the hallway, and she rolled her eyes as she glanced at the grill. "He's used it once." She hugged Brad's neck and kissed his cheek. "You look wonderful. How're the wedding plans?"

"Great." He smiled and then quickly pointed to his bag. "I'll get this up to my room." He didn't want his mother's scrutiny on why he was here. She would make more of his troubled heart than necessary. He shot a final look at the grill. "Chicken tonight?"

"Funny, Brad." His mom's tone was a mix of laughter and sarcasm. She looped her arm around Carl's waist and smiled at him. "You're a good sport, you know that, Carl?"

He hugged her in return. "I have to be with the likes of you two."

Brad took his bag to his room and stood for a minute in the doorway, remembering how it felt to lay sprawled on his twin bed, staring at the Michael Jordan poster on the ceiling, talking to Emma on the phone. Sometimes they talked through the night, holding the receivers to their ears even after they'd drifted off to sleep. "Spending the night together," they called it.

He blinked and the detail disappeared. He hung up his clothes and returned to the kitchen. His father had made him a meat sandwich with mustard and lettuce. They ate quietly, while Brad's mom tended to her vegetable garden outside.

When the kitchen was tidied, his dad put the metal detector in the truck bed. "Friday's a perfect day for beach hunting."

"Why's that?" Brad climbed into the front seat next to his father.

"Most people hunt targets as a hobby, so they hit the weekend mornings pretty hard. Friday midday means nearly a week's gone by without anyone running a detector across the sand."

"Hmm." Brad grinned at his dad. "I never thought about that."

On the drive to the Wrightsville Beach, Brad learned the finer techniques of metal detecting.

"First off ... go slow and low to the sand." Brad's dad stroked his chin, his eyes glued to the road. "People think the coil will break if they get too low, and maybe it will." He pointed to the backseat. "I keep a couple extra just in case."

"Of course."

"Thing is, you keep the detector too far up and you might save your coil, but who knows what you'll miss."

"You could leave a real find back on the shore."

"Exactly." His father jabbed his finger at the air for emphasis. "Another tip: Go slowly and turn down the discrimination gauge."

"The discrimination gauge?"

His dad cast him a quick look as if to say he thought everyone was familiar with discrimination gauges. "That's how the detector knows something's in the sand. The higher the gauge, the more metal the object has to have." He nodded slowly. "I turn the gauge way down. Something is better than nothing. That's what I say when it comes to beach hunting."

They parked at a spot on the far end of the beach and his dad said little as he readied his metal detector and placed two water bottles and the extra coils into his gear bag. Not until they'd combed half a mile of shore did Brad spot a bench at the top of the beach where the sand and grass came together. "Can we take a few minutes?" He motioned toward the bench. "To talk, I mean?"

His dad had already found an old Timex, a money clip, and two silver dollars. The goods jangled in his shoulder bag next to the water. He flipped a switch on the metal detector and the machine fell silent. "Yes." A layer of sweat shone on his forehead and upper lip. "I could use a break."

They took their places on the bench, and Brad's father handed out the water. Brad waited a few minutes, staring at the dark blue ocean, gathering his thoughts. "I'm having thoughts about Emma."

His dad rarely looked caught off guard, but at the mention of Emma's name, his surprise was evident even through his Blu-Blocker sunglasses. "Emma Landon?"

"Yes." Brad realized how that must've sounded. "I mean, no. Not like that." He braced himself against the edge of the bench and flexed the muscles in his jaw. "Thoughts about that last November." Brad hated telling this to his father, disappointing him even after so many years. But there was no turning back now. "Something that happened ... before we split up."

For a long moment his father looked at him and then at the water bottle in his hand. When he lifted his eyes, his brow was knit together—a mix of concern and thoughtfulness. "Your mother always said it was just time ... two kids who'd grown apart." He took a swig of water and rubbed the back of his hand over his weathered lips. "I didn't agree. I always thought something must've happened. You loved that girl too much to let her go. I remember."

His words cut deep at Brad's heart. "Why didn't you ask?"

"I did." His dad spoke deliberately, but with an unmistakable kindness. "I can't remember the day. You looked down. Very upset. I wondered if something was wrong with you and Emma, so I asked."

Brad felt the weight of what his father was saying. He didn't remember the incident, but it meant he'd been given a chance to come clean about what had happened and he'd missed it. He asked the next question even though he knew the answer. "What was my answer?"

"Everything was fine." His dad still looked puzzled. "You and Emma stayed together for a while after that, so I didn't ask again. Whatever was bothering you, why you broke up with Emma, figured if you wanted to tell me, you'd tell me."

"Makes sense." The defeat in Brad made him wish he could skip the whole conversation. But he couldn't. This conversation was why he'd come home. He straightened. *God … give me strength.* "You were right, Dad. Something happened, and I should've told you back then." He rubbed his hands together and stared at the white sand between his feet.

"Something with Emma?"

"With both of us." He looked out at the ocean again. "That summer, after I graduated … we made choices both of us regretted." He turned and looked straight at his father. "Emma got pregnant."

There was no condemnation, no immediate reaction except the slight way his father hunched forward. As if he'd been elbowed in the gut.

Brad could only imagine what his dad must be feeling. The baby would've been his father's first grandchild. A sick feeling ripped at him. "We were young. She had another year of high school." Brad hung his head, his eyes focused on the sand once more. "We didn't find out until she was three months along. She thought ... she was afraid ... and her cycle wasn't always regular." He shook his head. How hard it must've been for Emma. "She took the test and the school nurse made her an appointment at a clinic."

Until then, his dad hadn't broken eye contact. But at the mention of the word *clinic* he drew a quick breath and lifted his eyes to the sky. He muttered softly under his breath, "Dear, God ... no."

Again there was no accusation in his father's reaction. Just the heartbreaking awareness of what had happened. Brad understood. Speaking the words, reliving what they'd done even in these few details was gut-wrenching for him too. Brad's eyes were damp as he finished the story. The day he and Emma went to the clinic, Brad didn't have enough money. He'd called his dad for help. "Remember ... I called that day and needed money."

"For your car." His dad's memory was machine-like. He was the last person on earth to need lists.

"Right ... that's how I made it seem. But that was for ..." He couldn't finish the sentence. Couldn't come out and say it.

Again his father took the news with the courage of a military man. But the impact was there all the same. They were quiet for several minutes, and three times his dad sniffed hard through his nose. Again Brad knew. His dad was fighting tears, fighting the reality of his personal loss that day. The grandchild he'd never known or loved, never held in his arms. Finally he breathed in deep and put his hand on Brad's knee. "If I'd known ... maybe I could've helped you change your mind."

Brad's eyes welled up and a lump formed in his throat. He couldn't speak, so he only covered his father's hand with his own. Deep down Brad must've known that was what his father would've done. It was why he hadn't said anything back then. He hadn't wanted anyone to talk them out of their decision. It was easier to hold onto what the lady at the clinic told them. The procedure wouldn't take long and then it'd be over. Something like that.

His dad slid closer on the bench and moved his hand from Brad's knee to his shoulder. "Poor Emma." He gazed toward the beach. "After you left for school … I always wanted to call her. Have her over for dinner." He sniffed again. "Your mom thought it was better to leave her alone. Let the two of you work things out. But if I'd known …" His silence made it clear how helpless he felt about the situation. Even this many years after the fact. He was probably praying, asking for direction on what to say next. Finally he seemed to find a new sense of strength. "You're sorry. I can hear that in your voice."

"Of course." Brad couldn't bring himself to look into his father's eyes. Instead he stared at the sand and waited. "But there's something else."

"The reason you're here."

"Yes." Brad squinted at the sun lowering in the sky. "I never told her I was sorry." He clenched his jaw. "It's killing me, Dad. I mean, it's killing me. Like I can't move on until I find her and make things right."

"Find Emma." His words held a new soberness, as if he would need awhile to process all that was at stake. "Six weeks before your wedding?"

"Yes. That." Brad hated his timing, but he had no choice. He couldn't get past his guilt, couldn't see beyond his memories. A rush of unexpected emotion stuck in his throat, surprising him. "I can't believe who I was back then."

For a long time his dad only nodded, and then he gazed straight ahead at the sea. Finally he clasped his hands and looked straight at Brad. "Sounds like you never wrote the last lines to that chapter of your life."

This was why Brad was telling his father. The man brought no lecture to the table, but only a few simple words of wisdom. Something that would line up straight with the Bible and the character that his dad had tried to instill from the beginning.

Brad turned to his father. "I'm in love with my fiancée." He felt hopeless, angry with himself for being in this situation. "I want to finish that chapter without finding Emma. I mean, really. The wedding's in six weeks."

"With God, all things are possible. That's from Matthew."

Brad appreciated the reminder, and he believed it. He definitely believed it. But this time, he wasn't sure if there were enough days before the wedding to pull off all he needed to take care of. Even if God worked a miracle. "So that's what I should do, right? Find a way to close this chapter on my own? Without Emma?"

"No, son. Emma's in the chapter. I watched you write it. You loved that girl with all your heart." He paused, deliberate in his words. "If you have something to say to her, you have to find her and say it."

The beach below his feet seemed to fall away, and Brad felt his head start to spin. He blinked, forcing himself to stay upright. He wanted his dad's advice, but he never really imagined finding Emma. He could talk to his counselor friend, Jack, about making an apology face-to-face, but that didn't mean he ever really thought he would do it. "Talk to Emma now? Before the wedding?"

"You already know the answer. You came home to hear me say it." He adjusted his sunglasses. "Isn't that right?"

Brad stood and paced a few steps closer to the water. The day was warm, the sky clear except for a line of distant cumulus clouds. Jack had weighed in on what Brad needed to do, but still he hadn't wanted to think about the possibility. But now it was clear. His dad was right. This was why he had come. Because he knew he had to find Emma, had to look into her eyes and apologize to her. And he couldn't make that decision on his own. He rubbed his neck. What would Laura think, and how would he ever break the news to her? He walked back to the bench and sat down again. "So I have to tell Laura."

"What else is there?" His dad shifted his shoulder bag onto his knees. "You can't tell me a Cutler man would start something as big as a marriage without a foundation of truth."

Suddenly in that one statement, Brad understood what he'd been feeling and what he absolutely had to do. He had thrown a blanket over his past and built a lumpy foundation on top of it. He'd tried to pretend everything was fine, and he'd sidestepped yesterday on the way to the altar. But his daddy hadn't raised him that way, and now he could see that clearly.

"Then I have two things to take care of. Telling Laura and finding Emma. All before the wedding." He allowed his own words to simmer in his soul. What if Laura couldn't understand about the past? What if she called off the wedding and walked away? He held his breath and looked to the sky. *God, get me through this. Please. Go before me.*

With me, my son, all things are possible . . .

The verse from earlier in the conversation played again in his mind. He exhaled, weary from the assignment ahead.

"Looks like you're about to be very busy." His dad stood and patted Brad's shoulder once more. "This too shall pass."

"I don't know."

"It will." His dad checked his watch. "Let's do a little more hunting. Your mother's making dinner."

Like that, the conversation was over. There would be no emotional breakdown, no public prayer, no overt show of judgment. Brad was about to be very busy. If God allowed it, the coming weeks would finally bring an end to the most painful chapter of his life. But first he needed to talk to Laura. Then he would do the unthinkable, the thing he had never dreamed of doing.

He would find Emma Landon again.

Nine

EMMA'S ANTIDOTE FOR LONELINESS WAS A simple one: Stay busy. When she wasn't training for the half marathon or working on her old beach house, she volunteered. This weekend she was set to work with CCC, the Concerned Citizens of the Cape. The group helped disadvantaged kids—whatever the need.

Cape Fear was an hour away, and only a few minutes from Wilmington. Emma loved her work with CCC, but being this close to Wilmington was always hard for her. Too many memories, too much sorrow from her final year there—even memories from Cape Fear. One Saturday a month she was here, and that was enough.

That Saturday they were putting together care packages for a long list of families. Citizens had been collecting canned food and clothing for the past month, and now it needed to be sorted, organized, and distributed.

The day didn't figure to hold any surprises until Emma walked through the center door and saw Gavin Greeley, his sleeves rolled up, a baseball cap pressed firmly over his brow. He worked alongside a team of guys sifting through a mountain of canned food. He didn't notice her at first, so Emma took the chance to catch her breath. Why was he here? Wasn't it enough that she'd seen him yesterday at school?

Before she could busy herself in another part of the building, he spotted her. The instant surprise on his face told her he hadn't expected to see her either. For a few seconds their eyes held, then he lifted his cap, wiped his brow with the back of his hand, and stepped away from the table. "Emma ... what're you doing here?"

She laughed, amazed at her inability to escape him. "I've been coming here for the past three years. I'm a member."

"Very nice." He eased his cap back into place and walked closer, close enough that the faint smell of his cologne drifted in the air between them. Like always, his eyes sparkled with something that wasn't quite serious. "I'm currently seeking membership." He elbowed her gently. "Maybe you can put in a good word."

"If you're lucky." She studied him, fighting the attraction. This wouldn't be love, but maybe she could be friends with Gavin. There was no reason to be angry with him. He was merely spending his Saturday helping out—same as her. She pushed up her sleeves and tucked the layers of her long dark hair behind her ears. "Come on. I'll teach you the tricks of the canned food trade."

He laughed and followed her back to the table. They were an hour into arranging cans by food kind and size when Emma's cell phone rang from her purse a few feet away. Her mother had been gone for six years, and other than the staff at Jefferson Elementary and her neighbors, Emma rarely received a call. Especially on the weekend. She stopped and lifted the phone in time to see the name *Palazzo* in the Caller ID window.

In a sudden hurry, she pressed the Talk button. "Hello?"

"Ms. Landon? This is Steve Palazzo. I'm Kristin's uncle. The family wanted me to call you." He sounded strained, like every word was a struggle.

"What happened?" She moved a few feet away and leaned against the wall. From the corner of her eye she saw Gavin watching her. "Is she okay?"

"She went into cardiac arrest earlier today. She was crossing the street with my brother when she ... she just collapsed. Rick and Lynne thought you might want to know. She's at Brunswick Hospital in Supply."

Emma could feel her heart breaking. She finished the call and felt someone beside her. She looked up and Gavin was standing in front of her. "What is it?" Gone was the teasing from earlier. He took tender hold of her shoulders. "Emma, tell me. What happened?"

"One of my students." She pressed her fists to her forehead and tried to focus. "Not one of mine, but my high school volunteer. Kristin Palazzo. She's a junior. Her heart ... it stopped and she's ... she's in intensive care at Brunswick."

Gavin started to say something, then he held up his finger. "Wait here." He hurried to the group leader and checked both of them out for the day. Then he walked with her toward the parking lot, both of them moving at a fast, panicked pace. "I'll go with you. I came with a buddy. He's helping paint the gym." He stayed beside her until she reached her car. "Stay here. I'll be right back."

Emma leaned against her car door and stared at the ground. She was glad for Gavin's help. The hour drive would've been too much for her in this condition. Her hands were shaking and tears blurred her vision. *Kristin can't die ... not now. She's too young.* The girl had so many dreams, so much of life ahead. Emma paced a few steps away and then back again. Before she had time to think about what to do next, Gavin was at her side again. He helped her through the passenger door, then he took her keys and hurried around into the driver's seat.

They were back on the main highway, with Gavin clearly determined to get her to the hospital as soon as possible, when he glanced her way. "Cardiac arrest? For a high school girl?"

Emma blinked and ran her tongue along her lower lip. *Not Kristin ... please, not Kristin.* "She ... she has myocarditis. Her heart's been failing since she was ten years old. The ... result of an illness. She ... needs a transplant."

She pictured Kristin walking into her classroom the other day. Her smile was as big as ever, but her pace had seemed a little slower. Now Emma understood why — her heart had been about to give out. *No, not Kristin. Not yet. She's not finished making her picture project.* Her heart still had so much to give.

The ride grew quiet and Gavin didn't ask more questions. Emma was grateful. She couldn't focus, couldn't concentrate on anything but Kristin's face, her laughter as the students gathered around her just last Monday. *Keep breathing, Kristin. Hold on, sweetheart. Don't give up.*

This would've been a time when many people would've prayed. If she was any sort of decent human being she would beg God for a miracle, for Kristin to spring back and walk out of the hospital room later that afternoon. But God — if there was a God — wouldn't want to hear from the likes of her. She might even harm Kristin's cause by pretending to believe after all this time.

So she did the only thing she could do. She willed life into the pretty teenager as best as she knew how. *Please ... She wants to be a teacher ... please, let her pull out of this. She has too much love to give. Please ...* It occurred to Emma that if she was pleading, if she was begging for a hopeful outcome, then she had to be directing her request somewhere ... to Someone. She tried not to think about it. All that mattered was Kristin, and the fact that somewhere in a frantic hospital room, the girl was fighting for her life.

They were almost to Brunswick when Gavin broke the silence. "I'm not sure how you feel about this ... but would you mind if I prayed? For Kristin?"

How could Emma mind? Prayers coming from Gavin might actually help. She nodded quickly and squeezed her eyes shut, one hand shading her face.

Gavin waited until he was parked in the emergency room area. "Dear Lord, You are here with us. You never leave us, never forsake us. With that truth in mind, we beg You to breathe life into Kristin Palazzo right now. Please, Father. She has a weak heart, but a transplant could save her life. Please keep her alive until then and be with her family. Be with Emma, that she might be a strength and a source of light to Kristin's family." He reached for Emma's hand and squeezed it once. "In Jesus' name, amen."

He let go of her fingers as quickly as he'd taken hold of them, and they hurried into the hospital and to the third-floor ICU. Emma had spoken to Kristin's mother, Lynne, one other time, but she'd never met either of the teenager's parents in person. She was grateful for Gavin, that was all she could think of as they stepped off the elevator. Otherwise she wasn't sure she could face Kristin's family, a family fully rooted in faith.

She let Gavin lead her down the hall to the waiting room. A middle-aged man stood and introduced himself. He was Steve, Kristin's uncle.

"How is she?" Emma's heart raced, but she fought to stay focused.

"She's on life support." Steve's eyes were red, same as the eyes of everyone else in the room. Clearly the situation was dire. "The first few days are critical."

Emma wanted to scream, cry out to Whoever was listening, that none of this was fair. Kristin needed a heart transplant and another twenty years — not life support. She wanted to be a teacher … she hadn't seen the picture Frankie made for her … Emma swallowed, searching for her voice. "Is there … anything we can do?"

"Friends from church are on their way. We're going to have a prayer vigil — if you'd like to be part of it?"

She could feel Gavin beside her ready to join in. A prayer vigil would be perfectly comfortable for him. Suddenly Emma had a flashback, a time when she was in junior high and one of the girls in their youth group was hit by a car. The kids had come together at the hospital and prayed, and Emma's voice was one of the most vocal. She'd forgotten about that, and the fact that she'd believed in God back then, believed in the power of prayer.

When she didn't respond, Gavin quietly stepped forward. "We'll stay … of course."

"Thank you." Steve looked from Gavin back to Emma. "Kristin thinks very highly of you, Ms. Landon. It would mean the world to her that you were praying for her."

Panic coursed through Emma, and she struggled to keep her composure. Who was she kidding? She couldn't stand here and talk to a God she had walked away from about a girl so sweet and innocent as Kristin Palazzo. Steve moved across the room to tend to a woman who was crying softly. Probably his wife. Emma used the opportunity to take hold of Gavin's arm. "I need to talk to you. Please." She hissed the words as softly as she could.

Gavin followed her out into the hall and down a ways toward the elevator. Emma kept her voice as low as possible. "I can't do this."

"Do what?" Gavin's handsome face was masked with confusion. "Her family asked us to stay and pray. You can't do that?"

"Gavin …" she muttered his name, exasperated. Then she hung her head and braced herself against the wall. "You don't understand. I walked away from God. He wouldn't want me talking to Him now. Kristin deserves prayers from someone better than me."

A sad, single laugh came from Gavin, and this time he took firm hold of her shoulder. "Listen to me. God isn't going to penalize Kristin because you prayed for her. The Lord doesn't work that way."

"What if He does?" Her heart pounded inside her. She was the worst of all women, hardly fit to stand before God—whether He was listening or not.

"He asks everyone to come to Him. There's only one thing I want you to do." His look was as genuine as it was intent.

"What?"

"I want you to believe it'll make a difference. You have to believe, okay?"

Could she do that? For Kristin? Could she stand in a circle of people praying and believe that somehow those actions done in faith might make a difference? She didn't have time to sort through what she did and didn't believe. Kristin's life was hanging in the balance. She released a hurried sigh. "Yes. For Kristin I can do that."

"Good." He looked up. A group of frenzied-looking adults and teenagers exited the elevator. "Come on." Gavin led Emma back to the waiting room. As they walked, they watched a couple who might've been Kristin's parents meet the newest group of visitors. Gavin and Emma ducked into the waiting room, but they heard one of the girls in the group cry out loud.

"No ... not Kristin!"

Emma wanted to run, but Gavin's presence beside her steadied her, made her stay. Finally the group joined them in the waiting room. The couple approached Emma, and the woman seemed to struggle to speak. "I'm Lynne Palazzo. You're ... you're Emma Landon, right?"

"Yes, ma'am." Fear choked the strength from Emma's words. "I care very much about your daughter."

"She cares for you too." Lynne hesitated, then in a rush she gave Emma a desperate hug. "We need to pray." She stepped back and searched the eyes of everyone in the room. "Please, everyone. We have to pray."

The group formed a circle, linked hands, and one at a time people prayed out loud. Emma was certain they could hear her pounding heart above the sound of the prayers. She wasn't worthy to stand here, wasn't worthy to be in the presence of people with such faith. Yet, with her hand tucked in Gavin's, she found the strength to stay.

"You've kept her alive this long, dear God … please get her through the night."

A chorus of quiet yes's came from the group, and the strangest thing began to happen. Emma found herself doing exactly what she'd promised Gavin she would do. She was believing. Believing that with the intensity of their prayers and their certainty that God was, indeed, listening, that good news was bound to come. An hour later, that's exactly what happened. A doctor appeared at the doorway and hesitated.

"Excuse me." He looked at Lynne and Rick. "Can I talk to you?"

Emma was exhausted emotionally and physically. She wanted to run down the hall and check on Kristin herself. Instead she leaned into Gavin and waited like the rest of the prayer circle. After a minute, Kristin's parents returned to the room, their eyes bright with unshed tears.

"She's turned a corner," Rick put his arm around his wife's shoulders. "Her heart seems to be beating on its own. At least for now."

A collective gasp came from the fifteen or so people gathered in the waiting room. They took a brief break, celebrating the good news. And then they prayed for another hour before people headed home. Back in the car, Emma felt suddenly awkward alone with Gavin Greeley. She had relied on him completely over the last several hours. Emotionally and physically. Even spiritually. But that didn't mean she could allow herself to have feelings for him.

Gavin drove the two of them to his house, and the whole way she convinced him that she was okay, that she could get back to her beach house without his help.

"I can call a cab." He glanced at her, his hand steady on the wheel.

"I'm fine. Really, Gavin." They pulled up in front of his house. She left the car running. "Thank you. For everything. I couldn't have gotten through today without you."

"God has a way of doing that. He never gives us more than we can handle." Gavin managed a worn-out smile. "I'm glad she's doing better. Keep me posted, okay? And keep praying."

Emma didn't make any promises. She told him good-bye and thanked him again, but after he was gone, when she was alone and driving toward the Holden Beach bridge, she found herself doing just that. *God ... it's been a long time. I know I shouldn't be talking to You, but I have to. You see, Kristin's very special to me. She's special to a lot of people. So please, God ... let her heart keep beating. Help her get off life support so she can start the path to recovery.* A single tear slid down her cheek and fell onto her jeans. *The world can't afford to lose someone like Kristin Palazzo. Please, God.*

As her prayer came to an end, Emma wasn't sure what surprised her more. That she'd found the words and the strength to pray, or that she had done so without doubts. Either way, the moment was no longer about her and her shameful past.

It was about a beautiful brown-eyed girl with a heart of gold — no matter how sick — fighting for her life across town.

Ten

ON HIS LAST DAY BACK HOME, Brad decided he couldn't return to New York without making the trip to Holden Beach. He had enjoyed seeing his parents, and he'd needed the talk with his dad. But besides that, the time at home had given him crucial hours to figure out exactly what to do next. Every chance he had, he begged God, praying that Laura would understand and that he could find Emma quickly.

His mom was the first person he turned to. She kept up on the local gossip—who had moved on and who was getting married. That sort of thing. They were at the kitchen table yesterday when Brad brought it up.

"I need to talk to Emma Landon." He didn't want to tell her the reason, so he kept his tone relaxed. "Before the wedding."

"Emma?" His mom froze for a few seconds, her eyes on him. "That can't be good."

"It's nothing." Brad found his most convincing half-smile. "Just a few things I need to say before I move on."

His mom frowned. "I loved Emma, you know that. But you were kids back then. Laura's perfect for you."

"Exactly."

Her frown faded to mild confusion. "You and Laura are okay?"

"Definitely." Brad willed the answer to be true once he told Laura the truth. "This isn't about Laura. It's just something I need to do before the wedding."

His mother still looked mildly concerned. Then she seemed to relax. Brad wouldn't look her in the eyes and lie to her. She must've remembered that. "Okay, then," she tapped her fingers on the kitchen table. "Last I heard, Emma Landon was teaching near Holden Beach."

Her words had stayed with him in the day since then. Teaching near Holden Beach. The idea seemed almost impossible. What reason would Emma have for staying so close to the place where they'd both suffered such sadness? Still, the tip gave Brad a starting point.

But that wasn't why he was headed to Holden Beach now. He needed to be there again, walk along the sand and take the path to the end of the pier. So he could finally try to understand why he and Emma had given in when everything they believed told them not to. The day was mostly cloudy, and thunderstorms were forecast for later that afternoon. Brad didn't care. At this point he would've found his way back to Holden Beach in a hurricane.

The drive wasn't as long as he remembered, and just before noon he drove over the causeway and parked at the first public lot. For a long time he leaned forward on the steering wheel of his dad's truck, surveying the place. It was cleaner than before, more taken care of. Less wild and unexplored.

If he stared hard toward the surf, he could almost see the two of them, the way they'd been that summer. Their love as wild and untamed as the beach. They had plans back then, he and Emma. He would head to UNC, and she would finish high school. After that she'd join him at college and they'd take as many classes together as possible.

"I want to marry you," he had told her.

Her beautiful hazel eyes believed every word. That much was obvious. Brad squinted at the glare of the past. He had believed it too. They'd stay together the way they'd been since they were kids.

But suddenly, staring at the beach ten years later, Brad thought of something he hadn't before.

They didn't need to drive all the way to Holden Beach. They were Wilmington kids, after all. They had Wrightsville Beach just a few minutes from their homes. And a dozen beaches closer than this one. The answer brought with it a shame that fell like bricks on Brad's shoulders. Only one reason could explain their decision to come here over and over again that summer, to a beach an hour away from home.

Because here they had privacy. They had the freedom to act on the way they were feeling—even though their actions were wrong.

He needed to walk. His dad's truck was one of the last with a manual crank for the windows, and it stuck a little as Brad shut it. "Okay," he whispered, his eyes still on the distant beach. "Here goes." He climbed out of the truck, took off his shoes, and set them on the floorboard. Even with the cloudy skies, the beach was warm. He rolled up his jeans, and as he hit the beach, the sand filled in the spaces between his toes.

Slowly, as if he were pushing his way through a million moments from yesterday, Brad crossed the sandy slope to the surf. He stepped into the frothy tide and shifted his attention from the sea to the sky. The beach was still beautiful, still the sort of place for long thoughtful walks and star-gazing. That's what had gotten them in trouble. If only they'd packed up at the end of the day and gone home.

But August days had a way of wanting to stretch on forever.

Brad walked until he reached the pier. He wanted to walk out to the end, but without his shoes he wouldn't try it. Too many splinters. Instead he leaned against the footings and stared at the stretch of sand just ahead. The memories were so real he could touch them. The first time had broken both their hearts.

The years slipped away and he was there again, at the end of a long sunny day. She wore jean shorts over a white two-piece swimsuit, nothing too skimpy. But that didn't mattered. The two of them were alone with a blanket on Holden Beach in August. She could've worn a bathrobe and he would've struggled to resist his feelings for her. The sunset gave way to a starry sky, and after a while, Emma had fallen asleep. Brad could see the two of them lying there on the blanket, how they'd let one compromise lead to another.

"Hey," he touched her shoulder. The feel of her skin had rendered him unable to think for a moment. "Emma. We should go."

"Hmmm." She rolled onto her side. "Now?"

Brad tried not to stare at her. Instead he checked his watch. "It's after eight. We could get some food and head back."

"I thought … we had sandwiches." She was sleepy, her smile seductive though he doubted she meant it to be.

"Well … we do, actually." He could feel his heart begin to race. Inside his soul, a voice urged him to pack up the blanket and his backpack while he still had time, to escape the draw of the beach, the lure of Emma beside him. His throat was dry. "I mean … we have peanut butter and jelly sandwiches and … I have a few cans of Coke. Not very cold, though."

"I'm not hungry." She reached for his hand, easing him back down onto the blanket beside her. She lay on her stomach again. "Summer's almost over. Let's not go yet."

He stretched out, breathing harder than before, trying not to watch her. Every breath was a fight not to ease her onto her side again so he could cuddle up against her and kiss her. For a long time they stayed like that, him catching forbidden glances at her, longing for her. Looking away as often as he could. Somewhere along the passing of time, he uttered a lame prayer. Words he didn't mean at all. At least that's the way he remembered it. By then he was already running his fingers along her bare arm. *God ... help us not to fall. We can't let things get out of hand.*

But it was too late. Darkness had engulfed the empty beach, and with the bluff of sand and rock and grass behind them and on either side, their location was beyond private. The way they'd known it would be when they chose the spot earlier that day.

"Emma." He inched closer and kissed her bare shoulder. "Maybe we should go." It was his last-ditch effort ... he didn't mean a word of it. His breathing was still faster than before, and he could barely think for the way she made him feel.

She turned onto her side, and in a matter of seconds she was fully awake. "I'm cold," she whispered. "Pull the blanket over us."

Brad slid closer to her and flipped the other half of the blanket over them. "Is that better?"

He couldn't remember Emma's answer, or if they said much of anything after that. All he knew for sure was they started kissing. Somewhere along the next fifteen minutes, they tried twice to stop. Both attempts were made by Emma.

"We can't, Brad ... we should go."

But he only kissed her and pressed a finger softly to her lips. "Shhhh ... we'll stop. It'll be okay."

Again a little while later, she made a halfhearted attempt to push him away. "We need to get home. I can't ... Brad, please ... don't ... stop ... please, Brad."

By then, the tone of her voice sounded more like she was asking him to keep on, keep taking her higher up a mountain, keep filling her senses in a way she'd certainly never felt before. They gave in after that, no longer fighting the tide of emotions and sensations washing over them like so many wonderful waves.

Not until the act was done and they were lying on their backs side by side, staring at the stars, did Brad begin to sort out the horrific reality of what had just happened. He'd promised God and his parents that he wouldn't be sexually active until after he was married, but now … now he'd gone against everything he believed. And not just him, but Emma too. He wasn't sure how he could face her, how he could look into her eyes, and he had no idea what to do next.

Before he could move or say anything, he heard the quiet sound of Emma's tears. He dressed himself in a rush and she did the same. Then he sat up, facing her. "Em … don't cry."

"I can't believe it. That fast?" She covered her face with her hands and a sob came from her chest. "I thought it would … take longer. I thought we'd have time to stop."

Brad was just eighteen back then, and he was humiliated by her words. He tried to read through them to her real sadness. The fact that what they'd given up that night, they could never get back. "I'm sorry. I … I meant to stop."

She didn't speak to him until they were almost back to Wilmington. The whole ride, quiet tears slid down her face. Finally she turned to him and sniffed, her eyes red. "What … happens now?"

"I don't know." Nothing in all his life had prepared him for this moment. All he could think was that their youth pastor was right. Having sex before getting married changes everything, ruins everything. He grabbed for a question that might fit the awkwardness of the moment. "What do you want, Emma? You want some time?"

"No!" Her answer was panicky, a cry straight from her heart. "I want to pretend tonight never happened so that tomorrow we can wake up, and sometime after breakfast, we can swim at the pool and walk around the track at Wilmington West. I want to go to the beach again at the end of the week and never, ever let what happened tonight happen again." She settled back in her seat, worn out from the plea. "That's what I want." Fear clouded her eyes. "What about you?"

Brad wasn't sure whether to scream or cry, but he knew this: Nothing would ever be the same, no matter how well they pretended. "I want that too."

"Okay, then." She tried to smile, but her effort fell flat. She grabbed her backpack from the rear seat. "See you tomorrow."

"See ya." Brad hated himself for letting her go without telling her he loved her. He'd told her dozens of times before, but in the haze of guilt and shame, love seemed like the last thing they should talk about. They were a couple of kids who'd let things get out of hand, and now … now there was no going back.

Nothing about their plans changed over the next few days, and at the end of the week they went back to Holden Beach just like they planned. They pretended everything was alright, the way Emma wanted them to.

But back on this beach, they tried to find their way into a conversation and it was nothing but awkward starts and meaningless words. In the end there was nothing to say, because the desire in their eyes said it all. When the sun set that night, against everything they'd promised each other, they began kissing and touching, and again they gave in to the passion that had pulled at them all week long.

After that, they didn't bother lying to themselves. The lure of their physical connection was too great to ignore, too demanding not to give in. On the third time, Emma whispered to him in the moments before. "What if I get pregnant?"

He could tell by the way she said the word that it was the last thing she wanted to say. But they were crazy not to at least think about the possibility. Brad remembered what happened next, how he summoned all his wisdom and knowledge about such things and confidently, breathlessly pronounced that it wouldn't happen. "Girls your age don't get pregnant … not until they've been … well, you know … not for a few months anyway. I read that somewhere. Besides … I could get something from the store … next time, okay?"

Brad knew even as the words spilled from his mouth that he was lying. What he really meant was that he couldn't stop himself. Not for God or for Emma or for fear of getting her pregnant. They'd stumbled onto a passion bigger than both of them, a heady, whirling seductive range of physical feelings and emotions that had almost overnight become an addiction for each other that would not be denied.

No surprise then that November came with the news neither of them had wanted to believe possible. Emma was pregnant. She had him drive her to Holden Beach so she could tell him the news; mostly, he guessed, so they would have privacy — to discuss what to do next.

By then, Brad had already moved his things to the dorm at Chapel Hill, but in light of her announcement, he told his parents he needed more time. That he didn't want to be so far away from Emma, and that they'd go to college together when she graduated. In the meantime he'd earn money and create a savings for the next four years.

But all of that was only a ploy to buy time.

The wood against Brad's back pressed into his spine, pulling him from the tangled web of memories that made up his past. Right here on this beach, that's where she had told him the news. At first, of course, he could hardly believe it. She didn't look pregnant, didn't seem any different. He must've asked her a dozen times those first few days whether she was sure or not.

Brad started walking back toward the parking lot. Halfway there he spotted a white wooden cross in the midst of a section of wild grass. He hesitated but didn't move closer to it. Whoever had put it there, they hadn't intended it to be noticed by the public. It was too hidden for that.

He stuck his hands in his pockets and trudged back through the sand to his dad's truck. His time in the past hadn't helped resolve his feelings or give him a ticket to let it go. If anything, he knew better what he needed to say to Emma, why he had to find her before he could walk down the aisle with Laura. The way he'd treated Emma once they'd given in to their physical desires was appalling. Worse than that. His heart ached again, not for himself or the unfinished chapter from his past, but for Emma, his childhood friend and high school love. His precious Emma. He had to find her.

Otherwise the weight of the past would suffocate him.

Eleven

EMMA HAD BEEN HOME FROM THE hospital for an hour when she wandered down to the beach with Riley. The sandy stretch was empty except for an older couple walking hand-in-hand near the surf. Now that she'd talked to God, she had more to say. She'd wrestled with her own guilt and shame for so long, she figured she'd live this way forever. But now maybe that wasn't true.

She reached a stone wall separating Ocean Boulevard from the sandy beach, and with a graceful motion she eased herself up and onto it, hanging her tanned legs along the other side so she could face the water. Riley sat at attention beside her, ready to protect her if anyone dared get too close.

"It's okay, boy." She ran her fingers over his ear. "Lay down, Riley. It's okay."

Riley hesitated, then he yawned and moved in a series of tight circles before flopping down at her feet. She stared down the beach at the craggy place where small inlets of sand were hidden from view, the place where she and Brad had come that summer. The place where they lost control.

The thing was, she really believed him about getting pregnant, how it couldn't happen to her. Not right away. Or at least she wanted to believe him; after all, back then she had trusted him with her life. If she got pregnant, that wouldn't be the worst thing, right? Brad would stay by her and they'd have a quick wedding. They would live together while they finished school, and they'd raise their child the best way they knew how. That's what she pictured.

The day she took the pregnancy test would stay with her forever. Her mother was sick by then, very sick. She slept on the couch while Emma rushed quietly into the house with the bag from Eckerd's. She hurried upstairs and took the test kit from the bag. She wasn't sure how to use the contents of the box, so she was grateful that the directions were fairly straightforward. Two minutes later she had her results. She was pregnant, and there wasn't a soul on earth she could tell except Brad. Her best friend … the father of her child. She caught her breath, hating how she was drawn back to that time. They'd gone to the beach, of course. To the place right here where they'd lost control, where they'd compromised everything they believed.

"I'm late," she told him. They were holding hands, walking in the shallow tide. "I took a test."

At first her words didn't seem to register. But then slowly he stopped and turned to face her. "You're late … on your period?"

"Yes." She felt faint as she looked into his eyes. Like this had to be happening to someone else. Not her and Brad, because they were good kids, kids who didn't drink and party. Kids who had promised God they'd save themselves for marriage. She couldn't possibly be telling Brad she was pregnant. But she had no choice. She pulled the test stick from her sweater pocket. "I'm pregnant. The test was positive."

After that, the shock was more Brad's than hers. For a minute, he didn't seem to breathe, and then his skin grew pale and damp. "Really? I mean … you're sure?"

"Yes." She wanted him to hug her, to tell her everything was going to be okay.

Instead he turned from her and took a few steps toward the car. Then he stopped and doubled over his knees, heaving until everything he'd consumed for the past however many hours was lying on the afternoon sand. Gasping for air, still too sick to stand straight, he used his feet to kick sand over the mess. Then he turned to her, his mouth open. "What ... what are you going to do?"

She remembered how awful the question felt. What was *she* going to do? This was a problem they both faced, right? So why would Brad word it like that? Either way, it was a question with no answers. When he felt well enough, they drove home in her red ragtop with almost no conversation between them. Halfway there she took his hand and looked deep into his eyes. "Don't stop loving me, Brad. Please don't stop."

But love was the last thing on their minds after that. Emma didn't want to tell her sick mother, and Brad couldn't imagine telling his parents. They had been against Brad and Emma going to Holden Beach in the first place. This would be the worst admission of all, and Emma agreed they had to find an answer on their own.

At that time, her cycle hadn't been regular. She could miss a period and think nothing of it. For that reason she wasn't sure how far along she was, but since it was November she was terrified she might've been pregnant for a few months at least. That Monday in biology class, she was trying to figure out what to do when she remembered the school nurse and her promise to help any girl suffering with an unwanted pregnancy. Emma clenched her teeth, hating the words the nurse used back then. *Suffering from an unwanted pregnancy.* As if there was no baby involved whatsoever.

The nurse never for a moment considered any option but the one that made most sense to her. "You're at the start of your senior year. If you're a few months along now, a baby would mean you can't finish school or walk with your class at graduation. You can avoid all that heartache." It was as if the nurse were talking about a headache Emma was experiencing, not a baby growing inside her. "Having a baby is your choice, Emma."

She wished Brad had been there, but he couldn't bring him-self to show up on campus. His friends from the basketball team thought he was fully involved in his freshman year at college by then. He could hardly walk into an appointment with the school nurse, Emma at his side. The whole school would know the truth before lunch. Emma didn't blame him, but without his support, she felt very little resolve, little ability to do anything but be led through the process.

The nurse talked to her a few minutes longer before making the appointment. "They'll want to verify that you're pregnant. And they'll counsel you, of course. I don't want to assume any-thing. I mean, are you ready to be a mother?" The tone in her voice told Emma the question was rhetorical.

"No, ma'am." She sounded fifteen, timid and unsure of her-self. "I don't think so."

"And are you and the baby's father getting married anytime soon?"

"No, ma'am." Emma had sort of hoped so. That's what she had pictured, right? That Brad would seize his role in her preg-nancy, and that the two of them would find their way through the mess together ... they and their baby. But Brad hadn't mentioned marriage once since she'd taken the test. Before that summer, he'd talked about it all the time, how they were going to finish college and get married and live happily ever after.

But all that stopped with her positive pregnancy test.

The memories tore at Emma's heart, the way they always would. As much as she hated thinking back on that time, she couldn't pull herself from the past. Almost as if by staying with the series of memories she might finally understand what had happened, why she never made peace with the actions she'd taken that fall.

There were a few more questions from the nurse, and then Emma sat by while she picked up the phone and called a clinic in downtown Wilmington. "I have a student who may be pregnant," Emma heard her say. "From what I can tell, she's at the end of her first trimester." She scribbled something down on a piece of paper and finished the phone call. Then she turned to Emma. "Here you go. They're expecting you tomorrow at four o'clock. It'll be a preliminary appointment. You can work things out with them after that." She gave Emma a sad smile. "Any questions?"

Emma had a million. Was it really legal to walk into a clinic pregnant and walk out with an empty womb? Would anyone tell her whether the baby was a boy or a girl? And did an aborted baby have a funeral or just … or just what? Emma bit her lip and stared at her trembling hands. "No, ma'am. No questions."

Brad waited in the car while she went in for that first visit. Emma had called ahead and a woman had told her that this initial time wouldn't take long. She was right. A nurse performed another pregnancy test, and the results were the same. Positive. Then in a blur of discussion that felt entirely one-sided, Emma and a doctor at the clinic agreed she should come in on Saturday morning for an abortion.

She left the clinic shaking, terrified over what was about to happen. She couldn't talk about it at first, but that night she shared all her fears with Brad. They drove to the cape and held hands as they walked along a lighted pathway near the water, neither of them aware of anything but the conversation. Her "procedure" was set, and Emma was terrified.

"What if I die?" Emma shivered as a cool wind blew along the river. It was the third week of November, and the warmth of summer was long gone.

"You won't die." Brad sounded as terrified as she was, but he wouldn't say so. He tried to smile at her. "Come on, Emma. People do this all the time. It's not dangerous."

It's dangerous for the baby, Emma wanted to say. But she worried Brad might think she was forcing him to be a father. So she kept those feelings to herself. "I heard a girl talking about abortions in English last year. She said girls still die from them. They can bleed to death."

"That's at those back-alley places." Brad tried to sound informed, like he wasn't scared out of his mind.

"So you're saying I should do this?" An incredulous understanding came over her. "I thought you were a Christian?"

"I am." He stopped walking, his tone raised just enough to put tension between them. "I'm not telling you what to do."

"But you *are*. You're saying abortion's safe, but I thought …" her heart was racing so fast she thought she might drop dead there on the river-walk. "I thought Christians didn't believe in abortion."

Brad's silence in that single moment changed forever the way she viewed people of faith. It was one thing to take a stand against some societal wrong. It was another thing altogether to make tough decisions in line with that stand when the matter became personal. In other words, Brad's faith only allowed that abortion was wrong when it involved someone else. Emma had heard Brad's mother talk about their beliefs when the anniversary of *Roe v. Wade* rolled around. Back then Brad was very vocal about the subject, agreeing with his parents completely.

But now that the terrifying pregnancy was hers, Brad didn't have much to say.

They kept walking in silence, and a nausea came over Emma. She stopped and pulled her coat protectively around her middle. "You want me to have an abortion." It wasn't a question.

"It wasn't my idea, Em. It was the nurse's. She's the one who made the appointment." He released a frustrated sound and took a half step backward, away from her. He was acting detached, almost disinterested. "Look, we're too young to have a baby. You have to finish school. I have college. We'd be giving up all that."

There was no denying the fear in his eyes. "This is about our future."

She wanted to scream at him, ask him *what about our baby's future*. But she only hung her head.

He touched his hand to her elbow. "Look, I wanna do the right thing for you. Whatever that means I'll do it."

"Like what?" she tossed her hands in the air. "Drive me to the clinic? Pay for it?"

"I guess so." He hesitated. "Whatever you need, Emma."

She stared at Brad for a long moment and then spun around so he wouldn't see her cry. This wasn't what she wanted … it wasn't how she pictured this scene playing out. She wanted him to take her tenderly in his arms and stroke her back, promise her everything would be okay and ask her to marry him. Anything so they could get out of this nightmare together and whole. The three of them. But now … now he sounded like the school nurse, reminding her that they'd be compromising their futures if they had a baby now.

"Emma." He came to her, but not with an unconditional love and concern. Rather, his tone was marked by something new and uncomfortable. As if they hadn't grown up together. As if they weren't best friends who had gotten into serious trouble together. He put his hand on her shoulder. "I'm not ready to be a dad. If that's what you're looking for, I can't … I'm not ready."

So there was the real problem. She turned slowly, facing him, her heart breaking in half. When their eyes met, she realized something that only added to the sick feeling inside her. He looked like a stranger, like someone she didn't know at all. "So that's it." She sniffed, trying to keep from collapsing to a heap at his feet. Her voice was a tortured whisper. "You drive me to the clinic. I get an abortion, and we act like nothing ever happened. I go back to my senior year and you leave for Carolina and no one ever has to know. Right, Brad?"

"What other choice is there?" His voice broke, and for the first time since she'd taken the pregnancy test, his eyes filled with tears. "This is our only option."

Emma remembered putting her hand over her stomach, picturing the baby who would be half her, half Brad. Was it a boy with Brad's blond hair or a girl with her hazel eyes? She had one more question, and she struggled to find the right words as she stared at the boy she still loved. "What about us?"

"Us?" He swiped at the tears on his cheeks, and at the same time he turned toward the river. When he looked back, a hopelessness screamed from his expression. "Nothing's been the same. Not since ... not since August."

The world stopped spinning, and Emma couldn't breathe, couldn't speak. Was he breaking up with her? Were they finished because they'd made a mistake and gotten caught? No matter what happened next, she couldn't lose Brad. He was everything to her, every yesterday and a lifetime of tomorrows. There had never been anyone else for her but Brad, so he couldn't be saying what he was saying. She grabbed a series of quick breaths and shoved her fingers through the roots of her hair. "Are you ... breaking up?"

His answer was quick and defensive. "Of course not." Anger colored his tone. "I never said that."

"You said nothing's been the same since August." She was panting, struggling to exhale. In the distance a group of teenage guys walked by. They stared and snickered at them, as if the discussion were nothing more than a teenage lovers' quarrel.

"I didn't say I wanted to break up." He still sounded angry. "You're putting words in my mouth."

Emma hated that he was defending himself. She wanted him to fight for *her*, tell her he'd go to the ends of the earth for her. Promises of love and devotion and protection, that's what she wanted. Not this ... this frustrated guy making excuses and nervous accusations. But what was she going to do, order him to be kind, beg him to understand a little of the terror she was feeling? She forced herself to calm down, to breathe normally, and when she had regained some of her composure she reached for his hand. "I still love you."

His transition took a few seconds. But then for the first time since they'd reached the river, the look in his eyes was the kind one she was familiar with. He pulled her to him and breathed into her hair. "I love you too. Nothing's changed." He put his hand alongside her cheek and kissed her — not the passionate kiss that had caused them to lose control, but a kiss of tenderness and concern that said everything his words did not.

"We can get through this, right?" Her tears were back, blurring her eyes. She clung to him like she might otherwise fall off the edge of a cavernous cliff.

"Of course." His voice was heavy with relief. "We'll get through it together. Everything will be okay."

And like that, the decision was made.

Twelve

EMMA STOPPED THE MEMORIES COLD AND didn't think about them again until early the next morning. Even then she held them at a distance. What happened that terrible Saturday in November wasn't something she thought about — not ever. Instead she tried to focus all her thoughts on Kristin. A quick call to the hospital and Kristin's mother got on the line. Nothing had changed during the night. They were still praying for Kristin to come out of the coma. Emma promised to keep praying, but she kept the conversation short. She felt like a liar, talking about prayer to a woman with such strong beliefs.

Emma hung up the phone and looked around her house. She wanted to go back to bed and wake up a different person, someone without her wretched past. Instead she fed Riley, showered, and dressed in Capri pants and a loose-fitting sleeveless blouse. Sunday mornings she often stopped at Ace Hardware for paint or hinges, whatever her latest home improvement project required. But today she didn't feel like working on the house. Her worries for Kristin combined with the defeat and guilt of her memories made it impossible to feel anything but deeply discouraged.

Sunshine streamed through the front window, and for half an hour she tried to read the latest Grisham novel. But she couldn't get into it, not with the past breathing down her neck. She stood and stretched, noting the time on the old clock that hung on the wall by the window. Just after eight thirty. Coffee, that's what she needed. She made sure Riley had enough water, then she grabbed her purse and climbed into her old red convertible. She drove down Dolphin to Ocean, off the island onto the mainland to her favorite coffee shop. Cappuccino by the Sea was only a few minutes from her house. Maybe the short trip would jump-start her day and help put the memories behind her once again.

She pulled into the gravel lot and found the last open parking space. The place was tucked against a grove of towering trees, and outside sat a few white plastic tables and colorful umbrellas. Emma didn't see Gavin Greeley until she was nearly to the front door. He sat alone, stretched back in one of the plastic chairs, reading the paper. His khaki slacks and tan knit T-shirt were too nice for a casual Sunday morning coffee.

He must've sensed someone watching him, because he looked up, looked right at her. His eyes shifted quickly from surprised to serious. "Emma." He set the paper down and stood.

She wondered if there was some kind of celestial conspiracy against her. After all, this was the third straight day she'd seen him. She composed herself and walked closer. "Hi."

He looked like he might try to hug her, but then he seemed to change his mind. "How's Kristin?" His concern was deeply genuine. "Have you heard?"

"No changes." Emma wanted to get her coffee and leave. Standing here, looking into his kind eyes only added to her attraction to him — an attraction she would never give in to. "Her mom asked for more prayers."

"Definitely." He looked at the coffee shop door and then back at her. His tone softened. "Hey ... get your drink and let's take a walk. Talk for a few minutes."

Emma started to tell him no, she couldn't walk with him or get closer to him. But suddenly the idea seemed better than going home alone, just her and her incessant memories. "Okay." She took another step toward the door and tried to smile. Her determination to stay clear of him wasn't his fault, after all. "Just for a few minutes."

She bought a tall soy latte and returned to his table. "You're dressed nice."

"I have church in a couple hours. I like coming here first." He had folded the newspaper, and now he stood, unhurried. He pointed down a path that led from the parking lot through a grove of trees. "You ever walk back that way?"

"No." Emma narrowed her eyes, trying to see down the gravel path. "Where does it go?"

"There's a catfish pond back there. The path goes about half a mile in and then around the pond. It's a nice walk."

Again she was doubtful. She hadn't come here to take a walk with Gavin Greeley. But she couldn't think of a single reason to say no. "Hold on." She put her purse in her car and locked it. Then with her coffee cupped in both hands, she fell in beside him and they walked toward the path.

Gavin waited until they were under the cover of the trees before he glanced at her. "Can I ask you a question?" He walked slowly, clearly more concerned with the conversation than the catfish.

"You just did." She kept on, but she gave him a sheepish look and then turned her attention to her drink. "I'm not big on questions."

"See, that's what I mean." His smile was easy, but confusion shadowed his eyes. "You're always difficult like that."

"Difficult?" She never thought about how her actions might've made her seem. "Because I don't want to talk?"

"No." A breeze ruffled the higher tree branches above and sunlight streaked in along the path. "Because you won't let me be your friend."

"You wouldn't want to be my friend." She looked straight at him. "Not if you really knew me."

"You've said that." Gavin hesitated, his attention on her. "The other day at the hospital, that whole thing about your prayers somehow hurting Kristin, and how God wouldn't want to hear from you." He searched her eyes all the way to her soul. "Something must've happened to you, Emma. Whatever it is, it's stealing the life from you, and you won't deal with it." A tenderness filled his face and he hesitated a long moment. "Nothing you could tell me would make me run."

"You think that." She was trembling now, desperate to turn around and sprint back to the parking lot, drive away before the conversation went any further. "But you'd be surprised." She gave a quick look over her shoulder, but they were far enough away that she couldn't see anything but trees.

Gavin's gaze remained unwavering. "Try me, Emma. Give me a chance to be your friend."

Emma's mind raced, and she felt dizzy. What if she took him up on his offer? What if she told him what she'd done? Maybe then he'd leave her alone and they could avoid another scene like this one. She took a long sip of her latte, her hands colder than they should've been. "Okay." She started walking again, more slowly than before. "You want to know, I'll tell you."

He raised his brow a little and he stayed at her pace. "I'm listening."

She stared at her feet. Could she do this? Her stomach hurt and she still wanted to run. But she had to at least try to make him understand. She wasn't sure where to begin, so she decided to get to the point. That way maybe this talk wouldn't last longer than it had to. She forced herself to look at him. "It happened ten years ago. November 20, 1999." Her lungs felt tight, like she couldn't breathe right. Still she forced herself to continue. "I dated the same guy through high school, and … the summer after my junior year I got pregnant."

Gavin didn't blink, didn't change his expression whatsoever. They walked for a while without saying anything. The path wound into a small clearing, and wildflowers dotted a grassy field to their left.

The sun felt warm on her shoulders and it gave her confidence to continue. "I wasn't ready to have a baby, so ..." She stopped and stared at the blue sky for a long time. When she looked at him, she knew she had to tell him. There was no turning back. "I had an abortion." She felt like she might throw up. She hung her head and the ground beneath her feet felt suddenly liquid. The silence from Gavin was unbearable. She looked up at him again, at his complete lack of reaction. "That's it. See?" A sad sound came from her. "You need to meet someone at church, Gavin. Not someone like me."

Gavin's face held none of the shock or disgust she'd imagined, none of the condemnation. He took awhile, like always. Then he breathed in sharply through his nose. "I'll bet there was more to it than that."

"More to it?"

"Yes." He angled his head, sympathy in his voice. "Must've been the hardest thing you ever did."

His comment caught her completely off guard. She'd expected something along the lines of a mini-lecture, a talk about the value of life. That sort of thing. She felt her shaking ease some. "Hardest ever."

"Okay," he looked like he had all the time in the world. A couple of oak trees stood adjacent to the path and he leaned against one of them. "Tell me about it, Emma. I meant what I said. I want to be your friend."

A friend? A real friend? Emma hadn't considered such a thing since her mother died. There hadn't been anyone she could trust with the whole truth. She leaned against the other tree, facing him. The thing was, she had nothing to do, nowhere to go, and the memories would be there waiting for her at home if she didn't work through them somehow. "You want me to tell you about what happened that day?"

"Yes." Shade protected them from the glare of the sun. Again he looked deep into her heart. "If you'll trust me."

This was the last thing she'd ever imagined herself doing, telling Gavin Greeley the details of her abortion. But he was here and he was listening. Like earlier, she had the sudden urge to go ahead and talk, just tell the story and get through it this one time. Maybe if she did, she could figure out why she had never recovered.

"You really want to know?"

"I do."

The real way to tell him what happened was to start at the beginning. So she did. She told Gavin about Brad, about how they'd met and how they'd fallen in love. She told him about the trips to Holden Beach where they'd made the worst choice of all, and how she'd wound up pregnant. But she didn't stop there.

"Brad picked me up that Saturday morning and took me to the clinic." She stared off toward the trees, looking at nothing and seeing only the past. "We barely talked to each other on the drive there."

"What was Brad feeling?" Gavin's comments were few, but he was true to his word. He was interested and he wanted her to continue.

"I'm not sure what he was feeling. He told me I'd be okay. He kept saying that." Emma remembered Brad's knuckles were white as he gripped the steering wheel. His breathing was jagged and nervous. "He told me not to be scared."

In a rush, the memories took hold of her, each vivid detail. She didn't spare any part of the story as she told Gavin everything about that day. In the process, she didn't feel like she was talking so much as she was reliving that terrible morning.

When Brad told her not to be scared, Emma said nothing in response, because of course she was scared. Plus, she didn't want to talk. She kept her hand over her middle, over the place where the life was growing inside her. Did her baby know what was happening, that the tiny heart would only beat for another hour?

I'm sorry, little baby. I wish I were braver ... I wish I could walk away from Brad and have you on my own, but ... but I can't. My mom's sick and ... there wouldn't be anyone to help me. It's not your fault. Please forgive me. The tape played in her mind constantly as they reached the clinic and went inside. What sort of mother was she, caring more about keeping Brad than keeping her own child? She had worried that someone would see them, recognize them, but the parking lot was behind the building, surrounded by shrubs and trees. At that early Saturday hour it was empty but for two cars.

Before they walked in, Brad turned to her. "Tomorrow at this time, we can put this whole nightmare behind us."

Tomorrow at this time? She felt sick at the thought. She would never put this behind her. He moved in close to kiss her, but she turned her head. "Not now."

"Are you mad?" He took hold of her hand, his face riddled with shock. "Don't be mad at me, Em. Please."

He didn't understand at all. She pulled away. "I'm not mad." She crossed her arms in front of her. "I want it to be over, that's all." As soon as she said the words, she felt awful. What if her baby could hear her? She didn't want to do this, but she had no choice — no way out.

Still, even as she crossed the threshold into the clinic, she knew she was wrong. She could certainly have the chance to love her baby. All she had to do was turn around and demand that Brad take her home. He could walk out of her life today, and at least she'd have their child. The truth of that put her in a vice grip of guilt and shame, but still she entered the building, walked up to the desk, and gave the woman behind the counter her name.

"Emma Landon."

The woman smiled pleasantly, as if Emma were merely coming to get her nails done. "Emma ... yes, here it is. You're scheduled for a D and C procedure, is that right?" At the mention of the abortion, the woman's smile faded appropriately.

"Yes, ma'am." She barely spoke the words. She looked for Brad, but he was already sitting in the waiting area, his hands covering his face.

"You seem a little nervous." The woman put her hand over Emma's. "Don't be afraid, honey. This procedure is more common than you think. It's not something people talk about, but it's a fact of life."

Emma thought her choice of words was strange. This was abortion ... and abortion wasn't a fact of life, it was a fact of death. Emma closed her eyes for a long moment and then nodded at the woman. She didn't want a lecture or reassurance or anything, but to sit alone in these, the last minutes of her baby's life.

The woman gave her a clipboard with paperwork to fill out, and then another brochure, explaining the procedure and its aftereffects. "You haven't eaten this morning, right?"

"No, ma'am."

"Okay, let's take a look." She studied the paperwork. "You're eleven weeks along, is that right?"

"Something like that." Emma could barely make out her own voice.

"Okay, then. How would you like to make payment?"

The nausea was a regular part of her mornings by then, and suddenly the woman behind the counter reminded her of Judas, taking money in exchange for innocence. "I'm not sure ..." She gripped the counter and bent over, trying to keep from throwing up.

Brad must've heard the question, because he was at her side. "I'm paying." He pulled out his wallet. "I brought cash."

Emma straightened and reached for Brad's hand. "I don't feel good," she whispered.

"I know." He kissed the side of her head. "I'm here."

The woman behind the counter seemed slightly irritated by the delay. She waited until she had Brad's attention. "The cost for a D and C is three-fifty."

Brad's hands were shaking. "I brought three hundred."

"Oh." The woman's face fell. "I'm afraid that's not enough. This type of service is always more than three hundred."

Service? Emma grabbed onto Brad's elbow. Was that how they looked at an abortion? Just another service for women? Like getting her hair done or stopping in for a massage? She should turn around and leave. Brad didn't have enough money, right? So that was a sign from God to get out of there before anyone could harm her baby. She tugged on his arm. "Come on … let's go."

The woman realized their dilemma, because she handed Brad the phone. "Maybe there's someone you can call. We take credit cards over the phone."

"I … I don't want anyone to … to know we were here." Brad could barely get the sentence out.

"We know." The woman's smile seemed condescending. "The notation on the credit card statement will only say Wilmington Services."

Everything about Emma's life from that point on hinged on what happened next. Brad looked at her, a desperate look. But instead of acknowledging her request and taking her back home where they could figure out what to do next, he turned to the woman. "I'll call my father … if that's okay."

She smiled. "Go right ahead."

Brad swallowed hard, but despite his trembling fingers, he pushed the buttons in a hurry. His mom must've answered, because he asked to speak to his dad. Emma couldn't believe what was happening. She could never look Brad's father in the face if he knew what they were about to do. But as Carl Cutler came on the line, Brad didn't launch into a lengthy explanation.

"I'm in trouble, Dad. I need fifty bucks." There was a pause, and Brad muttered. "I know. I'll tell you later." A longer pause. "Okay, thanks. Here … I'll hand you over to the lady."

Emma didn't find out till later that Brad's father thought he was getting his car worked on. His billing statement would never prove otherwise. Carl Cutler hadn't for a moment thought the person he was giving his credit card information to was a clerk at an abortion clinic. Either way, the information was passed along, and a minute later the call was over and the woman was satisfied. "Have a seat. You'll be called back in a few minutes."

A cool breeze brushed against Emma's face, and she jolted free of the memory. Gavin was still watching her, his eyes marked with sadness. Had she really just told him all that? He must think she was terrible, but that was okay. At least now he knew the truth about her. She raised her shoulders a little. "That's as far back as I go. The rest … I can't …"

"I don't need to hear the rest." Gavin's attention was entirely on her, compassion filling his eyes. Again he was thoughtful with his words, taking his time before making any response. "Thank you. For trusting me."

"I've never told anyone." The slightest sense of freedom came over her. "I think … maybe I needed to."

"What happened … with Brad?" He wasn't pushing. His eyes were as kind as ever. "After, I mean?"

"We tried to make it work." She took a slow sip of her coffee, but it had grown cold. She lowered her cup and clenched her other fist. "Two days later he picked me up and took me to Wrightsville Beach." She could see them again, the distance between them that day. "We sat on a towel near the Sunspree and just … just stared at the water." She looked right at Gavin. "We had nothing to say."

"Hmmm." For whatever reason Gavin truly seemed to care.

"I couldn't stop thinking about the baby."

Gavin sighed and the sound was heavy in the morning air. He spanned the short distance between them, reaching out and touching her shoulder. "I'm sorry. For what you went through."

The feel of his fingers sent a shock through her, and again she felt like running. But she stayed. Against everything inside her, she stayed. She'd come this far and she wanted to finish the story. The part she was willing to tell, anyway. That, and she liked this — feeling like she had a friend in Gavin Greeley — even for an hour in the woods a world away from the coffee shop. "As for Brad … I think he felt guilty, but he didn't say." A sad sound more cry than laugh sounded lightly on her lips. "After that it was impossible to laugh or play on the beach or think about a movie." She felt suddenly awkward about Gavin's hand still on her shoulder. He must have sensed her discomfort because he eased his hand to his side again. She rested her head back against the rough bark of the tree. "I don't know … we were different."

"I'm sure."

"The holidays came and went and Brad left for college." Their last day together, their good-byes, none of it was heartfelt or drawn out the way it might have been. And of course not. The love they'd shared was long dead by then … dead since the twentieth of November. "A few years later my mom died. Brad came back for the funeral, but we barely talked." Emma drew a quick breath and drew her foot up against the tree trunk. "And that was that. I haven't heard from him since."

"It still hurts." Gavin's perception seemed to come naturally. He never looked away, never gave her anything but his complete attention.

"Yes." She looked down at her hands for a few seconds. "It still hurts."

He stretched out his legs, again unhurried. "Do you love him? Now, I mean?"

"No." Her answer was a little too quick, but it was the right answer. No matter how she sometimes felt on late afternoons when she ran along Holden Beach. "It's just ..." she squinted at the sky, trying to figure out her feelings. When she turned her eyes back to his she felt the same sense of freedom she'd felt earlier. "We never found closure. About the baby ... about us."

He smiled with a tenderness that warmed even the darkest corner of her soul. He took a few steps and nodded for her to follow. "Maybe this helped. Talking about it."

"Maybe." She was glad they were walking again. The pond glistened ahead of them.

"See?" A smile sounded in his voice.

"What?" The path narrowed, the trees on either side closer than before.

"I'm still here." His shoulder brushed against her as they walked. "You thought I wouldn't want to be your friend, but that's crazy, Emma. We all have a past."

"I know, it's just ..." this was the first time she'd ever spoken of these feelings, ever really understood them. "I should've been braver. I should've had the baby. I hate myself for it."

"You can't go back." Gavin's voice grew softer. They came into another clearing, and a few yards up the path they reached the pond. Three mallard ducks sailed in a lazy circle at the far end. Gavin paused for a long while, staring at the scene. Then he turned to her, looking straight into the part of her soul she never shared with anyone. "This is why you didn't want to pray for Kristin?"

Emma couldn't bring herself to talk about God, not in light of what she'd just admitted. She nodded and once more fought the urge to leave. "Brad made an impact in a lot of ways. It's ironic. Especially when it came to my mom." Emma felt a sad smile tug at her lips. "I started going to church with him when I was in middle school. My mom ... she became a Christian because of Brad's influence in our lives. She died with a very strong faith. But me ..."

"You have walls."

It was like he had known her forever. She looked down, unwilling to let him see inside her heart a moment longer.

"You know what?" His tenderness was like water to her parched, dry soul.

She looked up.

"I think inside those walls is a very bright light. You care, Emma. I can see that." He exhaled, long and slow, clearly wanting her to understand. "God forgives you." He wasn't preaching to her. He was doing what he said he wanted to do. He was being her friend. "Maybe you should take all this to Him. I mean, have you thought about it?"

The kind man beside her meant well. His comment about her touched her deeply. But Emma couldn't talk about turning to God in light of all she'd just revealed. A restlessness came over her. "You know what?" She smiled politely as she turned in the direction of the parking lot. "We need to get back." She started walking and again he stayed with her pace. "Thank you for listening."

"Emma ... I didn't mean to —"

"It's okay." Her pace was faster than before. Not rude, but definitely faster. "You need to get to church."

He slipped his hands into his pockets as they walked. "I still have an hour."

She didn't want to talk about it anymore. Instead she spent the walk back asking about his summer. He was leading a couple basketball camps at the school and another private camp — his own — in mid-August.

They reached her car and she felt like she could breathe again. He seemed about to say something, to stop her from leaving. But instead, slowly his expression eased and he gave her a sad smile. Before she could get into her car, he gently put his arms around her and hugged her. There was no logical reason why, but again, the way he cared for her came through in every aspect of his embrace. As he eased back he searched deep into her eyes. "I'm here, Emma. If you ever want to talk, I'm here."

"Thanks." She slipped into the driver's seat and pulled her keys from her pocket. Her heart was beating at double speed, pounding so loud she could barely hear herself talk. "I ..." she looked up at him, "this was good." She smiled so he wouldn't ask another question. "Thanks, Gavin."

He nodded and backed up a few feet from her car. When she pulled out of the gravel lot, he was still standing there, still watching her. Her hands felt damp against the wheel as she drove home. How could she have told him? She hadn't spared a single detail, so what must he be thinking about her now? On his way to church, of all things. He could say all the right things about still being there and about not being appalled, but he would never see her the same way again. He was a good man, a churchgoing man. His faith was as real as everything else about him. The conversation might've helped her process some of what she was feeling, but after today one thing was absolutely certain. Gavin Greeley might care about her as a person ... he might even pray for her at the church altar this morning.

But he would never ask her out again.

Thirteen

BRAD WAS BACK IN NEW YORK, but he'd been distant and evasive since his return and Laura was certain something was wrong. She had planned on using that Monday to shop with her mom for bridesmaid gifts, something special for the friends who had always been there for her.

But with Brad acting so strange, she wasn't in the mood to work on the wedding.

Instead she drove with her dad into the city so she could help him catch up on some marketing. She'd received her degree in public relations, but she'd mostly used it for the charity work she and her parents were involved in. She could write newsletters and send press releases to the local media when one of the ministries had an auction or a fundraiser. Only once in a while did she use her skills for her father's company.

"I have people who can do this, sweetheart," her dad smiled at her as they drove through the tunnel. "You should be focused on your wedding. Are you sure you and your mother have things under control?"

"Mom and I have done what we can, really. The wedding planner has all the details under control." *If only I did*, she thought. She patted his hand. "Besides, I like working with you."

The office had a long list of completed ad campaigns, and like other times when Laura helped at the firm, she would contact past clients, thanking them again for their business and offering the firm's services if they had any additional advertising needs.

It didn't hurt that she'd be near Brad all day. He'd mentioned he wanted to talk, so being at the office today might help make that moment happen. The sun was still coming up when they arrived at the building and headed for the elevator. Her dad's firm took up three floors, the nineteenth, twentieth, and the twenty-first. The executives had offices on the latter, and Laura intended to work from a laptop in her father's suite—the one next to Brad's.

"I like being the first one here," her dad grinned as they stepped off the elevator onto the plush carpet that marked his office space. "Gives me time to think."

It wasn't quite seven o'clock, but being early didn't bother Laura. She could organize her contacts according to product type and time zone. The extra hour would allow her to familiarize herself with the accounts, so she'd be ready to make phone calls well before noon.

They walked together past the office with Brad's name on the door, but her dad hesitated as they reached his office. "I have an early conference call with a new account." He motioned down the hall. "Why don't you work in Brad's office? At least until he gets in."

"Perfect." Laura loved the idea. She gathered a stack of client files and a laptop. As she opened the door to the place where he worked, she could smell his cologne. A feeling of peace and well-being came over her. Everything was okay … it had to be. They'd talked about getting married for years, right? But as she spread the files across the long table at the center of the suite, she couldn't help but think about Brad's recent trip to North Carolina and why his tone had sounded so ominous when he'd told her yesterday that he wanted to talk.

She forced all doubt from her mind. At the same time she noticed the poster-size baby photos spread around the perimeter of the room. That had to be it, right? His distance wasn't because of her or doubts he might be having about the wedding. He was struggling with the Kotton Kids campaign. Even after his meeting with the company's president, he still hadn't come up with the type of slogan the product deserved. Wasn't that what he'd told her?

Peace came over her again. Nothing was wrong. They were at the beginning of a wonderful life. Of course Brad would be upset by the struggles he was having with his current campaign. He didn't need her scrutiny ... he needed her encouragement. She turned her attention to the files and began arranging them. She would use the laptop to check back records on each account, but she needed something to write on, a place to jot notes about each file. The supply closet was all the way at the other end of the office, one floor down. She looked at Brad's desk. Surely he would have what she needed.

She crossed the room to his work space and pulled open the first drawer. But instead of paper and a pen, she saw an envelope, and on top of it, the small photo of a striking brunette. Laura's heart stopped and then thudded into a rhythm she didn't recognize. What was this? A photo of some girl she didn't know at the very top of her fiancé's desk drawer?

Dear God ... who is she? Please, God ... help me make sense of what I'm seeing. She was breathing faster than before. With everything in her she wanted to slam the drawer shut and pretend she'd never seen the picture. But she had, and that changed everything. Feeling like a trespasser in utter violation, she carefully picked up the photo and studied it.

Her fingers trembled as she examined the photo. The girl was stunning. Dark hair and hazel eyes framing an unforgettable face. The paper was slightly yellowed and worn, an older photo for sure. So why was it at the top of Brad's desk drawer? She turned it over and part of the mystery became instantly clear. A single name was written across the back.

Emma.

The realization hit her full force like a wall of freezing water, taking her breath and leaving her stunned. This was Emma? Emma Landon, of course. Brad's high school love. They met in grade school and became fast friends. Brad had talked about her one of the first times he and Laura went out.

"Sounds like you were destined to be with her," she had kept her tone light. "What happened?"

Brad's face gave away nothing. He smiled, a nostalgic sort of smile, and he shrugged. "We grew apart. Just because you share your childhood with someone doesn't mean you're right for each other."

"True." She didn't want to be nosy, but she had to ask. "Was it mutual, the breakup?"

"More or less. The last few months nothing seemed to work. The end wasn't a surprise to either of us."

His answer had satisfied Laura, leaving her convinced that Emma Landon was a part of Brad's past. Nothing more. Never again did Laura ask about Emma, and Brad brought her up only occasionally when he was telling a story from his past. Emma was pretty much a part of Brad's every memory until he graduated from high school. Laura was okay with that.

But now ... if Emma's photo was on top of everything in Brad's desk drawer, what did that mean? And was she the reason he needed to go back to North Carolina? Suddenly every certain thing about her life shifted onto shaky ground. Was this why he'd been so distant, the reason he needed to talk to her? If so, why? What had happened that a girl he'd left behind nine years ago would suddenly be on his mind?

Her heart was still racing, and she needed fresh air. She couldn't stand to hold the picture another moment. She set it back on top of the envelope and shut the desk drawer. What was she supposed to do now? How could any of this be happening? The picture and the trip to Wilmington had to be connected, somehow. A part of her wanted to call a car and go home, so she wouldn't have to face him in an hour.

Help me, God ... what's going on?

Peace, my Daughter. I am with you always.

The truth spoke calm over her soul, a truth she'd rested in since she was a little girl. God was with her. Even now, even when her relationship with Brad and their pending wedding was no longer certain. Her faith in Christ was, and He would be with her—whatever lay ahead.

She took a slow breath and steadied herself. No, she wouldn't run. She had to face him, had to find out what he wanted to talk about and take whatever came next with calm and confidence. Besides, maybe she was overreacting. This might not be anything more than a strange coincidence. Maybe he was cleaning his desk and found the photo. The picture might not have anything to do with Brad's trip home.

By the time Brad arrived, she had stationed herself in an empty office across the hall—not wanting to make small talk with her father or her fiancé. Brad seemed surprised by her presence. He came to her and shut the door behind him. "Hey ..."

"Hi." *Act natural,* she told herself. *Stay calm. Whatever today holds, stay calm.* She held her head a little higher. "How's your morning?"

"Good." He knit his brow together. "I thought you and your mom were buying bridesmaid gifts today?"

"No." She smiled, but it felt icy, even to her. "I wasn't in the mood."

"You weren't in the ..." He came closer and sat on the edge of her desk. "Laura? What's wrong?"

She wanted to give him a quick "I'm fine," play along like everything was okay between them. For several long, painful seconds she searched for a way to hide what she was feeling. But she couldn't pretend. Finally her smile faded and she studied him, trying to see his intentions. "You tell me." She pushed back from the laptop, her eyes still locked on his. "Tell me about North Carolina."

He hesitated. Not in a pronounced way and not for long, but his hesitation told her everything she needed to know. His lips parted and he shook his head. "I saw my parents." His lips stayed parted, like he might say something else to convince her. But then his expression changed. "Look, Laura. North Carolina … what I want to talk about … it has nothing to do with us. I promise you."

"What then?" She kept her tone kind, controlled. "Because if something's wrong with you, then it involves me. That's how it works when two people get married."

"I know." He exhaled hard and rubbed the back of his neck. "I'm sorry." A look that mixed resignation with trepidation filled his eyes and he checked the clock near the door. "I don't have an appointment until eleven thirty. How about a walk in the park?"

"Now?"

"Yes. Right now." Brad sighed. He held his hand out to her. "I need to talk to you."

She didn't want to take his hand. Whatever he had to tell her, she wanted to protect her heart. But she reached out for his fingers anyway. She left her purse and they walked to the elevator without saying a word. Central Park was a block away, visible from Brad's office. In three minutes they were on a secluded, tree-lined path, headed for the fountain.

"I want to be clear about one thing." Their pace was a slow saunter, Brad's entire focus on her. "What I'm about to say has nothing to do with you. But I realized something this past weekend. You need to know."

Laura couldn't keep walking. She moved to a bench on the side of the path and sat on the edge, waiting. Whatever was coming, she had a feeling it would change both their lives forever.

So before she could listen to another word, she needed to pray. Quickly and silently. *Lord, please be with me. I thought every-thing was fine …*

Brad was coming toward her, and the look on his face told her she would need to keep praying. Maybe constantly. Because Brad didn't look merely concerned or anxious as he approached her.

He looked broken, like someone she didn't recognize.

Fourteen

BRAD HAD DREADED THIS MOMENT SINCE he left North Carolina. His father had said he'd pray for him, and he'd said something else. "The sooner the better, Son. Truth doesn't like to be delayed."

That was certainly true here and now. He drew a slow breath, walked to the bench, and lowered himself to the place beside Laura. He'd prayed about this moment the whole way home and late into last night. Now he had no choice but to move forward. He took her hand and muttered under his breath, "Man, I hate this."

Laura was quiet, waiting. But there was no denying the fear in her eyes.

"Okay." He worked to find the right words. "So remember I told you about Emma? The girl I dated in high school?"

"I remember." The look in Laura's eyes changed a little. "The one you grew up with."

"Right." He shifted. "Her." For a moment he looked up through the trees, as if the sliver of blue sky beyond might somehow lighten the moment. But wide open broad sunlight wouldn't lift the mood here. He rubbed his free hand against his knee. "I didn't tell you everything about her."

Again Laura stayed quiet, her fingers cold despite the warm morning.

His stomach hurt and he wanted to erase everything that led to this moment. If he had it to do over he wouldn't have taken Emma to Holden Beach at all. Then there wouldn't have been a past to talk about. No August nights full of regret. No baby. No abortion. No reason to be anything but joyful here, five weeks before marrying his sweet Laura. Inside his chest, he could almost feel his heart growing heavier.

He had no choice but to say it. "Emma and I ... we let things get out of hand the last summer we were together. The summer after I graduated from high school. We had ..." He looked down at the ground between his feet. "We had every intention of staying pure. Really we did." He shook his head and lifted his eyes to hers. "But we didn't. We gave in."

Gradually Laura's fear gave way to a look of disbelief. "What?" It was a whisper. "You're not ..." She sat straighter, and in the process her hand broke free from his. "You *slept* with her?"

Another long sigh. Brad pictured his time with Emma on the beach, the way she was surprised and hurt that the moment was over so fast. They hardly slept together, but that wasn't what Laura meant. He nodded. "I did."

"Once?"

Her question flew at him, piercing him like an arrow through his soul. And this was only the beginning. Her questions were going to get more difficult for sure. He clenched his jaw. "A few times. Over the month of August."

Brad tried to fathom how this news was hitting Laura. It was one thing to realize that the man you were about to marry wasn't really a virgin. But to realize the fall wasn't one indiscretion, but a series of bad choices? He shuddered, not sure what to say next.

Laura allowed a few slow nods. Then she raised her brow and shook her head, the way someone might do after a blow to the temple. Her voice simmered with anger and betrayal. "Why didn't you tell me?"

His only answer seemed cheap even to him. "You didn't ask." He dug his elbows into his knees. "So I didn't offer." He locked eyes with her again. "I tried to forget about it. I wanted my past to be like yours. If I could change it I would."

"You think I wouldn't have dated you if you'd been honest?" Pain hung on every word.

"I don't know. I'm not the same guy I was back then." He felt defeated. "I wanted you to see me the way I am now."

Laura stared at him for a long time. Then she stood and crossed the path, keeping her back to him. Brad wasn't sure whether to go to her or stay seated. If she needed time to sort through her feelings, he understood. After nearly a minute she faced him again and slowly returned to her spot on the bench. "Is there more?"

With his whole heart, Brad wanted to say no. He stared at the ground again and muttered the words, "Yes. There is."

She bent over her knees and braced herself, as if she wasn't sure how much more she could take.

"Sometime in November, toward the end of November, Emma took a test and found out … she was pregnant."

Laura closed her eyes. "You mean …" she blinked and stared at him. Her expression had gone from shocked to horrified. "You're … you're a father?"

The question ripped through him. "No." He breathed out and willed the pain to go with it. But there was no way to minimize the truth, no way to feel less of the hurt. "I'm not a father." He thought about blaming their age or the school nurse or a culture that would endorse abortion in the first place. But if he was going to reckon with his past, he had to start by claiming it. "I … drove her to a clinic." The words sounded so foreign, the memory so far removed from his conscious thought, that he didn't recognize his voice. "I paid and she … she had an abortion."

An audible groan came from Laura and she covered her face with her hands. She stayed that way for a long time, and when

her hands dropped away, there were tears on her face. "I guess …
I mean I'm not sure what to say."

He had no idea what to expect, but he half hoped she would
tell him she was sorry, that she could only imagine the sort of
pain his past must have caused him. Not that he deserved that
reaction. He didn't deserve anything about Laura James. "May 15
would've been the birthday, and so …"

A dawning flashed in her eyes. "Kotton Kids." She looked
away. "No wonder."

"Yeah." His heart beat hard in anticipation of what was next.
"It started that day and by the next night nothing felt right."

"About us." Her tone was dead, her expression too shocked
to react.

"Of course not." He raised his voice just a little, then he
moved for her hand again, but he changed his mind. "About *me*,
the way I treated Emma back then." He found her eyes and willed
her to understand. "I never told her I was sorry. I never made
things right."

"She had an abortion, Brad. There's no way to make that
right."

"I talked to a friend of mine. A Christian counselor. He said
when it's possible, making amends with someone can be the first
step toward healing."

"Making amends?" Laura looked pale, like she might not survive what she was hearing.

"I don't know how else to say it." He stuffed his frustration.
He had to find a way through this. "Anyway … I went back to
North Carolina to talk to my dad and his advice was exactly how
I was feeling." He pictured his dad, gripping the metal detector,
intent on the targets beneath the sand. "He told me the last lines
to that chapter in my life weren't written yet." He hesitated, but
he was gaining conviction. The last thing he wanted was to hurt
Laura. But he needed to do this. "I have to find her so I can at

least apologize. So I can close that chapter before I start the next one. With you."

Slowly, Laura sat up straight again. She leaned against the back of the bench and slumped a little, her eyes vacant. "You're going *back* to her?"

He forced himself to sound patient. "Not like that. Only to do what I should've done when I left her."

"So," she turned to him and fire flashed in her eyes for the first time since they took the park bench. "Let me see if I have this right. You're not the guy I thought you were. You slept with your old girlfriend and got her pregnant. And you paid for her abortion. Now you want to take a few days and find her so you can tell her you're *sorry*? The way you should've before?" She was deliberate, her anger barely contained. "Five weeks before our *wedding*? Is that right?"

"I should've done all this a long time ago." He hoped maybe her careful, drawn-out analysis was for clarity, but he figured it was more in disbelief. "I can't move forward, Laura. Not without finishing what I left behind."

Laura's anger faded and again her eyes gradually filled with tears. She stared at her knees for several seconds and then breathed deep in a way that seemed to restore some inner strength. "Okay." Her voice was tight, strained to the breaking point. "I won't stand in your way." She pressed her fingers beneath her eyes, brushing away her tears. "I only wish we hadn't sent the invitations."

It took a few heartbeats to understand what she was saying. "Wait …" Brad put his hand on her shoulder and shook his head. "I'm not calling off the wedding. Not at all."

She paused long enough to collect herself. When she finally spoke, her voice was calm, more certain. "Maybe I am."

Brad sat back against the arm of the bench. He had dreaded this conversation and planned for it, thought it through and prayed about it. But for some crazy reason he hadn't once seen this coming. "Are … you serious?"

Her single laugh lacked any humor. "What do you think, Brad? I mean … I could live with the things you just told me. If I'd known from the beginning, we could've worked through the sad pieces of your past. But there are two details I'm not sure I can see past. Not in five weeks, anyway."

He waited, but he thought he probably already knew what she was going to say.

"You lied to me. You let me believe something about you that wasn't true, and you kept up the lie since we met. Four years, Brad. That's a long time to keep up a lie. And if I could handle that, there's the other reality." More tears filled her eyes. "You're going back to her."

"Not like that. I never—"

"Please." She held up her hand. "Let me finish." Her chin trembled, twisting her face from the sorrow consuming her. "You're going back. Who's to say what happens when you find her?"

Brad was ready for this. "Emma and I barely talked the last few months we were together. Neither of us has feelings for the other. That's not what this is—"

"Stop." She cut him off again, her voice more controlled. "You said that. But if you're thinking about *her*, this close to marrying *me* … maybe your feelings for her are stronger than you think. Maybe you'll reconnect and realize you've fallen in love with her again." Laura squeezed her eyes shut and pressed her fingers to her lips for a moment. When she opened them, her look was pure heartbreak. "You've known her since fourth grade, Brad. You could fall for her again and you know it."

"I couldn't." He felt suddenly desperate to convince her. This wasn't about some rekindled love for Emma. His voice rose with the passion of his conviction. "I don't love her. I love you. Please.

Don't do this." He stood, paced three steps, and then turned and walked back to her. "I want to marry you, Laura. I'm trying to be the right guy here. I made terrible mistakes in the past and I never told you. That was wrong." His words were as intense as they'd been since the conversation began. "I couldn't go another day letting you think the wrong thing about me. I don't want to marry you when I haven't been honest." He pressed his fist to his chest. "When I stand on that altar telling the world I love only you, I don't want any reason to look back. Not one."

An occasional tear still fell on her cheek, but she was listening, holding tight to every word.

"Sure, I wish I'd done this years ago. But marrying you is a beginning. The best beginning." He thought once more about taking hold of her hand, but he wasn't sure she'd let him. Instead he took a step closer. "What kind of man am I if I don't apologize to Emma ... for what I put her through?"

"You were a teenager."

"Yes, but I handled everything wrong. I can't move on without dealing with that, without making sure she's okay." As soon as he said those last words, he regretted them.

Laura's eyes grew harder than before. "Her?"

"And you too. All of us." Brad's frustration pushed his voice louder than before. "Look, I love you and I want to marry you. Please don't call off the wedding."

She waited a long time before she answered. Then a weariness settled in around Laura's eyes and mouth. "I'll wait till you come back." Her look pierced him to the depths of his heart. "But in my mind it's on hold. Come back and look me in the eyes and tell me you're really over her. Then we can talk about the wedding."

It took a few seconds for him to process what she'd just said. Hope soared through him, hope mixed with sorrow for what he was doing to her. Without hesitating he reached for her hands, and this time she responded. He eased her to her feet and looped his arms around her waist. She was stiffer than usual, but she stayed, their eyes fixed on each other. "I'm sorry. I'm so sorry, Laura. None of this is fair to you, and I know it." He stared at the far-off skyline, waiting for strength to continue. He found her eyes again. "I'm asking for your mercy … and your forgiveness. Two things I don't deserve."

She hugged him, but somehow the gesture felt like it came from a stranger. When she released him she looked defeated but more composed. "I need time, Brad. This is a lot for one day."

His hope evaporated again. Her faith was stronger than almost anyone he knew. But her forgiveness would not come easily. That much was obvious.

"Let's walk. I want to go home." She backed out of the hug and took a few steps. She crossed her arms tightly, but she waited for him so they could walk side by side even if they didn't hold hands.

The walk back was marked by silence. She needed time. What more was there to say? When they reached the firm, Laura bid him a hasty good-bye and she was gone. Brad watched her leave, and he had the horrible feeling he was free-falling, tumbling into an abyss with no way of knowing when he'd hit bottom. He didn't blame Laura for wanting time. In some ways his actions were borderline insane. But he had to be honest both to himself and her. Otherwise the past would haunt him, distract him from everything wonderful about marrying Laura.

A realization hit him. He had to be honest with someone else too, the one man who Brad dreaded facing more than any other. If he was going to make a change, if he was to be successful in dealing with his past, then even that most difficult conversation would have to take place.

But until Laura had brought it up, there was one part of the journey ahead he hadn't wanted to think about, wouldn't let himself acknowledge. The idea that if he found Emma, he might find his feelings for her too. The possibility might have scared Laura, but now it suddenly terrified him. He could downplay Emma's role in his life, but that didn't change the reality. They had grown up together, and for most of his childhood and teenage years he couldn't have imagined marrying anyone but her.

He'd told Laura the truth this time. The whole truth. He had no plans to linger around Emma Landon or spend more time with her than necessary. He wished there were another way to make things right with her—a letter or an email. But that wouldn't allow him to look in her eyes and make sure she absolutely knew how wrong he'd been. How sorry he was. He would have to keep his guard up, for sure. As long as he did, he wanted to believe that Laura was wrong. There was no possibility he would have feelings for Emma once he found her. Even if his search took him back to Holden Beach. But Laura had reminded him of something he would have to remember as he sought to find her in the coming days, a truth he couldn't deny.

He had loved Emma first.

Fifteen

Emma missed her mom, missed her the way she hadn't in years. Maybe because it was Monday and her kids had to hear the news that Kristin Palazzo was sick. Very sick. Or maybe because she'd taken a risk and told Gavin the story she hadn't shared with anyone. Talking about what happened reminded her of everything about that time. She'd thought about it a lot since then and the truth was clearer than ever. If her mom hadn't been sick she might've done things differently. She might be a mom today.

Again the school hours passed quickly—another day closer to summer and telling her students good-bye. Emma pulled into her driveway after a day at school, the sun hot on her shoulders. She cut the engine, stepped out, left the convertible top down, and went inside. Summer. That might be it. She missed her mom more in the summer, when the days stretched out and her loneliness was sometimes unbearable.

"Hey Riley … here, boy." She watched him thud down the hall, the cats in tow like always. "Want a snack, buddy?" She patted his head and scratched behind his ears and did the same to her cats. Then she led them into the kitchen, Pied Piper of her solitary household. A dog treat for Riley and a pouch of kibble for the cats to share, but still Emma didn't feel like herself. Her mom had been her best friend in those final years after Brad left. An afternoon like this, she wanted just one more day with her. One more hour.

Emma leaned against the kitchen counter, her back to the window. She could take the missing her out to the beach, pound it out of her system with a long run. But she had a feeling running wouldn't touch the ache inside her. Not today. She poured a glass of water and made up her mind while she drank it. The cemetery. That's where she needed to go. Her mom was buried at an old tree-lined cemetery just off the interstate, this side of Wilmington. The drive would take forty minutes, and maybe it would help clear her head.

She waited until Riley finished his bone, then she hooked a leash on him. "Come on, boy … let's take a ride." She led him out to the car and he leaped onto the front passenger seat. She looped his leash around a hook on the inside of the car door and they set out. Usually Emma would talk to Riley as they drove, but not today. She was lost in a place and time where her mother was alive and Brad was still a possibility.

Halfway there she stopped and bought red roses from a roadside stand. They reached the cemetery and Emma found her familiar parking place, just a fifteen-yard walk from her mother's grave. On this side of the quiet cemetery, no one would mind if she had Riley with her. Besides, dogs were allowed as long as they were on a leash. A cement bench sat close to her mom's tombstone — a gift from Emma's grandmother. Engraved on a metal nameplate were the words, "Jean Catherine Landon — loving daughter, devoted mother." Beneath that were her mother's birth and death dates. Emma sat Riley by the bench, then she walked the few steps to the marker. The wording etched into the light gray marble was the same as on the bench.

Emma didn't come here often. With her mother's deep faith, certainly she wasn't relegated to some underground grave. She was alive in heaven — that much Emma was sure of. But being here sometimes helped the memories come a little easier. Emma stooped down and brushed a few stray grass clippings and a layer of dusty dirt off the stone.

Carefully she laid the roses on the grave. Her mom had loved flowers … red roses especially. "Mom … you should be here."

The memories called to her, surrounding her and comforting her with the peace of the familiar. As they did, everything about those years came to life again. Her mother's pale face and cheerful voice, the way the house smelled faintly of her lavender lotion when she was alive.

Emma sat cross-legged on the grass, her hand on the stone. After graduation, she attended Cape Fear Community College so she could live at home and help her mother. The cancer diagnosis had come midway through Emma's sophomore year in high school. Sometimes Emma wondered if she would've been so quick to cross lines with Brad if she hadn't been scared to death about losing her mom. At first the cancer was in her lymph nodes, but a year later it was in her colon. After that she could take swings at the disease but she was honest with Emma.

She wouldn't beat it.

Emma had no relationship with her father—a surfer her mom had met at the beach and who had left their lives forever when Emma was one. When Brad left, Emma felt the way her mother must have felt when her dad walked out. Except for one glaring difference—her mother was brave. She'd kept her baby and raised Emma on her own. The irony, of course, was that Emma had chosen the abortion—at least in part—so that everything would go back to the way it was before she got pregnant. So Brad wouldn't leave.

But he left anyway, and nothing was ever the same.

Her mom got sicker, but because of the abortion, Emma walked around in a fog, numb to the pain that consumed her. The pain of missing Brad and knowing that her baby would be one and then two. The pain of knowing she could have turned around. She could have run out of that Wilmington clinic and everything would be different.

Emma pulled her knees up to her chest. Riley was sleeping a few feet away, a low rumble of a snore coming from him. She lifted her eyes to the sky. The air was still, not even the slightest breeze to ease the humidity. In the distance, the constant hum of the interstate was the only sound. Emma stared at the grave again and sighed. The spring of Emma's college sophomore year, her mother's breathing slowed and she could no longer get out of bed without a great deal of help. Emma was at her side, hiding her tears and doing her best to stay upbeat.

"We can get you through this, Mom. Keep believing, okay?" Emma would tell her. By then she no longer talked in terms of prayer or faith. "This is a setback, that's all."

But by then, the doctor had taken her off everything except her pain medicine and sent her home. No matter how positive Jean Landon remained, no matter how great her faith, the end was near.

Emma's heart warmed as she pictured her mother in those final days. Her beautiful, strong mother. She'd never been down or afraid, never been anything but concerned about Emma. The cancer could have its way, but her mom's faith was never stronger than in her final hours. Emma could still feel the wicker chair beneath her as she sat at her mother's bedside, still smell the dank scent of death in the room and feel the shadows casting a late afternoon darkness over her mother's bed.

"Mama ..." There had never been a great opportunity to say this, but now Emma was almost out of time. "I want to tell you something."

Her mom was deathly thin, her gray complexion drawn and pinched by the disease. Even still, she found the strength to reach out and take hold of Emma's hand. "What, honey?"

Tears choked Emma's words, but she pressed through. "Thank you ... for having me. You gave me your whole life, Mama." A sob caught in her throat and she hung her head, hung it so far down that her forehead touched the place where their hands held tight. "I know … how much it cost you."

"Baby …" her mom squeezed her hand in a show of love that screamed for more time. "You made it all … worth it. You were the best daughter."

Emma lifted her head, looking long into her mother's eyes, wanting the moment to last a lifetime. But all she could see was how hard it had been for her. The long double shifts, the countless nights when she must've known how Emma sat home alone longing for companionship, the way her mother's back ached at the end of the week. All of it came rushing into that single moment, and her mom's struggle was overwhelming. "Every sacrifice, Mama. You did it all for me."

"It wasn't a sacrifice." She eased Emma's hand to her dry lips and kissed it. "I never wanted to be anything but your mother."

"I love you, Mama. You've been the very best."

"Sweet girl … I would do it all again. You made every day worthwhile." Her mother's voice was scratchy, but her smile was young and full and unaffected by the disease. A smile that defied her pain and weakness, and even her imminent death. The same smile she'd had on Emma's first day of kindergarten and when Emma learned to ride a bike and when she brought Brad Cutler home for dinner the first time.

But then her smile faded and she squeezed Emma's hand again. "I know … it's been hard. Losing Brad … Hang onto Jesus, baby."

Tears streamed down Emma's face, and she gulped back a couple of strong sobs. "Yes, ma'am."

"Can you see it, Emma?" Joy painted an unearthly expression on her face. She turned her eyes toward her bedroom window. "A place with no more death or crying. No more pain. Where every day is bright with the light from the Son?" She seemed to linger on the picture, then she turned back to Emma. "When you get there … I'll be the first to greet you. Look for me, okay, baby?"

The sobs broke free and Emma buried her head once more against her mother's shoulder. "Oh, Mama. Don't leave me. Please, don't leave." *No, God … don't take her. She's all I have. Please, God …* But even as she prayed, she knew God wasn't listening. He'd already made up His mind about her mother.

"I can see it, Emma." Her words slowed along with her breathing. "I'll … be okay. I love you, baby. Always."

"Mama, don't go …" Emma sat up, terrified, but there was nothing she could do, no one to call. Cancer had gotten the final word. "Mama!"

Her chest rose two more times and then it stopped, still for all time. Emma wasn't sure how she'd handle the moment, whether she'd faint or scream or run from the room. Instead she sat unmoving, her mother's hand still in hers, and she let her mother's voice linger in her mind again.

I'll be okay … I love you, baby … always … I'll be okay.

Her mother wasn't gone for good. She was with Jesus. She had to be, because in her final minute she could see heaven. Actually see it. Her burial and memorial service were two days later, attended by a few neighbors and friends and a couple dozen people from the church she'd been attending. The church Brad's family attended. His parents and sister were there, and at the last minute, Brad also showed up.

When they had a few minutes alone, he touched her face, his expression thick with regret. "I'm sorry. She was a wonderful woman."

Emma nodded, angry with herself for missing him so much, for being attracted to him. She wanted to ask why he'd left and why they didn't try again. Why they'd let their love die right alongside their unborn baby. But with the wind in the trees and a cool shadow hanging over the cemetery and Brad ready to head back to Chapel Hill, she could only guard her heart. "Thanks." She pulled her long dark hair back so she could see him better. *I miss you, Brad*, she thought. *You don't know how much.* But her words came out differently. "It's been awhile."

"It has." He glanced over his shoulder, clearly anxious to leave. But then he looked straight into her soul. "I think about you. About us." He pursed his lips, as if he was frustrated because there was nothing left to say. "I'm sorry, Emma. About your mom." One more quick hug and he turned and walked away.

And that was it, the last time they'd seen each other.

The losses stacked up one on top of the other. Her childhood dreams ... her baby ... Brad ... and now her mother. It was inevitable, really, but God was the next and last loss. The only thing she had left to lose. The disconnect with the Lord was twofold. First, she was convinced He no longer loved her, no longer wanted the likes of her to go around calling herself a Christian. She was a horrific excuse for a woman, her baby's blood on her hands. She could have walked out of the clinic.

The truth screamed at her as often as she'd listen.

In time it wasn't only that God wouldn't want her. She didn't want Him either. He had taken everything from her, after all. What reason was there to feign an interest in faith or prayer or Bible reading when she had nothing left to pray for?

Cloaked with pain and sorrow, Emma had done the only thing she knew to do: She poured herself into her studies. Every day was the same, and Emma learned to live and work and breathe alone. She finished at Cape Fear with her associate degree and transferred to N.C. State—thirty-five minutes away, but it might as well have been a million miles away from UNC.

With every day of learning and taking tests and writing papers, Emma knew there was only one job that would help bring life back to her soul. The job of teaching. She earned her bachelor's in education, and after a year of intense studies, she was awarded her teaching credential. At the same time, she got word from her grandmother that the beach house was hers. A block away from Holden Beach, of all places.

She interviewed for the first-grade position at Jefferson Elementary and she'd been there ever since. Survival took over as the years passed. Yes, she marked every May 15th, remembering when their baby would have been five and then six, and then seven. But gradually she did her best to rewrite the past. The abortion hadn't really been her fault. The nurse had made the appointment, and Brad hadn't been supportive. She'd had no one to turn to. Besides, abortion was legal—the decision really had been hers, right?

Whatever it took to justify the past, because justifying it was better than blaming herself. Justifying the abortion meant Emma had permission to live. The alternative meant a lifelong debt Emma could never pay—even if no one but Brad knew what she'd done.

The air was cooling, and Emma stood. For a long time she stared at the gravestone, then she took a few steps back to the place where Riley was still sleeping. But before she might sit down, she remembered another gravesite a little ways from where her mother was buried. She took one of the red roses from the ground and walked slowly across the freshly mowed grass. Riley lifted his head, but she gave him a look that told him everything was okay and he returned to sleep.

The spot was closer than Emma remembered, the marker simpler, smaller. She stood at the foot of it and crossed her arms tight around herself. Even in the heat of the late afternoon a chill passed over her as she read the name on the stone. Cassandra Rae Armijo.

The name took her back, and Emma remembered the connection the way she hadn't in years. Her first fall as a student teacher, she worked alongside another Wilmington student

—Elisabeth Armijo. Though Elisabeth was married and a few years older than Emma, the two became friends. Early in the school year, Elisabeth was thrilled to find out she was pregnant. Only one problem clouded the picture. Elisabeth's husband was in the army, serving in Afghanistan.

"Maybe you could go with me to my appointments," Elisabeth suggested. She knew Emma had no family and therefore maybe more time to help out.

From the beginning, Emma struggled with the idea—walking with Elisabeth through the stages of her pregnancy. But she agreed—both to be a friend to Elisabeth and because in some way she had always wondered what she'd cheated herself of. Emma was there through the first appointment when the doctor used a sonogram to hear the baby's heartbeat, and the sonogram when the doctor pointed out the baby's arms and legs. "It's a girl," he beamed. "Congratulations."

Elisabeth contacted her husband overseas and they named their daughter Cassandra Rae. She was an active baby, and Elisabeth called Emma often to talk about the amazing feeling of having a life growing inside her. There were times when Emma felt like her friendship with Elisabeth was a cruel trick, a way for God to rub in her face what she'd done. But then she'd remind herself that she'd had a choice. She hadn't done anything illegal, only what any teenage girl in her situation would have done.

But sometime around Elisabeth's fifth month, she began having sharp cramps. She called Emma in a complete panic. "Please … come get me. I need to get to the hospital! Please, Emma!"

She arrived at her friend's house as quickly as she could, and they were at the emergency room in no time. "Stay with me," Elisabeth's eyes pleaded with her. "I don't want to be alone!"

The doctors did what they could to stop her labor, but in the end their efforts didn't matter. With Emma holding tight to

Elisabeth's hand, the tiny baby girl was delivered later that night, stillborn.

"Can … can I hold her?" Elisabeth was weeping, exhausted from the delivery and the loss of her baby.

Emma wanted to run, wanted to scream for someone to pause the picture while she removed herself as far from the hospital room as possible. But she was mesmerized by the beautiful dead baby girl. The nurse wrapped her in a pink blanket and handed her carefully to Elisabeth.

As the doctor and nurse discretely left them alone, Elisabeth cradled the infant to her face and let her tears fall on the baby's blanket. "Little Cassandra … Mommy loves you. Someday we'll be together again in heaven. I promise you."

No matter how much she wanted to leave, or how certain she was that she shouldn't have been a part of such an intensely painful, deeply private moment, Emma stayed. Rooted to the floor and drawn by a scene that was strangely familiar.

"Here," Elisabeth extended the lifeless bundle to Emma. "Hold her … So I won't be the only one who remembers her."

Again Emma wanted to be anywhere but there, but as if her body was running on autopilot, she reached out and took little Cassandra in her arms. She stared down at the baby's tiny, perfectly formed nose and hands, at the precise detail of Cassandra's cheeks and her beautiful long eyelashes.

And right there, in a way that was impossible to deny, Emma knew the truth. She could say what she wanted to about abortion. She could repeat the rhetoric about a woman's choice and the legalities of terminating a pregnancy. But a baby was a baby, no matter what stage of development. A precious life. Holding Cassandra, Emma knew she could never again justify her actions. She had killed her baby, and she would pay for her decision the rest of her life. Abortion was not a choice or a procedure or a woman's right.

The truth was cradled lifeless in her arms.

Emma bent down and placed the rose adjacent to Cassandra's name. Emma and Elisabeth still exchanged Christmas cards, but her friend was living overseas with her husband and two boys now. Emma lightly touched her fingers to Cassandra's name. Elisabeth would be glad she'd stopped by the grave. Glad that someone remembered Cassandra.

She stood and brushed off her shorts. The trip had been good for her, the reflection a way to reconnect with her mom even for a little while. She still missed her, but not with the ache she'd felt earlier. She went back to Riley. "Come on, boy. Time to go."

He stood and stretched and she picked up his leash. On the way home she wondered again what would've happened if her mom hadn't gotten sick, if Emma had found the confidence to tell her about the baby. The answer was suddenly an easy one. With her mom's help, she would've had the baby and everything … everything would've been different.

The baby would've been more than a life saved. If Emma had given birth, the baby would've been a bridge between her and Brad. Their nine-year-old would've been in the car with them right now, and later tonight their child would've been running and playing in the sand with Riley. They would've talked about the school year coming to a close and the adventures they would take over summer break.

If she would've had someone to confide in, someone to help her raise her baby, Emma and Riley wouldn't be driving home alone. Instead she would be holding the small hand of their son or daughter, the two of them headed home to a world that could've been—to a family and a future and a life with the only guy she'd ever loved.

If only her mother had lived.

Sixteen

LAURA TOLD NO ONE ABOUT BRAD'S confession. Two days had passed and she hadn't once even considered telling her parents. Brad was headed back to North Carolina to meet with an old girlfriend about an abortion they'd shared in? Now ... with the wedding weeks away? Her mom and dad would come unglued, for sure. This was the wedding they'd been dreaming about since Laura and Brad started dating.

Her parents wouldn't be so concerned with the financial aspect of canceling the wedding — if that's what happened. But the situation was so much worse than that. Laura worried that her father might never think the same of Brad again, which would absolutely affect his future at the firm. If they broke up altogether, Brad would have to find a position somewhere else. It would be too awkward to stay. That and the fact that all three hundred and twenty guests would need to be notified, which meant everyone in the family and her parents' entire social and business circle would know about the breakup. Laura would be pitied by all of them, and by association her parents would be pitied too.

The whole thing would be an embarrassment to the family and even the firm. So, instead of sharing the truth about what she'd learned from Brad, Laura had laid low, telling her mom she wasn't up for shopping or heading into the city to check on any of the wedding details.

"I need a few days to reflect," she said at dinner last night. Both her parents had noticed her drop in enthusiasm toward the wedding, and both had asked if she and Brad were okay. "We're fine," she had said more than once. What else could she say?

But today was Wednesday and maybe it was time to talk about what happened. She had to tell someone. The shock was wearing off, and in its wake were emotions Laura had never dealt with at this level—anger and betrayal, hurt and fear. Just last week she'd thought how hurt she would be if she—like her friend, Nelly—was ever betrayed.

And now—here—that betrayal had happened.

Laura drifted through her parents' house and out onto the front porch. The manicured grass stretched out an acre on either side of the driveway, and beyond that was part of the fairway from the country club. But that wasn't where they would hold their wedding. No, the ceremony and reception for the only daughter of Randy James would be at the world-renowned Liberty House, nothing less. The Liberty House had walls of glass three stories high. It was billed as "the view with a room," because every window provided a surreal vantage of the lower Manhattan skyline, the Hudson River, Ellis Island, and the Statue of Liberty.

Her parents had spared no expense working with a well-known wedding coordinator to pull together every detail. The reception—if it happened—would be something out of a fairy tale. Tables and chairs would be covered in fine linen, and the many chandeliers gracing the Grand Ballroom would be connected by strings of tiny white lights. An entire staff decked out in tuxedoes would tend to their guests' every need.

Her dress was breathtaking, an original that seemed made for her. Locally grown white roses would blanket the ceremony pathways and sitting area and every table in the ballroom. A Manhattan baker known for his artistic wedding creations had designed their cake. The prime rib and seafood dinner was being specially put together by a team of chefs who had their own daytime cooking show over the Hudson. There would be an orchestra and a DJ, and the dancing would go late into the night. When it was over, the guests would be invited back out onto the lush lawn for a private fireworks show. It should've been the wedding of the year.

But so what?

Laura sat down in one of the gliders on the porch and set the chair in motion. Without question she would've traded it all for the certainty that her fiancé was who he'd pretended to be, for the security in knowing that his ex-girlfriend wasn't distracting him this close to the wedding. A big, glamorous show. That's all the wedding was shaping up to be, and so she'd been honest with Brad. She really did need time.

And it was that final part that pulled her up out of the chair and pushed her inside for her car keys. The Bible study was at Megan's tonight, a few miles away, and suddenly Laura wanted to be there as badly as she wanted her next breath. Her friends had seen each other through far more painful things than a failed engagement. If that's what this was. Laura had supported her friends while they each experienced their various hopes and heartaches.

Now they would be there for her.

THE BIBLE STUDY COULDN'T START OFF with her news. Laura let the others talk, while she focused on what she was going to say, how she was going to say it. The girls gathered around the coffee table in Megan and Joey's condominium. Anna, Bella Joy, and Nelly sat on the sofa. Amy had the armchair, and Megan and Laura sat on dining room chairs pulled into the room for the occasion.

"My doctor wants to run some tests on me. One of my blood tests came back a little high." Megan sounded hopeful. "I'm not worried, but … I wanted you to know."

Amy leaned over and patted Megan's knee. "It'll be fine." She looked at the others. "We'll pray."

"Thanks." Megan managed a tentative smile. "I can't afford to be off my feet. Not with four little ones running around!"

"If you need help, I'll move in!" Bella Joy grinned at Megan. "I mean it. A month … two. Whatever you need."

"If it goes that way, I'll remember that."

Amy's eyes lit up. "By the way, I have good news about the twins. They got accepted to Orange Christian Elementary! The school offered us scholarships, so my mom and I can afford it!"

"I can't believe they're that old."

"They're five." Amy's pride over her girls shone in her eyes. She was a wonderful mother, never allowing herself to sound bitter or resentful over her own shattered social life or the sacrifices she'd made so that her girls would have a great life. "Kindergarten in the fall."

Laura looked around the room and saw she wasn't the only one feeling nostalgic over the fact that Amy's daughters were already school age, and that they would be attending the same school where the six of them first met. But today Amy's mention of the twins hit Laura on another level. How would Amy feel if she'd had an abortion? Laura felt an unfamiliar hurt for what Emma Landon must've gone through. Especially if Brad left her life without saying sorry.

"Time flies by after kindergarten." Anna smiled. She rested her hand on her pregnant belly. "That's what I've always heard, anyway."

Bella Joy and Nelly listened without saying much. They didn't have kids or husbands, so this sort of talk left them on the outs. Laura felt knots form in her stomach. She could picture herself — six months from now — having more in common with them than she'd ever imagined.

After another few minutes, Megan picked up her Bible. "We were in Luke, chapter 6. The part about loving our enemies."

Laura reeled at the sudden impact of the verses. Last week the Scripture had been so many more verses. *Love your enemies … be kind to those who harm you … show mercy …* Last week those were merely tough truths that framed the existence of the Christian life. Now they were personal. Brad had hurt her, and tonight she didn't feel like loving him. Even so, she needed the Scriptures. Life was crashing in around her, and she no longer knew whether Brad was the man for her, or even how she felt about him. Only with God's wisdom and direction would she get through whatever happened in the coming weeks. She didn't have to marry Brad, but she had to forgive. She had to love — no matter what. The thought made her angry, because it wasn't fair. She hadn't done anything to cause this, and right now she didn't want to love him.

Megan was talking about how often she'd thought about last week's lesson in the days since then. "Almost like God was giving me extra practice in loving the people who are harder to be around."

"Me too." Nelly looked down at her hands. "Did you see the tabloids? My ex married his back-up singer this week."

Laura's heart sank further into her chest. Would that be her one day, hearing from her parents or through a UNC friend that Brad had married? Maybe even married Emma? A shiver ran down her arms. *How could he keep his past from me all this time,* she thought. *It isn't right, God … I don't even know him.*

Only one response filled her heart. The Scripture from Luke, chapter 6.

Megan waited until they all had their Bibles open. "Okay, so let's have Bella Joy start with Luke 6:37."

Bella Joy was a happy soul, rarely feeling sorry for herself despite her loneliness. She held her Bible up and began, "'Do not judge, and you will not be judged. Do not condemn, and you will not be condemned. Forgive, and you will be forgiven.'"

The words fell on Laura like so many rocks, but she shielded herself from them. She had a right to judge Brad. Not for his past, but for not telling her sooner.

Bella Joy continued. "'… For with the measure you use, it will be measured to you.'"

"Whew! That's a lot." Amy sat back and lowered her Bible to her lap. "I mean, that's a pretty impossible list."

"Without God." Anna's face was pensive. "It's the same lesson my husband's been teaching the kids in his youth group. It's impossible without divine help."

"But just imagine if everyone lived like that." Bella Joy moved to the edge of her seat. "Forgiving each other, not judging or condemning."

"Sounds like heaven." Nelly smiled, but there was defeat in her expression. "I'll work on that list as long as I'm breathing. I'm not sure I'll ever really get it."

Her friends' comments both challenged her and scared her. She didn't want to think about her feelings toward Brad, or the call not to condemn. He had brought this on himself, right? Surely God wasn't talking about a situation like hers or Nelly's. She paused, focused on her pounding heart. Or maybe He was. She pushed the thoughts from her mind.

Amy read the next section, "'Why do you look at the speck of sawdust in your brother's eye and pay no attention to the plank in your own eye?'"

Laura tried not to tune out. A person had to have a plank in their eye in order to be guilty of paying attention to someone else's speck. Wasn't it possible that sometimes the plank really was in the eye of the other person? She tried again to focus on the verses.

"'… You hypocrite, first take the plank out of your eye, and then you will see clearly to remove the speck from your brother's eye.'"

Megan angled her head. "Joey and I were looking at these verses the other day." Her eyes were intent. "We noticed something we hadn't thought about before. If a person had a plank in their eye, of course their vision would be off. They wouldn't see anything right. Not their brother's mistakes or their own."

A series of nods went around the room. "I never thought about that." Bella Joy stared at her Bible again. "That's good. You wouldn't know you had a plank."

Laura sat back in her chair. Bella Joy's words hit her straight on because the truth was, she wasn't without fault. What was wrong with her faith that seconds ago she'd thought herself to have such clear vision? She was critical and judgmental, especially when she was crossed. She'd never been called to forgive anything like this, and she was struggling even to imagine it. What did that say about her? She hid her shame and listened.

Nelly released an exaggerated sigh. "Okay … but what if you're in a situation like mine. Your husband walks out on you and marries someone else. Am I supposed to look the other way, love him anyway, and do everything possible not to judge or condemn him?" She let her shoulders sag forward and her voice cracked. "The jerk broke my heart."

Bella Joy put an arm around Nelly and hugged her. She didn't say anything, didn't offer a spiritual insight to the verse or another Scripture that might help enlighten Nelly to a more godly attitude. She just held her. No one else said anything either. Because that's the sort of friends they were.

And it was why after they finished with the verses, Laura felt safe enough to finally say what was on her mind. She waited for a break in the conversation.

"Brad's going back to North Carolina." Her tone more than her words told them this was not the sort of trip he'd taken the week before. The girls turned toward her, surprise registering on their faces.

"To see his parents again?" Megan was the first to seek clarity.

Laura stared at her lap. She still couldn't believe this was happening, that the words she was about to say were actually real. "We had a serious talk a few days ago. He told me things I didn't know about him." She didn't feel like crying anymore. In this moment she felt nothing but betrayal.

"About what?" Anna's tone was kind.

"His past, things I never would've believed." She took a long breath and let it out slowly. "He made choices in his past that … that really hurt his first girlfriend." She didn't want to go too much into detail. "He talked to a Christian counselor, and Brad thinks he needs to apologize. Now … before we get married." She felt the heat in her cheeks. The story coming from her was so foreign she didn't recognize her voice. "He says he can't get married until he makes things right." She paused as long as she could. "He's going back to North Carolina to find her."

By the looks on her friends' faces, she might as well have told them she was joining the circus. The silence around her built until someone needed to say something. Nelly went first. "Wow. I think I'm in shock. Of all the guys …"

"Why did he wait till now to tell you?" Megan put her hand on Laura's shoulder. "I mean, couldn't he have worked through this a year ago?"

Laura felt void of any emotion but anger. "He says it didn't hit him. Not until a week ago."

"Have you told your parents?" Bella Joy looked nervous at the idea. "They must've flipped."

"I didn't tell them. You're the only ones."

More silence. Anna shifted in her chair so she was facing Laura. "What're you going to do?"

Sorrow worked its way into the mix. "I don't know. Brad doesn't want to cancel the wedding. He says he'll take care of this and come home. We can get married like everything's fine."

"Is that how you feel?" Nelly's tone was doubtful. "Because if he lied about that, who knows what else he's lied about."

"Exactly." Laura needed this, the chance to share what happened with her closest friends. "I told him I need time. I can't decide yet."

"The whole thing sounds shady." Nelly narrowed her eyes. "I have to be honest, I wouldn't marry him. Not after what I went through in Nashville."

Anna frowned. "That's hard." She clearly wasn't as one-sided as Nelly. "Maybe it's good he's being honest now."

"But he's going back to *her*." Nelly was amazed. "The writing's on the wall, girls. It couldn't be any clearer."

Laura nodded. Yes, she loved Brad. But that was the Brad she *thought* he was. Not this uncertain guy, a guy with a dark past and a desire to see his first love — for whatever reason.

"Joey always says every story has two sides." Megan seemed to choose her words carefully. The atmosphere in the room was already tense. "Maybe you're right. You need time before you can make any decision."

"Either way, we're sorry." Bella Joy looked like she could cry. "This isn't how the last weeks before your wedding should go."

They were silent again. Amy hadn't said much, but now she gave Laura a sad look. "Everyone has a past. That's the first thing that's obvious when I meet someone. A lot of times that's where our conversations start and end."

Laura hadn't thought about that either. She pictured Amy meeting someone — at church, maybe. Going out for coffee and getting into a conversation. If she was honest, then pretty early on she needed to explain her situation. She'd been raped and she'd given birth to twin girls as a result. For a lot of guys looking for a nice Christian girl to take home to his parents, that would be the end of the story. Even though Amy wasn't at fault.

Bella Joy held her hands out to the others. "Let's pray." She looked at Laura. "We're all here for you. Whatever you need, just call."

The others added their agreement. Nelly's look said if Laura was even thinking about taking Brad back she should call. Nelly would set her straight. Laura wasn't ready to think about any of it. But she was grateful to have the truth out in the open. The way Brad probably felt now. Anna led the prayer that night, asking God to grant all of them wisdom and kindness as the situation with Laura played out. "Help us—each of us—to apply what we've learned tonight to every area of our lives. And give Laura the comfort of knowing you're with her, Father. Even in the darkest times, you're with all of us."

Laura didn't want to stay and talk with the others. She'd said all there was to say, and she needed to be alone to process their comments and prayers. But when she got home, she found her parents watching a Sandra Bullock movie, the lights low. If there'd been a way to slip by them without being noticed, she would've found it. There was none.

"Hey there," her dad was always happy. He sat a little higher in the cushy leather sofa. "How was Bible study?"

"Great." She smiled, not quite stopping as she walked past them. The house smelled warm and clean, a mix of cinnamon and vanilla. Laura tried to focus on how good it felt to be home, and not the turmoil in her soul, but her parents seemed to be waiting for more, so she nodded in their direction. "It was at Megan's house."

"Honey," her mom turned to face her. "I was hoping you might have a minute."

Laura's heart raced in response. She stopped, her smile still in place. "Sure ... what's up?"

"Well ..." her mother seemed baffled, as if it was quite obvious what was up. They were in the final stages of planning a wedding for more than three hundred people. She released a nervous laugh. "I guess I'm wondering why we aren't working on the wedding this week."

"To be honest, Brad's been quieter than usual around the office." Her dad wasn't trying to pry. He was simply close enough to the situation to see when things weren't quite normal. "Everything's okay, right? With you two?"

She hated lying. It was the very thing she was most upset with Brad about. "We're working through some things." Her smile held. "Nothing to worry about."

But even with her happy assurance, their expressions both became subtly alarmed. "What could you possibly be working through?" Her mom slid to the edge of her seat, her brow furrowed. "You mean wedding details? That sort of thing?"

Laura felt like crying. But she chuckled instead. "Something like that."

"Oh." Relief filled her eyes. "At least you're working it out."

"Brad mentioned needing Friday off, maybe spending Memorial Day weekend back in North Carolina." Laura's father frowned. "Everything okay with his parents?"

"Definitely." She found her smile again. "Just something he needs to do, I guess."

There. She hadn't lied. But still she was exhausted from pretending everything was okay when her world was falling apart around her. "I'm kind of tired." She went to them and kissed them each on the cheek. She loved them deeply. She needed them now more than ever—that part was as real as the air they breathed. "Good night."

Her father hesitated, but not for long. A smile spread across his face. "Four and a half weeks." He touched his fingers to her face. "I'm so happy for you, honey."

Tears stung her eyes, but she blinked them back before he could notice. "Thank you, Daddy. You and Mom have been amazing."

"We always dreamed of this." Her mom touched her arm. "You get some sleep. We'll talk about favors later."

Much later, Laura thought. She gave them one last smile, hugged them both, and then headed for her room. She had told herself she'd look at the Bible verses again, ask God what He wanted her to take from that section of Scripture. But she was too worn out to do anything but brush her teeth and crawl into bed. She hadn't talked to Brad more than a few times since Monday, but she knew this much:

He was flying out to Raleigh tomorrow night.

Thinking about that made her ache for missing him. Lying in bed she was not the strong, indignant young woman she'd been with her friends earlier that night. She loved Brad Cutler ... she always would. Tears filled her eyes and streamed onto her pillow until the soft cotton was damp beneath her cheek. Why was he leaving her? And what if he never came back? She didn't need anyone to weigh in on how she should feel or what she should do. No matter how much his truth hurt, and regardless of what he found back in North Carolina, an ironclad realization came over her as she cried softly into her pillow. She wanted him back, wanted to spend the rest of her life with him because she loved him.

Despite every bit of anger and betrayal, she still loved him.

Seventeen

IN THE DAYS AFTER HIS TALK with Laura, Brad hadn't needed a private detective to figure out that his mother's information was right—Emma Landon lived and worked in Holden Beach. Brad called a buddy who owned a diner near the shore and the conversation gave him everything he needed.

Emma was a first grade teacher at Jefferson Elementary, single with no children. "She has a dog. I've seen them running on the beach a few times," the friend told him. "From what I hear she keeps to herself. A quiet type, sort of like she was in high school."

Brad thanked the guy, but he stared at the phone for a full minute after the call ended. A quiet type? Emma hadn't been quiet back in the day, not before that summer. She would race him down the beach, laughing her head off, or walk into a coffee shop pretending to speak only French, muttering foreign phrases and trying to gesture her drink order until Brad had to turn away so he wouldn't bust up. It had been her idea to walk up to complete strangers and launch into a conversation about some past shared experience that never happened.

"Harry, right? From the wedding last May? We sat together." She'd smile like she'd known him forever. "What a great time." She'd carry on for a few minutes—nothing rude or intentionally harmful. Then she'd leave the poor guy beyond confused. Brad would shake his head, embarrassed for her. But she'd walk off giggling and grinning, her face turned full to the sun. The old Emma.

Living alone? A quiet type?

He packed the knowledge in his hurting heart and enough clothes for the weekend in his carry-on bag. Thursday after work he boarded the last flight from LaGuardia to Raleigh. Nothing was certain with Laura, except his love for her. That would never change—no matter what he found on the shores of Holden Beach. But Laura hadn't wanted to talk to him much these last few days. Brad took his familiar window seat and stared into the fading sunlight. He didn't blame her.

The flight gave him time to transition from his world to Emma's, to the world she'd made for herself since he'd walked away. They'd made a baby together and lost it, and they'd never found closure. Of course he needed to go back. He should've done this years ago. Another memory came to life. It was April during his senior year and all the guys were asking girls to the prom.

He and a few guys from the basketball team decided to have a little fun with the process. They worked with the school's various coaches so that when Emma and two of her friends walked into their PE class first thing that Monday, Mr. Garrison, the football coach, met them near the door. Brad and his teammates were watching unseen from the coach's office.

"You're late," Garrison barked.

Emma stopped short, the hint of a smile on her lips. "Us?"

"Yes." His voice boomed through the gym. "Drop and give me twenty. All three of you."

One of Emma's friends pointed to the oversized industrial clock on the wall, and Emma lifted her arm and showed Coach her watch. From a distance, Brad and his friends worked to keep their laughter down as Garrison shook his head. "Ten minutes early is late around here. You know that."

Gradually, between stifled bouts of laughter and outrage, the girls lowered themselves to the floor and did twenty push-ups. Emma finished first, and as she stood, Garrison grinned and gave her a note. "You passed the first test. Report to Coach Black's history class." He pointed to the door. "Hurry. You have five minutes."

The girls looked at each other, not sure if he was serious. Emma started in with a question about whether this was a joke or some new physical fitness test.

Garrison only shrugged. "Four minutes."

The guys found a hiding place at the back of Black's classroom, where the girls were instructed to stand at the front of the room and sing the first verse and chorus of "Achy Breaky Heart," and when they passed that station, they had to dance the Macarena for Coach Wilson's math class.

A trip to the gym for twenty free throws, and finally Coach Baker pulled three Wilmington High jerseys from a box. He handed one to each of the girls. Emma's had Brad's number, and in a rush the girls understood what was happening. At that exact moment, Brad and his friends walked through a side door each carrying a single long-stemmed rose.

Brad remembered how his eyes found Emma's instantly, how there was a knowing that they would hold onto this day forever, and how neither of them looked away as he walked to her. Joy and laughter shone in her pretty eyes as she took the flower and moved into his arms.

"You big dork," she whispered. "I can't make free throws."

"I know." He pressed his cheek against hers, loving the way the smell of her shampoo mixed with a hint of her perfume. They both laughed, and he leaned back so he could see her eyes again. He asked her to the prom, and slowly his laughter gave way to the dizziness he felt being near her, the intoxicating way she made him feel back then.

The memory led to others and the flight passed in a blur. His dad met him at the airport, dressed to the nines as usual. "Bradley. You doing okay?"

"Not really." He hesitated. "Scared, I guess." Now that he was being honest, he wanted to tell the truth about everything. Especially to the people he loved. "After all this time ... she must hate me."

"No." His dad shook his head. "I used to watch that girl when she was around you. She could never hate you." He gave Brad a strong hug. "You'll get through this. I know you will." He stopped and punctuated the air with his finger. "By the way, I rented you a Jeep. Thought it might be more comfortable than the truck."

As long as he lived, Brad would never completely understand his father, the kindness of the man and the unique ways he had of expressing his love. "Dad ... you didn't have to do that. Your truck would've been fine."

"That's alright. I won a rebate in a sweepstake. Only had to pay the tax for the weekend rental."

"Okay, then."

"It's a nice Jeep. Good color. Deep sort of a blue."

So there it was. Brad would return to Holden Beach in a rented deep blue Jeep, compliments of his father's sweepstakes habit. "Thanks, Dad. That means a lot. You thinking of me and all."

"Besides, I want to load up the old truck for some metal hunting this weekend. People leave all sorts of things over the holiday."

"True." Brad smiled to himself. The subject of Emma didn't come up again on the drive home or the rest of the night. His mom cooked chicken and zucchini on the Finley grill, and while Brad was setting the table he noticed a package of Kotton Kids pajamas and blankets on the china hutch. "Dad?"

"Now, Bradley." His father's conviction was unwavering. "I believe in your future. I have to support your work."

Brad normally would've laughed, teased his dad about collecting more items he would never use in the foreseeable future.

But instead he went to the small stack and touched the soft cotton. All he could hear was Laura's question. *Are you a father?*

He grabbed a fistful of the blanket and gripped it, trying to find strength in the fibers of the material. *God ... I have so much to be sorry for. Prepare Emma's heart, Father. Please. And let Laura know I still love her.*

Old Carl came up beside him. Like other pivotal times in Brad's life, his dad didn't say anything or offer a lecture on past mistakes. He merely put his hand on Brad's shoulder. "I'm here, Son." His voice was quiet, so that from the kitchen, Brad's mom wouldn't notice anything unusual. His dad gave him a couple of firm pats. "If you need me this weekend, I'm here."

Brad nodded and gave his dad a side hug. Dinner was served, and after a little conversation with his parents, he went to his old room and turned in. Tomorrow he would see Emma Landon for the first time in nine years. Would she take one look at him and turn away, or would she listen? He had the feeling she would listen. Because maybe she needed this closure as much as he did. Brad stared at the ceiling of his room, remembering. He had blocked much of the memory of that terrible Saturday from his mind, the time in the clinic, the hurt in her eyes when she came back to the waiting room. But he remembered her asking only one thing of him on the way home.

"Please, Brad ... don't stop loving me. Please don't stop."

Her cry haunted him often through the years, but he'd never found the courage to act on it. Now, though, his buddy's words came back to him. Emma Landon, living alone. A quiet type. The picture made him wonder if she wasn't still somehow in the passenger seat of that car, silently crying on the way home from the clinic that day.

Begging him to never ever stop loving her.

The memory of his cowardly actions stayed with him through the night and sadness woke him up the next morning. Emma deserved so much more than he'd given her. So much more. The day was warm, eighty with at least as much humidity, warmer than usual for the end of May. Brad dressed in jeans and a white T-shirt and spent the day poring over his yearbooks and childhood photographs.

Emma was there for every stage, every milestone.

He was sorting through a box of pictures when he found one that stopped him cold. He was in fourth grade, his chest puffed out, skinny arms and legs sticking out from an Ellis Elementary School shirt and PE shorts. Next to him was Emma, her dark hair hanging in two long ponytails on either side of her face. Between them they held either end of a three-foot section of thick, braided rope.

The memory of that day wrapped its arms around Brad and made him smile. Until that point, he and Emma had constantly fought, bickering and name-calling, chasing each other around the playground the way kids did when they had no other way to express the fact that deep down they liked each other. Monday of that week, Emma ran to the playground supervisor and complained one too many times about Brad chasing her or Brad pulling her ponytail. Some such thing.

"Fine," the supervisor had said. "I'll teach you to get along."

The rope was a trick the staff rarely used, but the supervisor must've been tired of mediating. She brought the piece of rope out from the equipment shed and called Emma and Brad to her side. "Here," she held it out. "You'll each hold one end of the rope all recess long for the entire week. Whatever you do, you can't let go of the rope."

Brad had been humiliated by the punishment. His friends snickered at him and teased him, and Emma's did the same to her. Still they had no choice but to obey. At first Brad was sure the week was going to be the longest in his life. But by Friday, two things had happened. First, he and Emma were friends.

And second, he was convinced that as long as he lived he would never let go of that rope.

The playground supervisor had taken the photo, vindication that her punishment had worked, and proof of the beginning of a friendship neither of them thought would ever end. Brad stared at the photo, brushing his fingers lightly over the piece of rope that hung between them. He thought he remembered one of the staff members giving them the rope to keep. But he wasn't sure what had happened to it.

Like everything else about him and Emma.

At one thirty he left home and drove to Holden Beach, south on Seventeen toward the Intracoastal Waterway down Seashore Road. Along the way his sadness became uneasiness and then borderline panic. What was he thinking, reaching out to her now after all these years? She would probably laugh in his face. He doubled his determination and prayed the last few miles.

One more bend in the road, and there it was. The red brick of Jefferson Elementary. *You can do this ... You have to do this.* He pulled into the parking lot and something caught his eye, something that made him hit the brakes and stare, disbelieving. There among the other cars was an older model red Cabriolet. The very same one ... Emma's car. He had planned to start at the front office and ask for a visitor's pass. Walk to her classroom, and maybe wait for her outside in the hallway.

But now that he'd found her car, his plan changed. He parked as close as he could and waited. For the first time he wondered what she'd look like, whether she still had the long, skinny, tanned legs and enormous eyes or whether time had changed that. When she saw him, would she recognize him? He hadn't changed much, not physically, anyway. Brad settled back into his seat and pictured her, a thousand times with her. Was he really doing this, really about to see Emma Landon? He felt his heart going back, getting ready, bracing itself for whatever was ahead. School was set to let out in twenty minutes.

When it did he'd be waiting.

LAURA WAS IN THE DINING ROOM with her mother, and all she could think about was Brad and his trip to North Carolina. She wasn't sure how long she could keep the truth from her parents. Brad was gone now and she hadn't talked to him since he left. Which meant what? Was he thinking that maybe she was right? That there was at least a possibility he might fall in love with … with her again? Laura's mom was at the far end of the dining room table, sorting through wedding invitation responses.

"Not a lot of regrets," she smiled at Laura.

That depends, she thought.

"I'll say this," her mom didn't seem to notice her lack of enthusiasm. Yours is a wedding no one wants to miss."

Including me. She couldn't keep her heart in one place, couldn't settle on staying mad at him or missing him so badly she wanted to call him and beg him to come home. Let the past be the past and get back to thinking about the honeymoon. Before it was too late.

From the other side of the house they heard the sound of the garage door. Laura's mother frowned. "Strange. Your father planned to work late today."

Laura looked in that direction. If anyone might notice Brad acting out of the ordinary, it was her dad. The two were as close as any father and son, and with Brad taking time off work, Laura had to wonder.

She moved casually toward the garage door, looking over her shoulder at her mother. "Iced tea?"

"Oh," her mom's eyes lit up. "I'd love some. You sure you don't want to help me open these responses?"

"That's okay." She smiled. The same worn out smile she'd been wielding since Monday. "You've got a system."

"True." Her mom looked at the neat stacks in front of her, satisfied with her efforts. "You go say hello to your father and then bring the tea here. Keep me company. I've got that PDF of the flower layout. The wedding planner says the florist wants a faxed approval by five."

Laura was pretty sure she'd scream if her mother brought up one more detail about the wedding. There was no point in all this. The wedding was almost certainly not going to happen. Not with Brad off to spend Memorial Day weekend with his ex-girlfriend.

Her dad walked inside, his briefcase in one hand and a few file folders tucked under his other arm. His steps were slower than usual, and as he saw Laura he lowered his things onto an end table and froze. His lips were slightly parted, his expression dazed, like he'd just witnessed an accident. The kind you remember forever.

"Dad?" At first she thought that's what must've happened. Someone from the firm had been killed or a fire had ripped through the building. His face was etched with that type of shock. But as she came to him, she saw something in his eyes, a compassion aimed straight at her, and suddenly she understood.

He held his hands out to her. His familiar hands—older now, but still strong—her father's hands. The hands that had lifted her and swung her around when she was a little girl and tucked her gently into bed so many nights. She took hold of them and spoke in a voice that was barely audible. "You know?"

"Yes." The kindness in his expression grew. "Brad came in early this morning. Before his flight." For a long moment he searched her eyes. "He told me everything."

Laura felt her chin quiver. She looked down for a long moment and wondered if maybe she'd faint or fall over dead from the humiliation and pain. But a truth became gradually clear as she stood there. Her father wasn't falling apart. He wasn't launching into a tirade about Brad or making sweeping statements about firing him or canceling the wedding. He was simply holding her hands and standing.

Finally, she lifted her eyes to his. She couldn't count on her shaky voice, but she tried anyway. "What now?"

Her dad ran his thumbs along the tops of her hands. "You tell me." His voice was calm, marked by a quiet strength. "Do you still love him?"

The first tear rolled down her cheek, and then another. This was the question she'd asked herself a hundred times since the talk in Central Park. And always the answer was the same. She blinked a few times, struggling. "I do."

A weary smile lifted the corners of his lips. "That's what I thought." He sighed, a sigh that told her how much he hurt for her. He eased her into his arms and hugged her the way he'd done since she was little. "Baby, I'm sorry. I wish ... I wish he didn't have a past beyond you." Her father's voice was still understanding and resolute. "I wish you didn't have to learn about it now."

She leaned back enough to see his eyes.

"The hard thing about life is, well ... everyone has a past." He put his hand protectively at the back of Laura's head and stroked her hair. "He's sorry. I think you need to consider that."

Everyone has a past. The same words Amy had said at Bible study. Another trail of tears made their way down her face, and she nodded, dabbing at them. What would she do without her father? She had thought her parents would be furious if the wedding appeared to be in question. So much of what they'd paid for included nonrefundable deposits. Then there was the embarrassment factor. But here ... here her dad was extending grace and understanding to Brad, and to Laura—a way to survive.

"What about Mom?" Laura managed to say the words.

"I'll talk to her. She'll be upset, but we'll get through this." He leaned in and kissed her cheek. "We all will."

Laura wanted to be sure he understood. "He could ... go back and fall in love with her again. It's possible."

"I know." Again her dad didn't waver. "We'll ask God to show all of us the truth—whether this wedding should go on or not. And we'll get through it."

She sucked in a quick breath and hugged him tight, overwhelmed by his unconditional love and understanding. Her dad was right. They would pray for Brad, for his time in North Carolina, and for wisdom—so that Laura would know whether she should marry Brad or not when he came home.

If he came home.

She buried her face into her dad's shoulder. How could any of this be happening? Why hadn't Brad told her sooner, and how was he going to feel when he found Emma? She squeezed her eyes shut. She was glad about one thing. Brad had gone to her father and told him the truth, which was the right thing to do. He had saved Laura from having to tell them, and for that she was grateful. She winced trying to imagine Brad going to her father, telling him the whole story about Emma and the baby. The abortion.

"You okay?" Her dad's words soothed her jagged soul.

She nodded, but she stayed in his arms. Her heart might be broken, and the coming weeks might be the worst in her life. But she would have the love of God, and the love of her friends and family. Her father had proven that much.

Whatever happened next, that would have to be enough.

Eighteen

THE LAST DAY OF SCHOOL WAS never easy. Emma dreaded it almost from the time she stepped foot into her classroom each September. Nine months together and the kids went from darling straight-backed strangers to boys and girls who would run up and hug her around the waist when they saw her. This year was worse, because Kristin was supposed to join them today.

Emma had been by to see the teenager yesterday, but she was still in intensive care, still in a coma clinging to life. Her mother mentioned once more that they were trying to be hopeful as they waited for a heart for transplant. But she admitted that even if they located a heart, the surgery would be very difficult given her failing condition.

"Her doctor asked us to be ready," Kristin's mom whispered as the visit came to an end. "But God can work miracles." She gripped Emma's arm, her desperation tangible. "As long as we have her, we have to trust in that."

With all the grief in her heart, Emma wanted to believe for a miracle the way Kristin's mother believed. But if God were going to rescue Kristin, why did He let her slip into cardiac arrest in the first place? The facts screamed the truth—Kristin was dying. And the possibility cast a pallor over everything about this afternoon's last-day activities.

A few of the children asked about the gift Kristin was working on and whether she'd finished it and how Emma was going to get it now that school was out. Emma assured them Kristin would finish the project once she felt better. What else could she say?

Little Frankie came up to the front of the classroom before lunch and put her delicate hand on Emma's arm. "Teacher … is Kristin coming to the party?"

Emma glanced to the top of her desk, to a framed wallet-size photo of Kristin. "No, sweetie." Emma smiled and looked straight at Frankie. First graders didn't need a lot of details. "Kristin's still sick."

"Oh." Frankie's face fell. "I wanted to give her the picture I made for her." If anyone understood illness, she did. "I asked God to make her better."

Emma took hold of Frankie's hand. How long before life's disappointments created disbelief in this little angel? Two years? Five? When it happened, Emma would only say she couldn't blame the girl. But for now her sweet faith was so pure and innocent it brought tears to Emma's eyes. She grabbed a sharp breath, fighting for control. "Keep asking Him, okay?"

The concern in Frankie's face lifted and the beginning of a smile lifted the corners of her lips. "Okay."

Lunch that day was a pizza party, chaperoned by the five mothers who'd helped all year. Frankie's mom was one of them. Emma waited until they were alone near the food table before she came up to her and lowered her voice. "I saw new bruises on her arm." Emma gathered a few dirty cups, trying to look busy. Frankie would pick up on the seriousness of their conversation otherwise. "How's she doing?"

A weary shadow fell over the woman's face. "She won't be out much this summer. But the doctor's working with a new medication." A tentative smile broke through. "He's hopeful. It could help her quality of life quite a bit."

Emma felt the slightest encouragement. "Let me know if there's anything I can do."

In the final hours of the day, Emma presented the kids with the storybooks they'd been working on for the last month. A self-publishing company had bound the books and laminated the pages for the students, so this was a moment they'd been looking forward to all year.

"Mine looks cool!" A little boy waved his book at Frankie. "I drew the coolest car on the cover."

Frankie threw back her shoulders, not to be outdone. "I have two cars on mine!"

"They all look nice!" Emma laughed, one of the first of the day. "Let's look through our books. Then you can share them with the other boys and girls. We left blank pages at the back of each book so you can collect signatures from your classmates."

A round of cheers rose from the students, and even as they read the books, they talked and giggled and shared their stories with their neighbors. Emma savored the sound, her students no longer the timid children who had walked through the door of her classroom the first day of school. They were friends now, a family of sorts. Together they'd shared reading groups and making feathers for their Thanksgiving turkeys. They'd found friendships as they sang "O Little Town of Bethlehem" in the Christmas concert, and they worked side by side decorating Valentine's shoe boxes. Recently they could barely contain their excitement over the secret ceramic Mother's Day gifts they finished a month ago.

Now all they could think about was summer. They would move on with a quick hug and a happy wave, and that would be that. Only Emma would know the ache of saying good-bye, the certain knowledge that years from now, she would only be a slight mention in a conversation about elementary school. *Remember first grade? Who was our teacher?*

She looked from one face to the next, holding onto the moment. Every year on this day it was like saying good-bye to her own children. If she'd had children. *I might've been a good mother,* she thought. But as soon as the idea flitted through her mind, she quickly dismissed it. She didn't deserve to be a mother, not now or ever. What mother could walk through the doors of an abortion clinic and—

"Teacher," Frankie stood beside Emma's desk again. She lifted a small flowered gift bag and handed it over. "This is for you. 'Cause it's the last day."

Emma took the bag, her heart full. "Thank you, Frankie. That's very kind."

"You can open it." She grabbed a quick breath, too excited to slow down. "It's not like Christmas … when you have to wait."

Frankie's mom watched from a short distance away, giving the moment to her daughter. Everything about the child was endearing. Emma pulled the tissue paper out of the bag. Inside was a CD titled *Restored* by Jeremy Camp, a singer Emma had only vaguely heard about from Kristin Palazzo.

Frankie was bouncing up and down next to her. "My mom picked it out! Do you like it?" She glanced over her shoulder at her mother. "You got a card too. Inside the bag." She leaned in close, her head on Emma's shoulder. "The CD has a pretty picture on the front, right, Teacher?"

"Yes, it's so pretty! Thank you, honey." Emma stared at the CD cover. The title was intriguing. She opened the card and pulled the note from inside. On the left Frankie had written, *I love you, Teacher*. On the right, Frankie's mother wrote, *Your special class-helper Kristin once told me that this was her favorite CD. We're all praying for her recovery, but I thought this might help you feel closer to her.*

Emma blinked back tears and gave Frankie's mom a long smile. The woman's eyes were damp as well. Emma sighed and tucked the card and CD back into the bag. "This is very special." She hugged Frankie. "It's the best gift ever."

"That's what I said!" Frankie's eyes shone with limitless joy. She gave Emma a final hug and returned to her table where she sat down, careful not to bump her leg on the table. After years of bruising, Frankie knew her limitations.

The last hour flew by and a few times Emma caught herself watching the clock, willing it to slow down or fly in reverse. Willing the school year to include one more day with this class of kids. Ten minutes before it was time to go, Emma had the kids come to the front of the room and sit cross-legged on the floor. She found the box of last-day surprises at the side of her desk and she set it next to her as she stood and faced them.

"I always like to take a few minutes at the end of the last day to say good-bye," she smiled at each of them, moving her gaze slowly from one child to the next. A few of the girls already looked teary. "You have been a wonderful class. I've watched you learn and grow and become friends with each other. Even as you move on, you are always welcome here. You can come back anytime and tell me hello." She touched her hand to her chest. "In my heart, I know you'll have a wonderful summer, and I know you'll do very well next year in second grade." Her own eyes were brimming now. "But I hope you remember your time here, your days together in our first grade class."

She lifted the box and tucked it beneath her arm. "I have a gift for each of you. But please don't open it until you get home." Then she passed out the gifts—one for each child. They were small, stapled-shut party bags containing a few pieces of candy, a colorful pencil, and an eraser. But the best item in the bag was a custom bookmark Emma had made for each boy and girl. The bookmark was laminated with a photo of Emma and that particular student.

"Okay." She looked briefly at the clock. Two minutes. She motioned for the children to stand. "Everyone get in a circle."

The boys and girls did as she said. They were more subdued now, happy about summer but aware as best they could be that something special had come to an end. Frankie gave her an extra-sweet smile and so did several others. Emma sniffed, struggling for control. "Alright. Group hug!"

Emma had done group hugs with the class before, so they knew the drill. Everyone put their arms around the shoulders of the student next to them, and together they moved in to the center of the circle, giggling over this one last favorite routine.

"Here we go." Emma savored the moment. "One … two … three …"

Then together the children and Emma shouted one final word. "Hug!"

With that, the bell rang and Emma asked the children to line up at the back door, the one that led outside. One at a time, the boys and girls filed by her, some stopping to hug her, and others giving her a grin or a high five. When it was Frankie's turn, she held onto Emma longer than the others. "I'll come visit you next year, okay?"

"Okay, sweetie." Emma wiped discretely at her cheeks, smiling big to hide her sorrow.

Finally they were gone and Emma sat back at her desk. The silence surrounding her was deafening, very different from the silence at this time on other days. This was the sound of summer and second grade and the sadness of knowing another year was behind her.

After a while, she stood and walked the perimeter of her room, looking intently at the walls of her classroom, walls decorated with the efforts and achievements of an entire school year. All of it would have to come down, but not now. She could come back after Memorial Day weekend and spend a few days clearing out the room, cleaning it and readying it for the coming fall. For now, she would go home, change into her shorts and a T-shirt, and take Riley for a run. Then she'd try to imagine how on earth she was going to spend the next few months.

Emma stood slowly, gathered her purse and a file with paperwork she needed to fill out on behalf of each child. A supplementation to their report cards, with data from standardized tests and various writing assignments they'd finished that year. Then, without looking back, she stepped out into the playground area and locked her classroom door behind her.

The children had been gone for twenty minutes, so the parking lot was empty except for a dozen teachers' cars. The familiar path felt longer this time, the one that ran along the side of the school and toward the parking lot. She was halfway to her car when she saw a blue Jeep parked near her own. Leaning against the front grill was a guy who seemed to be watching her, staring at her. He had his hands in his pockets, one foot up on the bumper.

Emma slowed her pace. Was he a husband or boyfriend of one of the teachers? Maybe, because there was something familiar about him. His build or the way he held himself. Something. She looked behind her and to the left, at the school's main entrance. She was the only one leaving, and still his attention seemed completely on her.

She kept walking, and as she got closer, she shaded her eyes and squinted in his direction. He straightened and took a few steps closer, away from the Jeep. Only then, as she came near enough to make out his face, did she stop, unable to breathe or move or do anything but stare because … because this wasn't possible. He had moved on after college, wasn't that what she'd heard? That he was working for some big firm in New York City, right?

So how in the world was Brad Cutler standing thirty yards away?

She felt herself start to shake and she wasn't sure whether to turn around and run or keep walking. She half hoped he was nothing more than a product of her overactive imagination, and that maybe if she blinked hard enough he would disappear. But another part of her wanted to run to him before he did. Slowly, almost robotically, she kept walking.

He took another step toward her, and he shaded his eyes. She was close enough now that she could see his expression, his eyes, and how not once did they ever leave hers. No matter how many years had passed, she could read his look. Without saying a word he was telling her the same thing her eyes had to be telling him. That seeing each other now was proof they had not forgotten — not each other or the time they'd shared, or what it felt like to be in a moment like this.

She set her things down near her car and continued toward him, until she was just a few feet away. For a long time she didn't say anything. It was enough just to convince herself this was really happening, that Brad Cutler was really standing in front of her, his eyes as blue as ever, his look still enough to take her breath. Emma had no idea why he was here, but she could do nothing to stop the attraction she still felt for him.

Brad took another step closer. "Hi."

"Hey."

He didn't blink. "It's been … awhile.

A breathless laugh came from her. "Yeah." She looked away, but only for a few seconds. "You could say that."

There was an awkward few seconds, where Emma thought maybe Brad was going to hug her, but he stayed his ground. "I drove over from my parents' house. Flew in yesterday."

A terrible thought hit her. "Your parents …?"

"They're fine. It's not that."

She felt a puzzled look come over her. "So …?"

He let out a frustrated breath and turned away, searching the area almost as if he were looking for answers. Finally he turned back at her, and the sadness in his eyes was so rich and deep, it colored his expression. "I need to talk to you, Emma."

Her knees shook and again she felt the warring impulses—to run the other way or to run into his arms. He wasn't making sense. He'd flown in without calling, without warning, so that he could talk to her? "I … don't understand."

"It could take awhile." He raked his fingers through his still-blond hair. "Have dinner with me tonight?"

Emma had no plans, but in some ways she wanted to tell him no. She was busy now and she'd be busy the rest of her life where he was concerned. He couldn't break her heart and leave it for dead, then walk back into her life without warning. Whatever his reason. But this close, her senses were consumed by him. It was all she could do to hold her ground. She angled her head, looking past his eyes and straight to his heart. "Why?"

"I told you." His tone was thick with compassion. "I need to talk."

She hesitated, but her decision was already made. How could she tell him no? "I have to go home and feed my dog."

An intrigue passed over his expression, as if he wanted more information about her dog and her life and who she was now. But the moment passed and he crossed his arms, his legs anchored shoulder width. "Meet me?" A plea filled his voice. "Paradise Café on the beach? Five o'clock?"

That gave Emma an hour. She was curious now, wondering what was so important he would fly to North Carolina and drive here to ask her to dinner. Or maybe she'd passed out leaving her classroom and this was some strange, delusional dream. She blinked, but Brad was still standing there. "Okay. Five o'clock."

The awkwardness was there again. "Emma …" Brad uncrossed his arms, and once more it seemed like maybe he was going to hug her.

But before he could move a step closer, she backed away and held up her hand in a brief wave. "See ya." Then she turned and walked to her car. She opened the back door, set her things inside, and climbed behind the wheel. His eyes were still on her ... she could feel them. But she wouldn't look as she started her engine and drove off. She needed time to sort through her frantic emotions, time to collect herself before she did something she never expected to do again in her life.

Have dinner with Brad Cutler.

Nineteen

BRAD FOUND A QUIET OUTDOOR PATIO table at Paradise Café a half hour before Emma was due to meet him there. The patio would be full in a few hours, once people had time to go home and change clothes for dinner. This was one of the only restaurants right on Holden Beach, and it was popular with the locals. At least it was that long-ago summer.

But for now it was empty. A slight sifting of sand blew across the cement patio, the white metal tables and chairs worn and wobbly. The carved wooden sign in the back window of the café read, "No shirt, no shoes, no problem." The mantra of the beach crowd. A salty breeze drifted up from the water where it competed with the tinny PA system. Alan Jackson was singing about it being five o'clock somewhere.

Not yet, Brad told himself. *Soon, but not yet.* Five o'clock. When Emma would be here.

He sat with his back to the restaurant, his face to the beach. He needed this time because seeing her again had taken his breath, made him dizzy and angry with himself and full of guilt and regret. He could barely think straight until he climbed back into his rented Jeep and drove toward the shore. Even then all he could do was picture her, the way she looked now.

Emma Landon.

Brad leaned back in his chair and gripped the metal arms. He had memorized that first minute, the way she looked walking out of the building, and how he had known—absolutely known—it was her as soon as she rounded the corner. She wore cropped pink pants, a white shirt, and white sandals. Her dark hair was pulled back, the way she'd often worn it when they were dating. From a distance she didn't look any different than she had back in high school, and for a few seconds he was eighteen again, and she was meeting him at his car.

But as soon as she stopped he knew she was on to him. Their eyes held while she stared, almost demanding to know why he was there, what in the world had brought him. Then gradually she walked toward him. As she drew near he could make out her eyes more clearly. Her beautiful hazel eyes. Something was different about them, a greater depth. Or maybe she'd always had that faraway look, the look that warned a guy he could get past a lot of layers without ever coming anywhere near the vicinity of her heart.

Neither of them said much, because clearly the shock was there for both of them. Brad could barely think for the questions assaulting him. What they'd shared was rare and special, so what had happened? How could he have taken a treasure like Emma Landon and treated her like trash? Why had he walked away without ever telling her he was sorry?

And how come she was still so beautiful?

He wanted to rush ahead with his apology, but the timing was wrong. Her eyes were guarded, and she hadn't come closer than a few feet from him. No happy hug or lighthearted smile. The moment was as sad and lifeless as the one they'd shared the last time they were together—in the cemetery after her mother died.

Brad squinted at the water. A flock of seagulls hovered over the water diving at what must've been a school of fish. Their cries mixed with the pounding surf and the hum of traffic on the highway above the stretch of sand—the familiar sounds of Holden Beach. He lifted his eyes to the blue above the horizon.

Why, God ... why am I here? Maybe I should've sent her a letter and called it good.

Son, remember, anyone who knows the good he ought to do, and doesn't do it, sins.

How does that make sense? Brad shaded his eyes with one hand and rubbed his temples. The answer wasn't really an answer. It was the Bible verse that sat on his desk, the one that had convinced him to come. But was his being here really a good choice? Laura was back home worried that he was having cold feet about the wedding, or worse—that he didn't love her. But he did love her. He missed her terribly and wished he could have a quick dinner with Emma and be on the next flight home.

But none of this was going to be fast or easy. So was that really good for anyone? If he was going to pick at the wounds of the past, would that only make the scars worse? *God, I want to leave. Forget I ever saw her. I need to be with Laura, not here on the beach a world away.*

Be still and know that I am God, my son. You can do all things through my strength.

Brad leaned forward and planted his elbows on the hot surface of the round, wrought iron table. Was that really God's voice answering him? Or was a part of him merely looking for one last weekend with Emma Landon before he promised his life to Laura? He thought about that and found no truth in it. None whatsoever. This wasn't about seeing Emma. It was about making things right with her. If there was one thing he'd learned from seeing her earlier, it was this—she was still hurting. Like his friend had told him, she seemed quiet and distant—nothing like the happy, carefree girl she'd been before that one summer.

He stared as far out across the ocean as he could. *How do I know, God, that I'm supposed to be here? Help me be part of the solution for Emma ... for both of us, please, God.*

Leave your gift at the altar, Son ...

What? Brad fought his frustration. The answer that whispered across his soul wasn't clear, if it really was an answer. Leave his gift at the altar? But how did that apply to his decision to come to North Carolina? He would have to look up the words later in the back of his Bible. He'd brought it, but it was at his parents' house.

He checked his cell phone. Four fifty-five. He angled his chair so he could see the restaurant door, the one that led to the patio. What must she be thinking? It was the last day of school, so she probably had a lot on her mind already. Then she comes out to the parking lot to find him? Was she hurt by him for showing up unannounced? Had she agreed to come to dinner so she could tell him off, once and for all?

A pit formed in his stomach. Whatever happened at dinner, the conversation wouldn't be easy or marked with laughter. The pain of going back was about to begin. That's why he was sitting out here as close to the sand as possible. He wore sunglasses, but when the conversation started, he planned to remove them and look at Emma with honest eyes. He only had one chance to tell Emma Landon how he felt.

When that happened, the sunglasses would have to go.

EMMA PULLED INTO THE CAFÉ PARKING lot and checked her look in the mirror. She could hear her heartbeat, and she wondered if she was crazy. She could've easily told Brad she wasn't interested. He could go home to his parents' house and enjoy a holiday weekend with them. After so many years of Brad's silence, Emma had nothing left to say.

But being near him reminded her of every time she'd missed him over the years. The way she still missed him. And like everything else, seeing him reminded her of their baby. She thought about how long she'd carried the hurt of what had happened between them.

Nine years. Every day. Every single day.

Her life had moved on, and she tried her best to live in the moment. But their baby remained in the shadows, a constant presence, there in Emma's mind the way the date or day of the week was there. She didn't go through the hours reminding herself constantly that this was Friday. It simply was Friday. And that fact stayed subtly with her, coloring the background of everything else about the day.

It was like that with their baby.

Emma slipped her sunglasses on and blinked back tears. This wasn't the time to cry. That would come later. For now she needed to face Brad and see why he was here. Did he feel the same way she did? Was he mourning a loss they could never resolve, never make peace with? Or was he only curious about her life, and what time had changed along the way? She wore the same thing she'd worn to school that day, but her dark hair was down now, long loose layers that hung around her face and shoulders. She wore a hint of perfume and she'd retouched the light makeup around her eyes.

She was partly angry at herself for making even a little effort to look nice, for wanting to be pretty again for Brad Cutler. But if she was having dinner with him, she wanted him to struggle with the reasons why he left her. Another possibility existed. What if he had come looking to rekindle things? Then her efforts were important because they would tell him what she wasn't ready to admit to herself. That she would take him back again. She would always take him back.

His rented Jeep was parked a few spots away from hers, so he was already inside. She steadied herself and headed for the front door.

"Looking for someone, miss?" A tall beached-out teenager with a pierced brow grinned at her. "Because if you're alone I'll sit you in my section."

Emma gave him a polite smile. "I'm meeting someone."

"Try out back." He winked at her. "If he doesn't show up, I'm here."

"Thanks." Emma was vaguely used to guys hitting on her. She wasn't looking, so their advances meant nothing. She stopped at the back door and saw him, sitting alone at a table shaded by a weathered, oversized umbrella. Otherwise the patio was empty. She sucked in a quick breath and pushed her way through the door. He turned at the sound and she hesitated.

He was on his feet immediately—something he hadn't done as a teenager. He stepped out from beneath the umbrella and pulled out the chair across from him, so they'd be facing each other, the beach on one side, the back of the restaurant on the other. She sat down and he eased the chair in beneath her.

"Thanks for coming." He sat down and situated himself. The umbrella seemed to block out the feel of the restaurant, creating a sense that they were out on the beach, sharing a moment meant for just the two of them. "I'm sorry it was so last-minute."

A waiter descended on them almost immediately. They ordered sweet tea and chicken Caesar salads. The conversation stayed light at first. Brad talked about the products he'd been working on in Manhattan, and his dad's new fascination with the metal detector. The drinks came, and Emma mostly listened. When the salads were delivered, Brad told the waiter they were fine. They needed some time alone. He gave a happy shrug as he left. Brad waited a few seconds, then he turned to her, his words full and deep. "I … wasn't sure you'd show."

Emma waited, wondering if she would ever catch her breath as long as she was sitting across from him. She gripped the chair arms and studied him through her tinted sunglasses. "I was curious." She let the salty air wash over her face. *Relax, Emma,* she told herself. *He's just passing through town. Nothing more.* But her grip was so strong her knuckles were white. "Why now?"

He leaned his forearms on the table, closer to her than before. But he turned toward the water and for a long time he stayed quiet. She waited, because it was his turn. She owed him nothing. No explanation, no description of her life or her time since he'd walked away. He was the one who showed up ... let him do the talking. She studied him, his hands and arms, the toned muscles that showed through his rolled-up Carolina blue button-down shirt. He was still striking. Still the Brad Cutler who had stolen her heart on an elementary school playground a lifetime ago.

Finally he removed his sunglasses and set them at the center of the table. He leaned back in his chair and faced her, looking straight into her soul the way he'd always been able to do. "I'm engaged. I wanted you to know."

The ground beneath her seemed to open up and swallow everything but her body. At least that's how she felt. Like she was no longer connected to herself. What had he said? Had he really told her ... he was engaged? Brad Cutler was getting married. Adrenaline flooded her veins and her mouth went suddenly dry. For way too long she sat there, not remembering how to exhale, not feeling her heartbeat. Was this why he had come? To share this bit of cruel news with her? She finally inhaled sharply, and as she did she stood and walked to the cement wall at the edge of the café patio. Carefully, she stepped over it and sat down facing the beach. He was engaged? His news hit her in a crashing series of emotions, one with each set of waves that pounded the distant shore. She could feel him sitting there behind her, his ambiguity. She heard him slide his chair out, and then hesitate and slide it back in. Clearly he had no idea how to handle her reaction. Shock gave way to a fury Emma hadn't known since the week he told her good-bye. She wanted to grab her purse and leave. How dare he come here now and tell her this? She'd been fine, living her life, getting on without him. Why come now?

Her anger finally found the upper hand. She eased her legs back over the wall and returned to her seat. The crashing surf was nothing compared to the pounding of her heart. "You're engaged?" She sounded mystified. "That's why you came here? To tell me that?"

"No." He looked helpless, like he wanted to come around to her side of the table and hold her. But he stayed seated. "I needed to talk to you. I couldn't … I couldn't move on otherwise."

So that's what this was? Some sort of conscience-clearing exercise? She felt the sting of tears, and she gritted her teeth. "Maybe I don't want to talk."

"I can respect that." He seemed nervous — not at all normal for the unflappable Brad Cutler. He stared deeply into her eyes. "Please, Emma. Let me have this time. I feel like … we both need it."

The last thing she wanted to do was cry. He didn't deserve her tears or her time. But she stayed, her cheeks hot. Not because he asked her to stay, but because something he'd said had struck a chord. Maybe … maybe this was something they both needed. She forced herself to take calm breaths, and gradually the shock wore off and the threat of tears lessened. *Deal with it, Emma. Stay strong.* Brad was getting married. He wasn't here looking to start something new with her.

She reached into her purse, pulled out a hair band, and caught her hair up in a ponytail. Then she settled back into her chair, still fighting for composure. "When … when's the wedding?"

"Soon." Brad sounded defeated, like maybe he, too, was doubting his reasons for being here. "June 26."

Emma felt another ripple of shock. "Four weeks? You're getting married in four weeks?"

"I am."

A sound more disbelief than laughter came from her and she fought the urge to stand up again. Instead she gripped the chair arms once more and stared at him. "Your fiancée's okay with this? With you being here?"

"No." His eyes filled with a painful honesty. "I told her the truth. That I had to come."

"What … she's home working on wedding plans?"

Brad looked wounded, like she'd kicked him in the gut and now he was struggling to stay upright. "I'm not sure what she's doing. There might not be a wedding after this. I don't know."

Emma's head was spinning. Nothing Brad said was lining up. He was getting married in four weeks, but here he was, sitting across from her on Holden Beach. What did that say about his relationship with his fiancée or his feelings from their long-ago yesterdays? "Why, Brad?" Her voice was choked again with angry tears. For her, for the past they shared. For Brad's fiancée. "Why now?"

"Because," Brad's chin quivered, and his voice broke. He pinched the bridge of his nose, fighting for control. It took awhile for him to find the words, but finally he looked into her eyes again. "I can't start that chapter … until I finish this one."

For a brief instant, Emma wondered if he was going to mention their baby, if he would acknowledge the life they'd created, the life they'd lost. But he didn't.

He reached out his hand, desperation written into his expression. "Please, Emma. Give me this weekend. God alone brought me here. There are so many things I need to say."

Emma kept her hands to herself. She could feel her heart ripping apart. She watched him, the sorrow in his eyes, and some of her anger faded. However misguided, he wasn't here only for himself. He believed they both needed this time, and maybe they did. Maybe he was having doubts about his fiancée and he needed to find Emma to know whether he should move ahead … or find his way back.

She wanted to ask him if he truly loved her, this other woman he'd fallen for. The one he was about to marry. But she couldn't bring herself to say the words. She didn't want to know anything about her. Brad's fiancée. Not her name or where she lived or how they met. None of it. Maybe Brad was right about the chapters. Emma had loved him first, and if he needed this weekend to know whether he could move ahead, then she could give him that much. Maybe it would take that for him to see what he'd walked away from. If she did give him this time, she wouldn't ask questions about his fiancée. Brad was here now, where he belonged to her. Only her.

He still had his hand stretched out toward her, and suddenly she couldn't stop herself. The emotions were too strong, the memories too great. She slid her hand across the table and allowed his fingers to take hold of hers. His touch was electric and mind-numbing all at the same time. Because this was Brad Cutler across from her, his hand, the hand she'd held a thousand times, holding tight to her fingers once again. His eyes never left hers. "Please, Emma. Can we have this?"

Her words failed her, so she nodded and clutched his hand tighter than before. Then, drawing on all the strength she could summon, she released his fingers and withdrew her hand back to her lap. "When do you fly home?"

"Monday night."

His answer stood like the edge of a cliff in her mind. Monday night. Three days. Seventy-two hours to let Brad tell her whatever it was he wanted to say, to remember with him and allow her heart to find him again. He wasn't married yet, so maybe he was here because he still loved her. Emma hated feeling that way, because somewhere his fiancée was probably devastated by his trip here. But if he was going to marry her, Brad was right. They needed time now. After this they couldn't go back, couldn't have a weekend like this. Whatever they needed to say to each other, they would have to say it over the next three days no matter how much heartache it caused.

Because almost certainly they wouldn't have this chance again.

Twenty

BRAD TRIED TO EAT HIS SALAD, but his appetite was gone. Telling Emma about his engagement was harder than he had imagined. But at least he knew this much—Emma wasn't going to run away. She was giving him the weekend, which meant he could talk about the baby and make his apologies later. Tomorrow maybe.

For now he wanted to find common ground, at least. He wanted her to know he cared about how she was now, who she'd become. Holding her hand—however briefly—had bridged the distance between them, but it had done nothing to dim the hurt. With everything in him he wanted to take her in his arms and soothe away the sadness for both of them. Now that he was with her, he could see that she wasn't okay. The choices they'd made together had haunted her and changed her and left her broken. Whereas he had run from the past, allowing first his college days, then his relationship with Laura to cover up the damaged pieces of his soul ... she had done nothing of the sort. At least that's how it seemed.

"So you're a teacher." He smiled, wanting their time together to be marked by more than sadness.

"Yes." She kept her sunglasses on, not letting him in. "First grade."

"That's what I heard." He poked his fork around in his salad. "I remember how good you were with my little cousin. You were always good with kids."

She looked at him for a long time, but she said nothing. He'd only been making polite conversation, searching for a connection point. Her reaction was strange, not what he expected. Was she thinking about ... about what happened between them? He wasn't ready to ask. In the silence that followed, she ate a few bites of her salad and he did the same. Was this how their time together would be? Marked by awkward moments and misunderstandings?

He asked her about a few of the friends they had in common, including the buddy of his who now lived in Holden Beach. That part of the conversation lasted through dinner, and finally it was time to go. He thought about asking her to walk along the beach with him, but he sensed she was still processing the news of his engagement. Still wondering about his intentions. He didn't have the energy to get into it now. He needed to get back to his parents' house and talk to Laura. Before it got too late.

He paid the bill and they walked out to the parking lot together. The feel of her beside him — even though they weren't touching — was familiar and alluring. More than he wanted to admit. At her car, he slid his hands in the back pockets of his jeans and searched for the right words. "Thanks again. For being here." He kept his distance intentionally. Earlier he'd wanted to hug her, to create a bridge from yesterday to the here and now. But here he wasn't sure a hug would be good for either of them.

She opened her car door and set her purse and sunglasses inside. For the first time since dinner he could see her eyes. They were marked with both hurt and uncertainty, and she seemed in a hurry to go. "So ... what's next?"

"I can meet you here tomorrow. Your house or at the beach."

Emma looked out toward the beach for a moment. "No." She narrowed her eyes, as if she were seeing something far-off. "Where Dolphin meets Ocean Boulevard. Through the houses, there's a wall near the bluff." She glanced at him. "I can meet you there."

"Okay." He knew the place. His buddy had said she lived near the beach, but clearly she wasn't giving him that information. Not now, anyway. "What time works for you?"

"I have paperwork to finish up in the morning. How about three o'clock?"

Brad hid his disappointment. He had hoped to spend the whole day with her, but then … there wasn't really a reason why he needed so much time. He nodded, and again he resisted the impulse to hug her. "Three it is." He didn't hesitate. No sense making things awkward between them. They both said good-bye and climbed into their separate cars.

A minute later Brad was back on the road, headed home to Wilmington. The sun was setting, casting orange and blue light over the roadway and taking him back—the way everything about Holden Beach did. Even this drive. He remembered the first time, when he and Emma had gone too far. The ride home was silent, awkward. Much like the conversation over dinner had been tonight.

He rolled down the window and breathed in deep, the warm Carolina air filling his Jeep and his senses. What was Laura doing right now? Certainly she had talked to her dad, found out that he knew the truth. Walking into his office and talking to him had been one of the toughest things Brad had ever done. But there was no way around it. If he was going to take responsibility for his actions, he had to tell Randy James what he was doing.

Brad thought about their conversation. He'd expected Laura's father to be shocked and then angry—about the admission and the timing. All of it. Instead, he'd taken half a minute to walk to his office window and then back to the table where Brad sat. Then he'd said something Brad would never forget. "Everyone has a past, Son. Better that you deal with yours now than later."

How Laura's father had handled the news was further proof that marrying Laura was the right thing. She shared his faith and his views on every topic that mattered. And her family loved him. So then why was he driving back to Wilmington with plans to meet Emma at the beach tomorrow? He would get to the heart of the matter quickly, and maybe … maybe he would head home early. Tomorrow night even. He needed Laura to know that he hadn't changed his love for her.

Even if being around Emma had breathed life into feelings he thought long dead.

He dug around the passenger seat and found his cell phone. With a few clicks, he dialed Laura's number, but the call went to her voicemail. "Hey, baby, it's me. Just thinking about you. I'll try you again later."

But later never came. Brad pulled into his driveway and found his mom in the kitchen. He helped her can twenty-four jars of strawberry jam. His mom didn't really know why he was here, and she didn't seem interested in knowing. The entire hour they spent together that night, she said only this about the wedding: "I like Laura a lot."

"Me too." Brad grinned, keeping the tone between them easy. Laura had been back to North Carolina with him several times since they started dating. She and Brad's mother always got along well.

"Something I've learned about marriage." She gave him a knowing look, nothing too serious, but a look only a mother could give.

"What's that?"

"Once is enough."

He nodded slowly. "I agree."

"Just saying." She smiled at him and returned to her canning. And that was that. Her way of telling him that whatever had brought him home, he needed to be sure before he stepped up to the altar and said, "I do."

When they were done canning, Brad found his father in the TV room filling out sweepstakes forms. Brad sat opposite him, on the worn brown corduroy footstool they'd had for years. "Hey, Dad."

"Son."

Brad laced his fingers together. "I found her."

His dad looked up. "I figured you would."

"We didn't get into it. Not completely." He furrowed his brow, trying to imagine how the next day would play out. "I'm meeting her at Holden Beach tomorrow afternoon."

"Finishing the chapter?" There it was. The only bit of concern his father had shown since he brought Emma up on the last visit. The question mark in his voice.

"Yes." With his dad, he felt no reason to be falsely certain. Not when his heart was still wavering over having spent an evening with Emma. He sucked in a breath through clenched teeth. "I think so, anyway."

"You know what they say." His father lowered his pencil, the sweepstakes forgotten for the moment.

"What's that?"

"If you can't finish the chapter, then there must be more to the story."

More to the story. The thought terrified Brad. He wanted to have this time with Emma, tell her good-bye, and hurry home to his wedding. But what if that wasn't how the next few days played out? If he found feelings again for Emma, could he really return home to marry Laura? He felt sick at the idea, but he had to face the possibility.

He patted his father's hand. "I'll keep that in mind." He stood and smiled, more tired than he'd been in a long time. "I'm turning in."

"I'll be praying for you, Son." His dad meant the words.

Brad leaned down and hugged him. "Thanks."

He thought about calling Laura again before he went to sleep, but his mind was whirling with too many conflicting images. Laura's face, the way she beamed when she talked about her wedding dress, and the grief that had marked her expression when he told her the truth in Central Park earlier this week. Emma, as she'd walked out to her car from her classroom earlier today, and the way she'd kept her sunglasses on through dinner this evening.

Could he spend the weekend with Emma, tell her he was sorry, and remember again the most painful time in his life without finding feelings for her? *Please, God ... give me the strength. Help me know if I should be here.*

Remember to leave the gift at the altar ...

The answer was similar to what he'd heard earlier. Before he fell asleep, he reached for his Bible and found the verse about the gift. It was from Matthew 5:23 – 24, and reading it brought chills to his arms. He let the words wash over him like a soothing balm to his soul. *Therefore, if you are offering your gift at the altar and there remember that your brother has something against you, leave your gift there in front of the altar. First go and be reconciled to your brother; then come and offer your gift.*

That's what this was about ... it was why God had urged him to make this trip and why he had to see the visit with Emma through to completion. He was about to stand at an altar with the precious gift of Laura James. But he couldn't make a commitment to her while Emma had something against him. And she did — he could tell by the look in her eyes. This trip would be about reconciling with Emma — the way he should've done years ago. Only then could he return to New York City, to the gift that awaited him there.

To his place at the altar.

Twenty-One

LAURA SAT IN HER BEDROOM AND stared out the window at the expanse of grass that made up her front yard. Dusk was quietly giving way to night, and Laura planned to do little more than sit here and pray.

Her friends had been great. Offers had come in from three of them that night. Nelly invited her to dinner, and Megan called to see if Laura wanted to hang out, watch TV or play cards. Bella Joy knew a fellow dancer who had just joined the *Wicked* cast at the Gershwin Theater in Times Square. She had two tickets for the Saturday eight o'clock show, and she asked Laura to go.

"We can spend the day in the city, shop Fifth Avenue, and eat lunch at Tavern on the Green. We can even stop in at the Stardust Diner after the show. I know a guy who sings there," Bella Joy told her. "It'll be a blast."

Laura thanked her, but declined. She didn't want dinner or conversation, and she couldn't concentrate on a Broadway play this weekend. Not when she had no idea whether Brad was staying up late on a beach somewhere talking to Emma or whether he'd even found her yet. He'd left a message, but Laura hadn't called him. She hated the thought of sounding jealous, of asking the wrong questions. It was easier not to call.

Her parents were downstairs, and they'd been great about the whole thing. Her father, especially. Her mother had a harder time understanding why Brad needed to take care of his past now—right before the wedding. But both of them had given her the grace of having time to herself.

She stood and slid her bedroom window open. All her life everything had gone the way it was supposed to. Other than the usual petty differences between friends, high school had flown by with the sort of charmed memories she would smile back on as long as she lived. She'd dated, of course. There were prom dates and the occasional nights out to the movies. But she hadn't fallen in love. The guys in her class were friends, nothing more. College had been the same way.

"What if I never find the right guy," she'd asked her mother the summer after she graduated.

"You will, honey." Her mom's confidence had been reassuring. "God has someone out there for you. He wants you to be ready. Be strong in your faith and yourself. That way you'll recognize him when God brings him along."

Her mother's advice turned out to be right on. Laura stayed close to God, and when she spotted Brad at her dad's company picnic, she had the strangest feeling she'd seen him somewhere before. Like they'd known each other for years. Even so, she wouldn't have made the first move. She didn't chase guys — that had never been her style.

But when he talked to her that day, she had a feeling, a knowing. Their quick dialogue turned into a full-blown conversation — since neither of them had anything planned for the day, they spent the next two hours walking around the party together and pulling off to themselves as if they were the only people there. By the end of the day, Laura was starry-eyed and giddy — even if she didn't show that to Brad.

A month later, after she and Brad shared conversations like that one every day, she told her parents about her feelings. "I think Brad's the guy."

They couldn't have been more thrilled. Laura's dad had never had a young ad executive as promising as Brad Cutler. He shared her faith and sense of humor, and in no time he was part of the

family. "God must've known about the two of you from the beginning of time," her mom would tell her.

Until a week ago Laura agreed, heart and soul.

Brad seemed to share her faith. He cared about getting his
MBA and climbing the ladder at her father's firm, and he made
her laugh every time they were together. Sure they talked about
their pasts. Laura's was simple and straightforward. Her heart
had never been tangled up with love and loss, so Brad was her
first everything.

As for Brad, he admitted his relationship with Emma. "We
were kids. We grew up together," he told her. "Over time we grew
apart."

Laura had studied him, watched the look in his eyes. Growing up with someone was a powerful draw. "Why didn't it work?"
She asked the question in different ways on a handful of occa-
sions when the topic of his past came up.

"We were different," he told her. "We wound up with nothing
in common."

The answer always felt honest and truthful, and it always satisfied Laura's curiosity. Emma Landon was a part of his past. End
of story. By the time Christmas rolled around that year, Laura
and Brad were a serious item. On New Year's Eve, he told her
something she would never forget.

"It's not just the start of a new year," he told her as they
watched the snow fall outside her parents' front porch. "It's the
start of a new life. Because I never want to live a day without you,
Laura. I've never loved anyone like I love you."

His words rang in her mind again now, but in light of the
truth they seemed false, phony. She lifted her face to the breeze
drifting through her screened window. He'd never loved anyone
like her? That wasn't true. In fact, he'd loved Emma with a sort
of physical love Laura and Brad had never shared. Even if they'd

grown apart, the truth was Brad had never loved anyone like he'd loved Emma Landon.

Laura had to admit that now.

She looked at the calendar on her wall. The end of May. In all her wildest dreams and imaginations about the weeks leading up to her wedding, she could never have imagined that she'd be in this situation now. No matter that they hadn't called off the ceremony, their wedding was most likely not going to happen. Brad hadn't come out and said he had doubts, but what else could explain the timing?

She glanced at her cell phone on the bed and saw a text message from Amy. She clicked her phone on and read what it said. *Laura … check out Psalm 119:81 … I read it today and thought about you.*

Her phone had an electronic application of the Bible, so she quickly clicked to that verse. *I am worn out waiting for your rescue, but I have put my hope in your word.* Laura read it again and tried to believe that somehow God's Word would rescue her. The promise soothed her hurting soul, even if she couldn't imagine how it might apply to her. Was it really possible that God's Word would be her rock? She hoped so, because she wouldn't get through this otherwise. But right now His promises seemed written for someone else. She saved the verse to her bookmarked page, then she moved back to the text message and tapped out an answer to Amy. *I read it. Thanks, friend.*

That's all. She didn't want a long conversation, not with Amy or anyone else. *I want Brad, the way things used to be, God … how can any of this be happening?*

Remember, Daughter … the verses in Luke?

Laura blinked the soft response away from her heart. She would delve into her Bible study notes later—especially the part about forgiving. The heartache she was feeling now had her a long way from forgiveness. She wasn't even sure Brad was coming home after all. God's divine rescue, that's what she needed. Nothing short of a miracle.

She was about to lay down, crawl under the sheets and cry the way she'd done on the nights leading up to this weekend. But before she could make a move, there was a knock at her door. "Come in."

Her mother entered the room slowly, tentatively. "Hey."

"Hey." She smiled. Even now, when they knew the truth, Laura didn't want to look or feel like the victim. That's why no one but God had seen her cry these last few nights.

"Can we talk for a few minutes?"

"Sure." Laura patted the spot on her bed next to her. "Come sit."

Her mom looked more tired than usual. Gone was the excited peppiness that had marked her countenance since Laura and Brad had announced their engagement. "You've been up here most of the night."

"Thinking." Laura pulled one leg up onto the bed and angled herself so she could see her mom. "Not sure what happens next."

"I can imagine." Her mother covered Laura's hand with her own. "I keep praying. That's all I can do."

Laura thought for a while. "Bella Joy invited me to see *Wicked* tomorrow in the city."

"You should go." Her mom's tone was laced with sympathy.

"Really?" She pictured a day in the city, the brilliance of the show, and the fun she always had when she hung out with Bella Joy.

"Sitting here can't be helping much." Her mom tilted her face, her eyes hopeful. "A diversion might give you some perspective. Clear your head so you can get through the weekend."

Laura was quiet, considering the possibility. She had to admit, the idea sounded appealing. She hated being the victim, the jilted bride. "Maybe you're right." She sat straighter. A person could only stay sad for so long. This was Brad's doing, not hers.

If his actions were going to result in a cancelled wedding, in a called-off marriage, then at least she could go to Times Square with Bella Joy and have fun for a night.

"I was thinking." Her mom kept her hand over Laura's in a way that seemed to give them both strength. "I know you're worried about the wedding, but ... well, Brad's not saying he's changed his mind. He wants to have things in order first."

"I understand." Laura waffled back and forth between hoping nothing more than for Brad to come home and for the wedding to go on as planned, and being angry at him for waiting until now to handle this. Tonight she leaned more toward anger. "I keep picturing him spending this weekend with her." She met her mother's gaze straight on. "Why a whole weekend? Wouldn't it be enough to find her and tell her he was sorry?"

Her mom didn't look away. "The more I think about what's happening, what Brad's doing, the less I feel it's about this old girlfriend of his."

"What then?"

Her mom tilted her head, her eyes softer than before. "The baby." She breathed in deeply and folded her arms. "I've done some research online, about Post Abortion Syndrome. Brad and this woman made a choice that ended the life of a child." Her mother's eyes welled up. "Have you thought about that? About what Brad might be feeling?"

"Some." Laura felt her heart sink. "Maybe not to that extent."

"When you have a minute, look it up this weekend. Read about what people go through after having an abortion." Her mom looked intent. "Some people who've taken part in an abortion have trouble committing to another person until they find healing. Even if years or decades go by." She bit her lip. "I really think, Laura ... Brad needs to do this. He should've done it sooner, but he would've been wrong to marry you without going back. The situation is that serious."

She held her arms out and hugged Laura for a long time. When she pulled back, she had tears on her cheeks. "I know this is hard for you. For all of us. But maybe it's the only way."

Laura nodded and thanked her mom. After she was gone, she took her laptop from the dresser beside her bed and ran a Google search on Post Abortion Syndrome. A website called *It's a Life* showed up in the first few options. Laura scanned the top of the page to a section called Depression and Guilt. She began to read. *Many people who suffer from Post Abortion Syndrome deny ever having an abortion until years later. Only then do they begin to wonder—was it a boy? Was it a girl? How old would he or she be today? The questions come in a rush for some people—especially men.*

The words surrounded Laura's heart and opened her eyes in a way she hadn't felt before. Was that what Brad was going through? Some sort of post abortion syndrome where he was being overcome by questions about the baby? Laura tried to imagine what it might be like, knowing that a baby had died because of a decision she'd made. The reality came over her in full vivid force, and she imagined the child. A nine-year-old by now.

She returned to the website and kept reading. Another section was titled Forgiveness—a Gift Worth Giving. Laura felt her fingers shake as she scrolled down the page. *There are two stages to healing and forgiveness after an abortion. First, you must admit what you've done to your child and the person you conceived the child with—even if you were coaxed or led into the abortion and convinced it was the right thing to do. Still you must admit the action, and then you must seek forgiveness if you are ever to have healing.*

Laura closed her eyes and imagined Brad, the love of her life. She pictured him finding Emma and having this sort of intimate conversation. Talking about the baby they'd lost, and finding forgiveness together. How could they experience that much closeness and not fall in love again? But after having an abortion together, how could they not have this weekend? Her mother was right. Brad would never be whole without this time.

She brushed away her fears and kept reading. *Forgiveness from each other isn't always possible. People move on, and in many cases a feeling of disdain or embarrassment remains for the person you shared the abortion with. Either way—whether you can find forgiveness with that person or not, you can forgive yourself. This is only the beginning of healing from Post Abortion Syndrome. True healing only happens with God's forgiveness. Admit this wrong to Him, and allow Him to extend mercy to you. You will find unbelievable freedom as you allow Christ to forgive you. He died for this very reason, and He loves you enough to heal your pain. He doesn't want His people burdened by guilt and regret. Especially in this.*

She closed her computer, turned off the light, and lay there in the dark, staring at her ceiling. Disdain? Was that how Brad felt about Emma? Laura didn't think so, not based on the way he talked about her. Pity might've been a better word. She thought about Brad, the guy she knew and loved. His firstborn child was dead. There was no other way to understand the situation. A sorrow overwhelmed her, and she closed her eyes. For the first time since she'd heard the news, she grieved the loss of Brad's child, grieved like she hadn't expected she ever would.

If by some miracle Brad was able to walk away from Emma after finding her, if he returned to Laura and the two of them decided to marry, then one day down the road they might have children. And those children would never know a boy or girl who would've been their half-sibling. A part of their family. Laura rolled onto her side and felt the loss a fraction of the way Brad must be feeling it.

Perhaps thinking about marriage had led him to think about having children, and that, in turn, led him to thoughts of his child with Emma. The baby who would always be his first. Maybe now—for whatever reason—he was finally taking ownership for his role in her abortion. Finally seeking forgiveness, the way he tried to explain it to Laura in Central Park. Brad and Emma had been childhood friends, and even if they had barely known each other, he couldn't dismiss the harm he'd caused her. The words from the website came back to her. *Forgiveness with the person who shared in your abortion ... is only the beginning.* In that sense, Laura finally understood why Brad had to find Emma and apologize.

Because for him, he couldn't find healing with God until he did.

Twenty-Two

EMMA FINISHED HER PAPERWORK EARLY, REFUSING to think about the reality of what lay ahead in a few hours. When she'd completed the forms for every one of her students and submitted the package to her principal by email, she took a shower, dressed in shorts and a long-sleeve V-neck T-shirt. She didn't bother with her hair or makeup. Whatever happened with Brad, he wasn't here to fall in love again. That much had washed up on the shore of her heart overnight.

Yes, he had something to say. Emma willed herself to understand that, to keep her expectations low. She didn't have to know how he'd fallen in love or why he'd gotten engaged. The fact remained. He was here for a weekend, and then he was returning to New York and getting married. She found the path between the two beach houses at the end of her street and crossed the bluff to the cement wall on the other side. She was early, so she sat on the sand facing the water. Waiting.

What had Brad said about his trip? God alone had brought him here, right? Yes, that was it. God alone. She let her head fall gently back against the cement wall. So Brad Cutler had kept his faith in God—after all they'd been through he still had that. Which meant what? That he'd found peace with the choice they'd made ten years ago? That he had pretended he was a nice Christian boy long after leaving her?

No matter how long Emma thought about God, she couldn't think of a single reason why He'd want anything to do with either of them. Not after what they'd done. If there even was a God.

Emma thought about Kristin Palazzo. She'd gotten a call from Kristin's mother that morning midway through her paperwork. No changes. The sweet, vibrant teenager was still on life support, still being given almost no hope from her doctors.

Emma squinted at the sunlight reflecting off the water. *God ... if You're there, I'm sure You're angry with me. I don't blame You. But in case You're listening, please be with Kristin. Please let her live ... the way her mom and her church friends are praying for her. I'm not sure if You're real or if You can hear this. But if You can, I need to ask. I deserve nothing. But Kristin ... Kristin deserves to live. Please.*

Her prayer faded as easily as it had begun. She uttered the prayer only because Kristin would've wanted her to. Times like this Emma longed once again for her mother, for someone to sit across from her and hold her hands and help her understand why she should believe in anything other than what her eyes could see. Her mother had believed, certainly. Emma watched the waves roll in. Maybe the only thing standing between her and the faith of her mother was guilt. The shame and regret and guilt that were woven into the fabric of Emma's very being.

She stood and stretched, brushing the sand from her legs. She'd brought a bag with water bottles, sunscreen, and a couple beach towels. For a long time she leaned against the cement wall, watching the surf, remembering. A few years ago one of her young students — Alan — took a shower before going to bed. Only instead of standing up, he laid down on the shower floor to rest a little. And with the warm water hitting his face, in almost no time he fell asleep. His body blocked the drain, and water flooded out onto the floor and into his upstairs bedroom. His mom didn't notice the problem until water began pouring out of the light fixtures below. Screaming his name, she ran to him. "I thought he was dead," she told Emma later. She pushed his bathroom door open and saw him lying on the floor of the shower. One last time she shouted his name. This time the boy blinked and woke up, completely fine. Sleepy and embarrassed, but alive. The next day at school a discouraged Alan told her all about it, and how worker guys were at the house fixing the damage.

"You ever wish you could go back and do a day over again?" he asked her.

She hesitated, and then smiled. "Yes, Alan. I think we've all wished that."

A day to do over again. His question had stayed with her, haunted her since then. Especially as November 20th came and went. If ever there was a day she would do over again it was that terrible morning at the abortion clinic. A thousand times she'd played the scene again in her mind, and this time when the woman explained that she needed more money, Emma would've run from the building, run for her life and the life of her unborn child.

But do-overs didn't happen except in her dreams.

Something caught her eye and she glanced over her shoulder to see Brad making his way along the path from Ocean Boulevard between the houses. He wore shorts and leather flip-flops, a white T-shirt and sunglasses. He hadn't changed much, but he looked different, better somehow. He had a man's build now, strong and filled out. That and the way he carried himself, with a confidence and dependability that hadn't been there before.

He hesitated when he saw her, and his steps grew slower. She wondered whether he'd sit beside her and explain the real reason why he'd come or if he'd make small talk again the way he had yesterday. But as he reached her, he did neither. Instead he took a full breath and looked toward the surf. "Walk with me." He turned to her. "Okay?"

No answer was needed. She fell in alongside him as easily as she had when she was a teenager. When she was a child, for that matter. They trudged through the sand to a spot closer to the water, where they left their sandals and Emma's beach bag. Then they set off away from the pier, the same direction where they'd gone that summer. The private side of the shore.

"This was never our beach." He kept his hands in the pockets of his khaki shorts, his pace relaxed. "Not until the end."

His comment made her feel foolish, as if maybe she should've said something back then about avoiding Holden Beach. She lifted her chin, refusing to let herself feel guilty. "I always liked Wrightsville."

"I know." He was closer to the water, and he turned to her, slowing nearly to a stop. "It was my fault, Emma. I'm the one who chose Holden Beach."

His comment caught her unaware. She didn't expect for a minute that he was going to take blame for the two of them winding up here, on this secluded, romantic beach. But that's what he was saying. They had come to Holden Beach by his choosing. And what if they hadn't? She could've said something to stop him, right? She could've told him no, she wasn't interested in an hour-long drive just to find a stretch of shoreline. Wrightsville was in Wilmington, minutes from their houses.

She stared at her sandy feet and for a while the two of them walked in somber silence.

"Remember Wrightsville?" Brad looked to the sky and the sun reflected against his Oakleys. A smile stretched across his face. "We were kids, a couple of fourth and fifth graders, but we'd ride our bikes on the loop over to Johnny Mercer's pier. Our parents never cared as long as we were together."

Emma felt her mood lighten at the memory. Brad's tan legs pedaling as fast as he could ahead of her, a towel draped around his shoulders, backpack full of peanut butter sandwiches and a Frisbee. "Then in middle school. Remember that?"

Brad's chuckle got lost on the sound of the surf. "What were there, ten of us? Twelve? All caught up on some volleyball kick?"

"Every day the whole month of July. We thought we were headed for the Olympics."

"Me and Tommy Winters for sure."

"You guys actually got in a fight that one time. Over whether a ball was in bounds or not."

"Old Tommy Winters." Brad stopped and faced the water. "Wonder what ever happened to him."

"Tommy?" Emma stood beside him, but she kept her distance so there was no danger of their arms touching. "He'll Facebook me every once in a while. Married with two little boys. Lives in Raleigh. Works for the county planning department."

"Hmmm. Sounds like a good life." Brad turned briefly to her, and even though his eyes weren't visible through his sunglasses, he looked surprised. "You're on Facebook?"

"Sometimes." She crossed her arms in front of herself. The chill inside her had nothing to do with the temperature. "You?"

"I have a profile, but I'm never on it. Too busy." He chuckled. "I'll have to friend-request him."

She was quiet for a moment, imagining how different this reunion could've been. If they'd made other choices a decade ago, they might've found each other through Facebook—the way lots of old friends did. And maybe they would've messaged each other for a season and met up again. Before the other girl came into his life. Maybe they would've even met here at Holden Beach, where an afternoon like this could've been warm with promise. Instead of cold from the reality of all they'd lost.

"Who else have you seen?" Brad started walking again, slower than before, still west away from the pier, away from the public. "Online, I mean."

Emma kept even with his pace. "Sara Schumacher. She's still in Wilmington. A pediatrician, now."

"Sara?" Brad shook his head, in a way that said he wasn't surprised. "She was smarter than every guy in our math class. I remember her saying she couldn't wait for trigonometry."

"That's Sara." Emma felt her guard slipping. She hadn't expected to enjoy herself this much. "Paul Bond is a coach at Wilmington High. Varsity football. And Max Maynard is on the school board."

"Max? Mr. Party?" Brad's brow lifted and again he glanced at her as he walked. "The guy couldn't complete a sentence our senior year."

"He was kicked out of prom for drinking. Remember?" Emma had the sudden urge to link arms with Brad, to walk with him along their beach the way they'd done that August. She chided herself. *Be careful, Emma. Watch your heart.*

"Someone told me he gave his life to God." Brad's tone softened. "That would do it, I guess."

The chill was back. Emma ran her hands over her arms and kept them crossed. She felt eighteen again walking beside Brad Cutler. It took everything she had to remind herself that nothing was like it was back than. Absolutely nothing.

"All those people … you found them on Facebook?"

"Everyone's on Facebook. Half the parents of the kids in my class friend-request me the first week of school." Emma smiled. "It's good, I guess. Gives people a way to stay in touch."

"I guess."

"Of course … then there's your way." Emma wore sunglasses too, so he couldn't see the sudden way her eyes danced. But he could certainly hear the laughter in her voice. The sound caught even her off guard, like everything about the past hour. How long had it been since she and Brad had found anything to laugh about?

"My way?" He gave her an easy smile and again he stopped walking.

"Wait a decade and show up like a ghost at the end of the workday."

For a few seconds she thought he was going to turn serious on her, say something about how he couldn't post whatever he had to say on someone's Facebook. "Yeah." A gradual chuckle came from his throat, as if he wasn't any more ready than she was to talk about the real reasons he was here. "I always had to be different."

"Which was usually a good thing." Emma remembered dozens of times when kids from their class took beer to the beach or drove out to the country to party. Brad didn't drink. Not ever.

"Our class could get pretty crazy."

They were quiet again, and Emma figured Brad was probably as lost in the memories of yesterday as she was. The sun was warm on their shoulders, and the blue sky was quietly being consumed by clouds—the type that could quickly turn into thunderstorms. Back near the pier, a long ways down the beach, Emma saw that families had arrived with oversized coolers and folding chairs, towels and umbrellas. A couple kids ran together, releasing a kite slowly into the ocean breeze and watching it take flight. The holiday crowd.

But the place where Brad had led her was both familiar and private, the atmosphere they would need for whatever was coming. Emma had a feeling it was time. They could only talk about the past for so long without running into the reason why he'd come.

Brad motioned to a bluff up on the sand, a few yards farther from the water. The spot was marked with long sections of beach grass, the kind artists tried to capture in paintings of the Carolina coast. "Come on."

Emma followed him, but in response her heart skittered into a strange rhythm. *Relax,* she told herself. What could he say that would be worse than last night's news—the fact that he was engaged. She sat next to him and stretched her legs out, crossing them at her ankles.

Was this really happening? She stared at the ocean, trying not to notice him, but it was impossible. His presence heightened her senses in every possible way. Brad Cutler, a foot from her. His mannerisms, the smell of his shampoo as it mixed with the salty air, the way he pulled up one knee and casually leaned toward it. The familiarity surrounded her, consuming her. The two of them sitting here, breathing the same air, staring at the same old shore. Her heart wanted to believe she was still his ... he was still hers, and this was just one more summer day in a lifetime of summers she might share with him.

She leaned back on her hands, again careful to keep her distance. *Just say it*, she wanted to scream at him. *Get it over with.* Then this moment could be finished. He would go home to his fiancée and never find his way here again. Because every moment he lingered beside her made it harder to convince herself of the truth.

The truth that she must never, ever fall for Brad Cutler again.

BRAD WAS ENJOYING HIMSELF TOO MUCH, forgetting the adult he had become and the life he had back in New York City and everything else except Emma beside him. The sound of silence between them jolted him back to reality, reminding his heart that they weren't teenagers anymore. Never mind the attraction he still felt, or the easy way they had when they were together. He wasn't here to catch up on old times and remember once more why he'd fallen for her all those years ago.

He loved Laura now, and he needed to get home. He couldn't waste another hour reminiscing.

For a long minute he gathered his thoughts. The broken pieces in his soul needed to be laid out on the sand between them before he could begin to find a way to make them whole. For either of them. He was still trying to find a starting place when she shifted her position, just enough so she could see him better.

"You didn't come here to talk about Tommy Winters or Max Maynard." Her tone was softer than before. The humor completely gone. "Why don't you just say it Brad. Tell me why you're here." A massive cloud shaded the beach, and she removed her sunglasses.

Brad did the same, and he could see clearly into her soul. The way he always had been able to. The hurt in her eyes made him feel sick, made him doubt the wisdom in sharing any of this. He could've written her a letter or dismissed the idea, assuming Emma would be too hard to find. Anything so he wouldn't have to be here now, aware of her brokenness, trying to find a way to talk about the most painful part of their lives. He looked as deep and far into the blue sky as he could. He had to tell her. He had no choice.

The clouds were darkening the sky, but the forecast hadn't predicted thunderstorms until later that night. Brad looked into her eyes. If he was going to tell her how he felt, then he wanted her to know he was genuine. She watched him, waiting. *Please, God … give me the words …*

I am with you, Son. This is where forgiveness begins.

He filled his lungs, willing her to understand. "I remember bringing you here instead of Wrightsville. And I remember taking you to this part of the beach." He paused, the past vivid and painful. "I remember losing control."

Her cheeks grew hot, but she didn't move, didn't say a word.

"I can still see myself driving you to the clinic and then …" regret weighted his words, and he fought against a sudden rush of tears. "I remember driving out of town to UNC, but …" he looked down at the sand. What sort of jerk had he been back then? He clenched his jaw and then lifted his eyes to hers again. "I don't remember … saying I was sorry." He shrugged, helpless to change the facts. "I never said I was sorry, Emma. That's why I'm here."

For a few heartbeats she stared at him, motionless. Then she pulled her knees up and circled her arms around them. As she did, she faced the ocean once more, her back straighter than before. It took a minute, but gradually tears began sliding down her cheeks, falling to her bare legs and rolling down toward the sand. Finally she brushed her fingers across her face and swallowed a few times. "I loved you since I was in fourth grade. Since that week when that ... that teacher made us hold onto that stupid rope."

"I thought about that. The rope." He sounded beyond sad. "On the flight here."

"After that, I told you everything, you knew all that my heart held. Every detail. You were ... you were my best friend and my brother and my boyfriend." Another tear slid down her cheek, but Emma didn't seem to notice it. "You were everything."

Brad wanted to reach out to her, but he knew better than to take her hand again. Last time the feeling had stayed with him long into the night. Instead he allowed himself to think back to every long afternoon and endless weekend. Emma wasn't the only one. He had shared his heart with her, too. Whatever he was feeling, he told her. Until ... "Until we came here ..."

"All I wanted ..." Her hand shook as she lifted it to her face and dabbed at another tear. Her eyes were lost in the past, trapped in that terrible time when life changed for both of them. She looked right at him, straight through his soul. "All I wanted ... was for you to ask me what happened that day." She let her head fall slowly to her knee for a few seconds. When she looked up, her eyes locked onto his once more. "I never told anyone, not a single person. Not my mom or a friend or a counselor." Anger simmered in her tone, but she didn't raise her voice. "Because if I couldn't tell you ... who could I tell? You let me walk down the hallway of that clinic and when I came back you didn't say a *word*. You never asked me what happened."

Brad felt the truth hit him like a hollow bullet, shattering his heart into a thousand tiny bits. She hadn't told anyone what happened at the other end of that hallway? Not ever? Brad hadn't asked her because he hadn't wanted to know. Not then and not now. But he'd come all this way for that reason — to apologize and so they could both grieve. "Tell me, Emma." He spoke the words he should've said ten years ago. As he did, his conviction grew. He needed to know what happened because the baby wasn't only Emma's. It was his child, too. "Please tell me."

"Brad ..." She started to shake her head, new tears spilling from her eyes. "It's too late."

"No. That's why I'm here." He reached out his hand because he needed her. They needed each other. This wasn't about finding new feelings for each other. It was about figuring out the past. When she didn't seem like she was going to take his hand, he slid a little closer and tenderly took her fingers in his.

She didn't fight him, though her spirit seemed more broken than before. As if she wanted to resist his efforts at kindness, but she simply wasn't able. "Please tell me."

A few seconds passed, but she clung to his hand tighter than before, and he knew. The story was coming. She was about to tell him the details he hadn't wanted to hear or know. All these years Emma had held the truth inside her, and now that Brad was here, he could see that she'd never found peace or healing. She was still crippled by the trip she'd taken down the hallway of that clinic, and she desperately needed healing. While Emma wrestled with what to say and how to say it, Brad hurt for her ... and he hurt for himself. Because whatever the story involved, he was suddenly certain about one thing.

After this, nothing would ever be the same.

Twenty-Three

A CHANCE LIKE THIS WOULDN'T COME again.

Emma understood that as she wrestled with the truth, with how to tell him. The part of her story she needed to tell Brad was something she couldn't tell Gavin the other day, because she could barely admit the details to herself. For ten years she'd wanted to tell Brad about that day, so he'd understand how awful it had been. Now—in the wake of his apology—Emma knew this was the only time she'd have to tell him.

"I was scared to death. Sitting in that waiting room." She found strength in the way her hand felt in his. Safe and protected. The details of her story wouldn't kill her, not with Brad there sitting strong beside her. "I wanted to run back to the car and beg you to take me home."

"Emma …" A quiet groan came from him and his shoulders fell a little. "You should've."

"No." She shook her head. "You knew, Brad. You could tell I was scared."

At first he looked like he might argue, but then he closed his eyes for a moment. When he opened them, he looked stripped of any self-defense. "Yes. I knew. I didn't want to talk about what you were feeling." His eyes grew watery, but he didn't look away. "I didn't want you to change your mind."

The admission was what Emma had known in her heart, but it hurt all the same. He had taken her to the clinic, and not for a minute had he wavered in what he wanted from that visit. He wanted Emma to walk out no longer pregnant. He wanted no baby to complicate his future, nothing to change the course of his life, nothing that would tell the world what he and Emma had done.

"I was terrified by the time they called my name, but I guess …" Emma blinked back fresh tears. The breeze was cooler than before, so she inched closer to him, borrowing from his warmth. "By then I figured it was too late to change my mind." She couldn't tell the story in small fits and starts. With her hand holding tight to his, she allowed herself to be back there again, young and pregnant and walking down the cold, impersonal hallway of a clinic toward the back room where babies died. Steeling herself against the pain of the past, she began. And once she did, she told the story until it was finished.

An older woman with tight features and short gray hair led her down the hallway and Emma looked back just once. In the waiting room, Brad had his forearms on his knees, his focus on the floor.

"This way," the woman said. She seemed to notice that Emma was distracted, so she stopped and put her hand on Emma's shoulder. "Don't worry, dear. This will all be over soon."

Emma allowed the woman's words to stay with her, guiding her the rest of the way to a small white room at the end of the hall. The woman opened the door and nodded to Emma. "Remove your clothing and slip into the gown on the table there. Keep it open in the front. I'll need you to fill out another form before the doctor will see you."

The doctor? Emma remembered feeling confused. She hadn't considered even once that the person performing the abortion would be an actual doctor. All her life she'd thought of doctors as people who help others. The woman closed the door, leaving Emma alone. In some ways the boxy room looked like any other Emma had seen at her doctor's office growing up. A table, a sink, a round stool on wheels for the doctor. But this room also had a small table covered by a paper cloth. On top of the cloth were several frightening-looking tools. A machine stood nearby with a number of black switches, and a clear tube hooked to the side.

Emma looked away from the machine, and a cold feeling came over her. She began to shiver, first her teeth, then her shoulders and arms, until her whole body was shaking. Freezing to the core of her being. In all her life she couldn't remember ever being that cold before or since. Fear moved through the room, sucking the air from it, and Emma couldn't draw a full breath.

Do something, she told herself. *You can't just stand here.*

She could hear voices out in the hall, but none of them were clear enough to understand. Her heartbeat echoed in her chest, her head. It was so loud she was sure the nurse would hear it when she returned. Mindlessly, still shaking with fear and cold, still struggling to breathe, Emma kicked off her tennis shoes and peeled away her clothes. She set them in a small pile near a corner of the room, and then she slipped on the gown. It was white with small blue flowers. *The kind you might see in a baby nursery,* she told herself. She pulled it tightly around her, and the smell of bleach filled her senses.

What was she doing? And what about her baby? Was it too late to run from the room, to leave the office and the matter-of-fact woman and Brad and flee the building? The questions came at her like so many razor-sharp arrows, but before she could think of a single answer, the door opened ...

The woman stepped in, shut the door behind her, and handed Emma a clipboard.

"Counseling is mandatory before the procedure." The woman leaned against the door and smiled. "You've had your counseling appointment, is that right?"

"Yes." Emma didn't recognize her voice. She noted two things about the moment that would stay with her all her life. The woman never called the abortion an abortion. She called it a procedure. And second, her smile never came close to touching her eyes.

Not sure what to do next, Emma stared at the paper on the clipboard. Consent Form, it read. Emma looked up, her teeth clattering. "Is … is it cold in here?"

"You're just nervous." The woman came closer and felt Emma's forehead. "You don't have a fever. You need to relax, dear. Really." She took a step back, surveying Emma. "Has anyone gone over your options?"

"Options?" A glimmer of hope fanned through Emma's heart. "What are my options?"

The woman hesitated. "How old are you?"

"Eighteen." Emma set the clipboard next to her and hugged herself tight, trying to ward off the cold in her bones. "What options?"

"Well … they should've talked about this at the counseling appointment. Those options."

"Oh." Emma nodded. The option of having the baby and giving it up for adoption, or raising it herself. "I … think I know about the options."

"Very good." She smiled at Emma again. "A lot of girls are scared when they come in here, but I need to tell you. This is very routine. The procedure is performed on hundreds of women each month right here in this clinic." She looked intently at Emma. "You're what … twelve weeks along?"

Twelve weeks? She gulped, not sure what that meant or how she had let so much time go by. "I … think so. My cycle isn't … I'm not very regular."

"I'm sure you're not much further along than that." She patted Emma's shoulder. "At twelve weeks we're not talking about a baby, dear. You have a mass of cells inside you. The procedure removes those cells so that a baby doesn't grow. Then you can move on and put this whole thing behind you."

A mass of cells? Emma clung to the definition, and in a blur of comforting statements and reassurances from the woman, Emma signed the paperwork. She signed her name to a paper promising that this was her choice, her decision, and that no one had forced her into having the abortion, like she'd gone over in her counseling session a few days ago.

She gave her consent.

The temperature on the beach was falling again, and Emma felt as cold now as she had that day in the clinic. She turned to Brad and saw a shame and guilt in his eyes that she'd never seen before. He ran his thumb over the top of her hand. "I should've gone to the counseling meeting with you."

She wanted to believe that if he had, if they'd listened to the woman's explanation together, then they would've decided against the abortion. But she knew better. "It wouldn't have mattered. We'd made up our minds by then. This wasn't only your fault, Brad. I walked down that hallway."

"What ... what happened next?"

Emma slipped back to that moment. Once the paperwork was signed, the woman had little else to say. She collected her clipboard and left Emma alone again. In that final minute with her baby, Emma put her hand over her stomach. It was all going to be over soon, right? Wasn't that what the woman had said? But if this was the last time she would ever be alone with her child, she felt the desperate need to say something. A final good-bye of sorts. Tears spilled onto her cheeks, but the hot streams did nothing to warm her. "Little baby," she whispered. The shivering made her whispers sound like a series of strange clicks and breaths. "I'm sorry, baby. This isn't your fault."

She was still trying to talk, still crying when there was a knock at the door, and a middle-aged man walked inside. The doctor must've told her to lay down, because the next thing she remembered, she was on her back and he was easing the heels of her feet into stirrups. Everything started to blur and Emma's mind began to spin. The woman appeared and stood near the wall, but she seemed to look anywhere but Emma's eyes.

She squeezed her eyes shut. *I'm sorry little baby … I'm so sorry. Please forgive me. This isn't your fault.*

The doctor gave her a shot. She gasped, and her shivering grew worse. "It's … it's s-s-s-so cold."

"You'll be warmer in a minute."

Again the edges blurred and the room seemed to be in constant motion. The woman swaying by the door, the doctor looming over her.

She blinked and the memory eased up. The feel of Brad's hand in hers gave her strength to go on. The worst was yet to come. She took a long breath and told Brad what happened next. Every detail — every single painful, horrific detail about what she felt and heard and the heartbreak she felt.

"The memory is so clear, like it happened yesterday," Emma squinted toward the horizon, wishing for a way to go back and change the past. "But after a while I began to lose consciousness. Maybe the medicine, or the reality … knowing what was happening."

She heard bits and pieces of the doctor's conversation, something about being further along. By then, she didn't feel like she was on a cold abortion table in a clinic in downtown Wilmington. Rather she was holding her baby in her arms, protecting her baby. *Everything's okay, little one. No one's ever going to hurt you again.* Someone touched her shoulder … once and then again. Go away, she wanted to shout. But she was too tired to speak. She didn't want to be roused awake, not now and maybe not ever.

But eventually she heard the doctor's voice. "It's over. You can open your eyes."

Emma blinked, not sure where she was. She gasped as the realization hit her full force. She was in a clinic having an abortion, and now … "My baby?"

"The pregnancy is terminated." He looked satisfied with himself. "Your procedure was successful." He stepped back. "You were a week or so past the twelve-week mark." He paused, and then almost as an afterthought he said, "It was a girl, by the way."

They were words that stayed with Emma while the doctor cleaned her up and dismissed himself. Words that haunted her and mocked her while she rested for the next half hour and after she dressed herself and walked — with the help of the older woman — back down the hallway to the place where Brad was waiting. The baby was a girl.

Words that would stay with her forever.

Thunder rumbled in the distance and Emma looked at Brad through dry eyes. The pieces of the story were only just hitting him. He hung his head for a long time, and tears began falling to the sand. He still held her hand, only now his grip was much harder than before. Sobs began to quietly hit him, flexing the muscles in his back.

Emma wanted to do something to help, but there was nothing. Every day since then she'd grieved the loss of their little girl, but for Brad the grieving was only just beginning. He had lost a daughter, something he hadn't really understood until just now.

He dragged the back of his hands across his cheeks and finally lifted his head and looked at her. "It wasn't her fault ... our baby girl." He breathed in three quick times through his nose, clearly fighting the heartache. "I'm sorry, Emma. You've ... carried this loss ... all these years."

"I would've told you." She released his hand and put her arm around his shoulders. Her first love, her best friend. The man she had come to view as an enemy. Her strained voice was barely louder than the crashing surf. "You didn't ask about any of it. I figured ... you didn't deserve to know about her."

Brad's face twisted in a mask of unbearable grief. "Our daughter ... our little girl."

"Yes." Emma removed her arm from his back and covered her face. Her own tears had stopped as she told her story, but now the loss welled up inside her like a bottomless ocean of sorrow. "She … she would be nine."

A sound, part sob, part guttural cry came from Brad. "We never got to hold her." Brad slid closer and put both his arms around Emma, cradling her, clinging to her. "I'm sorry. I'm so sorry."

There was nothing more they could say, nothing they could do. Their baby girl was gone, and no amount of tears or pain would bring her back. Still they stayed that way, lost in the moment, unaware of anything but the tragedy they'd shared, the tragedy they'd lived with ever since.

Another clap of thunder sounded, this one closer than before. Brad released his hold on her and helped her to her feet. He sniffed and seemed to try to get a grip on his emotions. "We need to get inside."

Emma looked at the sky just as a bolt of lightning flashed out over the ocean. There was only one place they could go, whether it was smart to bring Brad Cutler there or not. "My house. We need to hurry."

With tears still on their faces, they grabbed their sunglasses and jogged along the packed wet sand near the water. The storm was getting closer, and as they neared the pier they saw families packing up in a hurry, grabbing blankets and picnic baskets and children and running for their cars.

"My bag." Emma pointed ten yards ahead and Brad ran to get it. He snatched the bag and both their shoes. There was no time to put them on.

"I'll follow you." Enormous raindrops were beginning to fall, and they both dropped their sunglasses in Emma's bag.

She raced up the sand with Brad close behind, toward the path between the houses and straight up Dolphin Street, up her front porch steps and safely inside her house, both of them out of breath and soaking wet. The screen door slammed shut, but Emma didn't close the other one. The sound of the storm raging outside mixed with their jagged breathing.

Brad set the bag down and he came closer, his eyes locked on hers. Rain dripped from his dark blond hair and hung in his eyelashes, but only then did Emma realize that the water on his face wasn't only from the rain. He stared at her, studied her. "It's still hitting me. That you've lived with this," his sides heaved from the run up the beach, from the news he'd just learned. "All these years you've lived with it."

"Who was I going to tell?" Her chin quivered, and she brushed her wet hair off her face. She was still catching her breath too. "You left, Brad. You wanted to get on with your life."

At first it looked like he might say something, try to explain himself. But then he looked at her for a long moment, and he did the only thing either of them could do. He came to her and wrapped his arms around her, holding her close the way two parents might hold each other at the funeral of their only child. "If there was a way back …" he breathed the words into her hair, holding tight to her. "I'm sorry, Emma. Our little girl … our baby."

The lightning was closer now, the crack of thunder more pronounced. As if all of heaven and earth were grieving right alongside them. In all her life she never expected to share the details of that awful day. But Brad had come back to her and he was sorry. He wanted to know, and she was glad she'd told him. But there remained a question for both of them. The question that consumed Emma as she stood lost in the moment, locked in Brad's tormented embrace. She'd told him everything there was to say.

So … where did they go from here?

BRAD COULDN'T BRING HIMSELF TO LET go of her. His sweet Emma, the girl he'd harmed so greatly. He wasn't sure what he'd expected by coming here, but now he knew the whole story. Emma's fear and doubts, her terrifying experience at the clinic, and the most difficult truth of all.

The baby was a girl.

Like the toddler in the photograph in his office. All along he'd wondered if maybe he and Emma would've had a daughter. And now that she was real, the pain of losing her was more than he could bear. For several minutes they stayed in each other's arms, a few feet away from the screen door of her small house, the storm raging outside.

He stroked her back, holding her, as if by doing so they could find their way to the moment before, as if they could run back to the car and life would be completely different. They could change their mind and today there would be a precious nine-year-old girl in place of the guilt and sorrow and regret. But there was no way back, and a decade of tears flooded out any other thought in Brad's mind. All along he'd told himself he was coming here to make things right with Emma, to apologize. But he knew better now. This trip was about his own healing as much as it was about hers. It was about acknowledging a life that never had a chance because of the choices they made.

This trip was about their daughter.

Emma pulled away first, wiping at her eyes. "I need water."

He let her go, but he followed her into the kitchen. Neither of them said anything as she poured two glasses and they drank them. Every thirty seconds or so lightning flashed around them and sharp thunder crackled outside. Emma set her glass down and stepped into an adjacent utility room. She grabbed two towels, one for each of them. They dried off and then Emma walked slowly back into her front room. She sat on a threadbare floral sofa, and Brad took the spot beside her.

Her eyes met his and she looked eighteen again. "I miss her." She wasn't crying anymore, but her lip quivered and her soft voice broke. She looked weary and worn out. "You don't know how much I miss her." Thunder rattled the house, and Emma's eyes searched his. "Stay with me, Brad. For a little while more."

She took a pillow from the far side of the sofa and set it on his knees. Then as if she couldn't bear to sit up another minute, she curled onto her side and set her head on the pillow. Brad stroked her hair, and it occurred to him that the thing he'd come here to do wasn't possible. He couldn't make things right with Emma. Only God could do that — for either of them.

Without taking this loss to Him, they would only find a never-ending, exhaustive source of grief and sorrow. There would be no healing short of the miraculous healing that would come from Christ alone. Brad was suddenly glad they still had tomorrow. If Emma was willing, he wanted to take her to church. Maybe stay afterward and talk to the pastor. What they'd shared today was important and it was a first step. But rather than healed and whole, both their hearts were ripped open, the loss of their daughter too overwhelming and crippling to move beyond. Now or ever.

Brad ran his fingers along Emma's hair for another hour, long after she'd fallen asleep, until the storm moved on and night fell over the beach. Here he was alone with Emma Landon, a million miles away from Laura and his life back in New York. He still loved Emma, he knew that now. But not the way he had before. The love he felt now had more to do with the shared loss of their daughter, and the weight of the mistakes they'd made ten years earlier. They never should've gone to the clinic, never should've had the abortion. Maybe then he never would've said good-bye, and today — this stormy afternoon — would've been marked by the laughter of a nine-year-old girl.

"I'm sorry, Emma … you don't know how sorry I am," he whispered the words, not loud enough to wake her. There were moments today when he wasn't sure how he could walk away from Emma again, but watching her now he was more clear-headed. He did not want a new love with Emma. He wanted the old one, along with their daughter and everything that would've been so different if they hadn't had the abortion. He wanted a way back.

But there was none.

When he was sure she was okay, and that she wouldn't wake up, he slid off the sofa and looked around the room. He found a quilt in a wicker basket beneath the windowsill a few feet away. He carried it back to her, unfolded it, and carefully spread it over her. Then for a long time he looked at her, the striking features and damp dark hair.

He would call her in the morning, ask her to go to church with him. He needed to know she was going to be whole and well after this. To the degree that it was possible. As he left her house, as he silently closed the door behind him, he realized something that terrified him. They only had one day left together. They needed to find closure and healing tomorrow, with God and each other. If they didn't, he couldn't imagine getting on a plane and returning home to Laura. Not because he didn't love her, and not because he had doubts about marrying her.

But because unless she was okay, he wasn't going to leave Emma Landon again.

Twenty-Four

LAURA MADE THE DECISION EARLY THAT morning to take Bella Joy up on her offer and head into the city. She was tired of feeling sad, tired of lying in bed crying, and most of all, tired of her new role as victim. She didn't want to talk about centerpieces or flowers or whether it was time to at least warn their hundreds of guests that the wedding was in jeopardy.

She wanted an escape. A trip into Manhattan seemed like the perfect answer.

They met up at Laura's house around noon and the two of them were taken into the city by one of the Towne Cars from the service Laura's father used. Bella Joy waited until they were in the car, a glass panel separating them from the driver, before she turned to Laura. "Have you heard from him?"

"No." Every hour that passed without a second call made Laura more certain things were not going the way Brad had planned. He had clearly found his old girlfriend, and they'd stumbled onto some still-strong connection. Otherwise he would've at least left her another message. "Monday's coming." Laura refused to get emotional. She patted her friend's hand. "I'll know more then."

Bella Joy studied her for a long moment and then smiled, her expression marked by compassion and understanding. "You don't want to talk about it?"

"Not now." She sucked in a sharp breath, keeping her sadness and uncertainty at bay. "Today I don't want to think about Brad or talk about him. If it's over between us I need to know I can be okay without him."

A deeper knowing filled Bella Joy's eyes. "Got it." She smiled again and gave Laura's hand a quick squeeze. "Today it's just us and the city."

"Exactly." Laura swallowed the fear and hurt. She was only saying what she wished were true. She couldn't really stop herself from missing Brad Cutler any more than she could stop her heart from beating. But she could pretend for a day. Even that much would be better than hiding away in her room.

Bella Joy filled the rest of the ride with a story about her friend who'd landed the ensemble role in *Wicked*. The details were just distracting enough, and by the time the driver let them off at Fifth Avenue and Central Park, Laura was fairly sure she could get through the day without dwelling on Brad, without imagining what he was doing. Even if she still missed him.

"Coffee?" Bella Joy's eyes sparkled.

Laura was grateful to her friend. Not only was Bella Joy willing to let the subject of Brad die for the day, she would do everything in her power to make their time together as fun and normal as possible. Laura hung her long purse straps across her body and grinned. "A trip down Fifth Avenue without Starbucks?" she laughed. "Impossible."

They walked past Tiffany's and ducked into the lobby level of Trump Tower, up one floor in the glass elevator, and into a busy Starbucks. They ordered a couple of grande soy lattes, extra hot, and then set out south on Fifth Avenue. Laura was glad this wasn't where she'd purchased her wedding dress. Instead they window shopped for handbags at Louis Vuitton and Gucci, and a Father's Day tie for Bella Joy's dad at Bergdorf Goodman.

Laura's only purchase was a short-sleeve polo at Lacoste for her mother. "For her golfing dates with my dad." Laura smiled at Bella Joy as she paid. She loved looking at the stores on Fifth Avenue, but she rarely felt right buying anything. Many of the stores had clothing items well over a thousand dollars. Ridiculous, really.

Their shopping led them to H&M across from St. Patrick's Cathedral. The store was three stories high, full of the newest fashions at rock-bottom prices. Bella Joy found two pairs of shorts and three summer tops for under a hundred dollars total, and Laura bought two jean Capri pants and a summer dress for less money than the tax on other items along Fifth Avenue.

Laura glanced at St. Patrick's as they made their way south, but she didn't mention stopping inside and Bella Joy didn't either. Laura looked up at the blue sky overhead. *God ... be with Brad. Whatever he's doing today. I don't know what's happening, but You do. For today that has to be enough.* She uttered the silent prayer, but she kept walking past the ornate church. She didn't need a reason to lose her composure. They passed NBC's headquarters and Rockefeller Center, and they spent half an hour in Anthropologie, where Bella Joy bought a colorful tablecloth for the summer picnics she hoped to have with Laura and their other friends. "Sometimes it's all in the setting."

"That's true." Laura loved this, loved these few hours where she didn't have to think about Brad or their wedding or her life with or without him. She wanted to hug her friend. Bella Joy had spent the day doing exactly what Laura had asked—keeping things light and avoiding any discussion of Brad. Before they left Anthropologie, Laura picked out a pair of sandals for herself and a candle for her mother.

Once they were back out on the street, she called for the car. They set their bags inside but declined his offer of a ride to the theater. "We'll call you after the show," Laura told him. "Sometime around midnight." The driver promised to stay on call if the girls changed their mind or needed him sooner.

They walked farther west on Forty-Ninth toward Broadway and ate dinner at Sbarro in Times Square. It wasn't fancy, but they ordered salmon and baked ziti and took their food to a table downstairs. Bella Joy talked about the guy she knew who worked at the Stardust Diner up Broadway a few blocks. "He's been going to Times Square Church, the one that meets in that old theater. Bunch of Broadway people attend. He says it's a great worship service, great preaching. I'm sort of interested."

Laura raised her brow, again happy for the diversion. "In the guy or the church?"

A sparkle lit up Bella Joy's eyes. "I'm not sure." She took a sip from her bottled water. "You're the first person I've told."

The conversation moved from that to the idea that Bella Joy still intended to audition for dance roles on Broadway. "It's something that never really leaves you."

"Mmmm." Laura's mind flitted to an image of Brad, the two of them walking hand-in-hand through Central Park in happier times. "Some things in life never do."

Their dinner flew by and they walked north to Fifty-First, west to the Gershwin. The show was set to start in fifteen minutes, and a flood of people gathered near the door, buzzing with excitement as they made their way into the theater. Laura had tried to see *Wicked* a number of times, but for one reason or another her plans never worked out. She and Brad had seen most of the other shows — even the new hit sensation, *In the Heights*. But this would be Laura's first time to see the prequel to the *Wizard of Oz*, a show that had become one of Broadway's biggest.

Inside, the theater was decorated with an enormous map of Oz and other items that looked like they'd been plucked from the set of the original movie. Laura hadn't read *Wicked*, the book — most people said it was a very dark story and not anything like the Broadway play. But she knew the premise. *Wicked* told a story that explained what happened before the twister hit Dorothy, the story of the friendship between the good and bad witches of Oz.

Their seats were amazing, fourth row center. Bella Joy leaned close as they sat down. "It helps having a friend in the show."

"No doubt." Laura leaned back in her seat as the house lights went down around them. From the first note, Laura was swept into the beautiful story. She felt tears in her eyes when Elphaba —the green girl—sang about the guy of her dreams falling for Glinda and not her. The actress playing the role had a brilliant voice, and as she sang the line, "I'm not that girl ..." Laura felt herself relating. That's what had happened with Brad, right? He had left and returned to his first love. No matter what his reason, or how he'd tried to justify his time in North Carolina, the fact remained. Right now, no matter how much she loved him, she wasn't the girl he wanted to be with.

Just like the song.

Bella Joy quietly pointed out her friend, and Laura was impressed. The girl was a beautiful dancer, and it was easy to see why she'd gotten the part. After intermission, the other moment that hit her was at the end when Glinda and Elphaba find each other again and share a good-bye song. "It well may be ... That we will never meet again." The words hit Laura square in the heart. Was that how it was going to be with her and Brad? They would have one last time together and then they'd say good-bye? The song played out, and Laura dabbed quietly at her tears. "Because I knew you ... I have been changed ... for good." The song told about moving on and finding forgiveness, knowing that what the two had shared was never going to last. But it would never be forgotten either.

Laura watched through eyes blurred with tears. That's how it would feel with Brad. If she were forced to walk away from him, she would do so believing that the experience of loving him had changed her for good. Bella Joy must've recognized that Laura was crying, because she slipped an arm around Laura's shoulders and gave her a side hug. Laura was grateful for the show's final number, when she had time to compose herself. When the lights came up, she dabbed her fingers beneath her eyes. "Amazing. I'd see it again tomorrow."

It was Bella Joy's third time to see the play and she nodded her agreement. "This was the strongest cast yet. The show gets better every time you see it."

They filed out with the crowd and crossed the parking area to the stage door. Bella Joy's friend had left their names on a list, and they were ushered inside and up a service elevator to the stage level where they met the dancer. For half an hour she gave them a tour of the wings and the costume area. Then she had a meeting with the cast, and Laura and Bella Joy left the theater and walked back toward Broadway and the Stardust Diner.

The place was packed, bustling with tourists and theater-goers. A waitress was singing "Ain't No Mountain High Enough" as they walked in. "There he is," Bella Joy had to shout to be heard, but she pointed at a waiter across the diner. "That's my friend. His name's Adam."

Adam was tall with pale-blond hair and a tanned narrow face. He noticed them right away and met them at the door. Bella Joy introduced him to Laura, and though he was polite, his interest was entirely on Bella Joy. Laura was suddenly very aware of her engagement ring. She was proud of it, proud of all it stood for. But was she really still taken? She twisted the ring nervously and followed Bella Joy and Adam. He took her hand and led her through the madness. "Come on. I've got a table for you in the middle of the action."

As he was seating them, another waiter, a tall guy with curly dark hair and flirty eyes approached them. He walked up to Laura and accompanied her to the table, the two of them trailing Bella Joy and Adam. He held out his right hand to shake hers as they walked.

"Hi." He yelled over the loud singing. Their fingers connected briefly. "I'm Donny." His eyes held hers. "The most beautiful girl in New York City walks through the door, I figure I should at least introduce myself."

Laura felt her cheeks grow hot. She hadn't thought of herself as being attractive to other guys in years. He mustn't have seen her ring. The chaotic restaurant was brightly lit and very loud. She leaned in close enough to be heard. "I'm Laura."

Donny locked eyes with her. "Nice to meet you." He looked toward the back of the restaurant at another waitress signaling to him. "Looks like I'm up."

He wove his way past the tables and took a microphone from the waitress. At the same time, the music from "Lean on Me" started through the restaurant. Laura took a spot at the table across from Bella Joy, who was still talking with Adam. Now though, Adam promised to be back in a minute to take their order, and the attention of everyone in the diner was on Donny. The guy was charm and charisma personified, and he had a voice that belonged on a stage. He made eyes with a number of older women and children as he worked his way around the restaurant. But very quickly he sang his way to the booth where Bella Joy and Laura sat.

Before Laura knew what was happening, Donny sat in the booth beside her. "If … there is a load … That you can't carry …" he put his arm around Laura, playing to the crowd and hamming up the moment. But in his eyes he seemed to be singing the song to her alone, "I'll share your load … If you just call me."

Laura laughed along with the crowd, which clearly assumed he'd chosen her at random for the impromptu moment. But the feeling was more unsettling than she wanted to admit. She was engaged, after all. She had no right flirting with a stranger at a diner in Times Square. No matter what Brad was doing right now. Donny ended the song by passing the microphone from himself to her. "Call me ..." he'd sing, and then it would be her turn. "Call me ..." Back to him, "You just call me ..." And so on until the song was finished. He leaned in close. "You look like Reese Witherspoon, anyone ever tell you that?"

"Once in a while." Laura's heart beat faster than before. She didn't want to lead him on. The diversion was fun, but a part of her felt like she was betraying Brad.

"I'll be back later." For a second it seemed like he might kiss her cheek, but instead he winked at her, stood, and returned to his work waiting tables. Throughout the night when it was his turn to sing, he found a way to stop by her table. Laura did her best not to encourage him. Bella Joy didn't say a word, but several times she raised a single eyebrow in Laura's direction. "He likes you," she mouthed once.

"Just what I need." Laura made a face, trying to keep things light. They both laughed, but Laura felt sick to her stomach. What was she doing here? She should be home, praying for Brad. They ordered milk shakes and stayed until the restaurant closed at midnight. By then the place had emptied quite a bit, and Donny had been by the table as often as Adam. When Adam brought the check, he grinned at Laura. "Donny's my buddy. He thought maybe the four of us could hang out later."

A sudden wave of panic seized Laura. She couldn't do this. No matter what was happening with Brad, she couldn't waltz into the Stardust Diner and let herself be swept off her feet by some singing waiter. No matter how cute or kind he was. She shook her head. "I can't." She shot a look at Bella Joy. "We have to get back."

Adam hesitated, but then he smiled and shrugged. "Okay." He lightly touched Bella Joy's shoulder. "We're still on for church tomorrow?"

"Definitely." Bella Joy seemed anxious to steer the attention away from Laura. "I'll be there early."

Laura was grateful for her friend's sense of perception. It was time to leave. She said a quick good-bye to the guys, and once they were in the car, she slumped against the backseat. "I feel terrible."

"You didn't do anything wrong." Bella Joy seemed calm, happy with how the night had played out. "You wanted a diversion, and that's what it was. Nothing more." She talked about Adam most of the way home, but after they were back at Laura's house, Bella Joy hugged her. "I've met Donny before. He didn't mean anything."

"It just made me miss Brad." Laura couldn't explain how she felt. She wanted to be alone. "No big deal." Laura smiled. "Thanks for everything."

"Okay." Bella Joy hesitated. "Just because I didn't bring up Brad today doesn't mean I'm not thinking about him. I haven't stopped praying for both of you."

Again Laura reminded herself how fortunate she was to have friends like Bella Joy and the others. Laura wished Bella Joy well with Adam the next day and then watched her drive off. But before she turned in for the night she sat in a chair at the end of her parents' covered porch. The stars were out, and she wondered if they were out in North Carolina too.

Suddenly she was almost certain she hadn't spent the day the way she should have. She hadn't done anything wrong, true. But what had she done to help? Her fiancé was in the midst of a crisis. There was no other way to describe it. He hadn't called not because he didn't love her, but because he must've been an emotional wreck. Memories of what Laura had read on the Post Abortion Syndrome website came back to her. She wasn't the only victim in the situation. Brad was hurting, and it was time she stopped taking that truth like a personal attack. However this all ended, Brad never meant to hurt her.

Like she needed her next breath, Laura needed her Bible. She crept inside, found it in her parents' office, and returned to the porch. She used the light from her cell phone to read the words as she turned to Luke, chapter 6. She and her friends had read about loving their enemy and refusing to judge. They'd read about getting the plank out of their own eye so they could see clearly to help their brother with the speck in his. But what about the last part of the chapter?

Laura flipped through the pages until she found the section she was looking for. Quietly and with a growing sense of alarm, she began to read. *Be merciful, just as your Father is merciful. Do not judge, and you will not be judged.* Laura closed her eyes, and beneath her the ground no longer felt steady. She felt sick over her initial reaction to Brad's admission. She hadn't been merciful at all. She'd been critical and judgmental. As if she could never be capable of falling prey to sin or disappointing someone she loved.

But again, that wasn't the section of Scripture that was calling to her. She pressed on to the end of the chapter, to verse 46. *Why do you call me, 'Lord, Lord,' and do not do what I say?* The words felt reverent, like God Himself was standing here speaking to her. She had studied this section of the Bible for weeks with her friends. *Love when it's difficult to love … don't judge others … be merciful.* But never until now had it occurred to her that she hadn't put these words into practice.

I will show you what he is like who comes to me and hears my words and puts them into practice. He is like a man building a house, who dug down deep and laid the foundation on rock. When a flood came, the torrent struck that house but could not shake it, because it was well built. But the one who hears my words and does not put them into practice is like a man who built a house on the ground without a foundation. The moment the torrent struck that house, it collapsed and its destruction was complete.

What else was marriage if not two people laying a foundation for a life together? If she let Brad forever more take the blame for the heartache of this weekend, then she would walk around the rest of her life with a log jutting from her eye. Haughty and self-righteous. And in that way she would be the worst of all sinners. Because the thing God hated the most was the very pride that had marked Laura's recent feelings toward Brad. *How dare he be less than a virgin ... how terrible that he hadn't talked about his past sooner ... how wrong of him to have an abortion with his ex-girlfriend.* Proud and arrogant, grain by grain she was laying a foundation for the two of them on nothing but shifting sand. Even the slightest storm of life was bound to tear them apart if she forced him to be the bad guy, if she made him feel lucky because she took him back. How could Brad lead her into the future if she made him feel somehow lesser because he had made mistakes? As if she were somehow perfect.

Suddenly a picture filled her mind, something she needed to do when Brad returned. If he returned. Laura read the words at the end of Luke once more, and this time she didn't feel sorry for herself at all. Rather, she imagined Emma, a young woman who hadn't only lost her purity, but who had experienced an abortion, the loss of a child without so much as an apology from the guy she loved. The bigger picture was this: There was no shortage of victims in the situation. Laura looked up to the stars. *Dear God ... I tried to run away from the pain today, but it didn't go anywhere. It's still here waiting for me.* She thought about Donny, the singing waiter. She had no right flirting tonight, not even a little. *I would've been better off here, talking to You.*

Pray without ceasing, Daughter. Pray for your beloved.

Yes, that's what she would do. She would pray that Brad would come home, and that he would forgive her pride and arrogance. And she would plan to bring to life the picture God had given her. More than that, she would pray for Emma to forgive, and for Brad to be strong. Strong enough to make things right with her, and strong enough together with his first love to grieve the loss of their child. Strong enough with God's help to put the matter behind them. By praying this way, Laura would build the beginning of a firm foundation for Brad and herself. Of course, she would pray for one more thing—pray for it as if her life depended on the outcome.

That after spending a weekend with Emma, Brad would be strong enough to come home again.

Twenty-Five

BRAD WAS UP AT SUNRISE, AND by seven o'clock Sunday morning he parked his Jeep along Ocean Boulevard at the end of Dolphin Street. He climbed out and walked onto the sand. All signs of yesterday's storm were gone, and the sun sparkled off the water. It was too early for the holiday weekend crowd, and other than a few metal detector junkies and a couple lone joggers, he was alone. Which was what he wanted. He needed to think, and he couldn't imagine a better place.

The reality had kept him awake, haunting him through the night. He and Emma had been parents to a baby girl, and their decision had cost their daughter her life. Their little girl ... the child that would never be. If he had that day to do over again, he never would have driven Emma anywhere near the clinic. They might've kept the baby or they might've given her up for adoption. But she would be alive.

He carried the burden of their decision like a blanket of lead around his shoulders. Without really knowing where he was going, he crossed the beach, walked up the stairs to the pier, and slowly headed to the far end. He leaned against the wooden railing for a long time, staring at the water, remembering. What sort of person had he been back then, taking her to the clinic and then never asking her what went on?

The truth about his actions made him feel sick to his stomach, and again he was convinced there was only one way to move forward. He checked his cell phone. It was seven thirty already. He'd looked up churches in the area earlier that morning at his parents' house, and he'd found a nine o'clock service at Holden Beach Community Church—a small congregation a few blocks from Emma's house.

He didn't want to wake her, but he needed to give her enough time to get ready. If she was even willing to go with him. He dialed her number, and she picked up on the third ring. "Hello?" Her voice sounded groggy.

"Hi. It's me." He pressed the phone to his ear so he could hear above the sound of the wind and waves. "How are you?"

A long silence followed before she answered him. "You left."

"You needed to sleep."

"Yes." She sounded more awake now. "Where are you?"

"On the pier. I was up early so I took a walk."

More silence. "So ... what do we do now?"

He was glad he wasn't with her in person. All he wanted to do was take her in his arms again and protect her from another hour of pain. But that sort of protection couldn't come from him. He understood that now. "I was hoping ... you might go to church with me. There's one close to your house. Service is at nine o'clock."

"Church?" Her tone sounded weary at the idea. "Really, Brad? That's what you want to do today?"

He understood her cynicism, but he had to press on. Had to find a way to make her understand where he was coming from. "Emma ... I came here to apologize. I wanted to find closure and healing for both of us." His voice was thick, remembering her story from yesterday. "It's just ... I've been thinking about it and ... I don't think it's possible without finding peace with God first."

He half expected her to laugh at him, tell him she didn't want anything more to do with him. Or maybe she would hang up without another word. But instead he heard her sigh—a long, drawn-out, sad-sounding sigh. "Fine." She had her guard up again. He could hear it in her voice. "Meet me here at eight thirty."

He felt his heart grow light with gratitude. God had done this. There was no other explanation. "I'll be there."

Most of the next hour he spent talking to God. *Lead us, Father … show me how to make amends with her and with You. I've failed so completely, Lord. Please lead me now.*

When it was time, he walked slowly back to his Jeep and drove up to Emma's house. Along the way he thought about Laura. He wanted to call her, assure her that he was working through the situation with Emma as quickly and completely as he could. But the timing felt wrong. He was in Emma's world now. He needed to tend to the matter at hand before he could look ahead to Laura. Still, he prayed for her too. That she would have the grace to understand. He never meant to hurt her with any of this. That was just it. He was tired of causing pain. That's why he was here.

He knocked on Emma's door, and he remembered hundreds of times when he'd done this very thing at her mother's house — times when he'd ridden his bike to her front door and times when he'd driven to see her after he bought his '65 Mustang the year he turned seventeen. Her red Cabriolet was parked in the driveway, so it was easy to feel lost in an old scene.

She answered the door, sunglasses firmly in place. She wore a short-sleeve sundress, one that flowed down around her knees but was completely modest. The way her long hair hung around her shoulders, Brad had to force himself to remember the reason he was there. He gave her a quick hug. "Thank you."

"I'm not sure why I'm going." She gave him a weary smile.

"Maybe we'll know afterward."

They said little as they rode in his Jeep to the church a few blocks away.

The place was made of red brick, small but friendly looking with large trees framing the grounds. Already people were milling about, children chasing each other and parents standing in small clusters of conversation.

"I can't do this." Emma held tight to the door handle. She removed her sunglasses and pleaded with Brad. "I don't belong here."

"Neither of us do." Brad looked out at the people already there. "No one belongs here." He smiled sadly. "I think that's the whole point."

"People will recognize me, Brad. Everyone knows me in this town."

He hadn't thought about that. "We'll sit in the back."

Again she reluctantly gave in. He climbed out first and held open her door. Together they walked in, exchanging greetings with several people as they moved inside the church building. "You know any of them?"

"Not yet." Emma kept her eyes down, even after they found seats near the back.

Brad opened the church bulletin and the title of the sermon hit him with a force he hadn't expected. *Forgiveness — The Missing Peace.* Only God could've done this ... brought them here for a sermon that seemed written for them alone.

He nudged Emma and pointed at the title.

She read it, and he watched her eyes well up with tears. As the service began he had the feeling the room held just the pastor and the two of them. The message was from 1 John, chapter 1, and the words seemed to be for Brad and Emma alone. Brad took hold of her hand and wondered if she felt the same way about the message.

"If we claim to be without sin, we deceive ourselves and the truth is not in us. If we confess our sins, he is faithful and just and will forgive us our sins and purify us from all unrighteousness."

The purification process, the pastor went on to say, was where peace came from. "Forgiveness is the missing peace, the peace we're all seeking."

Beside him, Emma hung her head. Her tears slid down her cheeks and onto her dress, and Brad no longer had to wonder. The sermon was hitting her the same way. When the service ended, the pastor talked to a dozen people and waited for the church to clear. The whole time, Emma and Brad stayed seated. Again, no one approached them, and Brad guessed it was painfully obvious that they needed their privacy. But when the pews were empty, the pastor walked back and stopped a few feet from them. Kindness marked his smile. "I'm Pastor Dave." He held out his hand, and Brad shook it. "You're new."

Emma barely looked up, so Brad took the lead. "Yes, it's our first time. I'm from out of town." He looked at Emma, at the brokenness that emanated from her. "My friend here, Emma, she lives near the beach."

"The next service doesn't start for an hour. I can talk if you'd like."

Brad had expected Emma wouldn't want a conversation. She was clearly not crazy about being here, and the message had been difficult for both of them—even if it seemed directed right at them. But she looked at the pastor. "I have a question." She wasn't crying anymore, but her voice was laced with fear and sorrow.

"Ask it." The pastor was in his late forties. His smile was warm and he didn't seem the least bit judgmental. "That's why I'm here."

"Okay." She tightened her hold on Brad's hand. "Can God forgive *anything*?"

The pastor waited a few seconds. "Yes, definitely." Compassion lightened his expression. "When a person confesses their sins, when true sorrow is expressed toward God, then yes. God will forgive. That's why Jesus went to the cross."

It seemed like Emma might add greater detail, but then she must've changed her mind. "If … I wanted to talk to someone some other time … not today, but later. A woman, maybe. Would there be someone you could recommend?"

"Several people." His body language was open, inviting, his hands at his sides. "There's a wonderful Christian counselor in town, and a few women's support groups meet here. My wife's another resource. She heads up the women's ministry."

Emma nodded. "I might … need to talk to someone." She narrowed her eyes, her heartache spilling into her expression. "I want that peace … the peace you talked about."

"It's available. Jesus offers it to everyone." He pulled a business card from his coat pocket and handed it to her. "What's your last name, Emma?"

"Landon." She moved to the edge of the pew and Brad sensed a new sort of strength inside her. "Emma Landon."

If he recognized her as one of the teachers at the nearby elementary school, he didn't say so. Instead he asked for her number. "I'll have my wife give you a call. If you don't mind."

Emma hesitated, and silently Brad prayed for her. He was witnessing a breakthrough. *Please God, don't let anything stand in the way. Emma needs to be set free. We both do.*

"Okay." She looked quickly at him and at the pastor again. Then she cleared her throat and rattled off her number. Pastor Dave scribbled it on the back of another one of his cards. He shook Emma's hand and then Brad's. "Nice meeting both of you."

"Thanks." Brad released Emma's hand. "We needed to be here."

"It's that way with all of us." He hesitated. The small church was empty except for the three of them. "Would you mind … if I prayed for you?"

Brad looked at Emma, at the way she still seemed nervous and uncertain. It truly was a miracle that she'd even stepped foot in a church after so many years. He didn't wait for her approval.

Instead he cautiously nodded at the pastor, and he slipped his arm around Emma's shoulders. "We'd like that. Thank you."

"Okay." The pastor smiled. "Let's pray then." He put one hand on Emma's shoulder, the other on Brad's. "Dear Father, these two young people are hurting. I can see that and certainly You can see that. I pray that whatever path has led them here, You would help them believe that this is where they're supposed to be. Every moment in all their lives has led to this one, and You, Lord, are calling them, asking them to step into Your loving embrace." He paused, his prayer unrushed. "You alone offer the healing we all need, Lord. The peace we all seek. You know the story of these two people. So please let this be a beginning for Brad and Emma. Where forgiveness is needed, let there be forgiveness. Where confession is required, let them confess. Be with them, Father. Let Emma find a point of connection with the women of our church, and let her feel Your love in this place and as she leaves here." His smile sounded in his tone. "Thank You, Lord, for You are the Lifegiver. You alone. In Jesus' name, amen."

Pastor Dave thanked them again for coming, and he promised Emma that someone would call her soon. As they left, he looked deeply at her. "You're going to be okay, Emma. Now that you're here, you're going to be okay."

Emma didn't say anything, but she stepped away from Brad and hugged the pastor. In a tortured whisper, she uttered the only words that seemed appropriate. "Thank you."

Brad had no idea what to say to Emma as they left. He somehow felt silence was stronger than any words he might add to the pastor's prayer.

When they reached the car, Emma turned to him. "I want to show you something. Down on the beach."

"Now?" He wore long pants and a short-sleeve dress shirt. His shoes still had sand in them from his earlier walk. "I have other clothes in the Jeep. Maybe we should change and meet at your house in half an hour."

Emma agreed, and the ride back to her house took place in reverent silence. Something was happening—and Brad hoped it was the healing he'd prayed for. Whatever it was, Emma was different than she'd been that morning or yesterday. Stronger somehow. He smiled at her when he pulled up in front of her house. "I'll be back."

"Okay." She held his eyes for a long moment. Then she climbed out and ran lightly up the stairs to her front door.

Brad found a café in town with a restroom where he switched into his khaki shorts and a navy blue T-shirt. He bought a bottle of water and drove through town, killing time, thinking of what Emma might want to show him. The hour passed quickly, and Brad returned to her front door. She opened it, wearing white Capris and a red shirt. She looked beautiful, though he wasn't about to say so. She had something to show him on the beach, and he prayed they might talk about the sermon, about her thoughts on God and what came next in their healing. He had to stay focused.

"Come in for a minute." Her dog was beside her, and she smiled down at him as she rubbed behind his ear. "Riley's a good dog."

"Hi, boy." Brad patted his head. He'd been too distracted to pay Riley much attention the other night. "He's huge for a lab."

"It's all muscle." She laughed, giving the dog a hearty side rub. "Right, buddy? You're all muscle."

Brad liked seeing this, a happy part of Emma's new life. "You run with him, right?"

"All the time." She looked at him, and the transparency in her eyes took his breath. Whatever distance had built up between them over the years, it was gone now. "Go sit in the living room. I need to let Riley out."

He did as she asked, finding his place on the floral sofa, the place where they'd cried in each other's arms the day before. When she returned, she was carrying a cardboard box. She sat down and put the box on the floor in front of her.

Brad wanted to slide closer, take a better look at whatever was inside the box. But he held his ground, maintaining the slight distance between them. In some ways this was dangerous territory, here alone with Emma Landon. He was enjoying himself, enjoying the way he felt beside her. He reminded himself to keep his heart in check. Today there was a sense of urgency, a determination to make the most of the time they had left. Brad was pretty sure they both felt it. "I thought … you wanted to show me something on the beach."

"I do." The sadness that was a part of her now was back. "I found this box after church. I wanted you to see a few things in it."

Brad angled himself so he was facing her. The first thing she pulled from the box was a weathered teddy bear with a pink ribbon around his neck.

"Remember this?" She handed it to him. "You won it for me at the fair the summer before you started high school."

He touched the worn fur and a rush of memories came back. "I told you to sleep with it every night through eighth grade. Until we could be at the same school again."

Emma carefully took the bear from him and cuddled it close, in a way that made her look like a young girl again. "I slept with it until the day you left for college. Every night."

He pictured her laying next to the old bear and longing for a way to keep what they'd once shared. The picture made him want to hold her again, tell her once more how sorry he was. But she didn't seem to want his pity today. She breathed in deep the smell of the bear and then she set it gently back in the box.

Next she pulled out a high school yearbook, its red cover emblazoned with the words, Wilmington High — Class of 1999. The year Brad graduated. "We brought these home at the end of May." She lifted her eyes to his and the message was unmistakable. The end of May. Before they started taking trips to Holden Beach. Before everything changed.

"Emma ..." He wasn't sure he could do this. No amount of looking through yesterday's treasures would take them back. Tears welled in his eyes. "I'm not sure ..."

"Please." Her eyes held a strength he didn't feel. "I want you to remember us ... the way we were ... before. What happened that summer, our choices ruined everything. But when I found this box." She looked down for a moment, and a fondness shone in her eyes. "When I found this, I remembered how great it really was before. Please ... remember it with me."

He didn't need to be coaxed into remembering. He was already there, as soon as she brought the teddy bear from the box. He nodded, his throat too tight to say anything.

Emma ran her hand over the cover of the yearbook, and then as if the pages were somehow sacred, she opened it to the front cover. "Here," she handed it to him. "Read what you wrote."

Brad didn't want to, but he had no choice. He needed this, needed to remember how much he had truly loved her. The past nine years when he looked back, all he saw was how things ended. How terribly sad and awkward they'd been when they parted ways for good. But this ... this would tell the truth about his feelings. He took the yearbook onto his lap and saw his familiar handwriting. Emma watched as he started at the beginning, his own voice playing silently in his mind.

My sweet, precious Emma ... how can I be leaving high school already? Remember when our days together seemed like they'd go on forever? Like the routine of waking up and heading off to school felt like it would never end? But here it is, and I have to tell you a few things. First, nothing's going to change between us. I'll go to UNC, and you'll join me in a year. You have your bear, so he can keep you company when I'm not here.

Brad blinked back tears. He reached for Emma's hand and held it as he continued reading. *Every memory I have is colored by you, by your laughter and love. I thank God that you and I have put Him first. We've stayed away from the stupid stuff everyone else is doing, and we'll stay away from it until the day I marry you. And I will marry you, Emma. No one ever loved you more than I do.*

Tears trickled down Brad's face and splashed onto the page. He dabbed at them, struggling to keep control. He had loved her. This was more proof than he needed. He blinked and found his place again.

Graduation is just another phase. We've been through grade school and middle school. We even survived Wilmington High. I know with all my heart we'll survive what's next, and one day … one day I'll give you that ring we always talk about. You are my other half, Emma Landon. I love you and don't you forget it. Always and forever … your love, your best friend … Brad.

"See …" Emma was still stoic, still not crying. As if by showing him these things she was somehow vindicated in the pain she'd carried all these years. "See how much you loved me, Brad."

He wiped at his eyes. "I did. More than I wanted to remember."

"The ending was ugly, and I think … I think you wanted to forget what happened before all that. But it happened." She smiled, her eyes glistening. "We were something back then."

"We were." His eyes found his signature once more, the date he'd scribbled at the bottom of the page. May 26, 1999. When all of life seemed carefree and forever stretched out with all the certainty of the seasons.

Emma took the book from him. She touched the page, smiling as if she were seeing it for the first time again. Then slowly she closed the cover and set it back in the box. "One more thing."

He wasn't sure how much more he could take. They couldn't go back to what they'd had, no way to undo the ugly ending. So why torture themselves now? Brad swallowed, but in a way he understood. Emma wanted him to remember the good times, the way they'd loved before they lost control. However hard it was, he owed her this.

She reached into the box and pulled out a coiled section of rope, and immediately Brad knew what it was. He felt fresh tears in his eyes. "Our rope."

"I kept it."

Brad looked at it, then he lifted his eyes to her. "I have a picture. The two of us holding onto the ends." He sniffed, unable to believe that this was it. The rope that had brought them together. "I always wondered ... what happened to it."

She stretched it out, running her hand over the soft fibers. "Craziest idea, making a couple of kids hold opposite ends of a rope for a whole week of recess."

"I'm not sure ..." he took hold of the other end. "I'm not sure I ever really let go."

For the first time since they'd sat down, there were tears in her eyes too. "Me either." She held tight to her side of the rope. "But after today ... we have to. We both have to."

He nodded and squeezed his eyes shut. "I know." He kept his hold on the rope and clenched his fist around it. Emma had kept the rope all this time? If he'd known that, would he really have left her after that awful summer? Holding the rope in his hand now made him wonder how they ever said good-bye, how they let life tear them apart. If only they'd found their way back to the rope, maybe ... a million maybes.

"I'm ready." She eased the rope from him, looped it, and held it to her side as she stood. "I want to take the rope to the beach, to the place I have to show you."

She reached into the box and pulled out one more thing. A small envelope. Only this time she didn't open it, didn't let him see what was inside. She set the rope and the envelope in her beach bag and lifted it onto her shoulder. Outside, the clouds were back, but there was no rain in the forecast. They had only a few hours left. "Walk with me, okay? One last time, Brad."

He wondered if his heart could take it. Gone now were all the lies he'd told himself, the lies about how Emma was someone he'd outgrown and how the relationship they'd shared was something young and less than serious. He had loved her more than life. They'd planned on forever, and they'd thrown it all away. He stood and nodded.

He would take this walk, wherever it took them.

Twenty-Six

EMMA LED THE WAY, AND BRAD followed at her side. When they reached the sand, she held out her hand to him and his heart melted with all they'd been through. All those years ago and again here—this weekend. Until now Brad had held her hand the polite way people held hands in prayer circles. Keeping his fingers together. But now as he took her hand, their fingers intertwined in a way that felt right, fitting for the moment. This time belonged to Emma and him. There was no room for pretending, not after all she'd reminded him of in the past hour.

They walked past the pier, toward the same parking lot where he'd left his dad's truck the first time he came here a week ago. He'd passed by this very area, and suddenly Brad had a slight idea where she was taking him. It couldn't be, could it? The beach was empty as they walked up the sandy hill, the area private and removed from the beachgoers far below. Gradually he could see he was right. She was leading him to the small white wooden cross. The very same one he'd seen when he was here before. Shock rang through him and he stopped, staring at the cross and then up at Emma. "I saw this. When I came here a week ago."

"You did?" Emma searched his face, as if she were trying to understand.

"I saw it, but I walked by. It ... it caught my eye ... that's all." He stooped down and saw something he hadn't before. The date etched into the weathered white wood. November 20, 1999. He touched it, ran his fingers over the letters and numbers. The wave of sorrow hit him unexpectedly. November twentieth. The day their daughter died. He gripped the top of the cross and slowly sank to his knees in the sand and grass. His head bowed in a canyon of grief deeper and wider than anything he'd ever known before.

She knelt beside him and put her arm around his shoulders. "I come by here all the time." Her voice was steady. "Whenever I run."

He looked at her and saw that her eyes were dry. She had already spent a decade grieving at the foot of the small white cross. "She was a real person. Our little girl." Emma covered his hand with her own, and together they clutched the top of the cross. A cool breeze rustled the long sea grass on either side of them. "I had to have some way to remember her."

Brad gripped the cross with all his might, with everything in him. As if by holding tight to it he could will himself back to that moment at the clinic, back to the place where they still had the chance to walk out. Back when their baby girl was still alive. But they hadn't backed out, and their daughter had died that day. November 20, 1999.

He covered his face with his free hand and he wept for the loss of this precious girl. For the way they'd missed holding her as an infant and watching her take her first steps. For the little voice they would never know and the smile they would never see. For every first and last they'd cheated themselves out of because of one very terrible, very final choice.

Brad had no idea how long he stayed that way, kneeling in the sand, Emma's arm around his shoulders, a lifetime of tears watering the place where the cross was planted. Finally, weary and worn out, he looked at her. "I miss her." He felt fresh tears, as if there would never be an end to the sorrow he'd caused. "How can I miss her when I never knew her?"

Still Emma's eyes were dry. "I miss her too. Every time I stop here. Every morning when I walk into school and pass the fourth-grade classroom. I miss her, Brad. This was all I ever wanted from you. That you might miss her too. We owe that to her, don't you think?"

He had a headache from crying, but he looked at the date again, the pitiful single date. "Yes." He wiped at his face again. "We owe that to her."

"I brought this." She removed her arm from his shoulders and took the envelope from her beach bag.

Inside was a small photograph of a little girl, one that looked familiar to Brad. Emma held it out so they could both see it, and he knew immediately who it was. "It's you. Back in grade school. Back when we held onto the rope."

"Yes." She smiled sadly at the photo. "I was nine. I think maybe this is what our little girl would've looked like. It helps me know she was real."

Brad brushed his fingers along the image of the young Emma. He didn't want to ask, because he was almost certain of her answer. But he'd come this far, and now he had no choice. "Did … you give her a name?"

"Yes." Emma slipped the photo back in the envelope and put the envelope back in the bag. She stared at the white cross again. "I named her Amanda. It means worthy of love. Because she was innocent. In every possible way, she was worthy of our love."

"Amanda." Brad wasn't sure he'd survive the pain, or the way his heart lay in countless pieces around the foot of the small white cross. Worthy of love. Yes, she was worthy.

"I like to believe," Emma's voice cracked, and for the first time since they'd set out toward the beach, tears filled her eyes, "that somewhere in heaven, my mom and Amanda are together. My mom loved children, and Amanda … she would've loved my mom." Emma's face contorted, and she squeezed her eyes shut. When she opened them, she ran her fingers over the date on the cross, and then she looked at Brad. "God would let them be together, don't you think?"

"Yes." Brad was absolutely certain. "Amanda and your mom are together. I'm sure they are."

"Good." Emma nodded. "I like believing that for her. For both of them." She sniffed and dried her cheeks. Again she seemed to find a control that amazed him. "We were wrong, Brad. No matter what people say about it being legal or a choice or anything else. What we did was wrong."

"It was."

She lowered herself to the ground, cross-legged, and faced him. "Pastor Dave said we need to confess our sins. That's the first step to forgiveness."

"Yes." This was what Brad had prayed for. Healing and forgiveness for both of them. But he had no idea how hard it would be once they reached this place.

Emma looked at the cross. "I've fought against God ever since that day. When my mom died ..." she inched herself around, her back to the cross.

Brad dropped down to the sand too, but he pulled up one knee and faced her.

The wind off the ocean sheltered the moment, making it feel private, almost dream-like. Emma gazed at the water, "I told her I'd hold onto my faith. So the two of us would see each other again." She found Brad's eyes again. "But I didn't mean it. My mom never knew what I'd done. I figured I'd go to my grave guilty, so I stopped believing in God. Because how could I let someone kill my baby?" Her voice was thick with pain. She breathed in slowly, as if she were finding a new sort of strength she hadn't known before. "But I can't live like this anymore. Feeling guilty. Running from life."

Brad understood how she felt. It was the same reason he was here today, and not being fitted for a tuxedo in New York City. They were still facing each other, their feet almost touching.

"This morning at church ... for the first time ... I heard God's voice. I felt Him calling me. I don't want to overthink this, or analyze it. But I'm tired of arguing against God." She reached out both hands and once more their fingers joined. "I only want to obey. I want the peace Pastor Dave was talking about today at church."

Brad felt a sunbeam of joy burst across the dry and barren landscape of his broken heart. "I want that too."

"I don't know how this works. I don't think God wants us to make it complicated." She held tight to his hands. "So I'll just say this." Quiet tears built up in her eyes and spilled onto her cheeks. The long sea grass around them blew in the breeze and sheltered them from the looks of any passersby. They were alone, the two of them and God and the memory of Amanda. Emma coughed a little and continued, her eyes never wavering. "I walked into that abortion clinic by my own free will, Brad. It was wrong—no matter who made the appointment, and no matter what the law says. I made a decision that killed my baby." Her voice broke and she hung her head. "That's my confession—before you and God."

Brad had never loved her more than he did in that moment. The strength she'd needed to say those words, was something that only could've come from God. Now it was his turn. He ran his thumbs along the tops of her hands and he searched for the right words. "Emma, when you told me you were pregnant, I wasn't brave. I didn't look to God for wisdom or help, and I thought only of myself." He looked straight to her heart, even though it felt like doing so might kill him. "I knew … I knew you were scared that day, but I only wanted everything to be how it was. I didn't care about you or the baby. I pushed you into the abortion and I caused the death of our little girl." Again the sorrow overwhelmed him, but even so he felt the freedom in his words. "That's my confession—before you and God." He searched her face, her eyes. "I'm sorry, Emma."

"I'm sorry too."

Brad didn't have to ask her. Their next step was as obvious as inhaling. "Pray with me."

She nodded and bowed her head, her eyes closed. He looked once more at the cross, and then he did the same thing. "Dear God, we come before You the way we should've a very long time ago. We were wrong. We've confessed that to You and to each other." Brad felt holy hands on his shoulders, and he was certain beyond anything in all his life that here on the hidden bluff along Holden Beach, they were in the presence of God Almighty. "Please forgive us, Father. Let us move on from this place healed and whole. And please," his tears choked his voice, but he pressed on. "Please let Amanda know we love her. And let her be with Emma's mother. Until we can see her one day in heaven."

"In Jesus' name ..." Emma's voice picked up where his left off. Then their voices came together. "Amen."

They opened their eyes, and for a while they said nothing, just looked at each other, basking in the moment. Brad was the first one to speak. "Do you feel it?"

"Yes." She smiled, and there was a light in her eyes that hadn't been there earlier. Not since before that summer. "I feel God."

"He's here." A burden lifted from Brad's shoulders, and despite the sadness that still marked the moment, he understood the gift they'd been given. "This is the peace that passes understanding. The one the Bible talks about."

While they'd been praying, the clouds had broken apart. Like the sky, the answers were clear now, all of them. And how could they not be? God had brought them together again and He'd forgiven them. Nothing would ever change that, and Brad was certain he would remember this moment as long as he lived. He and Emma and the cross.

And the presence of God all around them.

Twenty-Seven

EMMA SHIFTED HERSELF SO SHE WAS facing the beach, and Brad did the same. The sea grass danced on either side of them, the white cross behind them. "Look at the water, there ... where the sky is blue above it."

"It's beautiful." Brad's voice no longer rang with unbridled pain and loss. The peace he had spoken about was there for both of them. Brad breathed deep, as if he wanted to drink in the way he felt here on the shores of Holden Beach. "I've missed it."

Their elbows and knees touched, but there was nothing strange or uncomfortable about that now. A breakthrough had happened in Emma's heart, and she was certain about one thing. She would never be the same again. Not ever. The joy that had marked Kristin Palazzo's life, and the light that always shone from Frankie's smile, the forgiveness Gavin Greeley had told her about—that joy and light was hers now too. And Brad had been a part of that. No one could change what they'd shared on this beach today. No matter what tomorrow brought for the two of them.

A comfortable silence fell around them, and to their right, the sun was starting to set. Emma leaned her head on Brad's shoulder for a minute or so, and then she sat straight again, her eyes still on the shoreline. "Tell me about her, Brad. Your fiancée."

His answer didn't come quickly. "Really, Emma?" He turned, his eyes finding hers. "Now?"

"Yes." She wasn't ready before. Seeing Brad again, being near him, she had only wanted to remember the two of them the way they'd been before that summer. But now … now she was different. If they were going to say good-bye, she wanted him to have her blessing about his future. "Please, Brad. Tell me."

His eyes changed, and Emma could read them as easily as she had when she was a kid. Whoever she was, however they'd met … Brad loved her. He couldn't hide the fact if he wanted to. "Her name's Laura. Laura James." Brad looked away, turned his eyes back toward the ocean. "I work for her father. Her dad owns the ad firm in Manhattan. Where I work." He paused. "We met at a company picnic at her parents' house and we've dated ever since."

Emma allowed herself to feel the hint of jealousy. It was strange, hearing Brad talk about this other woman, and how he'd dated her for so many years. Until today Emma had been stuck back on the day Brad Cutler walked out of her life. Sure, she'd gotten her education and a job, moved into the house and picked up a few animals along the way. But she never dared let her heart move on. It was her way of punishing herself for what she'd done.

Not so for Brad. He had run from his pain, away from Emma and toward this other love, this Laura James. "She didn't know about us?"

"She didn't know about … about the baby. The abortion."

Emma hesitated, her back straighter than before. *Can I do this, God … can I get through this?*

I am with you, Daughter. I will never leave you.

The answer came like spring rain, watering her parched soul and assuring her of the change inside her. Yes, she could do this. With God's help she could hear the truth about Brad's life, about his fiancée. It was Sunday evening and his flight was set for the morning. There would be no other time for this conversation. "You told her?"

"I did." Brad sounded tired, as if he didn't want to go into great detail about this. "I told her father too."

Emma tried to imagine the shock Laura and her family must be feeling. Her wedding to Brad was supposed to happen in a month, but here he was at Holden Beach, lost in a moment with his first love. She didn't want to ask, but she was more ready for his answer now than she'd been on Friday. "You want to marry her, right? You still want that?"

Brad looked deep into her eyes, and the truth was plain without him saying a word. "I've wondered about that a lot this weekend."

"But you do." The wind blew at her hair, and she tucked a stray strand behind her ear so she could see him in the fading sunlight. "Right?"

He brought his fingers to her cheek, touching her with a gentleness that could never be mistaken for anything but fond feelings from the past. "Yes, Emma. I still want that."

Her eyes welled up, but she smiled and nodded. She had known this. All along she had known it. She thought back to how she felt when she first saw him, standing there in the parking lot of her school, and how she'd taken the blow when he told her he was engaged. But today, even while God was healing her soul, she had known they were going to say good-bye. That this was not a new beginning for the two of them together, but for the two of them separately.

In the separate lives they would lead from this point on.

Emma stared out to sea. Then slowly she removed the section of rope from her beach bag and held it close to her heart. "You and I ... we used to be the same, Brad. Our love was more brilliant than all the colors of summer combined."

"It was." Brad reached out and almost absently he took hold of the rope.

"But after … after what we did, after you left, I came here to the beach and I sat by the cross." She smiled, ignoring the tears that welled up in her eyes again. "I looked out at our beach and I realized what had happened. We weren't the same anymore. You were sky and I was sea, and we'd never ever be the same again. Never find our way back no matter what. Never again that same brilliant color."

"No." He listened, clearly caring for her, loving her. Not in the way she had known before, and not in the way she had hoped he might love her at the end of this weekend. A different love, but love all the same.

She savored the feel of his eyes on hers. "Shades of blue, you and I now. Nothing more."

He angled his head, searching her eyes, almost as if he were memorizing her. "Shades of blue. That's where we'll always be." He looked out at the ocean again. "Here in the shades of blue."

She didn't want to cry anymore. It was getting late. They needed to get back and say their good-byes. She took the rope and turned it over in her hands. "I'm leaving it here, our rope. It doesn't belong to me anymore. To you, either."

With little effort, she eased it from his hand. She rose up onto her knees again and she turned. Then very carefully, she looped the rope around the base of the cross. "It belongs here. With the memory of Amanda." She stood, staring down at the cross. Time could take it from this place. A strong storm or hurricane winds. A couple of kids passing by and glad for the discovery of an old bit of rope and a wooden cross.

Even so Emma had no reservations about leaving either of them. The memory of what she shared with Brad, the memory of Amanda's brief life wasn't anchored here in a piece of wood and a length of rope. The memory was in her heart, where it would always be.

She dusted the sand off her shorts and held out her hand, helping Brad to his feet. He stood beside her, their shoulders touching, and he stared one last time at the cross, at the rope. "I'm not sure …" he looked up, his eyes full of the richness and depth they'd shared here this afternoon. "I don't know if I'll be back."

"I know." His words hurt, but not nearly like they would've on Friday. Now, in light of all he was going home to, they were the right words. The way he should feel. She crossed her arms in front of her and nodded once more. She hoped her smile felt reassuring to him. "I was just thinking that." She looked down again. "And how we don't need anything to help us remember."

"No." He put his arm around her shoulders. "Not after today."

He lowered his arm and linked hands with her, their fingers intertwined like before. Emma tried to memorize the way it felt, the wonderful sensation of being with Brad this way. Not because she wanted another chance with him, but because this good-bye was so much better than the last one. So much more complete. They turned without looking back and walked slowly, silently along the beach. Their beach. The setting sun cast orange and yellow streaks across the blue, as if God Himself were drawing the curtain on yesterday. It had all come to a close—their guilt and sin and shame. Their time together this weekend.

Everything about the two of them. Finally and fully over.

Too quickly they reached Emma's driveway. They stood by his Jeep and faced the ocean a final time. Brad still had hold of her hand. "I came here to tell you I was sorry. To make things right with you." He faced her and took her other hand as well. "But God had much bigger plans."

"He did." She smiled at the freedom in her heart and soul. "I found the chance to tell you what really happened … to tell you about our daughter." She sniffed. "And I found a church." She felt herself smile. "I think I'm about to find a friendship with Pastor Dave's wife. And together we found forgiveness." Her smile faded and she stepped closer to him. For a long moment she let her forehead fall softly against his chest. When she looked up, she wondered if she could really do this ... tell Brad Cutler goodbye for all time. She swallowed against the pain that was sure to come. "I found something else too."

"What's that?" He linked his arms around her waist, holding her the way he might hold a sister or a close friend. Nothing more. "What did you find, Emma?"

"I found the old you," she touched the place above his heart. "The one I knew was still there somewhere."

"Promise me something." He touched his hand to the side of her face. The sun had finished setting, and dusk was falling around them.

"Anything." Emma let herself be lost in his eyes this final time.

"I want you to love again. You didn't tell me ... if there's anyone in your life."

"There isn't." Gavin Greeley's handsome face filled her mind, and her cheeks felt suddenly hot. "Nothing I've allowed, anyway."

"Allow it, Em. You have to. God's forgiveness means you have permission to live your life."

She thought about that, and for the first time ever, the idea appealed to her. Which could only mean that God truly had worked a miracle in her heart. His forgiveness was complete, indeed. "We'll see." She tilted her head, not willing to get into details about Gavin here and now. This moment belonged to Brad and her and God. The three of them alone. "Can I pray for you, before you leave?"

Brad looked mildly surprised, but instantly his expression filled with gratitude. "Please." He held her close, their heads bowed together, cheeks brushing against each other.

"Dear God ... I've run from You all these years, but now ... now I'm ready to live the rest of my life with You. I'll celebrate life from this point on. Mine and any other life You let me be a part of." Their good-bye was moments away, and the reality was suddenly sobering. "I pray for my friend, Brad. He's heading home to a wonderful girl, a girl he loves very much." Her eyes stung at the thought, but she didn't cry. "Please be with Laura and help her forgive Brad. Help her understand in a way that draws them closer." She paused. "In Jesus' name, amen."

Their eyes met again, and Emma felt the miracle still playing out in her heart. Had she really just prayed for Brad's fiancée? That she would forgive him and understand what this weekend was about? She breathed in deep and took a step back. "Thank you, Brad. For coming here. For risking everything so we could have this time."

"I told you Friday. I needed to finish this chapter."

"And you did." She smiled at him, hiding the ache already spreading through her heart.

"Yes." He looked intently into her eyes. "Because of you, because you were willing to find forgiveness with me."

She nodded, wanting to draw out the moment. But it was already over. It was time to admit as much and move on. "You better go." She pictured him standing at the front of a beautiful church, dressed in a dark tux, waiting for Laura James to walk up the aisle. "Go to her, Brad. Go make things right with her."

He nodded, but he didn't look like he wanted to talk about Laura. Again he brushed the side of her face with his fingers. "Thank you. For telling me about Amanda. For taking me to the cross."

A sound that was part cry, part laugh sounded on her lips. "That was God's doing. He took us both to the cross."

"He did." Brad narrowed his eyes, looking all the way back into the long-ago parts of her heart. Emma had the feeling he was seeing her as she'd been in third grade and in middle school, the way she'd looked her first day at Wilmington High, and the innocence in her face when he handed her back her yearbook in May, 1999. "I'll miss you."

"You, too." She wanted to run into the house before she started crying again. He deserved a happy send-off, one that assured him she understood about his wedding and his Laura. But all she could see as she looked at him was the boy he'd been, the one she'd planned on loving forever. "Brad …" his name came out as a cry, and in a rush she clung to him. For a long time she stayed that way because she didn't want him to see her tears, and because this was her last chance, the last time she'd ever hold him. Finally she tore herself away and took a step back. "Go. Please, Brad. I can't do this."

Only then could she see how very much he still cared, how much he would always care. Because he was crying too. He came to her and hugged her again. "If you're ever in New York, you can always —"

"No." She spoke the word against his chest as she moved away again. Her smile came from the depths of her soul, because this was how she wanted him to remember her. "I won't look you up, Brad. You go live your life, and I'll live mine."

He hesitated, and in all the world there was only the two of them. He reached for her hand once more. "I won't forget our Amanda."

She felt the sobs strangling her heart, but she held them off. "Thank you. She deserves that."

He looked deep into her eyes for a moment she would remember always. Then he tenderly touched her cheek, searching her soul. "I love you. I always will."

"I love you too." She held tight to his fingers, and then she let go and backed up toward her house. She raised her hand in his direction. Her aching heart wouldn't let her speak, so she mouthed one last word. "Bye."

He did the same, and then with a final look he was gone. As he drove away, she wondered if she might die there on her sandy front lawn. The pain of losing him this time was that great. But instead she forced herself to hold onto the good, the miracle of their time together.

They had found forgiveness and peace and even love. But not the sort of love they'd known before. Even with God's healing, there was no way to undo the consequences of their actions that November day. No way to love the way they'd loved before. Brad would go home to Laura, and if she would forgive him, in four weeks they would be married. And she would find her way too. A new life that hadn't seemed possible before this weekend.

Even so, she would never forget him. She would see him when she ran past the white wooden cross, and she'd remember him when she looked through her cardboard box. She would see the wide-eyed boy in the lines of what he'd written in her yearbook, and on occasion when she stopped in the middle of a run on the beach, she would feel his hand at the other end of the rope. And she would see him when she looked at the place where the sea met the sky. Where she would always see him.

In the shades of blue.

Twenty-Eight

BRAD WASN'T SURE HOW FAR HE drove before his tears stopped falling. With all they'd found together these past few days, he had to allow for the possibility—that he might've fallen in love with Emma Landon again. But that wasn't the type of love he felt for her, not even after all they shared this afternoon.

It wasn't the type of love she felt for him either. He could see that much in her eyes. They shared a beautiful past and a terrible mistake, a lifetime of regret and a healing that could only have come from God. But he wasn't in love with her. Not the way he was in love with Laura. With every mile that took him away from Emma, he became more and more consumed with hope and anticipation.

How much he must've hurt Laura with this decision. He could only imagine what she'd been thinking, or how she and her parents must've felt about him. Either way, he had absolutely needed to do this, to find Emma and finish that part of the story of his life. Like his dad had advised him. He smiled and realized his cheeks were dry. Good old Carl Cutler. The man's wisdom had changed his life this time. Saved it, even.

Now he could only hope Laura still loved him the way he loved her.

He pulled his BlackBerry from the passenger seat and disconnected it from the charger. Her number was at the top of his favorites list, so he barely needed to glance at the phone to call her. The night was pitch dark around him, the traffic almost nonexistent heading north on Seventeen back to Wilmington. Not like it would be tomorrow night, when the holiday was over.

Her ring-back tone was new, something she must've added over the weekend. Brad listened intently, trying to make out the song. *I don't wanna go through the motions ... I don't wanna go one more day ... without Your all-consuming passion inside of me ...* The lyrics were familiar and immediately he recognized the song. Matthew West's recent hit—"The Motions."

His heart skipped a beat and he let his hope double. Then just as quickly he reminded himself not to get too excited. A song like this could mean that she was looking to God to get her through the weekend ... but it could mean that she needed His help to get her over an inevitable breakup. *Answer ... please, Laura. Answer the phone.*

But after another few lines of the song, the call went to her voicemail. He didn't want to explain himself or what happened in a message, but he had to give her at least a hint about what he was feeling. At the beep, he grabbed a hurried breath. "Hi ... I'm on my way back to my dad's house. I'm coming home tomorrow to tell you the only thing that matters." He paused. "I love you, Laura. I want to marry you in four weeks. I hope ... I can only hope you feel the same way. I'll see you tomorrow."

He clicked the End button and dropped his phone back on the seat. Maybe he should've called her more often while he was gone. But there were moments in the past weekend when he wasn't in any position to talk to her. Besides, she hadn't returned his call from Friday. Which meant what? He gripped the steering wheel and stared straight ahead at the red taillights in the distance. Could their relationship really be over? Would he come home to find that she'd cancelled the wedding?

His heart beat faster than usual as he considered the possibility. *No, dear God ... please help her understand.* He pictured Emma praying for Laura—something he hadn't imagined might ever happen. Certainly if Emma could pray for Laura to forgive him, Laura could understand about Emma, how he'd needed to go back?

Or could she?

His mind hurdled from one side of the fence to the other until he pulled into his parents' driveway. If Laura was going to call off the wedding, he needed to pray tonight for a way to change her mind. Going back to North Carolina had only made him more ready to marry her.

He felt worn out from the emotion of the weekend, and he was pretty sure his eyes were red from crying down at the beach, near the white wooden cross. But he wasn't worried about seeing his parents. They wouldn't ask questions unless he felt like talking. And he didn't.

It was after nine o'clock as he walked inside. He found his mother folding clothes on the living room sofa, an old Roger Whitaker CD in the stereo. His dad sat across from her, sifting through a basketful of metal items. A trashcan on one side of his chair, a few lone items already inside. "Bradley." He looked up, but only for a brief moment. Then he returned to his sorting. "Lots of targets on the beach this evening."

"Your father thinks there's a nugget of solid gold somewhere in all that junk." His mom grinned at him and shrugged. "As long as he's happy."

"I found a World War II pin and an Australian coin. Vintage 1954." His dad jabbed his finger in the air. "And I found a good use for that Kotton Kids blanket." His dad pulled the soft blue cloth from someplace tucked in the chair beside him. "Makes a good polishing rag. I'll say that much for it."

Brad took in the scene and chuckled—for the first time all day. "I'm glad it's good for something." He moved to his mom's side and helped her finish folding the load of laundry. "Want coffee?"

"No, thanks." She looked straight at him. "I didn't see you last night."

"I wasn't here long. I couldn't sleep."

"How's Emma?" Her question was loaded, but that was okay. Brad didn't mind. He was slated to get married in four weeks, after all. His mother had the right to ask about Emma. He nodded. "She's good. We needed this."

"And," his mother raised an eyebrow. "Will you see her again?"

This time his dad lowered the Kotton Kids blanket and looked his way too, waiting.

"No." Brad leaned down and kissed his mother's cheek. "We both said what we needed to say. God met us in the middle of it all."

His mom hesitated long enough to search his eyes, his expression. When she must've been satisfied with his answer, she smiled at him. "I always liked Emma." She stood and picked up a stack of dishtowels. "But you're marrying Laura. There's a reason for that."

If she'll have me, he wanted to say. Instead he waited until his mother was out of the room. Then he crossed the floor and stopped at the trashcan. The bin held a few dozen scrap pieces of metal—tinfoil balls and broken metal pens. A half-missing belt buckle and a number of other unworthy targets—as his dad called them. Brad put his hand on his father's shoulder. "It was good advice, Dad. Finishing the chapter."

"Yes." His father stopped and briefly looked up at him. "You ready for the next one?"

"I am." He wanted to add that he was praying Laura was ready too. But he didn't want to alarm his parents. Not until there was an actual reason to be worried.

"The Jeep work out for you?" His father reached for a recipe box stationed near his chair. Organized by category inside were coupons and rebates, reminders of sweepstakes he was still waiting to hear about. "I can get another weekend if you need it. I read the fine print."

"No, thanks." Brad smiled at his dad's thoughtfulness. "I won't be going back to Holden Beach."

His father smiled. "Good." Then his smile faded into a more thoughtful look. "Even if we could get the Jeep for free." He shrugged. "We'll find another use for it one way or another."

"That's right. One way or another."

Brad bid his parents good night and turned in. He wanted to sleep well tonight, but as he lay in the dark he remembered the campaign for Kotton Kids. He pictured the photos of the babies around his office, and little Amanda. Precious Amanda. Suddenly the winning slogan was obvious. *Kotton Kids — Because You Only Have One Chance to Love.*

It was a line parents around the country would go crazy over. Not because it was clever. Because it was true. A sad certainty worked its way through Brad. This was what he'd been looking for, the perfect tagline to build his campaign around. One chance. Brad knew that better now, after spending the weekend with Emma. Through memories of his past with her and the stark reality of all they'd lost at a cold abortion clinic, the reality remained.

One chance to love.

As he fell asleep, he could only pray that somewhere that night Laura James was feeling the same way. He had done the two things God had asked of him, or at least he'd tried. He had known the good he ought to do, and he'd done it by making amends with God and Emma Landon. And he'd reconciled with her in a way that meant he was free to attempt the one thing he desperately wanted to do.

Return to his gift at the altar.

SUNDAY NIGHT PASSED SLOWLY FOR LAURA. Sometime after she was in bed, she heard her cell phone ring across the room. Whether it was Brad or not, she didn't want to talk. Not until she could see him in person. Look him in the eyes and tell him exactly how she was feeling.

Her parents had given her plenty of space—asking no questions about her night out with Bella Joy or what she might be feeling about Brad. Even she hadn't known until late Saturday night. She skipped church that day and spent much of her time in her room—poring over old photo albums and letters from Brad. Then she spent a solid two hours reading from her Bible, studying the Scripture in Luke, chapter 6. Reading it and rereading it and finally writing six pages in her journal over what she thought God was trying to tell her.

Everyone knew Brad was coming home Monday—at least he planned to come home then. And in the morning, when Laura listened to her messages she felt a rush of relief hit her. He still loved her. He was coming home. Now she needed to do her part, otherwise the wedding still might not happen.

Give me strength, God ... I can't be mad at him or ask fifty questions about Emma and his time with her. I have to do what You've told me to do. She felt a sense of strength in response. God would help her get through this. Now it was simply a matter of doing it.

She had a key to Brad's New York flat, because when Brad traveled for business, she watered his plants and fed his cat. As Monday wore on, Laura collected everything she would need and had one of her father's cars take her into the city. Early that evening, she made it into Brad's apartment—half an hour before he was due home. Working quickly and carefully she set up what she wanted to do and then she waited. Fifteen minutes became a half hour, and that became forty-five. She wasn't sure if his plane was late or if the traffic was heavier than usual because of Memorial Day. Either way she would stay.

Finally, thirty minutes later, she heard the sound of a key in the door. Laura waited, watching.

Brad stepped inside and flipped on a light switch. He took an immediate step back, his eyes wide. Realizing someone was inside his apartment must've surprised him, because he stood stone still for several seconds. Gradually, his eyes must have adjusted to the candle-lit atmosphere in the next room. He set down his bag and moved closer. "Laura?"

"Come here, Brad." She was sitting on the floor near his leather couch, waiting for him. "Please."

His face was a mask of confusion, but still he came. He walked into his living room and found her at the foot of the sofa. A few seconds passed before he must've understood what he was seeing. She rose to her knees next to a bowl of warm sudsy water, a thick white towel, and a washcloth.

"What ... baby, what are you doing?"

"Take off your shoes." She heard the brokenness in her own tone. She pointed to a spot across the room. "Take them off and set them over there."

Brad hesitated. "I don't under—"

"Shhh." She held her finger to her lips. "Please, Brad. This is something I have to do."

"Laura ..." Brad looked from the soapy water back to her and at the water again. But however confused he was, he took his shoes off and returned to her. "Baby, could you explain this? Just so I know what's going on."

"I will." She stood and took his hand. The feel of his skin against hers was intoxicating. "Sit here, on the couch."

He did as she asked, his eyes never leaving her face. Then she took the cuff of his jeans and rolled it up to the midway point on his calf. She did the same with the other leg, and slowly she helped him lift his feet into the tub of water.

Suddenly he must've truly understood what was happening, because he jerked back from her, his expression alarmed. "You're … you can't do this." He started to pull his feet from the water, but she put her fingers lightly around his ankles.

"Let me … God gave me the idea."

Brad's face looked pale, as if the idea of Laura serving him in any capacity was not only crazy, but horrific. "I brought this trouble on us. You did nothing." He put his hand to his forehead, massaging his temples. "I don't understand."

She steadied herself; then she took the white washcloth and slowly, with all the love in her heart, she began to wash his feet. Inch by inch she washed them, soothing her hands over the smooth skin at the top of his foot and the bones in his toes and the rougher patches along his heels. Washing his feet was only part of what God wanted from her. The rest wasn't an action, but something she needed to say.

"When you told me about Emma … about your past with her, my immediate reaction was very wrong. Very selfish. I wanted you to be pure for me, because I saved myself for you. I didn't think about how you were feeling, and I didn't … I didn't think about the baby you lost. How horrible that must've felt, and how sad that would be for you. So I felt none of your pain, Brad. I felt only mine." She felt her hair sticking to the side of her face, but she pressed on, looking at him, running the cloth and her hands slowly over his wet feet. "But God used this weekend to teach me something about being a Christian." Her voice was heavy with emotion, but she found the strength to go on. "Sitting back, head high, judging you." She shook her head. "That's not what God wanted from me. When you left here, you were far more the follower of Christ than I ever was."

"Laura … no one could blame you for any of this." His eyes were practically frantic for her to stop, to see this his way. "I was wrong. This was my fault, not—"

"Brad, please." She held up one soapy, wet hand and waited until he was listening again. Then she resumed washing his feet, running the washcloth over the sides and tops of them. "You knew you'd done wrong. Whatever happened this weekend, that's why you left. So you could make things right with God and her." She felt her eyes well up. "I'm washing your feet because true love forgives. When Jesus forgave those closest to him, he served them. He washed their feet. I couldn't think of any other way to illustrate to you how deeply I forgive you, and how deeply I need you to forgive me. For my judgmental heart."

She was done washing, so she dried his feet, one at a time. When she was finished, she took the wash bin to the bathroom, dumped the water into the sink, and washed and dried her hands. As she returned, she found her Bible on the coffee table and sat next to him. Before she could show him the verses God had used to change her heart, he eased her to her feet and embraced her. The sort of desperate embrace that told her how worried he was that she wouldn't be here when he came home.

"I love you, Laura." His words were a heart-gripping whisper spoken straight to her heart. "Forgive me for waiting so long to take care of the past. Marry me. Please."

"Yes." She whispered the word and it sounded more like a cry from the deepest place in her soul. "I'll marry you and I'll spend the rest of my life loving you and serving you. Because this weekend you showed me the lengths you'll go to apologize. If you love me that way, if you love us that way ... we have only the happiest life ahead of us. You and me, together." She laughed, even as two tears dropped onto her cheeks. "Yes, Brad. I'll marry you."

The alarm in his expression faded and his eyes began to dance. "I prayed for this."

"Me too." She let herself get lost in him. She loved Brad Cutler more than ever before. "Will you forgive me for my narrow view of love, for the way I judged you?"

He hesitated, as if even after all she'd said and done he still struggled with the idea of her being sorry for anything. But he must've understood the look in her eyes because he pulled her close and kissed her forehead. "I forgive you. Of course."

"I need to show you something, a verse." They sat down together, and she opened her Bible to Luke. She found the section that had opened her eyes, and with a love she hadn't known before, she began to read to him.

"'Be merciful, just as your Father is merciful. Do not judge, and you will not be judged.'" She felt sick over her initial reaction to Brad's admission. But she pressed on, because those feelings were behind her now. "'Give, and it will be given to you.'" She read through to the end of the section, to the part where the verses had suddenly and completely come to life for her. The part about building the foundation.

When she finished, she saw in his eyes that he understood the transformation in her. "I love you, Laura. I'm in love with you."

"I love you more." She smiled at him, and she could feel her face glowing, feel the way her eyes filled with life because this was the outcome she had prayed for.

He kissed her again, this time tenderly on her lips. Not a kiss intended to stir passion in either of them, but a kiss that told her he had come home to stay. No words were needed, really. The Scripture had said all there was to say. The life they were about to start together would take decades to build, and some seasons would be tougher than others. But this weekend God had taught them how to ride out the journey of life together. How to let the hard times bring them closer together. They had each listened to God, each sought forgiveness and found it. They had acted on His words, and in doing so they hadn't only come closer to the Lord.

They'd laid the first bricks in a rock-solid foundation that would last forever.

Twenty-Nine

KRISTIN PALAZZO WAS DEAD.

Emma could accept that now. The Lord took her home on a soft summer day the ninth of June with her family gathered around her. Today—two weeks before Brad's wedding—was Kristin's memorial service in a packed church not too far from the one where Emma was now a regular. Memorial service wasn't the right term, really. Her life celebration, that's what Kristin's family called it. Emma sat near the back, and a few minutes before the program began, Gavin slipped quietly into the church and joined her. He hadn't known Kristin, of course. But he had been there in the hospital with Emma after Kristin's cardiac arrest. He'd prayed for her ever since.

The church was so full people stood two-deep on either side aisle. The building held Kristin's friends and family, and even most of the children from Emma's class—including Frankie and her parents. Kristin was very loved in this life—today was further proof. People were still filing in, still signing the guestbook at the back of the church, still taking their places. Music filled the church—the songs from Jeremy Camp—the ones Frankie had given Emma the last day of school. Kristin's favorite.

She'd listened to the CD again and again since Brad's return home. Twenty times through at least. Frankie's mother was right; when Emma played the collection of songs, she could hear Kristin's voice, see her smiling face as if she were still only an arm's length away. Emma's favorite song was one that was playing now. It was called "Take You Back."

Emma listened to the words now, and like always they seemed written for her alone ... *A heart that bleeds forgiveness ... replacing all these thoughts of painful memories ... But I know that your response will always be ... I'll take you back ...* That's exactly what God had done for her, and he'd used Brad Cutler to make it happen. The Lord had taken her back and she would never, ever leave again.

Beside her, Gavin sat straight and tall, strong in every possible way. He'd called a few times, and with each conversation she felt herself falling for him a little more. She understood better now how he could care for her—even after he knew about her past. Before, she had needed all her effort to resist him—back when she didn't share his faith or his belief about God's forgiveness. Now ... now there was no telling where God would take their growing friendship. She smiled at him, and he did the same. His eyes told her that he was there for her. If today became too difficult, he was there.

A hush fell over the crowd and the service began. A slideshow presentation showed Kristin as a little girl with her black lab, Mollie, and with her grandma and her cousins. There were photos of Kristin arm-in-arm with her father, her hero, the man who had been with her in her final conscious moments on earth. Other photos showed her with her arm around her younger sister, Stephanie. Several pictures showed Kristin on a trip to the American Girl doll store, and at her family's cabin in the mountains of West Virginia.

The six hundred or so people in attendance chuckled when the photos showed her stirring a pot of spaghetti, red sauce splattered up along her shirt and her face, Kristin grinning, having the time of her life. Emma realized as she watched that they were still learning from Kristin, still drawing from her humble, easy way. The life pattern she had of trusting God in all that came her way, even long after she was sick.

Emma appreciated that about the slideshow. Her parents didn't include pictures of Kristin looking sick or frail. Nothing from a hospital bed, because that wasn't Kristin. The girl loved life and honored God with every breath. The slideshow focused on that truth alone.

When it was over, the pastor said a few words about Kristin's life, about the legacy she would leave behind. "I want to read you the first few verses of Psalm 46, the Scripture Kristin loved most." He opened his Bible and began to read. "God is our refuge and strength, an ever-present help in trouble. Therefore we will not fear, though the earth give way and the mountains fall into the heart of the sea." He closed the Bible and smiled at the crowd, at the people on the sides and in the back, and at her family in the front row. "The mountains have fallen into the sea, because Kristin Palazzo is no longer with us here, where we want her to be. But today she would ask you not to fear. God was her refuge, and He is ours."

Yes, that was exactly what Kristin would want. Emma could almost see her, smiling at them from her place beside the Lord in heaven. She leaned closer to Gavin. "I wish you could've known her."

His eyes shone with the love of God. "I feel like I do." He gave Emma's hand a single loving squeeze. "And I will … someday."

The service continued with a string of people coming to the front and talking about Kristin's life, how she never talked about being sick and how she was always more focused on others than herself. Friends laughed about the silly pictures she would take and her way of making people happy. One friend spoke through teary eyes. "I'd like to think that Kristin will be a much bigger part of my future than she was of my past." She struggled, her voice tight with sorrow. "And she was a very big part of my past."

Finally, the principal of her high school came to the front with an impressive wooden plaque. "This fall we will have a new art gallery in the main hallway of our school. For the first year it will display only Kristin's artwork, and after that it will hold the artwork of generations of students like her, with an eye for life." He held out the plaque toward the place where her parents were sitting. "If you'd accept this on behalf of Holden Beach High School, in commemoration of the Kristin L. Palazzo Gallery."

Kristin's father, Rick, stood and accepted the plaque as the crowd of his daughter's friends and family rose to their feet, applauding the way Kristin lived, the legacy she left behind, and the fact that Holden Beach High had chosen to honor her memory the way she deserved to be honored.

When the service was over, Gavin hugged Emma for a long time. He didn't say anything trite or try to pretend he might understand the personal way Kristin's loss had touched Emma. It was one more thing she liked about Gavin — his ability to be her friend without saying a word. Before they walked out of the church, Lynne Palazzo — Kristin's mother — motioned for Emma to wait. The woman's eyes were tearstained, but her smile was full and without reservation.

"Here." She handed a package to Emma. "Kristin must've made this for you before … before that day. We found it beside her bed when we were going through her things."

Emma was stunned. She took the gift and thanked Kristin's mother. The two shared a hug, and Lynne Palazzo looked intently into Emma's eyes. "She prayed for you all the time. That you would come to know Jesus the way she did. And something tells me you've done that."

"I have." Emma's heart warmed at the memory. She pictured Brad and everything the Lord had done to change both of them over that single Memorial Day weekend. "Kristin's prayers were answered."

Lynne smiled. "Let's stay in touch. I think Kristin would've wanted that."

"Definitely." Emma thought so. "I have something I'd like to bring by your house this week. A painting one of my kids did for Kristin."

Her mother's eyes filled again, but her smile was bigger than before. "Please ... bring it by."

Emma thanked her again for the package, and then she walked with Gavin outside and down the church steps. When they were a distance from the crowd, Emma opened the gift and put the pieces of pale floral wrapping paper carefully into her purse. Only then did she realize what she was holding. This was the present Kristin and her students had been working on. The picture book of her time with the class throughout the school year. She must've somehow had time to finish it before her collapse.

And now Emma would have it always, a reminder of Kristin's life and the prayers she'd said on her behalf. This would be proof of the miracle God had worked in her life in a few short days. A reminder that all life was to be celebrated. The Lord had taught her that lesson with her friend's little stillborn Cassandra, in the determination of Frankie, and finally in the death of Kristin Palazzo. But He had also used her own losses as well. Life was precious—every day. She would spend the rest of her time believing that.

Gavin walked her to the parking lot and her red convertible. He looked intently at the sunny blue sky. "I'm still training for that half marathon." He grinned at her. "You?"

She made a funny face, enjoying how he made her feel—as if she was going to get a second chance to truly live her life. "I've slacked off a bit. I have to admit."

"Which means ... if you go get your running shoes and meet me in an hour at the pier, I might have a chance to keep up with you."

She laughed out loud and the feeling was as free as her heart. "Okay. I'll try to go easy on you."

His eyes sparkled as he waved good-bye and walked toward his car at the other end of the church parking lot.

The hour flew by and he was waiting for her when she jogged up to the base of the pier. "Ready?"

Emma would always miss Kristin, but this was somehow as much a reminder of her life as anything Emma might do this afternoon. Running with her new friend, Gavin. Believing that God wasn't finished with her yet.

They set out to the west and then around past the pier and toward the far side of the beach. Emma had figured she would keep as far from the white wooden cross as possible. But she changed her mind as she drew near to it. With Gavin jogging beside her, she ran up the hilly slope and stopped short at the place where the cross stood. The length of rope was still looped around its base. She hadn't told him about Brad's visit. That could come later. Catching her breath, she stared at it, her hands at her sides.

Gavin looked curious, first at the cross and then at her. "This is yours?"

She nodded, her sides heaving from the run. "It is."

"I've seen it before." For a long while he said nothing, allowing her this time without needing all the answers. Then he looked closer at it and an understanding came to his expression. "November 20, 1999."

"Yes." Emma looked once more at the cross. She had always felt sad when she looked at it, but not this time. Now the cross represented more than a loss of life. It meant the redemption of her soul. She smiled at Gavin, trusting him with a softness she hadn't allowed before. "I thought you'd want to see it."

Gavin held her eyes for a moment and the look on his face told her he understood. He squeezed her hand for a few seconds. Then they set off running again, and Emma looked long down the length of Holden Beach. Yes, this was where life and love had ended. But today—Kristin's day—Emma chose to see this beach as something else.

The place where life began again.

THE LAST SATURDAY IN JUNE, SUNLIGHT shone over Manhattan, casting a brilliance on the Hudson River as a breeze blew over the neatly trimmed lawn at the Liberty House. Brad wore a tux that was both elegant and understated, and he stood next to his best man—his father, wise old Carl Cutler. The pastor stood on Brad's right, and on the other side of his father, the groomsmen were lined up, ready for the big moment.

His father leaned in. "You ready?"

"Absolutely." Brad winked at his dad.

Discretely, his father tapped on his tux pocket. "I have a list of songs here, numbers I want your mother and I to dance to later on. You and Laura, too."

Brad grinned and put his hand on his dad's shoulder. "Sounds good." Together they turned their eyes to the opposite end of the aisle, to the side of the building across the yard. As they did, the hundreds of guests did the same thing, and a hush fell over the crowd. None of them had known that the wedding was ever in jeopardy, which was just as well. No matter how the last few months had gone, there was never any real doubt in Brad's mind that God would give them this moment. This wedding day.

The music changed and the guests turned and watched, as one after another, Laura's best friends made their way up the aisle to the gazebo. He appreciated their smiles, the way each of them made eye contact with him, silently approving of Brad and the wedding and whatever details they'd worked through to get to this point.

Finally the guests rose and turned toward the Liberty House. Again the music changed and Laura walked out, her father at her side. Even from this far away, she was a vision—the dress she'd talked about for so long, breathtaking. *You did this, God...* Brad felt a lifetime of love well up in his heart. He loved her and only her.

He would love her until the day he died.

A quiet sound of awe came from their family and friends as Laura and her dad drew closer. The dress was designed for her, no question. But that wasn't the main reason she was so stunning. She seemed to see none of the guests, but only him. The look in her eyes made his heart beat faster—innocence and devotion and purity, love and understanding. Combined, they made her the most beautiful bride ever.

Her father's smile was never bigger, despite the tears in his eyes. He walked Laura to a spot just short of Brad and then Laura's mother stood and moved beside him.

"Who gives this woman to be married?" the pastor's voice resonated with joy.

Randy James smiled at his daughter and kissed her cheek. Then he linked hands with his wife on his other side. He turned his attention to the pastor and cleared his throat. "Her mother and I."

This had been practiced, of course, but every detail meant so much more here—on the actual day of the wedding. Laura's mom hugged her and her father did the same. Then her dad took Laura's hand, and with all the love of a lifetime, he gently placed it in Brad's. "Take care of her," he whispered.

"I will." Brad smiled at him for an extra second or two, his look unwavering. Then he tucked Laura's arm in his and they turned to face the pastor.

The ceremony was tender and heartfelt, and in a blur Brad and Laura were saying their vows and exchanging rings. Not until they walked into the gazebo to light the unity candle did it seem to hit them both at the same time. They exchanged a look of thrill that they could barely contain. "We're married!" he breathed against her cheek as they leaned close to light the flame.

"It's like a dream."

They let their eyes linger on each other for a long moment after the candle was lit. Then they returned to their places and grinned at the pastor.

"With the power vested in me by the state of New Jersey, I now pronounce you husband and wife." He smiled big at them. "Brad, you may kiss your wife."

He took her in his arms like the precious gift she was and he kissed her, a kiss that held both love and lasting commitment. When it was over, their guests clapped and the pastor made his final announcement. "I present to you for the first time, Mr. and Mrs. Brad Cutler."

Walking back down the aisle, Laura's hand in his, Brad had the wonderful sense that there might never be a moment as perfect as this one, that the Lord Himself was walking beside them. Or maybe it was simply the feeling of God's favor, because He had to be pleased with the way things had turned out — for all of them. Brad had done what he needed to do. He had gone back to Holden Beach and made things right with Emma. Laura had gone through a transformation, too — as painful as it was. Yes, there would always be heartache when he thought of Emma Landon and their daughter, Amanda. But there would be forgiveness as well. For all of them. And because of that, this wedding was exactly what it should be.

The first page in the first chapter of the rest of their lives.

Dear Reader Friends,

I remember where I was when I heard the song for the first time.

It was a Tim McGraw hit called "Red Ragtop" and it stopped me in my tracks. The song talked about a guy driving down the road and coming to a red light next to a red Cabriolet. Behind the wheel was a girl with green eyes, a stranger. And suddenly the guy is drawn back in time to the most painful memory of his life. Years earlier he had been in a relationship with a girl who drove a car like that, a girl he'd loved. As the song goes, the two were young and wild and when the girl became pregnant, they decided not to have the child.

Rather than have a baby, they had an abortion.

Around the country, some radio stations banned the song. They thought it held a pro-abortion message. But the song spoke to me in the exact opposite way. I believe "Red Ragtop" is a song about regret, about a guy being years removed from such a decision and still knowing that it would haunt him all his life.

The first time I heard that song, I knew that one day—if God allowed it—I would write a novel about a guy like that. A guy smothered with regret. Brad Cutler is different in many ways, of course. Brad is a Christian—so the story involves faith, whereas the song does not. And the song gives us no background on the man, no way of understanding what led to his decision. But the song was a starting point. The regret ... the lifetime of guilt and remorse ... was something I desperately wanted to explore.

I have not had an abortion, and I am strongly in support of life—all life. We are active supporters of Crisis Pregnancy Centers, and I believe God has a purpose for every breath. But this topic is very personal for me, and so I feel I must confess something to you, my reader friends.

My story is this: Once, a lifetime ago on a sunny Saturday morning, someone close to me called me frantic with tears. She was young and afraid and alone, scheduled to have an abortion that day. But her boyfriend hadn't shown up.

"Please, Karen … will you take me? I have no other way to get there!"

I was seventeen. I did not have the relationship with Christ I have today, but I knew abortion was wrong. I knew it because my dad had been passionate about the Right to Life movement. I cannot blame her desperate cries on the other end of the line or the fact that it wasn't my problem. The sad truth is, after very little debate, I agreed. I wasn't happy about it, but I drove to her house, picked her up, and took her to an abortion clinic. I sat in the waiting room for an hour or three hours. Whatever it was. It passed in a blur, and as I drove her home we said absolutely nothing.

To this day I think about how I might have handled that morning differently. I was not a friend to this special girl, no example, no beacon of faith. I could've picked her up and taken her to a park or a coffee shop instead. I could've prayed with her or taken her to a counselor. I could've helped her change her mind.

But I did none of those things.

Somewhere in heaven today is a child who died too young because I didn't have the courage to act differently. Earlier this year when I was writing *Shades of Blue*, I researched various types of abortions and exactly how the sad procedure plays out. Somewhere in the middle of my research, every detail about that long-ago Saturday morning came rushing back and I began to weep.

I wept because that child might've grown up to find the cure for cancer or maybe to be the amazing older brother or sister for this woman's other children. Because I didn't act differently, the world will never know who that child might've become, and I was overwhelmed with guilt and remorse.

Days later, I contacted her—a grown woman now. I asked her if we could talk, and I went to her. On a sandy path, we took a walk similar to the one Brad and Emma took on Holden Beach, and I told her I was sorry for my actions that day. "You looked up to me back then, but I did not act like a Christian or a friend," I told her. "I never should've taken you there." I could barely talk for my tears. "I pray you can forgive me."

We both cried and we hugged, and together on that beach we prayed and we found God's forgiveness and healing like we hadn't found it before. Like Laura's father said, everyone has a past. This book caused me to deal with a piece of mine — a piece that is real and devastating and not very flattering. But I wanted to be honest with you about this. I can't suggest that you can find healing in Christ without telling you that I, myself, have found that same healing.

Abortion is a very difficult topic. Regardless of God's precious view of life, abortion is legal, and many times women are counseled that their pregnancy does not involve a baby, but only a mass of tissue. They are often encouraged to have abortions. I know of cases where mothers insisted their daughters have abortions, and in many situations an abortion happens through very little fault of the woman.

Even so, it is the woman who suffers the loss and oftentimes lifelong guilt and regret. The fact that abortion remains so personal is one reason why I haven't written about it before. I remember talking with Christian author Francine Rivers several years ago. "I'm so glad *you're* handling the abortion topic," I told her, referring to her wonderful novel *The Atonement Child.* "I'm not sure if I could do it."

Francine looked deep into my eyes. "You can, Karen. You must. We need more stories that talk about it." She went on to say, "Women hide this, but they'll never find healing so long as they're hiding." Then her voice became almost a plea. "Pray about it, please. I think God is asking you to write about this."

And so I have prayed every year since then. From the time I heard "Red Ragtop" for the first time, I knew I was absolutely supposed to write this book. But I've held off for three years since then, held off even though the storyline was practically bursting at the seams of my heart.

Here's the reason I wasn't sure about writing it—I wouldn't want one person reading this to feel condemned or judged. More people have had abortions or taken part in them than we could ever imagine. It's a secret that stays silent within groups of friends and within families. But God's truth tells us we cannot find healing without confession, without admitting our wrongs and asking for His forgiveness. Even if we didn't know the wrong we were doing at the time. Then ... and only then ... can we walk in His amazing grace and live in His redemption.

If you have suffered from any aspect of abortion, I wrote *Shades of Blue* especially for you. Please know that there is healing for us all and for anyone who would give their burdens to Christ. Lay your sorrows at the foot of the cross, the way Brad and Emma did. Jesus is waiting with open arms to grant you perfect healing and forgiveness. And to give you a new, restored life in Him.

If you are a woman facing an unexpected pregnancy—for any reason—I pray that this book will help you choose life. If you are unable to care for your baby, adoption is a beautiful choice. There are countless parents waiting even at this very minute for news that a baby is available for them to adopt. Christian adoption agencies are ready to help you and counsel you. Look for one in your area and pick up your phone. Most of them offer free pregnancy tests and even ultrasounds. Or perhaps God is calling you to raise your baby with the help of family and friends.

Pray and listen for His voice, and please choose life.

With abortion, the saddest truth is you can never go back. A life hangs in the balance and the choices made are irreversible. I've known that since that sad Saturday morning in my past. There is no going back. Please know that I have prayed for each of you that as you read this book you will be touched and changed—that in some way life will become more precious to you because of the characters in this book. Laura and Brad and Emma. Kristin and Frankie and Cassandra. Even little Amanda.

Okay. Big breath … Originally I wasn't sure I was going to share this with you. But you are honest with me, and I want to be honest with you too.

As always, I look forward to hearing your feedback on this book. Take a minute and visit my website at *www.KarenKingsbury .com*, where you can get to know other readers and become part of a community that agrees there is life-changing power in something as simple as a story. On my website you can post prayer requests or pray for those in need. You can send in a photo of your loved one serving our country or let us know of a fallen soldier we can honor on our Fallen Heroes page.

My website will also tell you about my ongoing contests, including "Shared a Book," which encourages you to let me know when you've shared one of my books with someone in your life. Each time you email me about this, you're entered for the chance to spend a summer weekend with my family. In addition, everyone signed up for my monthly newsletter is automatically entered into an ongoing once-a-month drawing for a free, signed copy of my latest novel.

Also on my website you can see which women's conferences I'll speak at next and whether you might live close enough so we'll have the chance to meet, to share a hug, or take a picture together. In addition there are links that will help you with matters that are important to you—faith and family, adoption and ways to help others.

Of course, on my site you can also find out a little more about me and my family, my Facebook page and YouTube channel, and my Karen's Movie Monday—where I release occasional Monday

YouTube clips dealing with some aspect of my family and faith, and the wonderful world of Life-Changing Fiction™.

Finally, if you gave your life over to God during the reading of this book, or if you found your way back to a faith you'd let grow cold, send me a letter at Office@KarenKingsbury.com and write *New Life* in the subject line. I would encourage you to connect with a Bible-believing church in your area and get hold of a Bible. In addition, if you can't afford a Bible, write *Bible* in the subject line. Tell me how God used this book to change your life, and then include your address in your email. If that applies to you, I'll send you a Bible at no cost.

One more thing. I've started a program where I will donate a book to any high school or middle school librarian who makes a request. Check out my website for details. Again, thanks for traveling with me through the pages of this book. I can't wait to see you next time. My next book will be the third segment of the Above the Line Series. It's called *Take Three*, and I think it will answer a lot of questions you might have about Bailey and Cody and the future for the producers in that series.

Until then, my friends, keep your eyes on the cross.

In His light and love,
Karen Kingsbury

www.KarenKingsbury.com

READER STUDY GUIDE

Please use the following questions for your book club, small group, or for personal reflection.

1. What do you know about Post Abortion Syndrome (PAS)? If you don't know about this, look up the symptoms online. Share about this.

2. Do you know anyone who has gone through an abortion? If so, talk about that person in general terms (careful to keep their identity private). Did that person suffer any signs of PAS?

3. What did you initially think of Brad's decision to go back to Emma Landon and seek her forgiveness? Talk about what Brad might've been feeling. What did you think about his decision by the end of the book?

4. Was there a time in your life when you needed to seek forgiveness from someone? How did you go about this, and what were the results?

5. Is there someone in your life to whom you need to extend forgiveness? What is holding you back? Talk about what might happen if you offered an apology to that person.

6. Laura was part of a very strong Bible study. Did you relate to one of her friends more than the others? Which one and why?

7. Are you part of a Bible study or small group? Explain how your group works and how the group's study and interaction is a benefit to you.

8. Laura's father heard the news about Brad's past from Brad. How did Laura feel about this first sign of Brad's desire to take responsibility for his actions? Have you ever taken part in a difficult conversation, one that wasn't easy but was the right thing to do? Talk about it.

9. How do you think you'd react if you found out someone you loved had hidden an important truth from you? Can you relate to Laura's reaction? How would you have handled the news differently?

10. After he had told Laura and her father the truth about his past, Brad chose to talk to his father. Which of your parents are you closer to, and which one might you choose to share something like this with?

11. In what ways was it evident that Emma Landon was still trapped by the pain and regret she carried from her past?

12. Talk about a time when you struggled to find healing and forgiveness. How did that hurt carry over into your life or the life of someone you know?

13. How did Emma react to the idea that Brad had come to Holden Beach to apologize? Has anyone you know ever told you they were sorry for something grievous? How did you react?

14. Emma hadn't told anyone about what actually happened at the abortion clinic. Why do you think it was important that she shared this information with Brad? How did the news change the way Brad viewed their decision to have an abortion?

15. Christians can get a bad reputation for being judgmental, but many times Christians are actually very understanding. Explain how Emma must've felt when

Gavin Greeley was willing to listen without judgment when she talked about her abortion.

16. Tell about a time when you or a Christian you know did *not* pass judgment on someone who was struggling. Explain how love and grace was extended to that person, and talk about the outcome for the person who was struggling. Share, also, about a time when a Christian was judgmental. How did that situation turn out?

17. Share your favorite "life" story—proof that life is God's alone, and that all life is to be treasured. This might be the story of the birth of a child or the miracle story of someone you know or love. Talk about the gift of life.

18. Psalm 139:13–14 says, "For you created my inmost being; you knit me together in my mother's womb. I praise you because I am fearfully and wonderfully made." What does this mean to you?

19. Emma and Brad created their own moment of confession and forgiveness on the beach. Talk about what it means to confess your sins to one another. Why do you think God asks His people to confess their wrongdoings as part of the healing process?

20. Laura washed Brad's feet upon his return to New York City. Explain why this act of humility was a critical part of her transformation. How can you serve someone you love as a way of showing Christ's love and grace?

READ AN EXCERPT FROM THE FIRST BOOK
IN THE ABOVE THE LINE SERIES: *TAKE ONE*

One

CHASE RYAN DOUBTED THERE WAS ENOUGH oxygen in the plane to get him from San Jose to Indianapolis. He took his window seat on the Boeing 737, slid his laptop bag onto the floor space in front of him, and closed his eyes. Deep breaths, he told himself. Stay calm. But nothing about the job ahead of him inspired even a single peaceful feeling. On Monday Chase and his best friend Keith Ellison would set up shop in Bloomington, Indiana, and start spending millions of dollars of other people's investment money to make a film they believed would change lives.

Even during the rare moments when that fact didn't terrify him, Chase could hear the quiet anxious voice of his wife, Kelly, splashing him with a cold bucket of reality. "Only two million dollars, Chase? Seriously?" She had brought it up again on the way to the airport. Her knuckles stayed white as she gripped the steering wheel. "What if you run out of money before you finish the film?"

"We won't." Chase had steeled his eyes straight ahead. "Keith and I know the budget."

"What if it doesn't go like you planned?" Her body was tense, her eyes fearful. She gave him quick, nervous glances. "If something happens, we'll spend the rest of our lives paying that off."

She was right, but he didn't want to say so. Not when it was too late to turn back. The actors were arriving on set in two days, and the entire film crew would be in Bloomington by tomorrow. Plans were in motion, and already bills needed to be paid. They had no choice but to move ahead and stick to their budget, trusting God that they could make this film for two million dollars, and illustrate a message of faith better and stronger than anything the industry had ever seen.

Failure wasn't an option.

They reached the airport, but before she dropped Chase off, Kelly turned to him, lines creasing the space between her eyebrows. She was only thirty-one, but lately she looked older. Maybe because she only seemed to smile when she was playing with their two little girls, Macy and Molly. Worry weighted her tone. "Four weeks?"

"Hopefully sooner." He refused to be anything but optimistic.

"You'll call?"

"Of course. Every day." Chase studied her, and the familiar love was there. But her anxiety was something he didn't recognize. The faith she'd shown back when they lived in Indonesia, that's what he needed from her now. "Relax, baby. Please."

"Okay." She let out a sigh and another one seemed right behind it. "Why am I so afraid?"

His heart went out to her. "Kelly ..." His words were softer than before, his tone desperate to convince her. "Believe in me ... believe in this movie. You don't know how much I need that."

"I'm trying." She looked down and it took awhile before she raised her eyes to his again. "It was easier in Indonesia. At least in the jungle the mission was simple."

"Simple?" He chuckled, but the sound lacked any real humor. "Indonesia was never easy. Any of us could've been arrested or killed. We could've caught malaria or a dozen different diseases. Every day held that kind of risk."

The lines on her face eased a little and a smile tugged at her lips. She touched her finger to his face. "At least we had each other." She looked deep into his eyes, to the places that belonged to only the two of them and she kissed him. "Come on, Chase ... you've gotta see why I'm worried. It's not just the money."

He caught a quick look at his watch. "You're afraid we won't finish on time and that'll put us over budget and —"

"No." She didn't raise her voice, but the fear in her eyes cut him short. "Don't you see?" Shame filled in the spaces between her words. "You're young and handsome and talented …" Her smile was sad now. "You'll be working with beautiful actresses and movie professionals and … I don't know, the whole thing scares me."

She didn't come out and admit her deeper feelings, those she'd shared with him a week before the trip. The fact that she didn't feel she could measure up to the Hollywood crowd. Chase ached for her, frustrated by her lack of confidence. "This isn't about the movie industry. It's about a bigger mission field than we ever had in Indonesia." He wove his fingers into her thick dark hair, drew her close, and kissed her once more. "Trust me, baby. Please."

This time she didn't refute him, but the worry in her eyes remained as he grabbed his bags and stepped away from the car. He texted her once he got through security, telling her again that he loved her and that she had nothing to worry about. But she didn't answer and now, no matter how badly he needed to sleep, he couldn't shake the look on her face or the tone of her voice. What if her fears were some sort of premonition about the movie? Maybe God was using her to tell Keith and him to pull out now — before they lost everything.

Once on the plane, he tightened his seatbelt and stared out the window. But then, Keith's wife was completely on board with their plans. Her father was one of the investors, after all. Besides that, Keith's daughter, Andi, was a freshman at Indiana University, so the shoot would give Keith a window to Andi's world — something he was grateful for. Andi wanted to be an actress, and apparently her roommate was a theater major. Both college girls would be extras in the film, so Keith's entire family could hardly wait to get started.

Chase bit the inside of his lip. From the beginning, all the worries about the movie came from him and Kelly, but now that he was on his way to Indiana, Chase had to focus not on his fears, but on the film.

He ignored the knots in his stomach as he leaned against the cold hard plastic that framed the airplane window. The movie they were making was called *The Last Letter*, the story of a college kid whose life is interrupted when his father suffers a sudden fatal heart attack. The kid isn't sure how to move on until his mother reveals to him a letter—one last letter from his father. That letter takes Braden on a quest of discovery in faith and family, and finally into a brilliant future Braden had known nothing about.

The story was a parable, an illustration of the verse in Jeremiah 29:11: "'For I know the plans I have for you,' declares the Lord, 'plans to prosper you and not to harm you, plans to give you hope and a future.'" The verse would be their mantra every day of the filming, Chase had no doubt.

He closed his eyes, and in a rush he could hear the music welling in his chest, feel the emotion as it filled a theater full of moviegoers. He could see the images as they danced across the big screen, and he could imagine all of it playing out beyond his wildest expectations.

But the way from here to there could easily be a million miles of rocky back roads and potholes.

They were still at the gate, still waiting for the plane to head out toward the runway. Chase blinked and stared out the window, beyond the airport to the blue sky. Every day this week had been blue, not a cloud in sight, something Chase and Keith both found fitting. Because no matter what Kelly feared, no matter what pressures came with this decision, here was the moment Chase and Keith had dreamed of and planned for, the culmination of a lifetime of believing that God wanted them to take part in saving the world—not on a mission field in Indonesia, but in packed movie houses across America. Oak River Films, they called themselves. The name came from their love of the first Psalm. Chase had long since memorized the first three verses:

Blessed is the man who does not walk not in the counsel of the wicked or stand in the way of sinners or sit in the seat of mockers. But his delight is in the law of the Lord, and on his law he meditates day and night. He is like a tree planted by streams of water, which yields its fruit in season and whose leaf does not wither. Whatever he does prospers.

Oak River Films. That everything he and Keith did would be rooted in a delight for the Lord, and a belief that if they planted their projects near the living water of Christ, they would flourish for Him. Chase shifted in his seat. He silently repeated the Scripture again. Why was he worried about what lay ahead? He believed God was sending them to make this movie, right? He pressed his body into the thinly padded seat. *Breathe. Settle down and breathe.*

In every way that mattered, this film would make or break them in the world of Hollywood movie production. Easy enough, he had told himself when they first began this venture. But as the trip to Bloomington, Indiana, neared, the pressure built. They received phone calls from well-meaning investors asking how the casting was going or confirming when the shoot date was. They weren't antsy or doubtful that Chase and Keith could bring a return for their investment, but they were curious.

The same way everyone surrounding the film was curious.

Keith handled these phone calls. He was the calmer of the two, the one whose faith knew no limits. It had been Keith's decision that they would make the film with money from investors rather than selling out too quickly to a studio. Producers who paid for their projects retained complete creative control—and the message of this first film was one Chase and Keith wouldn't let anyone change. No matter how much easy studio money might hang in the balance.

Moments like this Chase worried about all of it. His wife and little girls back home, and whether the production team could stick to the aggressive film schedule they'd set. Chase massaged his thumb into his brow. The concerns made up a long list. He had to manage a cast of egos that included an academy award winner and two household names—both of whom had reputations for being talented but difficult. He had to keep everyone working well together and stick to his four-week schedule—all while staying on budget. He worried about running out of money or running out of time, and whether this was really where God wanted them—working in a world as crazy as Hollywood.

Chase took a long breath and exhaled slowly. The white-haired woman next to him was reading a magazine, but she glanced his way now and then, probably looking for a conversation. Chase wasn't interested. He looked out the window again and a picture filled his mind, the picture of an apartment building surrounded by police tape. The image was from his high school days in the San Fernando Valley, when a major earthquake hit Southern California. The damage was considerable, but the Northridge Meadows apartment symbolized the worst of it. In a matter of seconds, the three-story apartment building collapsed and became one—the weight of the top two floors too great for the shaken foundation.

A shudder ran its way through Chase.

That could be them in a few months if the filming didn't go well, if the foundation of their budget didn't hold the weight of all that was happening on top of it. Chase could already feel the weight pressing in along his shoulders.

"Excuse me." The woman beside him tapped his arm. "Does your seatback have a copy of the *SkyMall* magazine? Mine's missing."

Chase checked and found what the woman wanted. He smiled as he handed it to her. "Helps pass the time."

"Yes." She had kind blue eyes. "Especially during takeoff. I can usually find something for my precious little Max. He's a cockapoo. Cute as a button."

"I'm sure." Chase nodded and looked out the window once more. Pressure came with the job, he'd known that from the beginning. He and Keith were producers; with that came a certain sense of thrill and awe, terror and anxiety, because for every dollar they'd raised toward this movie, for every chance an investor took on their film, there was a coinciding possibility that something could go wrong.

"You ever wonder," Chase had asked Keith a few days ago over a Subway sandwich, "whether we should've just stayed in Indonesia?"

Keith only smiled that slow smile, the one that morphed across his face when his confidence came from someplace otherworldly. "This is where we're supposed to be." He took a bite of his sandwich and waited until he'd swallowed. He looked deep into Chase's eyes. "I feel it in the center of my bones."

Truth and integrity. That's what Keith worried about. The truth of the message when the film was finally wrapped and they brought it to the public, and integrity with the cast and crew, the investors and the studios. For Keith, every day was a test because God was watching.

Chase agreed, but the pressure he felt didn't come from being under the watchful eye of the Lord. That mattered a great deal, but God would accept them whether they returned home having completed their movie mission or not. Rather Chase worried because the whole world was watching to see what sort of movie the two of them could make on such a limited budget. And if they failed, the world would know that too.

They were in the air now and the woman beside him closed the *SkyMall* magazine and handed it back to him. "I've seen it all before. Nothing new for Max." She shrugged one thin shoulder. "I've been making this trip a lot lately. Trying to sell my house in Indiana."

Chase still didn't want to talk, but the woman reminded him of his grandmother. She had a warmth about her, and something else … a sadness maybe. Whatever it was he felt compelled to give her at least a little time. "Moving to San Jose?"

"Yes. It's time, I guess." She looked straight ahead at nothing in particular. "Lived in Indiana all my life." Light from the window fell on her soft wrinkled skin, and for a few seconds her smile faded. She had to be eighty at least, but she seemed a decade younger. Then, as if she suddenly remembered she'd begun a conversation with a stranger, she grinned at Chase again. "What about you? Heading home?"

"No." He angled himself so his back was against the window. "Going to Bloomington for business."

She looked delighted that he was talking to her. "Business!" She raised an eyebrow. "My husband was a businessman. What line of work?"

"I'm a producer." Chase fought with the sense of privilege and headiness that came with the title. "We'll be on location four weeks."

"Produce! Isn't that wonderful." She folded her hands in her lap. "My great nephew works in produce. Got a job at the grocer not too far from his parents' house and now he unpacks tomatoes and cabbage all day long."

Chase opened his mouth to tell her he was a producer, and not in produce, but she wasn't finished.

"He's only been at it a few months, but I don't think he'll end up in produce long term. He wants to finish school." She angled her head sweetly. "Did you finish college, young man?"

"Yes, ma'am. But—"

"Well, of course you did." She laughed lightly at herself. "You must be a produce manager, heading to the farms of Bloomington for harvest season, making sure the crop's coming up good and going out to stores across the country." She gave as hearty a nod as she could muster. "That's a mighty important job." Her finger gave a quick jab in his direction. "The public takes it for granted, the way we need produce managers. We walk into a store and just assume we can buy a pound of red apples or Vidalia onions." She settled back in her seat, but she looked straight at him. "Farming's the American way." Her grin held a level of admiration. "Thanks for what you do for this great nation ... what'd you say your name was?"

"Chase. Chase Ryan."

"Matilda Ewing. Mattie."

"Nice to meet you, ma'am."

"Well, Mr. Ryan," she held out her bony fingers. "It's a pleasure to meet you too. But what about your family back home? Four weeks is an awful long time to be apart. My son nearly lost his marriage once because of that. He was in sales ... had to figure out a different territory to save his family." She barely paused. "You do have a family, right?"

"Yes, ma'am. It's hard to be away." He was touched by the woman's transparency. "My wife, Kelly, is home with our little girls. They're four and two."

She sucked in a surprised breath. "And you'll be gone four weeks! You must have a peach for a wife. That's a long time to tend to a family by yourself."

"Yes, ma'am." Chase wondered if the woman was slightly confused. Seconds ago she was singing his praise, claiming the virtues of his being a produce manager, and now she was practically chastising him for daring to take such a long trip.

"Don't get me wrong," she was saying. "Farming's a good thing. But be careful. Fences pop up when you're away from each other that long. Nothing on the other side of the fence is ever as green as it seems." She chuckled softly. "Even in produce."

The flight attendant peered into their row. "Something to drink?"

Matilda ordered ginger ale, and in the process she fell into a conversation with the person on the aisle. The diversion gave Chase the chance to stare out the window again and think about the old woman and her wisdom. Never mind that her hearing was a little off, Chase almost liked the idea that the kind woman thought he worked producing vegetables and not movies. But more than that, her words were dead on when it came to his family back home. Especially the part about fences.

With all his concerns and worries, he hadn't thought about how the four weeks away would feel to Kelly and their girls.

He must've fallen asleep as he thought about his conversation with Matilda, because in no time she was tapping him on the arm again. "Mr. Ryan, we're landing. Your seatback needs to be up."

He stretched his legs out on either side of his laptop bag and did as he was told. "Thank you."

"My pleasure." She adjusted the vent above her seat. "You were sleeping pretty hard. You'll need that rest when you hit the fields."

"Yes, ma'am." Chase rubbed his eyes and ran his fingers through his hair. When he was more awake he turned toward her again. "So ... why are you moving to San Jose?"

At first she didn't seem like she intended to answer his question. She pursed her lips and stared down at her hands, at a slender gold wedding band that looked worn with age. When she looked up, the sadness was there again. "My husband and I were married fifty-eight years." She wrung her hands as the words found their way to her lips. "He passed away this last January. My girls want me to live closer to them." She smiled, but it stopped short of her eyes. "We're looking for an apartment at one of those … senior facilities. Somewhere that'll take Max and me, both." Her expression told him she was uncomfortable with the idea, but she wasn't fighting it. "I can get a little forgetful, and, well, sometimes I don't hear as well as I used to. It's a good idea, really." A depth shone from deep inside her. "Don't you think?"

"I do." He wanted to hug the woman. Poor dear.

"My girls say I'm dragging my feet." She shifted her gaze straight ahead once more. "And maybe I am. When I close up that house and shut the door for the last time, that'll be that." She looked at him through a layer of tears. "We spent five decades in that house. Every square inch holds a hundred memories."

"Leaving won't be easy."

"No." Matilda sniffed. "That's why I'm saying," her composure gradually returned, "look out for fences, Mr. Ryan. Produce or no produce, home's the better place. Kids grow up and God only gives us so many days with our loved ones."

"Yes, ma'am."

The captain came on, advising them that they'd be landing soon, and the announcement stalled the conversation with Matilda. She started talking to the passenger on her left once more, and not until they were at the end of the jetway did she turn and flash her twinkling eyes his way. "Good luck with the produce, Mr. Ryan. And remember what I said about fences. The greenest grass is back at home."

Chase thanked her again, and then she was gone; between the gate and baggage claim he didn't see her again. He rented a Chevy Tahoe and headed for Bloomington. Once he arrived, the first thing he did was call Kelly.

"Hello?"

"Honey … it's me." Chase felt a sense of relief. His words spilled out far faster than usual. "There's something I should've said, back at the airport when we were saying goodbye. I mean, we stood there all those minutes, but I never really told you what I should have, so that's why I'm calling."

She laughed. "Someone's had too much coffee."

"No." He exhaled and slowed himself. "What I mean is, I appreciate you, Kelly. You have to handle the house and the girls for a very long time, and I never … I never thanked you."

For a few beats there was no response. "You really feel that way?" A tentative joy warmed her tone.

"I do." Another picture flashed on the screen of his heart. The two of them holding hands in front of a church full of family and friends, and Chase knowing that in all the world he could never love anyone as much as he loved the beautiful bride standing before him. "I love you, Kelly. Don't ever forget that, okay?"

"Okay." She laughed and the sound was wind chimes and summer breeze, the way it hadn't been for a while. "You don't know how much it means … that you'd call like this."

"I miss you already. Give the girls a kiss for me."

"Okay. Oh, and Chase … one more thing." She laughed again. "Go get 'em tomorrow … I know you can do it. I've been praying since you left and I feel like God cleared some things up for me. This is going to be bigger than Keith and you ever dreamed."

Her confidence breathed new life into his dreams. "Seriously?"

"Yes." The sound of the girls singing about Old McDonald's Farm came across the lines from the background. "I believe in you, Chase. I promise I'll keep believing."

"Thank you." He thought about old Matilda and how she would smile if she could see the conversation Chase was having with his wife. "Okay, then … I guess I'm off to the harvest."

"The harvest?" Kelly still had a laugh in her voice. "What on earth?"

"Nothing." He chuckled. He told her again that he loved her, and he promised to call that evening to tell the girls goodnight. After he hung up, he caught himself once more drawn back to the sweet woman's words. In some ways he really was headed out to the fields, out to a crop that needed harvesting—the crop of human hearts and souls that might only be found if they created the best movie possible. But more than that, he thought about the fences.

With Keith and him producing, the months ahead figured to be crazy at times. But no matter how bumpy the ride, he vowed to stay on the same side of the fence as Kelly and the girls. Because Matilda was right.

God only gave a person so many days with their family.

ABOVE THE LINE SERIES

Take One

Karen Kingsbury,
New York Times *Bestselling Author*

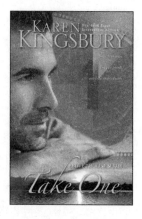

Could they change the world—before the world changes them?

Filmmakers Chase Ryan and Keith Ellison left the mission field of Indonesia for the mission field of Hollywood with a dream bigger than both of them. Now they have done the impossible: raised enough money to produce a feature film with a message that could change the world.

But as Chase and Keith begin shooting, their well-laid plans begin to unravel. With millions of dollars on the line, they make a desperate attempt to keep the film from falling apart—even as a temperamental actress, a botched production schedule, and their own insecurities leave little room for the creative and spiritual passion that once motivated them. Was God really behind this movie after all? A chance meeting and friendship with John Baxter could bring the encouragement they need to stay on mission and produce a movie that will actually change people's lives.

In the midst of the questions and the cameras, is it possible to keep things above the line and make a movie unlike anything done before—or is the risk too great for everyone?

Hardcover, Jacketed: 978-0-310-31843-9

Pick up a copy today at your favorite bookstore!

ABOVE THE LINE SERIES

Take Two

Karen Kingsbury,
New York Times *Bestselling Author*

Filmmakers Chase Ryan and Keith Ellison have completed their first feature film, and Hollywood is buzzing with the news. In the wake of that excitement, the producers acquire rights to a novel that has all the ingredients they want for their next project. At the same time they cross paths with a well-connected player who introduces them to the right people, and suddenly every studio in town wants to talk to Chase and Keith. The producers' dreams are on the verge of coming true, but Chase's marriage is strained and Keith's daughter — Andi Ellison — is making questionable choices in her quest for stardom. The producers are gaining respect and are on the verge of truly changing culture through the power of film—but is the change worth the cost?

Hardcover, Jacketed: 978-0-310-31893-4

Pick up a copy today at your favorite bookstore!

Every Now and Then

Karen Kingsbury,
New York Times *Bestselling Author*

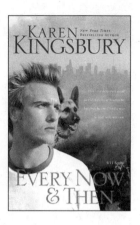

A wall went up around Alex Brady's heart when his father, a New York firefighter, died in the Twin Towers. Turning his back on the only woman he ever loved, Alex shut out all the people who cared about him to concentrate on fighting crime. He and his trusty K9 partner, Bo, are determined to eliminate evil in the world and prevent tragedies like 9-11.

Then the worst fire season in California's history erupts, and Alex faces the ultimate challenge to protect the community he serves. An environmental terrorist group is targeting the plush Oak Canyon Estates. At the risk of losing his job, and his soul, Alex is determined to infiltrate the group and put an end to their corruption. Only the friendship of Clay and Jamie Michaels — and the love of a dedicated young woman — can help Alex drop the walls around his heart and move forward into the future God has for him.

Softcover: 978-0-310-26615-0
Unabridged Audio CD: 978-0-310-288183
Audio Download, Unabridged: 978-0-310-288190
ebooks:
Adobe® Acrobat® eBook Reader®: 978-0-310-28821-3
Microsoft Reader®: 978-0-310-28823-7
Palm™ Reader: 978-0-310-28825-1
Mobipocket Reader™: 978-0-310-28822-0
Sony® Reader: 978-0-310-29045-2
ePub: 978-0-310-29623-2

Pick up a copy today at your favorite bookstore!